A Thorough Seaman

To Peter Hunter Blair, loving partner in the search

A THOROUGH SEAMAN

The Ships' Logs of Horatio Nelson's

Early Voyages Imaginatively Explored

Pauline Hunter Blair

◆

CHURCH FARM HOUSE BOOKS
CAMBRIDGE

Distributed by Gazelle Book Services Limited
Falcon House, Queen Square
Lancaster, England LA1 1RN

British Library Cataloguing in Publication Data
A catalogue record for this book is available from the British Library

ISBN 0-9536317-1-0

Typeset by Amolibros, Watchet, Somerset
This book production has been managed by Amolibros
Printed and bound by T J International Ltd, Padstow, England

Contents

...he was frequently in fine weather indulged by the officer of the watch to tack the ship, which he performed like a thorough seaman ... His ardent ambition was to make himself thoroughly acquainted with the most minute part of a seaman's duty.

J Clarke & J M' Arthur, *The Life and Services of Horatio, Viscount Nelson*, quoting the Master of the *Seahorse*, Mr (later Captain) Surridge.

Preface

Ships' logs rank with journals, diaries, letters and accounts as documents of unparalleled immediacy. And the first thing I learned from a kind Greenwich curator was that there are almost certainly half a dozen or more logs of the same voyage. For each of Horatio Nelson's early voyages, I studied two or three logs, kept by captain, master, lieutenant, or midshipman. (Sadly enough, though Horatio's Passing Out Certificate, 1777, stated that 'he produceth journals kept by himself' and mentioned the '*Carcase, Seahorse* and *Dolphin*', none seems to have survived.)

Only the first voyage has no logs, the sugar ship, the *Mary Ann*, plying back and forth to the West Indies. Horatio himself tells us that she belonged to the house of Hibbert, Purrier and Horton, and, from Lloyd's Lists of goings and comings over the period, her identity was established. For another early incident also, we depend on his and William's memory, not on logs. A sea captain, unknown forever, though said to be an acquaintance of Captain Suckling (never a man of words) spotted the forlorn boy wandering about the Basin at Chatham, fed him, and got him aboard the *Raisonnable.* I allowed this kind man to introduce Horatio Nelson to HMS *Victory*, with no factual grounds save only that she was lying at Chatham at the time. The boy and this most famous first-rate were conceived in the same year, 1758.

Other extraordinary coincidences of date in Horatio's career – 21st October, Cap François as well as Trafalgar; the King's call for men in the Falklands crisis of 1770, on his birthday, 29th September – bring a sense of an inexorable pattern of fate, a pre-destined glory and tragedy: yet they can only be coincidences.

For the most part the logs are spare, giving us bare hard facts from which to determine the likely course of events, provide possible details, and suggest a conclusion. Could I by any means decide on the most likely date of Horatio's joining his first ship? All accounts say he joined at Chatham. William remembered that he left school 'very early, and in a cold and dark morning' in March or April. On Friday 15th March at 10 a.m., the *Raisonnable* sailed from Chatham for Sheerness: so we are confined to the first half of March. Allow a week in London fitting him out. They probably went straight for Lynn and London, hence the early start. Supposing he left school on the 1st or 2nd March. The ironical log entry about the one man and the quantities of beef is for Friday 8th March, p.m. Entries for the day before refer to one man and ten men by what must be a transport ship: and no other entries for a single man (under his own steam) appear for the first half of March. Meanwhile the Muster Roll, while showing that he was 'Entered' (on the books), 1st January 1771, gives his 'Appearance' on the list dated 1st March/30th April 1771, when he shows up as Horace Nelson, Mid, from Wells. The storyteller accepts that he is less hag-ridden by exactitude than the historian. Yet it may be the exact date.

Because the very spareness of a log leads to long stretches of repetitive dullness, one leaps to attention to follow any startling, dangerous or tragic action that befalls a ship. Such is the sad tale, in which I have involved Horatio, of Joseph Riddall drowned in the Kitthole, by sudden wind, a swinging beam, or sheer carelessness. He had sunk like a stone in the cold, cold water, the crew never even found his body. Captain Suckling, though knowing the sailor's name, could not fit a face to it, an attempt on my part to express the horrors and hardships of the eighteenth century seaman's life in general and the anonymity of his manifold sufferings in particular. Such also is the happier incident of a man overboard on the return from India. While Captain Pigot no doubt kept the bobbing head in his glass, the master and crew brought the ship around so smartly that the flounderer was safely rescued and joy filled the ship. (The man perhaps could swim, as so many could not.) The crowning irony is the blank space left for his name, never filled in. How one longs to know that seaman's name! I let Horatio exult in the rescue for a particular reason: the story called up another much later incident, when Captain Hardy had taken a jolly boat over to search for a man, and was being swept away. Nelson is said to have ordered the ship to be brought about with equal urgency, crying, 'I'll not lose Hardy!'

The *Triumph* log, Tuesday 29th September 1772, p.m.:

Sent Mr Boyle [sic] 4th Lt, a Mid: and 26 Men; Victuals for 4 days to the Defiance at Woolwich.

My chapter four title is from Horatio's own *Memoir*, and, more fully, it reads:

'Thus by degrees I became a good pilot...from Chatham to the Tower of London, down the Swin, and the North Foreland, and confident of myself amongst rocks and sands...'

No other entry in the log indicates another such journey, and Horatio remembers its geography. I have therefore assumed 'a Mid' to be he, and 'Mr Boyle' to be Charles Boyles, perhaps acting 4th Lt (the *Naval Chronicle* does not give the date he became Lieutenant). Maybe the coincidence of its being Horatio's fourteenth birthday is a corroboratory detail.

And who does *not* know the tale of Horatio and his polar bear? Yet in timing it fits no bear incident recorded by James Allen, master of Captain (later Admiral) Lutwidge's ship on the Arctic voyage, the *Carcase*. Allen was an assiduous recorder of bears. Nor can one argue with such a strong traditional tale. I had to find the occasion in the log which best fits the details as usually given: ships in the ice and bears ubiquitous; a foggy night-watch to allow the two boys' escape, clearing in early morning to allow their furious recall; and *after* the crews had been issued with muskets for their possible traipse over the ice. Perhaps for once Allen was turned in and missed a bear. Perhaps the dire circumstances were simply too pressing.

This Arctic voyage has a particular interest now since John Harrison and his 'Time Keeper' or 'Sea Clock' have come into the limelight. The *Racehorse* log notes the visit by people from the Board of Longitude, who sent '2 watch machines' – 'one by Mr Kendal on Mr Harrison's principles, the other by Mr Arnold. Also Mr Arnold made [Captain Phipps] a pocket watch, very exact – which varied only 2' 40" in 128 days'. The *Carcase* also reports that Mr Arnold brought a timekeeper on board: but in three days it had stopped. Arnold was summoned to see to it: all it needed was winding up. However, within a day or two of sailing, this timekeeper began to lose, and lose it did the whole way.

It is also a most interesting fact that despite the great lunar-versus-sea-clock debate, which lasted from Harrison I in 1737 to Harrison 4, the Watch, in 1760, we find Thomas Surridge, the master of the *Seahorse*, an unconverted and unrepentant lunar man, working out the ship's longitude at sea by lunar observations and sums which took four hours each day (despite Mr Maskelyne's tables, even if he had them). Indeed Horatio declared that he thought Mr (later Captain) Surridge's logs were amongst the best the navy ever received.

Horatio's invaliding home from the East is usually assumed to have been due to malarial fever. The log of HMS *Dolphin* and her watchful captain have provided a framework for this monumentally important yet nebulous journey, during which, if the boy had not conquered the fever, the course of history might have been different. The *Seahorse* Muster Roll reports his discharge 14th March 1776. The captain's log of the invalid ship, the *Dolphin*, reports that she received '10 invalids from [Bombay] hospital' on 21st March from the various ships in the squadron; and 'our' [my quotes] sick men on the 22nd. If there were four *Dolphin* sick, making fourteen when the ship sailed, and one died at the Cape, it fits with the largest number of sick ever mentioned being thirteen. For from 14th July, in a more temperate climate, the captain's log noted the numbers of sick daily rather than occasionally. (John North, late bo'sun of the *Seahorse*, seemed to be counted always as bo'sun, not invalid, though he died on the way home.) Of the thirteen, Horatio must be one, so he is still ill at 5th July when all thirteen are sick (no individuals are identified). Twelve only are sick at the 27th August, and I have taken Horatio to be the non-invalid, his last bout possibly being 23rd July – 1st August, finishing around 4th August. His depression (quite understandable), followed by his 'vision', would be after 4th August and before the 27th: at which time his physical recovery is established aided by his renewed spirit, and what he calls Captain Pigot's kindness. This fits the likely six-month duration of a malign tertian malaria followed by acute pernicious malaria (with cerebral effects like loss of the use of limbs), if it has started about the end of January, and nowhere quarrels with the sick figures in the log: and although it has to be only a working hypothesis, it is a very tempting one.

Pauline Hunter Blair
Bottisham
Cambridge
2000

CHAPTER ONE

Sheerness and the Nore

Despite ambition, there was to be much anguish for young Horatio Nelson, twelve and a half years, and setting forth on his life at sea upon the *Raisonnable* at Chatham. The forlorn flavour of these first days was to linger all his life, to eclipse all lesser memories.

'Well, Horace. How is Mr Nelson faring?'

'Thank you, sir, very well, sir,' replied that small person warily. His uncle had been piped aboard last evening, the red side-ropes rigged, all standing to attention, the mids and officers frozen upon the quarter-deck: the scene encompassed by the bo'sun's pipe ascending, a note that made Horace shiver, and that began its descent only when Captain Suckling had saluted the quarter-deck.

'There being no chaplain nor schoolmaster upon this ship, you will come to me for your lessons in such time as I can afford between nine o'clock and twelve. Have you your Robertson with you?'

Elements of Navigation by J Robertson was the book which the boys had used at school.

'Yes, sir.'

'How much of it do you know by heart?'

'Not all of it, sir,' said his nephew modestly.

'You will also keep a journal. The wind, the weather, and the events of the day. Mr Scott will show you how. We shall soon try to enliven your navigation lessons with some practical observations. Have you your own quadrant? Did you ever take an altitude?'

'No, sir, not yet.'

'Ah. You are acquainted with the compass?'

'Yes, sir.'

'The log and line? You will discover, upon your watch. As to practical seamanship, your chance to learn is with the seamen as well as the officers. Watch every action and see how it is done and why, when they are about the rigging or whatever else. The top men will teach you the ropes up aloft. But always remember you are—you will be—an officer. Regard your duty as befits your position. Pay

1

every respect to your superior officers, as you shall wish to receive respect yourself.'

'Yes, sir. I will, sir,' his nephew replied eagerly.

Captain Suckling, neither the most observant nor the most imaginative of men, could not help but see the boy's face become illumined with a positive ambition to do well. If his health only allowed it he thought that he might.

'And how was your papa, Horace?' he went on, becoming uncle rather than Captain.

'Much better, sir, thank you. The visit to Bath did him great good.'

'I am very gratified to hear it,' said the Captain.

The morning lessons proved fitful and often dreary: for if the Captain were engaged he would set Horatio and the other youngsters to study upon their own. Sometimes they were not sent for at all. Horace would pace the deck with no practical task to do, and would long for eight bells and whatever ill-cooked meat the meal provided; albeit that in the gunroom he was too much the greenhorn to be addressed by the gunner and his mates, and too much the Captain's nephew to join the fraternity of the servant boys. When the longing for home pierced him like a molten arrow, he learnt quickly to turn to his journal or his text-book; to hitches and bends and clinches and slings; to the lashing of hammock rolls (seven turns of the cord, clews at top and toe tucked tidily under it): an art which he perfected only by watching the seamen.

One happiness had warmed him fleetingly. Not long after his arrival, an unrecognised voice had reached him from outside the gunroom as he braced himself to meet another day.

'Horace? Psst!'

Who was this, calling him as he was called at home? Hovering by the capstan was Charles Boyles.

'Charles!'

'Mr Boyles, if you please.'

The near three years' difference in their ages was now more marked. 'Mr Nelson likewise,' replied the youngster perkily.

'When did you get aboard? I've but now heard someone mention the Captain's nephew: I thought it needs must be you.'

'A day or two ago. I came across with the casks.'

'Which watch are you? Have you seen Mr Anderson?'

Mr Matthew Anderson was the first lieutenant: he had summoned Horace that morning.

'Yes, I'm the starboard watch, Mr William Scott. And a mid called Swan.'

'Pity you and I are not together. But you'll find Mr Scott more agreeable than Mr St Alban Roy and Mr Faithful Adrian Fortescue,' Charles mouthed under his breath.

'Mr Fortescue treated me as if I were not there.'

'Ay, one of his common tricks. Are you snug in there with those brats? Watch your stuff, won't you?'

Horace nodded. 'Where do you sleep?'

'Cockpit. Orlop deck. Down below here.'

'How long have you been here? My papa heard you were perhaps gone to sea.'

'Yes, I came up to London to the Rendezvous, in the middle of December. It was when they all thought there was to be a war with Spain. When's the old man —your uncle, beg pardon—expected back?'

'I don't know.'

Looking at Charles, Horace thought of Burnham and Papa. 'How do we send letters?' he asked.

'Catch someone going ashore. I'll see to it when you have written it.'

'Thank you kindly, Mr Boyles.'

Charles waved as he descended the ladder.

And the bells, the bells! How the sharp sadness of the bells struck him in those empty spaces of loneliness: he counted them, longed for them as they split up the weary time. But after dinner, were it his watch on duty, Mr Scott would sometimes remember to instruct Horatio, as the men plaited rings, or set up the standing rigging, explaining the difference between shrouds and stays, or finding some not unfriendly man to slow down the work of his gnarled fingers, that the lad might see. Little by little Horatio came to recognise in the crowd a few kind and friendly faces, in those long melancholy days of his first week aboard ship.

Ten o'clock upon the morning of Friday the fifteenth of March, cloud with moderate wind from the west-north-west: Horatio (was it but one week after his arrival?) noted in his journal with satisfaction that the ship was sailing.

For the bleak north-easterly wind of his early days at Chatham had gone round to the south-west. By Tuesday afternoon a fresh gale had blown from that quarter: a noisy but controlled activity pervaded the ship upon Wednesday morning, as the sails were worked upon each mast together (Captain Suckling would say nothing was so lubberly as to hoist one sail after another) and a pilot and the master attendant came aboard. But the wind scanting, they were obliged to keep fast: and on Thursday morning loosed the sails again as they relinquished hope, and took on board fresh bread and beer and butter and cheese in a flat calm. Horace longed for the wind with impatience: too young to know yet that winds, like hope, spring up only when they will, but ever anew. Last night a wind had risen from the west-north-west, and now the *Raisonnable* in company with the *Resolution* was sailing.

Up the Chatham reach to Upnor Castle, due east under Cockham wood, due south down the Short reach, past Gillingham's fort and her church tower, visible inland. The river wound like a serpent. With every new coil came the shouting of orders and the trimming of sails to the wind. The three hours journey held him absorbed, straining to see ahead as the officer called out names: Bishop's Marsh, Ocam Beacon, Sharpfleet Marsh, Yantlek Creed, Stangate Creek, Saltpans behind Blackstakes, where guard ships lay at anchor. It would be a long time before he could carry that chart, those names, in his head! North-easterly at last towards the steep cliff of Sheerness: hulks floating before the quays, buildings rising above them, and many ships riding at anchor.

At one p.m., anch:^{d} at Sheerness with the best bower in 8f^m the Master Attendant came on board and bro:^{t} us to moorings.

Upon Tuesday the nineteenth of March, entering a north-easterly wind in his journal, Horace remembered with a pang of feeling that it was Papa's birthday and little Kitty's also. What were they doing at Burnham parsonage now as he crouched over his journal on a raw hazy day anchored off Sheerness? Mun and Suckling would have gone off to school, accompanied by Ann. Sukey would be in the kitchen with Mary, or upstairs about her linen; Papa and Kitty-Kat would be in the study, was Kitty of an age to begin her lessons? Horace calculated that she was four today.

A roll of the drum interrupted his dream of home. The drummer beat to muster. He hastened up to his place and watched the whole company fall in, two midshipmen of each watch calling over the men of their divisions. Then each lieutenant checked his own men, their gear and their clothing. All were now ordered up to the quarter-deck and sat upon buckets, mess kids, upturned tubs, the empty carriages of the small guns or simply upon the deck.

Mr Matthew Anderson stood forward near the afterhatchway. Horatio felt his heart begin to beat. Was some misdeed to be reported on? (Had he himself failed in his duty? Would he be sent back to Burnham in disgrace?) But the first lieutenant began to read the *Articles of War* and the *Abstract of Parliament*: and his voice soon dropped to a monotonous slowly enunciated catalogue.

What did the men, the boys, the idlers, the marines, the officers, the midshipmen think of, as Mr Anderson read out the conditions of their service in time of war or peace, the rules that governed them, the offences they would commit, and the meet punishment for each? Some ceased to listen; some found the lieutenant's voice more enlivening than their own minds; some winced at past crimes and the memory of punishment; some nursed hatred for the life they had been pressed into leading. Horatio (after a fleeting memory of Thomas reading the ancient oration at school) gave his whole attention to the sins chronicled with such dull particularity.

The next morning the people rigged out the mainyard so that it stood on end upon the deck, its base upon a block of wood. It was securely lashed and its head was held in place by guy ropes and tackles. Horace stood considering it and wondering. It looked as if it were to lift things on board. Sure enough, they were loading her guns, swung aboard one by one, their dumb hollow muzzles waiting to roar. By the afternoon of the second day, ranged along each side of the lower deck were twenty-six twenty-four-pounders, while the upper deck had as many eighteen-pounders; there were twelve small guns, nine-pounders, for fo'c's'le and quarter-deck. Horace now counted to his satisfaction that the ship carried her proper complement of sixty-four.

This was the gunner's hour. Back and forth he went with his mates, seeing each gun settled in her bed, upon her four-wheeled elm truck carriage, her breech lying upon the wooden wedge-shaped quoin like an effigy's head upon a tomb. Horatio observed the gunner pat each gun when it had passed his scrutiny: then she was hauled close up to the side by her pulleys, the breeching ropes were lashed together to keep her fast, the quoin was removed, and the muzzle, plugged with its red painted tompion, was lashed where it rested touching the upper part of the gun port. Horace thought he could by the end have fixed a gun himself.

He dared to ask why the guns were called twenty-four-pounders, or eighteen-pounders? The gunner was gratified by his attention.

'Look 'ee Mr Nelson, that is the weight of the ball she fires. A gun is named by her shot d'ye see, there they lie in the racks.'

The *Raisonnable* seemed now to assume more exactly the aspect of a man-of-war. But to what purpose? The settlement with Spain was accomplished weeks past. In his cabin the Captain kept his counsel, a silent man by nature. In the wardroom the lieutenants discussed their future, Mr Scott being of the opinion that what they all needed was a war: Mr Fortescue assuring him that they were very well as they were. In the after-cockpit Charles Boyles expressed some restiveness, which he soon communicated to Horace.

'What happens,' complained he, 'since the guns got in? Down t'gallant masts and up again. And I count in bread, beef, pork, flour, suet, raisins, butter, cheese, vinegar and ells of canvas, all to feed idle men—'

'The men are not yet reduced to eating canvas,' countered Mr Nelson brightly. 'And I would be happy to meet some raisins.'

'And men go and come to the hospital. And the muster master musters. And we dry the sails! It is well for you Horace, all is new and to learn.'

All that happened was the smoking of the ship. From the lower gun deck upwards, fires were made of dampened wood in braziers and the ventilator shafts were worked: the smoke curled all around, fore and aft and upwards, cleansing, purifying and drying between decks, often choking the unwary seaman.

Upon the afternoon of April the first there came down from Chatham the *Golden Fleece* tender bringing seventeen of the *Raisonnable's* men. No sooner were they aboard than some kind of quarrel broke out; a noisy fight followed, the ringleader was seized, and was ordered to be immediately and summarily beaten; Captain Suckling preferring to have such matters out of the way. He gave his order to Mr Anderson, who sent Mr Boyles to the bo'sun's mates, who piped and shouted all hands aft to witness punishment. Horace lingered behind the junior officers below the poop to windward. Above him the marines fell in. His uncle stood with the lieutenants on the quarter-deck. The purser and the surgeon were to leeward below the poop, the bo'sun and his mates before them. The ship's company fell in upon the boats, the booms, and any point of vantage forward of the mainmast.

'Rig the gratings,' shouted Captain Suckling: whereupon the carpenter and his men carried aft two wooden gratings from the hatchways and placed one flat upon the deck, t'other upright against the poop railings. The Captain called forth Hugh Wilson held by the master-at-arms, announced his transgression and asked him had he ought to say?

'Nought, sir.'

'Strip,' ordered the Captain.

Hugh Wilson pulled his shirt over his shaggy head and advanced to the grating.

'Seize him up.'

The boatswain's mates tied his wrists above his head. The Captain doffed his hat, and every man upon deck who was covered bared his own head. The Captain read from the *Articles of War* that rule which concerned fighting and quarrelling. Horatio watched and listened with an intensity of interest and concern that was later to disgust him. He saw men half-smile in a jocular attempt to make the affair seem of no consequence. He saw the faces of others screwed into anger or numb with subdued fear. The bo'sun's mate was untying his red baize bag, flicking out the cat, its handle red, its nine tails knotted. For the second or two that the Captain's voice ceased, the man stood bound and the cat waited, Horace was caught up himself in the expectation of the crowd.

'Do your duty.'

The bo'sun's mate put himself in the right position, advanced upon Hugh Wilson, drew the tails through his left hand, flung back his right, and laid on the first cut.

The newest boy aboard felt himself go hot and then faint. The force of the blow had jerked from the man's lungs a horrible, unwilling grunt. Blood sprang upon his shoulders. Each stroke drew more: Horatio could hear the gasping of his breath, the groan that became a sickening choke. He was given twelve lashes, untied, and led staggering below by the surgeon's mates.

Horace escaped, seeking the emptiness of the gunroom. He must not let the boys see he felt sick. He sat upon his chest, his head drooping. He supposed he should get used to it, was obliged to become hardened to it. Punishments there had been at school, but never anything like this. Was it not the being watched that was so hateful? He felt shame himself and some anger at the man being so shamed. Yet he supposed that one could not let a transgressor go unpunished. Would Hugh Wilson, when he was fit to face his fellows again, hold his head up? An obscure seed of doubtful sympathy with the victim arose in him which must surely either grow; or be ordered to die. His supper went down ill that night.

A great many ships came and went as they lay at anchor off Sheerness, their doings of the utmost interest to Horatio, matters of more immediacy than struggling with the positions of imaginary ships, whose latitude and longitude he was to ascertain by dead reckoning; or using the tables to reduce the sun's declination to a given meridian, to find the latitude of a place: or trying to puzzle out the rules for working a lunar. After such problems he would hurry up to gulp the fresh air, and look over the estuary. The *Crescent* had recently sailed away. The *Triumph* and the *Panther* had followed the *Raisonnable* down on the next favourable wind from Chatham. The *Augusta* was lying here, and the *Marlborough*, some of whose men came aboard their own ship. One Sunday morning early in April the King's fisher anchored near at hand. The sloop *Cruiser* anchored and the *Lynx* sailed hence. Then the *Somerset*

arrived. Horatio wrote them in his journal, whether they sailed on down to the Nore, or were bound back to Chatham.

He enjoyed keeping his journal, writing as neatly as he could on to a clean page. He thought that his papa also enjoyed it as he kept the records of his parish and checked and signed the overseers' accounts. Horatio and his brothers grew up with the sense of the importance of records. All his days upon this ship were now charted: he looked back over his month and more aboard. Papa would like to see how his time was spent. One day the purser, Mr Leigh, had served slops: seamen who wanted waistcoats or shirts or fur caps or an extra blanket, or a new straw mattress, gathered at the slop room on the orlop deck, presented a permit from their lieutenants, and purchased their needs out of regular naval stores. Not long afterwards they had loaded in three hundred and thirty-one barrels of powder. They were stowed in the fore-magazine, in the forward part of that warren of dark storerooms far below water which made up the ship's hold. The casks were arranged in tiers, one above the other. He had been stationed in the light-room just forward of the magazine, in charge of the lantern, which was lit to give the men in the magazine their only light. The light-room had double windows of glass, through which Horace could see not much, as the men crept about in their felt slippers on the rough fearnought which covered the floor. The magazine was protected so carefully, there was no ladder directly into it: you must go through a copper door guarded by a marine and along a narrow passage. The cartridges for the cannon were here, where they would be filled with powder from the casks, and stored in wooden tubs in racks. Horatio had pressed his advantage with the gunner who was beginning to be a friend of his, and asked about these matters.

Yesterday afternoon there had come on board a personage called the Clerk of the Cheque, who had paid the volunteers their bounty. The King's bounty! At the word, Horace was back in the school parlour, reading of the King's bounty! Charles was one of the fortunate ones who received it, for until January the first he had been rated an able seaman and only afterwards a mid.

The boy closed his journal, returned it to his chest, and went up on deck. Forward of the mainmast the carpenter and his mate planed and joined a coffin.

'Who's dead, Mr Carpenter?'

'Some poor fellow. Died at seven last night. I forget his name, sir.'

'What did he die of?'

The men shrugged. The mate said, 'He was flogged—'

'You don't mean Hugh Wilson?' Horatio asked, his heart leaping with a sort of guilt.

'Na. He's about again, I seed him. This was John Hollier. He was flogged some weeks past.'

'Do you mean he died because he was flogged?'

'Mebbe, young sir. Mebbe he was ill when they beat him. He only had twelve.'

Horatio stood watching, cold and quiet.

'What had he done?'

'He was a thief.'

'Will they take him ashore?'

'Oh, ay. After dark, sir.'

'Will his family come?'

'I reckon not, sir.'

Poor John Hollier, Horatio said under his breath. They looked up in surprise, and nodded gravely.

'Ay, sir.'

He heard their tools begin again. Another name flitted upon the outskirts of his memory. *Poor George Commin.* That was it. Papa had made them the clock with his, Horace's, name upon it. It was a hard enough life seamen led, enough hazards and hardships, without beatings. Who could he ask about John Hollier? All would soon forget him, who had no family near enough to come. He would not be forgotten however, if his death were written in a journal, as Papa wrote the names of those who died in Burnham to be there hundreds of years hence, forever. There was some comfort in this. He would write John Hollier's death into his own book.

Over the estuary came the longboat from Sheerness carrying water casks, Charles and other men aboard her. On the lower deck the men were busy scaling some of the guns.

On Monday April twenty-second, a cloudy morning with a moderate wind, Captain Suckling rose up at three bells and addressed his pupils early.

'Today we propose dropping down to the Nore if the wind keeps fair. Go you up now and observe all you can as the ship gets ready. It will do you more good than pestering your head with tides.'

'Yes, sir. Thank you, sir.'

Horace hurried on deck with glee. At ten o'clock the pilot came aboard from Sheerness, and in the next two hours the *Raisonnable* was transformed into a man-of-war ready to sail. At three o'clock they let slip the moorings and came to sail, in company with the *Resolution*, north-easterly, until the entrance of the River Medway lay behind them: and Horatio was to see for the first time in his life the wider entrance of London River. South of the Nore lights, which Mr Anderson discovered to him, was a stretch of good anchorage where several other ships rode already.

> At 4 Anch^d at the Nore with the best bower moor^d ENE and WSW a Cable each way; found here his Maj: ships *Augusta, Conquestador, Glasgow, Crescent* and *Tamer* Sloop...

'Now, young Mr Nelson, what landmarks shall we observe, do you suppose, to describe our position exactly?' said the third lieutenant to his charge when the *Raisonnable* lay calmly at anchor and all was in order.

'Sheerness point, sir?'

'Ay. And that lies to which quarter?'

Horatio observed the compass.

'West south-west, sir.'

'Ay. Now one to the north?'

'The Nore lights, sir?'

'Ay, good.'

'North-west-by-north, sir.'

'So. And a southerly landmark?'

'Is that a church we can see, sir?' Horatio said screwing his eyes southerly against a glint of sun over the Kent coast.

'It is Minster church. And it lies?'

'South by west, sir.'

'Good. You may enter our position in the deck-log.'

For the first time and with some pleasure Horatio wrote down the ship's new position.

Not much more happened as the *Raisonnable* lay at the Nore than had passed at Sheerness: but under cover of this tranquillity the youngest midshipman was learning. He had observed the worming, parcelling and serving of cables.

> 'Worm and parcel with the lay
> Turn round and serve the other way',

a bo'sun's mate had said to him, filling up the sheet cable with thin yarn, working with the lay of the rope, making all rough places plain. They cleared the hawse, they scraped the top masts and payed them with varnish of pine: they listened to the *Articles* and *Abstracts* (but never once upon a Sunday the service of the Church which Horace, son of the Church, sorely missed): they heeled and scrubbed the ship; they set up the standing rigging. The longboat with a lieutenant and a midshipman and several crew went across to Leigh for water and returned with Mr St Alban Roy looking distinctly uneasy.

'Three men run,' whispered Mr Boyles to Horatio in passing.

Captain Suckling was a mild man on the whole but was heard to raise his voice to the lieutenant upon these defections.

Three cutters arrived, the *Alarm*, the *Greyhound*, the *Meridian*. HMS *Cornwall* passed by for Sheerness. The *Glasgow*, the *Augusta*, the *Conquistador*, the *Tamer*, the *Crescent* and the *Bellona* sailed for Sheerness: the *Seaford* and the *Captain* anchored.

At the end of a morning's lesson his uncle again detained Horatio.

'I am going in the middle of the month to his Majesty's ship, *Triumph*, Horace. She is a guard ship at Blackstakes, at the present. You will of course accompany me, and Charles Boyles prefers also to stay with me. Whether she will further your sea career more than this, I doubt: but we will ponder that problem when we are there. In any event it will be a change, my lad. How do you do, with your life at sea? Do you wish to relinquish it? Now is the time: but you look not thus to me.'

'Oh no, sir, I am determined to pursue it, if you please, sir!' said his nephew without hesitation.

Captain Suckling was gratified: the boy had showed himself lively, eager and willing, the officers had confirmed his opinion.

At seven bells on the morning of Sunday May the twelfth, the order was given to man ship. The whole company, scrubbed, clean clad, shaved and neat, were ranged along the decks, the men at the guns were ready below.

At noon came down the *Augusta* yacht with Lord Sandwich. She wore the square flag with golden anchor at her main top-gallant masthead. Early in January Lord Sandwich had succeeded Admiral Lord Hawke, who in the midst of the crisis with Spain had resigned from the cabinet on account of bad health. In the spring Lord Sandwich had set about inspecting the dockyards to ascertain the number of ships of the line fit for service, those that were reparable, and the numbers of seamen available.

As the first gun boomed, Horatio fair jumped out of his skin. The *Raisonnable* saluted with fifteen guns; the *Resolution*, then the *Captain*, did likewise. The *Augusta* returned seven. Horatio knew that the numbers bore a significance (which he promised himself to discover) and that according to ancient custom a salute was always of an odd number. For the first time, inspired with the roar of the guns, his heartbeat strangled him with pride that he was part of so ancient and honourable a service.

On the fourteenth of May the *Namur* anchored near the *Raisonnable*. On Wednesday the fifteenth Captain Suckling, to the wails of the bo'sun's pipes, left the *Raisonnable* and went aboard her. At noon she anchored at Blackstakes near the *Triumph*.

Down at the Nore, Mr Edward Leigh, the purser of the *Raisonnable* (who had had so little to say to Horation upon his arrival) died just after the Captain left. At Blackstakes, the *Augusta* yacht anchored on Wednesday afternoon. The *Triumph* saluted the Earl of Sandwich with seventeen guns and manned ship on his coming on board, repeating the salute when the Earl and Lord De Spencer left. Upon May the sixteenth in the morning, the *Triumph* mustered the ship's company. Captain Pigot resigned the ship, Captain Suckling took command. Sailed the yacht *Augusta* for Sheerness.

No man aboard the *Triumph* was sorry to see Captain Hugh Pigot go.

On Friday May the seventeenth, there sailed past the ships at the Nore the *Augusta* with Lord Sandwich, and HMS *Cruiser*, to the eastward. The *Raisonnable* manned ship to see them go. On Saturday the *Edgar* hove in sight for Sheerness and ran aground, and the master of the *Raisonnable* sent the pinnace to her assistance. (Horatio wished dearly that he could have gone.)

On Monday the Hon Henry St John took possession of the ship *Raisonnable*, Captain Suckling being removed into the *Triumph*. On Tuesday May the twenty-first in the afternoon, six petty officers were discharged from HMS *Raisonnable* and hustled themselves and their chests into the cutter. Two were dropped off at the *Crescent*, now lying at Sheerness. Three, Mr Boyles, Mr Bromley and Mr Swan, with Mr Nelson in tow, were taken down the Medway a little further to Blackstakes, where their arrival upon the *Triumph* was so inconspicuous as not to be noted in the Master's log.

CHAPTER TWO

The Mary Ann

Over the amazing blue sea, dark as indigo yet translucent withal, beneath the amazing azure sky where young white clouds flocked on the horizon, the *Mary Ann* pursued her course, like a snorting sea beast breathing foam. The sun was hot and glorious, the breeze stiff but balmy as warm milk, the pace of the ship raised all spirits to a level of joy. No brace nor tack had been touched for several watches.

The youngest member of her crew, sprawled beneath the break of the poop upon the hot deck, thought about his good fortune with a smile upon his flushed face. He was bound for the West Indies! Of which Mamma had used to talk; for there Uncle Maurice (by a sea-change become his uncle again, not his Captain) had found fame in battle. Those half-remembered descriptions of his had remained in Horace's mind as of a fair and fabulous place beyond belief, an unattainable land: which he was now fast attaining.

Now that they were in the north-easterly trade winds, Horace had some difficulty in picturing the colourless life at Blackstakes at all; Charles and the others dropping over to Sheerness for water, and the people raising and lowering and drying sails for something to do. In a kind of ecstasy of present satisfaction Horatio looked back upon the dreary two months on the *Triumph*, little of which forwarded the sea career of a youngster not by nature lazy, and who preferred to be active.

Captain Suckling had thought much about it with some anxiety. What Horace needed first to learn, by practice, was the working of the ship: how could he learn this, stationary? And all this theory of navigation: it was not much use teaching the boy this yet: how could it be brought home to him, when it was not being used? He needed to be on the ocean, see the log hove regularly, begin to observe the heavens and see the use of the quadrant. Who was there to whom he would happily entrust his nephew while he himself was fixed here? Now that there was to be no war, what chance had Horace aged twelve of a good long summer's voyage? His best chance was upon a merchantman, perhaps a West Indian. Captain Suckling had pursued his thoughts, made enquiries, and broached the subject to Horatio.

Horace was now remembering the interview with satisfaction. *Horace, how am I going to turn you into a practical seaman, fixed here in the Medway?* I don't know, sir. *What you need is a voyage, my boy, which I cannot achieve for you myself, being ordered here.* No, sir, I am aware of that, sir. *What would you say to a voyage upon a merchantman? To the West Indies? Would you find that more lively, than to stay here in the doldrums?* Yes, sir! If you please, sir, but... *You are anxious about what your papa may say? We shall write and ask his permission, of course. You shall tell him that I purpose to put you with Mr John Rathbone, who was my master's mate in the Dreadnought, and as fine a master's mate as ever I had and is now Captain of a merchantman.* Oh, sir, I remember about the *Dreadnought,* there was that battle off Cap François! *There was: you may ask Captain Rathbone for his version!* (Dryly.) *Does this plan please you? Then write to your papa, at once, and I will write too. Captain Rathbone thinks to sail before the end of July.*

Papa had written by return, that he was agreeable: bidding Horatio learn all he could under so able an instructor, he sent love from all the family and his blessing. The letter brought a pang to Horatio. There was not even time to see Maurice in London. He was dropped down to Chatham on the tender, posted across from Rochester to Gravesend, and joined the *Mary Ann* there. Her cargo was already stowed. On July 25th she slipped her moorings and sailed for the Downs, anchoring in Leigh Road (where they had used to go for water, from the *Raisonnable* at the Nore). The next evening the Warp buoy, and the next, in Margate Roads with a whole flutter of other ships for the Channel. Weighing anchor early, they were passing the North Foreland before noon, abreast of Deal two hours later, hauling round the South Foreland by mid-afternoon: and Horatio stood clasping the side timbers, his forehead on his hands, clenching his teeth, fixing his mind upon landmarks, in an effort to keep down the sour, uneasy swill in his stomach. But the heaving, slapping Channel waves and the ship's beating across them were his undoing: he was sick, his brow was cold with sweat, he shivered all over. He was ashamed, humiliated, and anxious. It's often the way at first, the steward told him, lie flat, you will get over it. Or get used to it, he added. Leaving behind the Lizard the boy was no rosier: and over the Bay of Biscay felt distinctly worse. But he went about his regular tasks with a green face and tightly-pressed lips and no complaint but a rueful smile when twitted. Once I am got over it, sir, perhaps I'll not suffer it again? Captain Rathbone had stood over him in the cabin while he drank hot grog; the weak brandy warmed his flinching stomach. You can never be sure of that, the Captain had said.

Horace grew to love Captain Rathbone; there was every reason why he should. His uncle had entrusted him to the Captain, speaking of him in his *Dreadnought* days as the most stalwart of men, a daring seaman yet one who would always struggle to keep things ship-shape and cosy. To Horatio, his new Captain was half a hero before he met him. He was a man now in his thirties, tall and broad, his hair thick and dark, his eyes a sparkling grey, his countenance slightly sardonic. He was quicker to speech than Horace's uncle, and much quicker to laughter. He would have nothing slack throughout the ship, yet was a friend to all his crew. When he had got the measure of this determined, quick-witted wisp of a boy, realised his eagerness to learn and his single-hearted application, his disregard for comfort and his need for approval, he soon came to feel for him a warm natural affection which Horace responded to at once. His desire to please Captain Rathbone was a lively spur towards his beginning to master his seamanship. John Rathbone, eager to do Captain Suckling a favour, spared no pains with Horatio and saw that his crew did not either.

Counting the Captain at the head and young Horace at the bottom, there were eighteen of them. There was the chief mate, who had early announced to Horace that he had been a lieutenant in His Majesty's Navy, but had soon quit *that*. Horatio was astonished at the tone of his voice and had dared to ask did you not like it, sir? To which the chief mate had returned another question: Did you like it, lad, crammed on a man-of-war with hundreds of others? The boy was speechless, having never thought to question the disposition of a man-of-war. Give me a cosy little ship like the *Mary Ann,* the mate had said. Then there was the second mate, a seaman who had been a master for years. There was a bo'sun, a steward, and a carpenter, a cook and a sailmaker and a surgeon. Of gunners the *Mary Ann* had no need. The other eight were able seamen with a variety of special skills (including fishing). And that was all. Although Horatio took his meals in the cabin with Captain Rathbone and his officers, he worked constantly with the men and very soon knew all the crew as friends. It was almost like being once more in the bosom of the family. He had already begun to feel its warmth and security. He had a tiny snug berth of his own, one of those off the mess room where the company fed.

The *Mary Ann* was a vessel of between two hundred and two hundred and fifty tons burden, three-masted, ship-rigged, and being built in Britain some years ago for the trade, she had been designed with the greatest possible cargo capacity that could be achieved with a reasonable speed. Broad in the beam she might be, but she was no bad sailer: and in conditions that suited her, as now, she bounded along gleefully. She was considerably smaller than either of the warships Horace had been on. Beneath the quarter-deck was the cabin, with the Captain's berth off it, and other berths used by the officers, some single, some double, where passengers also would be accommodated. Below the main deck was another, which being unpestered (as the second mate had pointed out early to Horace) with guns and their carriages, contained comfortable space enough for the mess room and the men's berths and much else. All below this were holds, packed close with stores and cargo: though not near so close, the steward told him, as they would be coming back with the sugar. Horatio was down in the bowels of the ship helping to carry back the cook's stores. What is all the cargo, he had asked? Oh, there's bales of prints, cottons and linens, handkerchiefs and stockings and hats. And earthenware, and pots and pans, and crates of glass. And some soap and candles. But I heard say (went on the steward, weighing out the flour) that the main cargo this time is stuff for a new sugar plantation and its mill and boiling house: tools, you see, hoes for the slaves, and bills and axes to clear the ground and building materials, tiles and nails. And great old copper boilers. What are *they* for, Horace asked? They're for boiling the sugar in, once it's crushed. You'll not have seen sugar, lad? What's it like? Well, great tall grass only thick. That'll do now, that's enough for the duff. Though he'll be clever if it doesn't taste of paint.

For while the hands had little to do to work the ship, time was devoted to scrubbing, tarring, rubbing down and laying on fresh paint. The ship's sides were yellow with a band of black, her deck work was picked out in white or black or yellow according to the men's taste. She looked shining, smartened up during the run before the trades to arrive spick and span in the islands. Horace, yearning to try, repainted the ship's name upon the deck buckets. The *Mary Ann* belonged to a London West India house by the name of Hibbert, Purrier and Horton. When Horatio knew Captain Rathbone well enough, he had asked him if the *Mary Ann* belonged to him? The Captain laughed.

'Nay, lad, that she does not, I wish she did.' And he told Horatio how a merchant house grew up, and how very often the same family were not only ship owners (for what was neater than carrying your own merchandise in your own bottoms) but also planters, out there in the islands.

'The chief partners in this firm are the Hibberts. You'll meet Mr Thomas Hibbert, when we go to Jamaica. There were three brothers and he is the eldest, he's much older than the other two. He's got a great place in the north of Jamaica. You'll see Hibbert's house in Kingston, where we do our business: he built it. We're taking him a load of stuff for new sugar buildings.'

'Such as great old copper boilers?' said Horace innocently, in his best Norfolk.

'Ay. How did you know that?'

'I asked the steward what the cargo was, sir,' the boy replied.

The Captain smiled. He liked a boy to look about him.

'Do you find this more interesting and lively than the guardship in the Medway, Horace?' he asked.

'Yes, sir. Certainly I do. Though,' he added quickly, feeling at once guilty of ingratitude to his uncle, 'I have wished for years to be in the navy.'

'Oh? Well, I daresay there's something to be said for the navy. In wartime, that is, you won't get paid *off*. But there's a deal to be said against it,' he added reflectively: a sentiment which Horatio was now meeting with constantly. 'For example, you won't get paid so *much*.'

This was the first time Horatio had heard Captain Rathbone put his opinion behind that of his men. Noting his solemn frown, the Captain added: 'Oh, I daresay it is all very well for the officers, what the men do well redounds to their credit. It is a hard life for the people, though. Poor food, cramped quarters, little time ashore. And floggings. What thought you to the floggings?'

Horace considered his judgement. 'I felt sorry for the men even though they had done wrong.'

'Ay.' The Captain was short. 'Little good comes of it, much harm. I have seen good men broke and useless after it. You'll not impart my opinions to your uncle, my boy.'

'No, sir.'

Horatio reflected upon the whispered remarks that he and Charles had sometimes caught amongst the men of the *Triumph*. It seemed the men thanked providence for the change of Captains: that, compared with the man his uncle had followed, Captain Suckling was a just man, only roused with due reason. About the whispered tyrannies of Captain Pigot, the men knew the danger of letting their tongues go. But a feeling had pervaded the ship of some oppressive evil removed.

Pulled between his ardent pride in the idea of the King's Navy and these contrary new ideas aboard the merchantman, the boy said nothing of this further ammunition against a man-of-war: but considered it, nonetheless.

They were divided, as in the warships, into watches. Horace found himself in the starboard watch under the second mate, a fearless seaman, not impatient that his pupil had all to learn and glad to find that the young man longed to go aloft. Whenever hands were sent up to see to some line or other, Horatio would stand below the mast watching the men's progress up the ratlines as if he would impress every foot and handhold upon his memory. Wait a bit, lad, the second mate would say, you shall go: when she's steadier and you're steadier, we'll have you up.

Before the tropics they had shifted sail, having off the fine new ones with which the journey had started, and bending an old patched suit for the fair weather. The watch would tail on to the gant-line of the sail to be hoist, and run aft with it singing, and up would go the sail: then 'Aloft, and bend it!' the order would come. Now Horace ran with the rest, up the ratlines the weather side, straining to keep up with the man ahead of him. His pride was at stake, his longing to excel urged him on, he did not look down, being admonished by his fellows not to, and was fortunate in finding that he was not afraid. He took his place upon the foot-rope of the main royal yard, far, far above the *Mary Ann's* deck as she tossed them about like birds in a windswept tree. While the head of the sail was spread along the yard and the head earrings passed, and the buntlines and leech-lines clinched, the boy allowed himself one quick amazed look over his shoulder. The sea! The blue sea stretched for ever, for ever! He watched his neighbour. Never leave go, lad, one hand for yourself, one for the ship. Somehow, the rovings were tied with one hand; the sheet and the clew-line were shackled. When the sail had been picked up and furled in and made fast to the jackstay by short ropes called gaskets, they came right down to the deck, to hoist next the upper top-gallant. Then up aloft once more, where the whole process was repeated. This was the way to learn the ropes. You must watch every step upon the ratlines, every hold upon the shrouds, beware of every gust that might make a canvas lash and throw you off. What Horatio felt at those brief glimpses below was not fear but awe, for the vast, heaving, powerful, endless deep.

It was very hot, too hot often for bare feet upon the scorching deck. They were approaching the tropic, but Horatio got off lightly: Sails, wearing an oakum wig and beard for Neptune, appeared on the quarter-deck waving his sceptre after Horace, and upon the payment of half-a-crown by Captain Rathbone did nothing worse than plunge the boy's head in a bucket of sea-water, a penalty more pleasurable than otherwise. His hair bleached a pale gold and plastered upon his scalp, the water glistening upon his face, his chest and bare legs burnt dark with the sun, Horatio stood laughing upon the deck while all applauded. He had become the darling of them all, it was Horace this and Horace that, and Horace the other, as he hurried eagerly to oblige. They had seen him turn from a green-faced sufferer to a healthy, lively, useful apprentice who could haul with the rest, turn a rope the right way on the pin, do his share aloft, feel which way the wind blew. He was their creation, for all had had a hand in building his confidence. They were proud of him. He blossomed under it.

'Heave the log,' yelled the second mate now. The mysteries of the line had early been explained to Horatio, how it was marked off in fathoms by different pieces of cloth or leather with varying ends, or by simple knots, so that a man could recognise them by feel in the dark: the distance between each knot was the time the sand glass took to run thirty seconds. The reel which held the line was attached to a conical-shaped piece of wood called the logship.

The second mate hove the logship overboard, letting about twenty fathoms of stray line run out.

'Turn!' called out the second mate as soon as a piece of bunting reached the water.

Horace turned his glass sharply and watched the sand slide through.

'Stop!' he cried as the last grain vanished.

The second mate stopped the line instantly, counted the knots, and announced their speed to be nine and a half knots. Eight bells struck.

Horace lingered a minute or two to watch the flying fish. A silvery shoal leapt suddenly up into the sun, down again into the water with a thousand tiny splashes, up and down, and up and down again, attracting the attention of a cruising bosun bird looking for his supper. How should he describe them to Papa? He had begun a letter and should post it by the packet from Barbados. They were really quite like small herrings, with wings. But the mate had told him that they were very large fins, not wings, and when the fins dried out in the air, down the fish fell again into the sea.

Horatio was up on the fo'c's'le: he had possessed himself, after somewhat grudging permission, of the second mate's quadrant. It was the starboard watch below, but too stifling to say down: the winds were becoming more fitful, there had been some breathless calms, and now and then a hazy mist over the sun.

Horace studied the instrument, which was of the kind called Hadley's after its inventor.

'Don't you go fiddling with the screws now,' the second mate had said. 'Because it's all adjusted and screwed tight, how I need it.' He now ran his hands down the radial sides of the polished wooden frame, smooth with use and care. The thing formed an eighth of a circle, the shape of a slice of cake: the two sides being fixed into a third, an arc of wood called the limb, round which was fixed a strip of brass marked off from right to left into degrees and minutes. Fixed to the top above the join of the two arms was a movable, flat bar of brass called the index: and standing up perpendicular to the instrument was the index glass, a quick-silvered mirror which moved with the index and caught the image of the sun, or moon, or star, that you might be observing. The job of this mirror was to reflect the image upon one or other of the two horizon-glasses, fixed upon an extension from the frame. Then there were three coloured glasses to prevent the sun's rays from hurting your eyes. The sight vanes, one disposed at the right position for each horizon glass, had holes in them through which you directed your gaze. Horace had a great desire to try on his own. The simplest way of determining your latitude at sea was by observing the sun at noon, and failing that you must take a double altitude and work out sums by means of the tables. But all he wished to do was to capture the image of the sun, floating there misty but luminous halfway to the horizon.

He stood up, adjusted the two red glasses to protect his eyes, and, holding the quadrant flat before him, put his eye to the proper sight vane and gazed at the horizon. He must move the index, to find the coloured image of the sun in the horizon-glass. Slowly and with delicate care he moved the index along while he peered through the hole in the vane. The reddish glow made all look full of foreboding, like a storm or the end of the world. There it was: there was the coloured image of the sun, dancing up and down in the glass! Now came the tricky part; once you had caught the image you must give the quadrant what they called a slow vibratory motion about the line of vision. Horace was finding it difficult enough to hold the quadrant up steadily. Now he began to perform a peculiar swaying movement with the thing, which he fondly hoped to be what he had seen others do. The sun's image at once disappeared. A pox on the sun, he had had it perfect! He turned and swayed about until he found it again. Now then, while you were performing the vibratory motions, you were to move the index until you brought down the lower limb of the sun to sit upon the horizon. What a magical feat it seemed, to bring down the sun! He began once more upon his careful swaying movements, gently pushing the index along with his left hand. The image of the sun began to descend, and Horatio's excitement to rise, when the hot silence of the fo'c's'le was shattered by roars and whinnies of delighted laughter. The sudden noise made the boy start violently. His experiment all lost, Horace turned scarlet to the chest with fury.

The cook had come out of the galley behind him, and with a frying pan held before his eyes was performing an exact parody of the boy's vibratory motions. The port watch was unable any longer to contain its laughter. Horatio, tears in his eyes, almost choked with rage: for he hated to be laughed at. But his wits came to his aid, he lowered the quadrant, rubbed his eyes, and laughed with the rest.

'Oh, I nearly had it, I all but had it!' he wailed, stamping on the deck.

'Never mind lad. Try again. Get in, Slush. Leave the boy in peace,' said the chief mate.

Still chuckling, the men returned to their stations, and Horace to the far distant horizon.

Nearly a week after they had crossed the tropic, the mate calculated them to be in the latitude of Barbados, and the *Mary Ann's* course was set due westerly so that they should not run by unawares this low lying land, first of the tropic islands. Now the fish and the birds increased. Flying fish landed upon the deck, to be swooped upon and carried to the cook. Shoals of bonitos like huge mackerel made good fishing and good eating. On the fo'c's'le, Sails came upon a great brownish-purple grasshopper with grey spotted wings, live, and blinking its prominent eyes. 'That's a locust. Tasty to eat. Here, let me catch 'un.' And Sails did so, turning Horace's stomach at the thought. Tropic birds, and black fork-tailed men-of-war birds dropped into the water for fish. Huge duck-like boobies, grey and white, their faces innocent above their round yellow bills, perched in the tops to be stalked by the seamen. The noddy birds were equally confiding. Round the ship's bows plunged shining porpoises and blue dolphins. And sharks' fins would appear, cleaving the water with savage speed, a trail of phosphorescence behind them. This flaking phosphorus enchanted Horatio, who spent much of his free time watching and enquiring the names of the birds so that he might tell his papa, who had an unquenchable interest in the wonders of creation and would like to know.

When the look-out called the land, Horace rushed to look through the second mate's glass at the blurred blue outline low on the horizon. As they entered a sheltered bay at last, the prospect seemed like heaven: sand whiter than any he had ever seen, fronded trees of vivid green, fields beyond more brilliant still; white houses with green blinds, a fort with flags flying. Now he could see the people, in pale, bright clothes. Anchored in Carlisle Bay, the ship was besieged by shore boats crowded with baskets of glowing oranges, green bananas and fruits that Horace had never seen; with dried fish and eggs and chickens and much else. He longed to go ashore, but must instead watch the Captain's gig bobbing over the water towards the gleaming sand.

The *Mary Ann* was running down to Tobago, the wind steady upon her quarter but less fresh, all her sail crowded on. Tobago was Captain Rathbone's first port of call: he was in a hurry to finish there and get on up to Jamaica where there was more trade, more people, and more diversions of every kind. He had come off from Bridgetown with various pieces of news which he retailed at the cabin table.

'There's been a terrible plague of locusts in the bay of Honduras, ate up every green thing and starved all the Indians. They say they were lying a foot thick on the ground. The locusts, I mean.'

'No wonder that one Sails ate was so fat, sir,' said Horace.

'Sails *ate?*'

'Said he was going to, sir.'

'Sails will eat anything,' put in the chief mate. 'Did you get news of the Jamaica drought, sir?'

'Ay. Eased a little. Good rain in May. They think the sugar will be up to normal. There's trouble in St Vincent, where the Caribs won't exchange their land, protesting they are not subjects to the Kings of Great Britain.'

'But they are since 1763, are they not?' put in the surgeon. 'What's to do?'

'It's said we shall land troops to subdue them. How's your French, Horace?' he asked suddenly.

Horace was startled.

'Bad, sir. Very bad. I never could like French at school, sir.'

'Pity. Because plenty of folk still speak French in Tobago and I was counting on you as interpreter,' said the Captain, winking sideways. Horace thought of Jemmy Moisson at North Walsham and wished he had not wasted his time. Who would have thought that French would ever be of any use to him? He was afraid he would have to repair the breach.

Tobago, a hilly island clothed in forest, had rushing streams in every valley and a spine of higher mountains down the middle. In Courland Bay the *Mary Ann* put in, the Captain went to the custom-house: and black slaves appeared to unload her cargo. Tobago having ceased to be French at the end of the last war, was now filling up with British planters who needed British manufactures.

Captain Rathbone had business ashore, and took Horatio with him. It was the first time Horace had touched dry land for weeks (it was now towards mid-September) and despite the heat which met him like a wall, he could not suppress a hop and a jump. From the harbour side they took the road to the little town of Scarborough (where in the market were the nutmegs for which Tobago was famed), and on above the low shore to Sandy Point as the sea broke in foam far out: and at length to Plymouth, a smaller town still. Fields of sugar cane and fluffy cotton, coffee bushes in dark scarlet berry, forests of tall trees with brilliant flowers, and creepers strung with fruits, lay on the land ward side.

As they turned to go back, Captain Rathbone said, 'Did you ever read *Robinson Crusoe*, Horace?'

'Yes, indeed I did, sir!' Horatio said.

'I've heard it said,' went on Captain Rathbone, 'that this is Crusoe's coast. There's a cave I believe somewhere along the shore, which people call Crusoe's cave.'

Horace gazed up at the shore with rocks and trees above it, which might easily conceal the fortress and cave and summer bower of Crusoe: and was suddenly transported to King's Lynn on a cold February day, Papa at hand, and he himself calling out the sign of an auctioneer's shop.

From Tobago the *Mary Ann* sailed down Crusoe's coast, rounded Sandy Point, then set her course north-westerly across the Caribbean sea for Port Maria upon the northern coast of Jamaica. It was the nearest port to Mr Thomas Hibbert's estate at Agualta Vale, and the goods he had ordered were heavy. They arrived at dusk about eight days later, and Captain Rathbone wasted no time in sending a messenger to Mr Hibbert. Early the next morning, a train of mule carts was spotted winding down the road from the plantations. It was still barely five o'clock. Horace stood waiting in the delicious coolness, drinking in unconsciously the scents of vegetation, the salt surf smell, the bright colours misted with dawn, and behind all this the unrecognised cries of the approaching people, singing rhythmical snatches, urging on their beasts with sticks and exhortations, themselves urged on by an overseer on horseback, with a whip.

All hands worked feverishly to race the sun's might. The boxes, the crates of utensils and provisions were swung or handed out on to the quay, the carts were loaded and tied, the cavalcade prepared to move off, and the *Mary Ann* lay lighter in the water. The Captain, ordering Horace to carry his bag, entered the sociable that had been sent for him and the boy climbed in after. By nine o'clock the sun was fierce, but inland were sudden cool breezes. They followed wide forest tracks closed in by polished coffee bushes, and banana palms, with here and there a tree so tall that Horace's canvas hat fell off in craning to look at it. They came out into lush pastures where cattle grazed: and acre upon acre of green sugar cane waving its narrow leaves higher than Horatio.

'It looks in good heart to me, drought or no drought,' remarked Captain Rathbone to the driver.

'Ay, sir. All new sugar. Several months to go yet,' the man replied.

Mr Thomas Hibbert was a man in his early sixties, as dark as the famed mahogany wood of Honduras and the islands. He had arrived in Jamaica in 1735 and become one of the richest of Kingston merchants, establishing his business in an elegant house in Duke Street. This great estate of Agualta Vale he had purchased about ten years ago. This year he had got new sugar lands cleared and weeded and prepared by hundreds of slaves with their hoes and machetes, and had planted at the end of May the acres of canes through which the visitors had driven. They were taken up to his favourite hill-top by Mr Hibbert, whence they could see the sugar works a-building, for which much of the *Mary Ann's* cargo was awaited. To the south-east, the Agualta river wound towards the sea and the silver sweep of Anotta bay. More distantly rose the misty peaks of the Blue Mountains.

They had hauled down the top spars and heeled over the lightened *Mary Ann* in the careenage at Port Maria, and were slung or clambering along her upturned starboard side, scrubbing and scraping her under water timbers, hogging her bottom with stiff brushes. Horace had already lost one hog into the water, which had caused the bo'sun to roar. It was not unpleasant work, with a hat to keep off the sun and the breeze from the sea to cool one's back, but it made the arms ache.

Horatio puffed and sighed, stretching his right arm out.

'Watch that brush!' said the bo'sun from below him. 'Or I'll feed you to the sharks.'

'Ay, ay, sir. Shall we stay here in this harbour all the time?' asked Horace of his neighbour. 'Or shall we go to Kingston?'

'Oh, we shall go to Kingston all right. That's where all the trading goes on.'

'I thought we were to be full up with Mr Hibbert's sugar.'

'There's other Hibberts, sends their sugar into Kingston. That's where *we* have to be wary, in Kingston.'

'Wary of what?'

'Wary of the pressmen. Lurk on the quayside, in the inns, in the market. You never know where. Grab you, put you in irons, in the bottom of some goddam warship,' he said. 'And there you stay till out at sea. And our Captain left with not enough hands to sail her.'

Horace began to scrape again, remembering with a shock that he was in fact still a member of the crew of a goddam warship himself.

Now the sun was clouded over, the smell from the land was strong, a blustery wind blew athwart them. The sudden rain fell in sheets, plastering their hair and their shirts against the skin, blinding their eyes, drowning their shouts and laughter with its beating upon the deck. The second mate grinned down upon the starboard watch, drenched at their work. 'Up, lads. Watch your step, she's slippery,' he yelled. It rained increasingly throughout October.

Sailing down from Port Maria, they rounded Morant Point and approached Kingston from the east, by the good passage above the many islands large and small that lay before the mouth of Port Royal Harbour. As they approached the long spit of land which sheltered Kingston, the *Mary Ann* ran up her signal for a pilot: and a pilot boat was soon seen, beating across the sparkling water towards them. The sight enthralled Horace: the great expanse of blue water, whipped up into small waves merrily crested with foam; the fort of Port Royal with its flags fluttering; one or two large ships of war standing at anchor; frigates passing fleetly out towards the islets; fishing-boats, dug-out boats, pilot-boats, a tidy little cutter which came alongside, to collect the fee due to the officer of the fort: who even now was firing his guns to signal the *Mary Ann*. The ship proceeded into the huge sheltered expanse of Kingston Harbour where many merchantmen lay and lighters came and went. The *Mary Ann* lay out in the Channel, her Captain having an ever-present fear that those who nosed alongside were more at the mercy of the pressmen. Then Captain Rathbone went ashore to enter his vessel and pay the fees and duties and pilotage.

'Shan't see him for a few days,' remarked the second mate to Horace. 'He'll be up to Hibbert's house to find out our home cargo. There'll be sugar from the Hanover estates and the Albion estate, and coffee and cotton too. All Hibbert's. And maybe some Horton contracts and something for the Purriers.'

'And Mr Thomas's sugar?'

'Oh, ay. We always must leave room for that. At the top. His hogsheads take the best place.'

'Why is the top the best place?' Horace asked.

'Less likely to get washed out in a storm. We'll have no trouble getting her full, never mind all the foreigners.'

'The foreigners?'

'There are free ports in the islands now, where the foreigners can get our goods. They can get the slaves they need, too.'

'Who brings the slaves?' Horace asked.

'Why everybody. Depends where they come from.'

'Where do *we* get them? The British, I mean.'

'From West Africa. You've heard of the slave coast.'

'But how do we get them? They can't wish to come?'

'I daresay they're slaves already, and their kings and chiefs trade them. Mr Hibbert's are slaves, they're happy enough, aren't they?'

'They seemed so indeed.' Horace sounded doubtful, thinking how hateful to be a slave: his doubts pricked the seaman's conscience. Young and unworldly, the boy had a child's curiosity and an untarnished view of right and wrong. Was the whole trade in slaves wrong?

'Not but what it isn't disgraceful the way they're brought,' he added. 'All herded together under hatches. But when they're here, maybe it's better.'

'Have you ever sailed in a slaver?' Horace persisted.

The second mate was silent.

As January wore on, the sugar droghers began to arrive, small coastal vessels bringing the raw sugar round to Kingston. The harvest went on until May: all the slaves of a plantation cutting day and night; and the workers in the boiling-houses watching over their seething liquid. The muscovado went into the hogsheads for Europe, the molasses into the still-houses for rum, or else to North America.

Horatio went ashore with the second mate. They would walk along the waterfront, where British merchants sold cargoes to dark arrogant Spaniards dressed in striped gingham coats, who would pay in *pesos fuertes* carried in leather buckets upon the heads of their Negro servants. These were Spanish silver dollars: but there were French and Dutch and Portuguese merchants with their own coins and their own tongues. Jews there had been for generations. One day they passed a group of slaves standing for sale: those in front young and well, concealing those behind who shivered and looked grey, drooping to hide tears. Planters from inland walked round inspecting them. The second mate turned Horace quickly into a booth and bought rum.

By mid-May the *Mary Ann* was beating about into the teeth of the north-easterly trades making for the windward passage between the islands of Cuba and Haiti. (The Captain preferred it to the treacherous passage through the Florida Gulf, where the current was so strong that, though it might carry you along against the gale, it might too easily carry you on to the reefs which fringed the channel.) The ship was full-loaded and going home: coffee (carefully stowed by itself next to some bales and seroons of cotton wool, for coffee picked up the flavour of its neighbour); some fustic, some indigo, some ginger; some bales of hides, some puncheons of rum: but more than all, sugar, hogsheads of oozing, sticky raw sugar, with its sickly strong smell which turned the stomach. They had been more than seven months in the West Indies: any other life seemed as strange as an unknown continent. All minds, all hands were now upon the sailing. They were close-hauled upon the starboard tack.

'If this don't teach young Horace how a ship goes about, then nothing will,' the Captain had remarked more than once. For what seemed like the hundredth time that day, came the order for all hands, for the ship to go about. Horace knew which braces were his to loosen and coil down clear upon the deck when the moment came. Aft were the stronger members of his watch, at the mizzen-top-gallant and royal braces: forward, the other watch at their stations. At the break of the poop, the Captain, eyeing all about, calling out:

'Ready oh!'

Then Captain Rathbone silently motioned with his arm to the helmsman, who eased the helm down.

'Helm's alee!'

The *Mary Ann* turned her head up shyly into the wind, the cook let go the foresheet, the wind came out of the foresail, then the mainsail fell limp and fluttered.

'Raise tacks and sheets!'

All but the foretack were loosened while the Captain paused, judging his moment.

'Mainsail haul!' he bellowed.

The men hauled on the rope. The yards swung round prettily, quickly. Horace pulled hard upon the slack of the braces, he could scarce do it fast enough, and turned them tidily upon the pin. Then he leapt for the main deck, the crossjack and main braces. While the chief mate and the port watch were bracing up the foreyards and trimming them, the Captain himself trimmed the afteryards. Horace now helped his watch haul on the tackle of the maintack bringing the point of the sail right down, while the port watch saw to the foretack. When all the yards were trimmed, the tacks boarded, the bowlines of the course hauled forward, and the *Mary Ann* sailing trimly upon the port tack, the Captain called:

'Go below, the watch!'

Then the watch on deck coiled down all neatly and tidied up.

When it was well and quickly done (which was not always the case) there was great satisfaction after the effort, pleasure at working with skilful strong men. Horace was more aware of this than ever before as he stooped to coil down ropes. *Aft the most honour,* they were always saying to him, *forward the better man*. They said it in all contingencies: when you were for'ard yourself how true it seemed! The Captain or the mates might give the orders, but what use would they be without the men knowing, doing, hurrying, bending all their strength and skill to the hard exactitude of their tasks? Now at this minute the boy was entirely one of them: a huge love welled in his heart for all the men who had taught him, freely given him their hard-earned experience, the men with whom he worked. The moment seemed radiant and timeless. He exulted in working with his fellows. No less certainly he loved those aft, the Captain in particular. For a few more weeks he should have this pleasure, to live and work and feed and laugh with these men: what then? What should he do without them? How should he make out, lacking their affectionate concern? How should he return to the huge crowded loneliness of a man-of-war, the being alone yet never alone: the horror of the men's being flogged, the fear of a bad officer? He was in heart a midshipman no longer: he wished to continue in the warmth of Captain Rathbone's company upon their merchant ship. The Captain had implied more than once (casually, so that the suggestion was scarce noted the first time or two) that he would be gratified to keep him and make a first-class seaman of him. The suggestion now crystallised in Horace's mind. His conversion was almost complete. Though he did not realise this, he was fully aware of his dread at their approach steadily and surely to the English shore. Six weeks, seven, eight at the most, they must be there. How would he broach his feelings to Uncle Maurice and to Papa? He did not know. He turned his mind resolutely away from the future, determined to enjoy a fleeting present.

'Horatio!' called the Captain, from the poop. He seldom used the formal name: the boy sprang up, wondering how long he had stooped here over his tidy rope, thinking these warring thoughts and feeling such emotions.

'Sir!'

'If you have done, you may go up on to the fo'c's'le. To starboard ahead there, you will see Cap François my lad, where your uncle and I chased seven French and shot them about in 1757!'

Shot them to rags and tinder, the boy heard in his mother's voice.

The tug-of-war increased beneath his consciousness.

Chapter Three

'…a practical seaman, with a horror of the Royal Navy…'

Maurice Nelson, now turned nineteen, had been in London more than five years, Burnham only seen occasionally. On this warm July evening, he found his lodgings insufferably hot. He opened the window, took off his neckerchief, and flung himself into a wickerwork chair that creaked with complaint at his assault. It seemed as if there might be a good summer to come: already there had been spells of warmth, now came another.

He picked up Papa's latest letter and read it again. At Burnham, they would be haymaking. Papa would marshal Edmund and Suckling, on holiday from school for the purpose, and they would all four be mowing the glebe with stalwart Peter working the fastest. The remembered smell of the hay on the warm night air smote Maurice to the soul. What heaven to be there, amongst the summer flowers, moon daisies and poppies, pink campion and forget-me-nots and clover! To work till one's throat burned with thirst, to sit under the huge elm, and swill down great tankards of ale! It made him long for a drink instantly. Ann might be at work too, her skirts tucked up: and Sukey would come and summon them to supper, in the dusk when they could see no more. It was Sunday night, the twelfth of July: he remembered that today they would not work, they would have been to church, past roses and honeysuckle smelling like paradise. He had been for a long walk himself, down to the river and up towards Chiswick, out of the smells of the city.

There came the sudden sound of hooves and wheels stopping, then a spirited quick knocking upon the door of the house.

Now who would be that, upon a Sunday night?

Maurice bounded out into the passage and to the street door. He wrenched at the wobbling iron handle, and flung the door open. Two people stood there a man—and a boy. For the briefest instant, Maurice did not recognise him.

'Maurice!'

'Horace!'

They flung themselves, laughing, into each other's arms: there had always been this foolish jest about their names rhyming.

'Where have you sprung from? You look in splendid health!'

'Thank heaven you had not moved your lodging! This kind gentleman accompanied me from the coach, for I am green enough in London—'

'Will you come in, sir? And have some refreshment? How far have you come?' Maurice asked, heaving in his brother's sea chest.

'All the way from Plymouth, as has your brother. I will not linger, I have a family in London awaiting me, but I must first make sure Horatio found his brother, at the Captain's request.'

'Thank you indeed, sir, it is exceedingly good of you. From Plymouth, by heavens, you must both be weary. How many days?'

'Four, all but a few hours. Quite fagged out, and very hungry, are we not, sir?' Horace said perkily, shaking his companion by the hand and thanking him warmly again. The two brothers waved as he entered the chaise: then dashed, screaming with excitement, for Maurice's room. That young man's spirits had risen like a fountain, his loneliness and the heat were forgotten.

'Horace! How wonderful to see you, what a treat, I never saw you in better health! How sunburned you are! Though I can see you are tired—'

'I shall be as right as rain with a good night's rest. These inns, I did not care for them and I think I was bitten by fleas,' said Horatio strutting about like an experienced traveller, and tossing his jacket upon the creaking chair.

'I don't doubt you were. I was about to get supper, but I have only bread and cheese and a little cold meat—'

'Quite what I am used to, I need no more.'

'I am going to fetch a jug of ale, we shall at least drink to our meeting. Do you know, I was sat here, dreaming about the haymaking, and the ale at home, and longing to be there.'

Horatio let out a huge sigh.

'Sit down, rest yourself, I shall not be long. Oh, it is splendid to see you, brother. What news you must have to tell! We shall talk till we are hoarse, therefore, the ale!' And Maurice seized a pot and hurried from the house, and ran past the window waving it. Horace did not sit down, however, but roamed the room, and stared from the window, his joy at seeing his brother unable to subdue for long the turmoil in his mind and the anguish in his heart. The four days' journey with nothing else to think of had screwed up his anxiety and excitement to breaking point, he must let out his heart to Maurice or die.

The *Mary Ann* had made Plymouth on July the seventh, coming to port with some difficulty for the winds were contrary: and had been so,

Captain Rathbone was soon informed, for the last week or more. When no change had come within two days and the easterly wind still blew, he had decided to send his young charge by land. 'Why, we may be kept hanging about here another week or more lad,' he had said. 'You will report to your ship and talk to your uncle as to your sea career. You have done well with me, you are already a promising seaman, I would gladly have you back, Horace, to complete the task! You know where you can find me, should you want to: the *Mary Ann* will be a month or less, fitting and turning round.'

This was as near as he had ever come to proposing the change in Horatio's direction that was now causing the boy such heart-searching. Horatio had parted with his companions and the Captain in a state of stunned disbelief that he must leave them: and with a desperate determination to do no such thing, could he by any means compass otherwise.

Thus Maurice found him, standing glumly by the window, the airy joy of his arrival swallowed up again in his struggle.

'Look what I have found! Cherries! The first, from Kent. We seldom saw them in Norfolk,' and he set down the ale and placed a basket of the fat, gleaming crimson fruit upon the table, and quickly brought out the supper. 'Come Horace, you are exhausted. Sit and eat first, then we shall talk and you can tell me what wonders you have seen. And what it is that burdens your mind. As I can see, for you were in good spirits but now.'

'I am not hungry, but I'll eat a bite.'

'You will find you are when you begin. Here. And I am, for one.'

His brother's words proving to be true, they ate in quiet concentration together. Maurice poured out ale, they drank to each other with silent smiles. He pushed forward the cherries.

'Take a handful. Eat and spare not. There's no fruit so good, I declare.'

They began to eat the delicious fruit and continued ravenously, unable to stop eating. The polished skin's feel in the mouth, the soft firmness of the pink flesh, the sweetness of the juice which runs down the throat make the ripe cherry the most alluring of fruits. A race developed, as each clawed at the twinned and trio-ed cherries, pulling them off into their mouths, spitting the cleaned pips about the room in laughing abandon, expelling them through the open window from their fingers' tips.

'Mine!'

'Mine!'

'Yours, I think. I have had my share.'

Horace ate the last cherry, with lingering pleasure.

'You are sorry in some sense to be back,' Maurice stated at length.

'I have been so happy. I have learnt so much, I think I know all there is to know about the *Mary Ann,* there are only eighteen of us, and they all taught me, all helped me, I think I have had the happiest year of my life!' his brother blurted, his heart in his voice.

'And you do not wish to leave them.'

'No, I cannot bear to leave them. I dread going back to the *Triumph.* I had far rather stay in a merchantman, than continue in the navy! Captain Rathbone will have me, I am sure he wants to have me! And the places we have seen, and the people, and the islands!'

'Tell me.'

Horace talked till he was tired, but his heart relieved. He talked of Captain Rathbone, and his crew; of his first going up aloft, of bending sail, of learning the ropes, of going about, of high seas and torrents of rain, of the glorious steady trades, of sun and sugar cane and slaves and cocoa and rum, and scraping the ship's sides, and tarring and painting. Of incongruous Christmas feasts of too rich food, crabs and chickens and peppers and avocados, in too hot weather. And often, again, of Captain Rathbone. Maurice questioned him now and then, led him on, sighed: thinking of his office stool and his quill.

'What a fortunate fellow you are, Horace. What a life it sounds!'

'Do you suppose that there is any chance that Papa—that Uncle Maurice...' his brother stopped helplessly.

'You must return to the *Triumph* tomorrow I suppose,' Maurice said. 'Can you not talk with Uncle Maurice, tell him your feelings, ask his advice?'

'How can I ask his advice to leave him, to refuse what he has offered? Besides (fond as I am of our Uncle Maurice) I never can tell what he is thinking! He says so little, he seems to feel so little.'

'True.' Maurice remembered the quietness of his godfather from his earliest encounters with him. 'You can but try. Would he, do you suppose, let you have a week's leave? We might journey to Burnham together if I can arrange it! Then you may talk to Papa, explain yourself to him, you and he have always understood each other. Do try to get leave, you have not been home for eighteen months.'

'I will. I will try, by heavens. To be at the parsonage again, for a little! What bliss! I think Uncle Maurice must allow me. To see Papa!' he shouted.

'I'll request Uncle William tomorrow to let me go next Saturday! Do you do the same from Uncle Maurice. So soon as I hear from you I will take our places upon the diligence. I shall write to Papa in any event, and tell him of our hoped for arrival. Oh, I pray nothing happens to prevent it, it's a capital arrangement.'

As soon as he reached Chatham, Horatio realised that the stubborn easterlies had changed. The wind was coming from the west nor' west, this wind would blow the *Mary Ann* up the channel. His heart was fixed with the *Mary Ann*, with her Captain and her crew; yet he must needs find the *Triumph*.

Horace had joined the *Triumph* at Blackstakes, and sailed with her across to Sheerness: he returned to find her lying in Chatham reach, not so very far from where he had first come to the *Raisonnable*. He reported himself to the officer of the watch; and to the purser, with some pride, as an ordinary seaman: for this he now judged himself to be, though he had remained upon the roll as Captain's servant. The purser noted his appearance upon July 13th 1772, and the question of leave having been mooted, arranged for him to see his uncle.

'Well, Horace!'

'Sir!'

'You are grown taller, and you look in good health. Have you had a profitable voyage with Captain Rathbone?'

'Indeed I thank you, I have, sir, I was never happier in my life,' the boy burst out with a kind of defiance.

Captain Suckling noted it: it was new in his nephew.

'Good. And they have taught you everything you need to know?' he continued, dryly.

'Everything, sir,' said Horace with such emphasis and confidence that his uncle smiled.

'Then I hope we shall quickly see the fruits of it. I daresay you will find it a little slow here after your adventures—'

'I think I may, sir,' Horatio confessed, flushing.

Again, the Captain noted it. It was no uncommon thing, he supposed, for a boy to return unwillingly from a favourable voyage. He was not unaware of the general opinion of the merchant seaman against the king's navy.

'You still resolve to be a seaman?' he asked.

'Oh yes, sir, I am more than ever resolved to be a *seaman*—' the boy emphasised the word and hesitated, flushing again.

'You think perhaps a merchant ship is a more comfortable place?'

'It is not that, sir, I think little of comfort'—which was true—'I was very happy with Captain Rathbone and his crew, we were like a…like a family, sir!'

'Ah.' His uncle paused. 'The purser says you would like leave?'

'I have spent the night with my brother Maurice, I travelled up from Plymouth, sir. Maurice determines to ask Uncle William for a week's holiday from Saturday, and thought you might grant me the same favour so that we go together?'

'So you shall, Horace. Take a week, think it well over, you may feel differently when you have done so. Talk to your worthy papa. Before that you may feel at home upon the *Triumph* again. Nothing comes, but it goes, Horace: all is change in this life,' said his uncle in an unusual burst of philosophy, as he dismissed his nephew from the cabin.

The week began with the arrival of Lord Sandwich in the yacht *Augusta* and for the next four days salutes roared back and forth between the ships as the First Lord came and went. Captain Suckling entertained a fleeting hope that his reluctant nephew's enthusiasm and loyalty would be re-attached by this bustle: his nephew, beneath the forgotten rigours of manning ship and the roar of guns, heard but the voice of Captain Rathbone dismissing it all as so much flummery. By the morning of Saturday the eighteenth the *Augusta* was gone. So was the Captain's nephew, hurrying up to London in the dawn to join his brother.

Edmund Nelson was puzzled and anxious: and his anxiety made him stern.

The excitement of his two sons' arrival had at first overwhelmed them all: Horatio's joy to be home, to see Sukey and Nanny again; and the two schoolboys Mun and Suckling (usually quiet enough, but at this event run mad with boisterous enjoyment): and little Kitty who remembered him not at all, picked up and flung screaming into his arms by Maurice. William was home for the harvesting, from North Walsham: the two shook each other with shy laughter, William pulling one of his noted faces to hide his feelings of pleasure.

And how Horatio had talked! Papa, listening to the excited flow, realised how this son of his when roused had always been the most articulate. And how he boasted (as he had always been used to do) in his excitement: of what he had done and could do, of all he had seen, of his happiness upon the *Mary Ann*. Susannah, though laughing, encouraged him, Ann smiled primly, the two younger boys drank it in, dazed with their brother's adventurous life: Kitty, it was clear, was ready to adore him. The rector felt some concern for his eldest son, listening to Horace with such good-natured admiration, while bound to his office desk and with no ambition or capacity to better his own lot. After a day or so it began to dawn upon Mr Nelson that his son was far from happy in returning to the *Triumph*. This had been Horace's object (discussed with his brother in the coach)—to give his father a picture of the advantages of the merchant seaman before he voiced his prejudice against the navy. His father's uneasiness had increased as the boy's expressions against ships of war became more and more open.

'Why, I had far rather continue with Captain Rathbone, than return to the *Triumph*!' he confessed airily at last.

His father was conscious of his son's glance covertly upon him, but he said nothing, did nothing to relieve the sudden silence at the table. Later, he sent for Horatio to the study. A glance passed between Maurice and his brother before he went.

'Papa?'

'Come in Horace, shut the door, sit down. Your talk, my son, is that of a person with a divided mind about his future. Have I interpreted you rightly?'

'Yes Papa.'

'I had rather you had come direct to me than bandied this about in talk—'

'I was going to, Papa, I was waiting a chance...' he began eagerly.

'Now is your chance, Horace. What is it that disturbs you?'

The rector listened patiently enough while his son unburdened his heart: but his anxiety and distress were plain to Horace, who spoke the more desperately in consequence.

'But Horatio,' he began, 'even if we were so ungrateful as to spurn the help your uncle has offered us, how sure are we of your employment?'

'Oh Papa, I am not ungrateful! But Captain Rathbone made it plain he would welcome me back, and I was so happy with him...'

'Has he sent me a letter, to say he will employ you? Until you are trained, and of age to look to yourself?'

'No Papa, but I am sure he intends it—'

'I have no doubt of his good will towards you, my boy, but I think such a thing would be an apprenticeship, and I think your papa must find a premium? I have little money to spare, Horace, and six more of you to settle in life. Does it not seem foolish as well as ungrateful to forgo your uncle's help at this time? What is your future in a merchant ship?'

'When I am trained, Papa, I shall be Captain of a ship myself.'

'And where have Captain Rathbone and his mates received their training and experience? Was not Captain Rathbone in your uncle's ship, the *Dreadnought*?'

'Yes, Papa.'

'And what of his crew? Are they not some of them naval men?'

'Yes, Papa, the first and second mate are such, and others too,' Horace admitted honestly, with an increasing sense of defeat.

'Then does it not seem to you that you should take your naval training? If, when you are trained, you still wish to sail for a merchant company, I suppose it might be arranged you go with Captain Rathbone.

I have no interest in those quarters and shall have less wealth than ever by then to back you,' his father said helplessly. He was anxious upon his own account also.

Now, cried Horace in his heart, I long for it now, to return to my friends! I shall not care by *then*, Captain Rathbone will have forgotten my existence! But he did not say it aloud. With the helplessness of youth, he saw that circumstances were too much for him. He saw his bright dream of happy years learning his seamanship upon the West India run vanish as if it had never been. It had never been remotely possible. He realised it at once. They could not reject Uncle Maurice's help to give him a training: much as he now hated the notion he had no choice but to become a naval officer. His father saw his struggle, his face drained of hope for his darling schemes.

'And what of your future?' he asked, the question chiming with Horace's own thoughts. 'What would it be in a merchantman? To lay up treasures you would hope, for yourself—' his father paused.

'Papa, I have ever longed to earn money for *you* and the family—' the poor boy said with truth.

'I know it is so: you spoke to me of prize money I remember. Besides this, when you first told me you wished to go into the navy, you spoke of your desire to serve your King, and your duty to your country. Are these forgotten?'

Dull hard duty: where was its radiance now? It shone not at all, as did the warm pleasure of his past year. But he could still feel the pull of his duty to his family. Maurice had no choice but to labour in London. He had none either, it appeared.

'No, Papa,' he said despairingly, and seemed to see the *Mary Ann* slip below a silver horizon.

'You go back to the navy with a wealth more skill and experience,' Papa said encouragingly, knowing that he had won and sorry for his son's disappointment.

'Yes, Papa. I am a good ordinary seaman,' Horace said.

'Is that not the foundation for a good officer?'

How could he explain to his father that he loved the seamen, had no present desire to be an officer? That he loved Captain Rathbone?

'I think that you will find it so, my boy. I think it is clear where wisdom and your duty lie.'

It was.

His father observed with sorrow during the remaining days that the sparkling, buoyant talk had fallen quiet, disappeared into the darkness, like a memory of the trails and stars of some just-finished firework: and noted this loved son relapsed into quiet melancholy, as much a part of his nature as the other.

Chapter Four

'Thus by degrees I became a good pilot...from Chatham to the Tower of London...'

When he came to look back upon it from successful maturity, Horace would remember that it was many weeks before he got in the least reconciled to a man-of-war. Now, returned to the *Triumph,* his bid for freedom to follow his heart defeated by his father's necessitous arguments for common sense, the drab routine of life aboard seemed petty and useless beyond description, and was accompanied by that deep ache of resentment, like a weeping of the heart, which folk feel when caught in a life they hate. When this chances to coincide with the tormenting pangs of growing into adolescence, the strain may be all the worse. Horatio went about his business with an unsmiling face and clenched jaw, the bleakness within him soon showing itself in a pallor beneath his sunburned countenance: and even kind Charles Boyles had much ado to make him smile. Constantly tired, as if he laboured against an actual obstruction, as indeed he did, he needed some homely philosopher to tell him:

> Your willing heart goes all the way
> Your sad, tires in a mile-a.

Captain Suckling, aware of some of this by the expression upon his nephew's face, called the boy to him and did his best to hearten him. His brother-in-law had written a letter to enlighten him: begging him to overlook Horace's apparent ingratitude and inconstancy, asserting the goodness of his heart, his eagerness to do his duty and his pleasure in hard activity. Do but give him, Edmund Nelson had suggested, some goal, some object to work for, and you will find his natural zeal will be speedily employed.

'Now, Horace,' his uncle began briskly, 'your year at large has accomplished what we aimed at. Captain Rathbone writes well of your seamanship, and your papa writes that you like hard work' –Horace flushed at the mention of Captain Rathbone –'so now that you have mastered the foundations of how to work a ship, what is your next aim?'

Horace was braced, in spite of his gloom, by his uncle's tone. 'I think I have not progressed very much in my education, I mean in my knowledge of navigation, sir.'

Captain Suckling was pleased at this honest response.

'Quite what I supposed, because it was not incumbent upon you to navigate the ship. So now you must make yourself as proficient in those matters as in the others. As a coming midshipman, your aim is now to prepare yourself for passing your examination for lieutenant.'

Horace did not deny it, though his inclination was still far otherwise.

'How old are you?'

'Nearly fourteen, sir.'

'Yes. You have several years. While you are here in the Medway and the Thames you may learn these estuaries. Some of it is in your books and tables: the tides, the times of the spring and the neap, the depths at high water at different places. You must learn the effects of the winds upon the ebb and the flow, and of both upon the ship. And where the channels lie, and the sands and the swashes, making currents: and where buoys and beacons or lights are and the landmarks we use, such as Reculver's twin towers on the Kent coast. The depths of the channels also, and the width of water you have at different times of the tide, and the distances from one point to another around these estuaries. A great deal of this is to be had from those who know, and can navigate. So as soon as you show some grasp of the subject you shall go in the cutter or the longboat, and see the effect of the tide, wind, waves and currents with your own eyes.'

This was an immensely long speech for his uncle. Horace could not help but feel surprise, even while he found his attention held and his ambition pricked in spite of himself. He said in a subdued tone:

'Yes sir, I thank you. I shall do my best. How may I begin?'

'You shall begin now, by a study of my charts. Come nearer, I have laid out the best I have of Medway and Thames. Here are we, moored in Chatham Reach, in this deep quite close to Princes Bridge. Here, Blackstakes, and Sheerness, and down to the Nore. You have been to the Nore, Horace? So you have seen the Nore lights, and there is a buoy there. Here is the Warp, marked with a buoy—'

'We anchored at the Warp Buoy, setting forth in the *Mary Ann*, sir.'

'So you might. Here is the Shoe, there is a buoy and a beacon at Shoebury. Here is Leigh, a beacon upon the spit below. Did you ever go across to Leigh?'

'No, sir, but I saw them go from the Nore for water.'

'You shall soon be going for water yourself. Here, notice, in Sea Reach in Thames mouth is a note that the flood is very rapid. What means that?'

'That the tide runs in very fast, sir?'

'Yes. And why? Because there is a narrowing just here of the channel. If you force a flood into a narrow place it goes the faster, does it not?'

'Yes, sir. And I see in some places they give you the depth of the water?'

'Ay, the numbers are the depths at low water, spring tide. Does that tell you aught?'

Horace reflected. 'Does it not tell me the lowest, the shallowest, the water will ever be?'

'Good, so it does,' said Captain Suckling, pleased. 'And you will find some notes where the sands dry and where they partly dry. Look as long as you choose, ask what you will.'

Horace looked long, seeing in detail for the first time the pattern of the estuaries which he already knew slightly by experience. It was the first of many lessons administered by Captain Suckling, or by Richard Williams, the master; pursued sometimes by Horatio from his *Elements of Navigation*. Sums must now be done in earnest and with understanding, if he was to be allowed to go in the cutter and the longboat.

Dr Maskelyne's *British Mariners' Guide* and *Nautical Almanac* became his companions: Dr Hadley's quadrant transported him to a hot day upon the *Mary Ann*: the traverse tables and the tide tables engaged him, and the ways to find latitude (which was fairly simple) and longitude, a much more difficult problem: taking a double altitude, working a lunar, with all these mysteries Horatio, with furrowed brow and lower lip protruded, must now become more properly acquainted. But these days, he heard his uncle say, there was being investigated a much quicker and easier way to find longitude at sea than either dead reckoning by the tables (which sailors called 'working the day's work') or by observations of sun, moon and stars used to check the reckoning. Sea captains were beginning to hear of the merits of the new marine timekeepers which could keep accurate time to within a degree, whatever the heat, the cold or the buffeting: and if you had on a ship the right time at a fixed meridian such as Greenwich, the longitude problem was eased, indeed solved. The first few of these had been invented and made by a clock-making genius called Mr John Harrison in the thirties and forties of the century. He had been persecuted and belittled for years by that same astronomer royal (publisher of Horatio's *Almanac*), Dr Nevil Maskelyne. Captain Suckling, a man slow to make changes or take sides, had as yet had no occasion to try any timekeeper, being in home waters; but had been reminded of the long argument between the astronomers and the clockwork makers, when in January this very year of 1772 the ageing Mr Harrison and his son had appealed to good King George (very interested in astronomy himself) for help in the righting of long injustice. Years ago, a Board of Longitude set up in the previous reign had offered a prize for the solving of this ancient problem. Mr Harrison's clocks, four of them, the fourth shaped like a watch, had performed properly when properly treated. They had been forcibly taken away from him after he had received only half of the prize, on the grounds that they were public property. (He had had to agree early to this, for he had been given grants to pursue the work: but had clung on to his clocks in the hopes of bettering them, perfectionist that he was.) One precious machine had been dropped while being carried off from his house in Red Lion Square and transported without due care upon a cart. (Captain Suckling had heard of this from his brother, William, to whose office nearby the tale had spread.) They had been given false trials in the wrong conditions; one had been kept sequestered at Greenwich instead of being tested at sea. The maker's plans, instructions and drawings had been seized and published by the astronomer (in pursuit of the prize himself, with his lunar distance method and his tables) so that any other clockmaker could use them, and several did. Mr Harrison had never received until now the full amount of the prize, but only half of it.

This complex story Horatio overheard his uncle discussing with the master. For his part, he persisted with his studies, remembering Papa's words about giving his whole heart to a matter.

Edmund Nelson had known his son. After a month or two the hard work, interspersed with questionings and practical demonstrations, had begun to heal Horatio of his hatred for the navy, to awaken all his early ambition and interest.

About two weeks after Horace's return, upon Saturday August the eighth, a cutter came down from Chatham upon a fast setting tide, the wind west nor' west, but a baffling wind, ever dying away and changing direction. The cutter was hard put to it, drifting near the lee shore as the ebb caught her.

'That's the Wells cutter!' Mr Boyles announced, from Wells as he was, looking through his glass.

'Dang me, but what she 'ont be on the mud if she aren't 'ware.' The plight of his fellow Norfolkers had called up their language. The side of the ship was quickly manned by *Triumph* men eager to watch the performance of the cutter. A sudden shifting of the wind made her trim her sails, bring her head up into it: no sooner achieved than the wind died clean away, her canvas fluttered, the tide caught her, and set her broadside upon the bared mud below Princes Bridge.

An ironic cheer went up from the *Triumph's* men. Captain Suckling emerged to see what went on. The officer of the watch consulted with him. Horace gazed over the intervening water, straining to see if there were men he knew aboard her. She was going home! In a day or two she would be in Wells Harbour! If only he were upon her, going home! The memory of the recent hot, hay-filled days with the family was still near and sweet, his disgust with his present situation still at this time overwhelming him.

'Mr Boyles, take the longboat and six men, carry a hawser to the cutter. When she is attached, give the sign for us to heave.'

'Ay ay, sir.'

'Charles,' Horace whispered urgently as he passed, 'if you see folk we know send messages to Papa, to the family!'

'Ay that I will,' Mr Boyles replied under his breath, 'and to mine too. Owt in partickler?'

'Oh, I am well, I work at my navigation. Please to write.'

Perhaps Captain Suckling too felt nostalgia for the cutter's home port, and the days when he had taught little Nelson boys about ships. He sent for Horace up to the quarter-deck.

'You saw what happened, Horatio?'

'Yes, sir, the wind baffled her and the tide caught her. Was there aught she could have done, sir?'

'Not much. She lost her wind so she lost weigh, do you see, she was at the tide's mercy.'

'Yes, sir. But should she not have set out earlier?' said the boy, smiling palely.

Captain Suckling laughed.

Horatio's was as good a suggestion as it could be.

When the midshipman signalled the cutter was securely attached, the men tramped round the capstan with their rhythmical shouts and hove her into mid-stream. The wind favoured her, she quickly cast off the hawser and was away at once to the jeers of the *Triumph's* crew. Her men answered with laughter and the waving of striped caps. Horace watched her go, past Upnor and out of sight, on her way to Wells-next-the-sea.

But hourly, daily, weekly, monthly, the routine of the *Triumph* enclosed him. Once a week or at the most fortnightly was a cheque muster when every man must answer to the purser's call of his name. Every now and then, a man did not answer for he had run: and the master would note his desertion in the log. Twice a month they were mustered to hear what all knew as the 'Articles and Abstract'. Every so often, it was the *Triumph's* duty to fire the morning and evening gun at eight o'clock (save in the summer months when they did not fire it at night until nine). About every three weeks they exercised great guns and small arms. The Captain would take every opportunity also to exercise the guns for some public event: on the twenty-second of September they fired twenty-one for the King's coronation. Horace had always been interested in the guns. Now his interest was revived as the gunner's mates trained them how to load and ram and fire. Or he would practise the use of the musket, the marines' weapon that all must learn to handle. It was a flint-lock, muzzle-loading, its length from muzzle to pan three and a half feet. Horatio learned to bite off the bullet, to load the cartridge down the muzzle and ram it home, with the bullet on top. When he first hit the target, he swelled with heroic pride. Then there was the pistol, the weapon of the boarder of enemy ships. Gun drill included practice boarding-parties, the use of the cutlass, the boarding-axe and the boarding-pike. Horace surprised himself at the cracked roar from his lungs as he led the way madly towards the nettings, flourishing pike and cutlass. It was a welcome change from navigation.

And while he studied, the ship's people pursued their ever-recurring duties. They scraped and scrubbed, upped and downed masts and yards, dried sails, checked ropes, repaired pump chains, fetched supplies and went a-watering. Men from Chatham yard came, caulkers, carpenters, painters, helping the ship's people in their ceaseless struggle to preserve her against the elements.

All would rejoice at an interruption of the ship's day. The last day of August the *Prince George* was launched from Chatham yard. The *Triumph's* decks were manned with clean-shirted men straining eagerly to see her take the water from the slipway and add their cheers to the rest. The *Prince George* was a ninety-gun ship-of-war, a second-rate named for the King's eldest son, now a lad of ten years old. Next day forty *Triumph's* men were employed helping to ballast the new ship.

The interruptions were not always cheerful. Two or three times a month some seaman would be dealt out lashes, for drunkenness, or neglect of duty, or suttling, or quarrelling. One Saturday in September Thomas Hansell, a marine, was tried for desertion and sentenced to fifty lashes. The punishment began with ten lashes aboard the *Triumph's* longboat and continued alongside the *Resolution*. Then the longboat was sent down to Sheerness for the rest. The gloomy procession returned in the afternoon and it was much ado to get the prisoner aboard again and down to the surgeon, and a relief to all when he lost consciousness.

Monday the twenty-eighth of September came as a day of fair weather with a light wind from the south-east, though by the afternoon it had turned cloudy and the wind had increased a little, blowing easterly.

'All the better to sail her away,' sang Mr Boyles, now acting fourth lieutenant, to his midshipman Mr Nelson, shepherding his twenty-six men into the cutter, all cheerful and glad of the change. The cooks came along with canvas bags of bread and mess tins and billy-cans and a water barrel.

'Wittles for four days, sir.'

'Good. Hand them in. See them stowed, Mr Nelson.'

'Ay, ay, sir.'

'You'll sail her off, Mr Boyles?' called Captain Suckling, watching the proceedings from the pooprail. 'You'll only get as far as Cockham Wood. No matter, it may have gone round again by then. You have plenty of pullers at all events.'

'Ay, sir, I thank you.'

'Have you all the charts and instruments, now?'

'Ay, sir.'

'Mr Nelson?' the Captain addressed his nephew.

'Ay, sir,' said Horace eagerly. 'I have them, sir.'

'Then make the best use of the trip and your superior officer's knowledge. And I may drink your health tomorrow, Mr Nelson, is that not so?'

Horace flushed, smiling. He had not expected his uncle to know or remember. Tomorrow, the twenty-ninth, was his fourteenth birthday. Had this to do with his being named midshipman for this trip? He did not precisely know: but the Captain had expressed satisfaction at his two months' work and said that it was time he had some practical experience.

'Ay, sir, I thank you!' the boy replied.

They were going to Woolwich, to the *Defiance*. With the exploration of the harbour mouths they were to make, it was reckoned (with long stretches of pulling) that it might take them four days. Hence the allowance of food. In midstream, the boat caught the ebbing tide, just turning. The sail was hoist, the oars were shipped, the lieutenant and the mid raised a salute to the Captain, the *Triumph's* men raised an

43

envious cheer from the rails, and the cutter was away with the wind broadside on, past Upnor Castle, towards Cockham Wood reach. Here the river turned due east and the rowers must pull against the wind, but with the ebb tide to help them. Down the short Sovereign's Reach they found the breeze again but it was scarce in the sail before Medway turned once more, and the men must pull for a good mile along past Gillingham. By the time Mr Nelson had watched this operation several times, he had got the hang of sailing down Medway upon a falling tide against an easterly wind. After the two-mile pull of Long Reach they anchored at Ocam Ness below the beacon to get their victuals into them, for Lieutenant Boyles was intent upon making Sheerness that night. This done and the lanterns lit, the midshipman took the boat through the Kitthole himself. As they travelled, Charles had pointed out landmarks and buoys, sandbanks which dried, marshes and mussel banks, creeks and beacons: and Horatio had followed upon the chart.

As night fell, the men were pulling wearily along Salt Pan reach towards Blackstakes. Here amongst the swaying lanterns of many other craft the lieutenant was tempted to anchor and asked Mr Midshipman what thought he?

'Oh pray, let us go on, sir!' said that ardent young man. 'Will she not sail now, across to Sheerness? The river turns once more, I begin to feel the wind brisk. 'Twill be scarce an hour longer!'

'You'll not find your wind till Sheerness Hole. What say you, my men, will you pull Mr Nelson across to the Hole?'

The men laughed and agreed: it was difficult to disappoint him, there was magnetism in his eagerness. What is more, he began to handle the boat as a mariner should. They rowed on, found the wind for the last lap and anchored at the hulk dock under a half-awning. But the midshipman heaved the lead, recorded a sounding, noted the wind to be still easterly, and entered their winding course and distance in his log by lantern light before he felt free to think of turning in.

Lieutenant Boyles noted his assiduity with approval and decided to press it further.

'When is high water at Rochester tomorrow morning, Mr Nelson?'

Horatio had looked up the table, carried it in his mind. 'About half past three, sir.'

'Ay. Then when must we stir ourselves to benefit by the tide out of here in the morning?'

'Not a minute later than five o'clock if you please, sir! We must breakfast and get away by six at the latest.'

Charles laughed.

'Let us say half past five. Now with this wind, shall we get out?'

'We shall not get along the Cant to the Foreland, sir, for it's right contrary.'

'Ay. Then what shall we do?'

'We may at least drop down as far as the Little Nore, sir, I think,' Horace replied, holding the lantern to the chart.

'West of it, ay. And what then? The tide runs from London Bridge when?'

'An hour and three quarters later than Rochester. About a quarter after five will be high water, sir.'

'Then in Thames mouth we shall have the benefit of the slack until about ten of the clock—'

'But a wind clean contrary. How long does the slack water last?'

'It varies with wind and weather. About an hour or more. So what do you suggest?'

Horace studied the chart.

'We must beat back and forth across Thames mouth to make the Nore, must we not?'

'Ay, no other way. It is a good chance to show you where the sands lie. There will be plenty of water until about nine. Three boards should bring us down to the Nore. With this wind we shall be beating up the Swin likewise. We shall not get far!'

'I shall pray for the wind to go round to another quarter by eleven of the clock, sir,' said the midshipman with a prim smile.

'Ay, you do that an' all,' Charles laughed, bidding him goodnight.

Curled in his blanket at last, the chart still lay before Horace's eyes, his mind roved eagerly across it. Tomorrow was his birthday, Papa would be thinking of him. How surprised he would be could he see him now, lapped all round with the black water in this small vessel, about to make his first ascent of the Thames. The reflection caused him to see himself as if from very far off, an infinitely small being, at the start of an immense pilgrimage. With the dwindling of his size to a pinpoint, he fell asleep.

Quite chill, a cloudy sky had soaked up the sunrise, the wind stayed obdurately in the east. They were away by six o'clock north-easterly, beating across the current in the mouth of the Medway, half a mile west of the anchorage of the Little Nore. From the Isle of Grain lying between Thames and Medway a spit runs out, narrowing into the bank called Sheerness Middle: but Charles set his course over the deepest part of this shelf, then ordered the ship about on to a south-easterly tack which brought them down east of the Little Nore, avoiding the shallows of the bar. The next board carried them clean over Sheerness Middle where Horace took a sounding not much more than twelve feet.

Horace surveyed the great deep anchorage of the Nore, north of them. Hundreds of ships lay here held fast by the easterly wind: warships, merchant vessels, frigates.

Their next course brought them up between the Nore light-ships and the buoy. Then about they went once more, sailing south-east.

'Tedious mebbe,' Lieutenant Boyles said later as they were leaving the lightships on the west, 'but I reckon there aren't nuthen more useful for showing you where things lie, eh, Mr Nelson?'

Horace could not but agree: the chart was beginning to transfer itself to the expanse of the waters. This course should bring them up ready to enter the West Swin. If only the wind would go round, they would sail merrily out that channel! He raised his eyes to the sails.

'Saying yer prayers?' the lieutenant teased.

As to whether it were the midshipman's prayers, or whether the wind did what it often does and changed with the tide, the crew were divided. But, between eleven and twelve, it went round to the south-east, the sails were trimmed, and a light breeze blew the cutter up the West Swin. At the top of it they met the chopping waters of the swatchway running into the channel from between the Barrow Sands. By two o'clock they were up the East Swin level with Foulness, and the mouth of the Crouch just visible.

'How much further is it to the King's Channel, sir?' Horace asked, feeling the familiar desire of the sailor with a good wind to go on and on for ever.

'Twelve miles and more to Gunfleet Sand.'

'Too far do you suppose, sir?'

'What do you think, Mr Nelson? When is high water at London?'

'Five-thirty, sir. About three hours to go of the flood.'

'Three hours to Gunfleet too: and the tide against us coming back. Twenty-odd miles back to the Nore from this point here, four hours if we are lucky. That makes seven hours at the least. Will you go on or turn about, Mr Nelson?'

'Turn, sir,' said that young man promptly with a grin.

'Ay, I'm glad of that or you'll have a mutiny on your hands I reckon. We'll take her about.'

Horatio sighed somewhat gustily, as the men laughed.

'Another time, another time,' Charles said. ''Tis not your last visit to these waters! What you must watch here going about, is being set to leeward, with this wind and the flood strong. Never stand in too close.'

As it was, they were back at the Nore upon the rising tide comfortably before six of the clock, many another ship's lights answering to their own.

'A bumper for the midshipman's birthday!' said Charles at their supper. He had produced a small cask of wine from Horatio knew not where.

'Ay, the wind-changer!'

'May he allus pray as well, sez I.'

'A good helmsman an' all.'

'Mr Midshipman Nelson!' called the lieutenant.

'The same, God bless him,' answered the crew, pleased with their wine.

Horace was overcome with a joy he had not felt since he left the *Mary Ann*. He scrambled to his feet and bowed, thanking them, an awkward little figure, comical and touching.

Upon Wednesday morning they left the anchorage at about six, sailing for the Nore Buoy and along the Nore Sands. Horace had wished to rise at dawn to use the last hour of the flood.

'But there aren't no hurry,' explained the lieutenant over the chart the night before. 'However early we leave we 'ont get above Gravesend against the current. We're best to drop over to Holy Haven, and there we can bide for the noon tide. Once the tide flows we'll storm up the River. Do you see?'

Horace nodded. It was senseless to fight nature unless there was need: you waited for it to help you.

'Can you tell me the distances, now?'

'It is about four leagues or more to Holy Haven, sir.'

'Ay. So we'll leave at a Christian hour. And then?'

'It is something over ten leagues to Woolwich.'

'So 'tis. We shall do very well with this wind.'

'Supposing this wind stays, sir.'

'Ay, always supposing that,' Charles had laughed, turning in.

Horatio now kept his lead at hand and his eyes upon the waters. On the chart, a swash ran between the two parts of the Nore sands which would be dangerously shallow inside, and the surface of the water might show where it lay. Now they sailed northerly, rounded the tip of the bank called Nore Middle fifteen feet by the lead, and on into the deep anchorage of Leigh Road. Due west lay Sea Reach, its marshes and flats now all under water.

'You know where lies Leigh,' Charles pointed out, 'and below it is Chapman Sand, dries at low water. There's a beacon on the spit. Do you see where the water's ruffled? That is Leigh Middle Sand, lies opposite Nore Middle and below Chapman, dries at low water also. The colliers are coming, we'll stand in the middle, they'll take the northerly bank for the current you'll see.'

A procession of vessels sailed calmly down the river upon the setting tide. The colliers led them, showing their nature by their sails, blackened with coal dust: several large ships, three-masters with square sails, had the start. Behind them followed a group of barques, three, four or five masts apiece, the for'ard masts square rigged, the furthest aft carrying fore and aft sails. The first ships were now entering Leigh Road, almost upon them, passing them by, the swirl of their wakes rocking the cutter in midstream. Horace watched them going, watched more coming, looked up to the narrowing entrance to Thames and saw more and more and more.

'See those small ones, the two-masters with a gaff mainsail, coming into sight now: they are brigs, handy little ladies.'

'Are these all colliers?' Horace shouted, in the flurry of sails and the slapping of waves.

'Ay. They're usually the first down. Always in a hurry, the colliers.'

'Why so?'

'Paid by the voyage, they are. The faster you're back, the sooner you're off again. Right dextrous sailors, the coal crews. And always in a hurry.'

Ships of every sort slid down on the tide: small east coast craft, Baltic timber vessels, fishing fleets; cutters, pleasure boats, barges and wherries. Here came a splendid ship, gleaming with new paint and clean canvas, cleaving the water with pride.

'An East Indiaman I would reckon har to be,' Charles said.

The sands to the north and south were beginning to show as the cutter sailed up Sea Reach. They entered Holy Haven in the Isle of Canvey and moored there soon after nine o'clock. The lieutenant and the midshipman walked over fleshy, grey marsh plants, which reminded Horace of Overy, towards an inn called the World's End. The wind had gone light and variable, the morning was cloudy, marsh birds fed and gulls screamed.

After dinner, the flood flowing fast below the haven, their progress was less tempestuous than the lieutenant had hoped because of the fitful wind. The cutter idled out of Sea Reach past the flats and marshes of Mucking into the Hope where Thames turns southerly, past Tilbury to the north of them, Higham to the south, and so into the Gravesend Reach. Off Gravesend, Horatio stared at the tiers of ships moored there as if he might make out where lay the *Mary Ann* when he joined her last year. But the West Indiamen would be gone by now, the *Mary Ann* would be far away, she might even be there in Jamaica or Tobago below the sugar cane fields in the hot sun. He felt only a kind of tenderness like a bruise in his heart as he thought of this. Church, windmill, lime works, water mill: Northfleet, lying next Gravesend. Up Northfleet Hope, to the wharves at Grays Thurrock, and the river swinging in a great loop, and, as it swung, beware an eddy near the south bank with the flood tide. At Greenhithe it swung again into the Long Reach, past Stonemarsh and West Thurrock Marsh and up to Purfleet.

'How high does the water rise at Purfleet?' the lieutenant questioned.

'Seventeen feet at Purfleet, fifteen at Holy Haven, nineteen feet at London Bridge,' the midshipman repeated. Such things he said often in his mind.

Dartford Creek, Crayford Marsh, Erith and Cold Harbour Point, Hornchurch and Dagenham and Halfway Reach. Then Barking Level and Plumstead Marsh and Gallions Reach to Woolwich. They were there at dusk, and soon aboard the *Defiance*.

CHAPTER FIVE

The Killing of Edward Smith

The party from Woolwich consisting this time of two mids and forty-two men, arrived back upon the morning of Sunday the twenty-fifth of October. Lieutenant Boyles had not stayed on the *Defiance* at Woolwich but been lent with some of the *Triumph's* men to the *Romney,* where he still was. The cutter had been brought back by a midshipman of more experience from Woolwich assisted by Mr Midshipman Nelson. Horatio's month in the Thames and his navigation of the river both up and down, his trips from Woolwich to the Tower and London Bridge, had begun to establish that confidence in himself as a pilot which he was later to find of great comfort. Through hundreds of vessels of all descriptions coming or going to the Pool, sometimes on a fair wind and tide, sometimes beating against a contrary gale, he had practised picking his way, the dome of Saint Paul's looming out of the mist to guide him. He had marked where the buoys and beacons of the upper reaches were, seen Trinity House at Deptford whence the craft of the buoy wardens issued; learned how to evade the watermen, singing out as they ferried their passengers across Thames from the innumerable steps where they waited; and the lightermen, unloading countless commodities from ships which had not room to anchor at the quays.

A wild November with westerly gales and much rain followed. Horace's education in the handling of the ship's boats had plenty of opportunity. Now a fair hand at navigating the cutter, he was soon learning the ways of the longboat: and would now often go to exchange water barrels, or return boatswain's and carpenter's stores to Chatham, or fetch new casks of beef and beer. Just before Christmas, eight men were despatched to bring up the *Goodwill* cutter from Sheerness. She arrived the nineteenth of December, a neat little craft to be the commanding officer's tender. As she approached through the dusk of the winter afternoon, a south-westerly breeze bringing her close-hauled and prettily round from Upnor, Horace inspected her with approval, in some impatience to handle her.

Christmas Day, never a day for arduous work aboard a ship in the river, was spent that year in launching the longboat and rigging her. As soon as January was in, all hands began to ready the ship for going into dock. The first week of January 1773 was very cold. With hands often blue and senseless, the men scraped and cleaned between decks: and with the snow and frost came the mast-makers from the Yard and decreed the spritsail yard to be defective. The admiralty marshall, beads of foggy moisture upon his beaver hat, brought on board a wretched deserter by the name of Edward Smith missing since early September. The *Speedwell,* a ballast hoy, was loaded up with eighty tons of shingle ballast they were emptying from the holds. The guns were sent away to the gun wharf. The spritsail yard was sent to the mast house. All the ship's provisions went to the *Dunkirk,* a hulk near at hand. On the twenty-third of January the *Triumph* slipped the bridles and hauled for the dock. All the people went to the *Dunkirk:* and by Sunday at one o'clock they hove the ship in, with little purchase. Only some officers and a few needed men remained aboard the *Triumph.*

The wind turned due northerly on Candlemas Day and blew a fresh gale with snow. It was still frosty the next morning and a moderate north-easterly blew flurries of snow into their eyes. Horace was bidden with others to take the *Goodwill* with a party of marines to the *Portland* at Sheerness. Wind and tide favoured them, they unloaded the men and were turned for home by noon. A still coldness descended: the breeze dropped lighter and variable, and Horace at the helm had some trouble in keeping the cutter's head in the wind. Mournful sea birds rose up from the black water by the marshes frilled with snow. As they turned through Kitthole Reach a sudden wild gust from the east smote them, the sails went over hard, the cutter tilted violently to starboard, there was a loud cry cut off short and a heavy splash.

'Man overboard!' yelled several seamen together.

'Helm down!' roared the midshipman in charge.

Horace put the helm down, the cutter turned her head up, the wind was now in their teeth, and the flowing tide was bearing them backwards upstream. They made a tack to the far bank, came about, beat back to the side where the man must have fallen in.

'Have the rope ready!'

'Ease off the main sheet!'

'He's not here! Can he swim?'

'Is this the spot?'

'Ay, I marked the bank. He's gone under. I seed him wave his arms.'

'Who was it? What happened?'

'Riddall. I saw him go—he yelled. But I didn't see what happened.'

Whether the boom had hit him, or the sudden tilt of the slippery deck had simply unbalanced him, no one could say. It was very probable he could not swim. While they beat across and back, the icy water had quelled his struggles. There was no sign, no disturbance, nothing to show. The crew of the *Goodwill* beating wretchedly about the spot could not even find the body.

'There's no use in tarrying, we're doing no good. Set for home!' ordered the mid in charge.

Horace was overcome with horror and melancholy. They had lost Joseph Riddall, he had sunk like a stone. *He* had been at the helm. What could he have done, to save the boat gybing? And should he not have got her around faster? He did not think he had wasted time. Tender of conscience, he took the blame to himself. And to leave the poor man in the river, unblessed, unburied!

'It weren't your fault' said the older mid seeing his troubled face. 'We did all we could. He was caught unwary. Don't do for a seaman.'

Riddall, someone said, drank plenty. They could remember him being beaten for suttling last summer. Not that he had had the chance to drink today; but it dulls a man's wits.

The *Goodwill* returned in gloom. The master entered the event in his log, the purser crossed the name from the roll, wrote him dead. The Captain looked grave but was unable to fit a face to the name. Horace woke in the night, cold, and remembered. They never heard whether the body were recovered.

Almost a week later they hove the *Triumph* out of dock, and the ship's company came back from the *Dunkirk*. The next day the *Marlborough* who had arrived from Sheerness made the signal for a court martial to try Edward Smith, the deserter. Horace took Captain Suckling across; and news came later that the man had been sentenced one hundred-and-fifty lashes. Riddall by comparison was fortunate— *fortunate,* Horace said to himself, as he stood in the waist checking in all the stores back from the *Dunkirk*. They hoist in fresh water, starting out what was stale. By the next week the wind had gone round south and westerly and it was not so cold.

On the night of Monday the fifteenth of February when the men of the first watch had not long been relieved, Horace was on the fo'c's'le with another midshipman and the bo'sun's mate, when a sudden loud and increasing clamour of bells came over the water from Chatham Yard.

'What's amiss, Mr Mate?' called the officer of the watch from the quarter-deck.

'Fire! They ring the bells for fire, sir! I can see the smoke!'

'Raise the watch! And the officer of marines! Order the muskets fired! Waken up the sluggard *Marlborough!* Ring the ship's bell! All hands amidships, hands to the boats!'

The *Triumph* exploded into noise and action. The two mids on the fo'c's'le raced each other for the bell, the smaller (Mr Nelson) being elbowed out of the way as the larger smote it in ever mounting clamour. The officer of marines ordered his sentries to fire, which they promptly did, round upon round into the air. The boatswain's mate had run to the hatchways to blow the shrill call for All Hands, and was now bellowing to the watch below—Ahoy, Rouse out there. Hey. Out or down here! But there was no need of starters, for few men had yet fallen asleep. The ship soon echoed with running feet. The *Marlborough* had begun to ring her bell, fire her muskets, and the *Flora* lying at hand hers. The whole river was a pandemonium of shots and shouts and clangour. By now the master was out and up and several other officers. Captain Suckling himself emerged enveloped in brocade and nightcap, climbed coolly to the poop and raised his glass. The scene at the Yard was by now well lit and claimed his attention for minutes. Horatio, sent by the officer of the watch with a message, hovered uncertainly behind him.

'If you please, sir, Mr Parry intends to lower all the boats and send aid!'

'Ay, send immediate assistance, what're you waiting for, send all the boats and don't forget the buckets: I wonder you aren't there already, Mr Midshipman,' his uncle teased, hearing who it was.

'Ay, ay, sir,' muttered Horace, by now in great anxiety lest all the boats should indeed have set forth without him. The longboat was down, men were over the side and jumping aboard her in a hustling, shouting stream. His rival at the bell was to be heard in the jollyboat commanding the oarsmen. The yacht was got out next, the officer of the watch calling who should go in her. Then they were lowering the *Goodwill*.

'Mr Parry, sir, the Captain agrees every boat and don't forget the buckets and wonders I am not there already,' said the eager midshipman somewhat reproachfully.

'Ay very well, get you down, Mr Nelson, and the rest of the watch, look alive.'

They joined the bustle of the other ships' craft, all making for the south bank and the Yard. The south-westerly wind that forced them all to fall to the oars for Chatham was likewise fanning the flames. Smoke billowed towards them tinged rosily with flame. Several pumps were at work, and long lines of seamen and dockyard men formed chains from the waterside passing buckets in an endless stream. The boats arriving jostled with each other for mooring space. Horace leapt for the quay and joined a group of fast runners, mostly mids, carrying the empty buckets back from the fire to the waterside.

The fire was in the south-east end of the smithy. Horace waited with the rest, peering into its smoky shadows, alive with figures shouting orders, bringing up ladders, using fire-hooks. For the fire had got into the roof: occasioned by the sparks from the forges lodging in the rotten battlements. The boys ran back and forth with the buckets, the men on the ladders dowsed the smouldering timbers. A notable fire-engine from Rochester arrived and demanded room to operate; the commanding officer of the Yard strode about reprovingly in great agitation, blaming the smiths for blowing their fires too high and failing to extinguish them properly the night before. By three of the clock the conflagration was deemed to be mastered, the bustle subsided, the buckets were sorted, the boats returned to their ships. Horatio's watch were ordered straight below, which occasioned some grumbling from the unlucky men who had missed their rest. Horace rolled in and fell fast to sleep, the night's exertions being of an order that he thoroughly enjoyed.

On the Wednesday morning of the same week returned Lieutenant Boyles and the fourteen men who had been lent to the *Romney* since the twenty-ninth of September last.

'I'm danged but what you haven't growed a mite at last,' said Charles, greeting Horatio as he prepared to take the longboat for water. 'You're sartinly stouter. What is the news?'

'Why, the smiths set the smithy at the Yard alight with their sparks, and we dashed to their assistance. It's near five months since I saw you. I suppose I may be expected to be grown,' said that young man going down the side and into the boat. Charles watched his handling of her with approval.

Early on the morning of the twenty-fifth of February, while the watch on deck were swaying up topmasts and yards and beginning to take in stores, the marines and the master-at-arms prepared to punish Edward Smith. The man had been recaptured early in January, sentenced early in February, and kept in cold and misery in chains below deck. Hearing of the impending punishment, many men had saved him a little of their last night's grog which had been borne to him early by a sympathetic sentry of the marines; so that at least a slight curtain of numbness might stand between him and his torture at first. Before seven he was brought up, his face grey, his eyes red, and ordered over the side into the longboat which it had been Charles' melancholy duty to prepare. Captain Suckling appeared at the gangway of the quarter-deck. The prisoner's wrists were wrapped in old white stockings and lashed to a bar of the capstan. In the boat with him were the master-at-arms and the surgeon. Behind the longboat the cutter and the yacht waited, manned with marines: and likewise a small boat or two from the *Marlborough.*

Captain Suckling now stepped forward.

'Edward Smith, seaman, was sentenced one hundred and fifty lashes by court martial the eleventh February for attempted desertion,' he read in a loud voice.

'Do your duty,' he added to the bo'sun's mates who now went down the ladder to the longboat. By seven, the first blows in the killing of Edward Smith were being laid on: when the watch below were come up on deck, the sickening whistle and thud of the whip had become a part of the grey morning. When breakfast was over, half of the punishment had been inflicted, the prisoner having lost consciousness several times and been revived with spirits to bear the rest. His wrists were now untied, he was lowered to the deck and the raw crimson of his back concealed with a cloth. A marine began to strike the half-minute bell, the drummer to beat the rogue's march, the oarsmen to pull with the drummer's beat. The boats behind followed to the same sombre measure. The procession made its way to the *Dunkirk* hulk alongside which the remaining seventy-five lashes were to be inflicted. Bell and drum fell silent, the dying man was hoist up once more, the whipping continued. The day's work went on upon the *Triumph.* No one expected to see the victim alive again: it was more probable that what remained of him would be buried in the mud at low-tide. Eleven men had deserted over the last eight months: Edward Smith was made their scapegoat.

March came in with moderate fair weather, the commissioner and clerks came aboard and paid the ship's company to the thirtieth of June 1772 (nine months in arrears). March was remarkable in Horatio's mind for the arrival of a clergyman, the Reverend Mr Frew, on two Sundays, to take Divine Service upon the quarter-deck before all the company. He never appeared again. March also brought Horace his first turn of rowing guard. At midnight on two evenings in late March, one of the *Triumph's* small boats rowed silently round and about each guard ship in the river, being hailed alongside by the officer or a midshipman as to their identity, and shouting out in reply, 'Guard Boat!' Should they remain unhailed for long, by someone caught napping, it would be the worse for him.

By the middle of April, the general talk was that the *Triumph* would shortly be going to sea. The painters from the Yard were about her;

new topmasts and spars were received. The carpenters were busy round the hatchways: the people lashed the blocks of the necessaries. Boatswain's stores came in, anchors and cables and new sails. Caulkers worked about the wedges of the masts. Twenty-two upper deck guns were hoist aboard: only to be hoist out and sent away again ten days later not finding favour, for some reason which Horatio never heard and never enquired after. For his mind, quite suddenly, was turned to another sphere.

Somebody had brought the news to the midshipmen's mess that an expedition was fitting out for the Arctic. That it had all to do with a scientific gentleman who had wrote papers about earlier Polar exploration and read them before the Royal Society. That the Society had writ a memoir for the First Lord of the Admiralty Lord Sandwich to carry to His Majesty, urging upon him the sending of an expedition to try navigation towards the North Pole. That His Majesty had heartily approved the idea and agreed to every encouragement and assistance. That two ships, bomb vessels, called the *Racehorse* and the *Carcass*[1], had been commissioned on the fifteenth of April and were even now being fitted out at Deptford for their arduous voyage amongst the ice-floes, being double bottomed from the bows to the main chains and after parts.

'What are bomb ships?' Horace now asked.

'Used for bombardment of places from the sea: when they carry a quantity of guns in the bows. They must be built very strong, to resist the shock of their own guns,' said somebody.

'I think they are ketches, ketch-rigged. I once saw one.'

'What else says this account?' asked Horatio. 'Who are the Captains commissioned?'

His informant referred to his gazette. 'There's a Captain, the Honourable Constantine John Phipps...Wa Wa...And there's a Commander Skeffington Lutwidge...And there's ice pilots going, from the Greenlanders...And there's a gentleman called Dr Charles Irving going for surgeon, who has an ingenious contrivance for distilling fresh water from salt...Here, young Nelson, read it for yourself.'

The midshipman was eager to do so, while the rest discussed the discomforts of life amongst the ice and voted the expedition out of court.

'Too cold by far, says I.'

'No prize money. No fights, no prizes.'

'Nothing but whales and seahorse I daresay.'

Not so Horatio. Once the idea had struck him, he lay awake all the first watch thinking about it. Cold it might be, but it was adventurous.

---

1   The log spelling; the correct spelling is used hereafter.

He did not bother over much about cold, he was used to it in Norfolk. (He had no image of Arctic cold.) It was a fresh turning, an exciting chance, could he but compass it. The King had encouraged the venture, the bombships were getting ready. Unless he acted at once he would find they both had their full complement. (Neither had he yet learned that his own enthusiasms were no yardstick for the measurement of other people's.) Then he would have missed his chance and would regret it all his life. He resolved to go to his uncle in the morning to find out if he had any interest or acquaintance with either of these gentlemen with the grand names.

'Captain Suckling, sir.'

'Horace. And how is Mr Nelson faring?'

'Mr Nelson fares very well I thank you, sir, but he has a great idea to fare further!'

His uncle laughed. How he envied the boy his readiness of tongue! Had he but had such wits at that age, when he could scarce join one sentence to another, so tongue-tied was he!

'What have you in mind now, my boy?'

'Sir, I have just heard an expedition goes to the North Pole—'

'So it does to be sure. I have heard of it for some time.'

'Sir, I would greatly like to go!'

'They will never have you. All men, no boys, so 'tis said. Because of the hardship and danger, they must have effective men. Not waste berths on youngsters.'

The Captain had spoken straight out, without thinking to soften the blow: he had not the imagination to do so. Now he found himself quite sorry, to see his nephew's face.

Horatio's eagerness had wilted like a paper in the flames. His face clouded slowly over, as if he could hardly entertain the dashing of his hopes. A kind of incomprehension, almost of stupidity, came over him. He stood dumb, taken aback with disappointment. His uncle watched him.

'Well, there ain't no harm in trying, boy,' he said kindly. 'Nothing venture, nothing have.'

Horace came at once to life again, but cautiously.

'What can I do, sir?'

'I'm acquainted with Mr Lutwidge. Shall I write you a letter, will you go and see him? I know not where he is, whether at Deptford or elsewhere, but we will try to discover.'

'Oh if you please, sir! Could I not go as his servant?'

'He probably has dozens of sons and nephews wishing to do so. You might perhaps persuade him that you could navigate his gig. I will tell him I think you are trustworthy with that type of boat now. This will be the only position you might get, being under age as you are. Shall we essay it?'

'Yes if you please, sir. I shall be sorry to leave you, uncle, but I would greatly like to go.'

'It will be a change, a chance to further yourself. All *we* shall do is cruise about a bit. I will enquire and send for you.'

'I thank you indeed, sir...You are ever my good friend,' the boy said impulsively: and thereafter lived in an agony of impatience awaiting his uncle's summons.

When he at last came before Commander Lutwidge, that gentleman, considerably younger than his uncle, surveyed him with some amusement referring to the letter he had proffered. Captain Suckling had presented to him his shrimp of a nephew, but a lively shrimp he said, begging him to let not his diminutive size be a prejudice against him, for what he lacked in stature he amply made up in eagerness, dutifulness and ability. If he were not yet suited with a coxswain to his gig, here was the very young man he sought.

'So you think you wish to venture to the Arctic, Mr Nelson?'

'Yes, sir, I do, sir, I can think of nothing I should like better,' replied the unworldly midshipman.

'When you are frozen to the marrow of your bones and your fingers are dropping off, my boy, you may be able to think of plenty! It will be exceeding cold and uncomfortable at times, and dangerous, and often dull!'

'Yes, sir, as you say, sir,' said Horace brightly, not in the least dismayed.

'And can you tell me any sufficient reason why you will be of more use to me than a young gentleman of proper age?'

'I have been fortunate enough to be exceeding well trained in seamanship by the Captain of a West Indiaman with whom my uncle put me. And for the last year, near a year, sir, I have been taught to navigate Thames and Medway in small vessels belonging to my uncle's ship. And I have worked prodigiously hard at my navigation books, sir, also; I beg I may accompany you as your coxswain. I shall not take up very much room, sir,' he hazarded in a whisper, with a shadow of a smile.

This pleased Commander Lutwidge, who laughed in return.

'And you think yourself capable of navigating my gig?'

'Yes, sir, indeed I do, and any vessels of the same description.'

'Very well, Mr Horatio Nelson, I will have you. You are beforehand, I have not yet all the midshipmen I want, and you shall be rated as such since this is what you have been. It has not proved easy to find men as eager to go as you are. I do not think, by the way, that *all* your fingers will drop off my boy, since the Board of Admiralty are providing us warm waistcoats and mittens and fur caps and I know not what'—Horace beamed with pleasure and confidence—'and you may join the ship as soon as it suits your uncle to arrange your discharge from the *Triumph*.'

'Ay, ay, sir,' said Horatio with a salute.

Commander Lutwidge rose and shook the boy by the hand, beginning a friendship which was to continue for many a long year.

On the third and fourth of May, the *Triumph* herself getting ready for sea took a pilot aboard in the hopes of leaving Chatham for Sheerness, but was prevented by the wind veering against her. From now on her fortunes were less concern of Horatio's: for, upon Thursday May the sixth, the purser entered him 'paid off to the *Carcass*' in the muster roll, he said a warm farewell to his uncle, and was taken in the cutter to join his new ship at Sheerness.

CHAPTER SIX

Towards the North Pole
'...under...that good man, Captain Lutwidge'

Horatio was in the highest spirits. He welcomed the change, the chance, and the adventure: and was full of impatience, as was his wont, to make a start. He had had news of all his family: having written to his papa to say that he was for the wastes of snow and ice, to wit the North Pole, he had received a prompt reply with the rector's blessing. (Totally devoid of adventurousness himself, he always admired it in this son.) Everyone was well: Sukey was to go as apprentice to a good milliner in Bath this June; William was to leave North Walsham at the end of the year; good little Ann was rising thirteen and would soon go to school in Norwich; Edmund and Suckling, eleven and nine, struggled on at the Burnham school; Kitty, his joy and delight, was six and learning all accomplishments fast. All sent the adventurer their loving greetings, including Mary Blackett and Peter: the adventurer, reflecting upon their quiet lives, received these with complacency. It pleased him to be the one out of the common run. As to Maurice, still in the same dull office, he twitted him with the extremes of his existence: to be roasted in the Indies, frozen in the Arctic! Yet pronounced himself envious, and hoped to see him before he sailed from Sheerness.

Horace now surveyed his new home. Bomb-ketch though she may have been, she was referred to as His Majesty's sloop *Carcase*. Horace (ever quick to note opinions around him) soon became aware that in the estimation of some the sloop deserved her name. She had been double sheathed with planks of seasoned oak, from her wales down her sides and from her keel to her stern. He soon learned that after this operation she was leaking seven inches of water an hour, 'from the large nails drove into her sides to secure the doubling'. The wrights had had to rip this off and caulk between keel and sheathing. Her quarter-deck had been risen upon as far as the mainmast, and her fo'c's'le brought likewise further aft. Between the two, strong bulkheads were placed to keep out the water. All this made her look fit to resist shocks, if ungainly. She was three hundred tons burthen, and many cabins and berths had been built in, suitable to cold climates. She was a three-master: when Horace arrived, tops, crosstrees and yards were mostly up, and the rigging was a-finishing.

He was no longer the shy greenhorn of three years ago and he made his way to the purser Mr John Parry, who looked at him curiously, asking his age.

'Nearly fifteen if you please, sir,' said Horace promptly.

The pale purser delivered a slow wink.

'Near enough, eh.'

'Yes, sir, so Commander Lutwidge thought, sir,' Horace affirmed smiling: and pursued his way down to a kind of cockpit aft, glorified with some built-in berths. Here a boy of much his own age approached and hailed him. Robert Hughes was Welsh, and he and Horace were not long in finding out about each other's homes and histories: Horace had already more to his account than this lad of sixteen.

'But how old are you? You can't be—'

Horatio borrowed and performed the purser's wink, indeed fondly hoped he improved upon it.

'*Nearly* fifteen,' he said solemnly, rising to his full if exiguous height.

'Oh ay, I take you,' said the other. 'Then you and I are the younkers of the ship. The other mids are all older.'

Horace was soon to meet them. There was Charles Dean and John Creswell and Edward Rushworth, all ABs. By the end of the month a sixth had joined the midshipmen's berth, John Toms. The lieutenants were Mr John Baird, a Scot, slow of speech, kindly and much loved; Mr Joshua Pennington the second; and the third, Mr George Wykham, who had been aboard the longest.

Horace crept up upon Mr James Allen the master one day when the mates and men were fleeting the stays and shrouds aft.

'If you please, sir,' he began.

'Well, bor?' answered Mr Allen, thereby confirming the opinion Horatio had secretly formed.

'May I make a guess where is your home town?'

'Why, where be yours an' all?' said Allen smiling.

'Burnham Thorpe near Wells in Norfolk!'

'Oh ay! I'm a Cromer man myself, lad. It's a good old country and no mistake and breeds proper seamen.'

'So it does, sir. Though my papa is parson of Burnham.'

'Then you're brust out of your own furrow, to be sure. My folks be in the crab-catching since years agone. You and I'll not feel the cold I reckon, like t'other pore souls,' he finished.

The work of readying the sloop went on: they stowed the ground tier of water, counted in coals and wood; they got in the cables and the gunner's stores. They bent the sails, got the booms on board, took on the boatswain's and carpenter's stores. On Friday May the twenty-first, the provisions began arriving early in the morning: bread to the quantity of ten thousand pounds, porter, spirits, pork; a barrel of sugar, huge quantities of flour, and suet and raisins, bushels of pease and oatmeal, a great deal of rice; barley, butter in plenty, cheese, vinegar, pepper and mustard and a cask of tongues for the cabin table. The *Carcase* settled lower in the water.

'They aren't agoing to let us starve!'

'It'll sink the old *Carcase!*'

'We shall all get stout. Perhaps I shall grow,' Horace suggested, his voice cracking as he laughed.

Everyone was the whole day stowing them.

In the evening, HMS *Triumph* passed by, just arrived from Chatham. Horace had his new glass up scanning her, reclaimed fleetingly by that different world upon the ship he had left. There was another reason why he scanned the dock and the shore: Maurice had promised a visit.

Next morning they were marshalled to salute the French ambassador, sent on board as a consolation prize to visit the *Carcase* from the *Modena* yacht, in which Lord Sandwich himself was on his way to bless the *Racehorse* at Woolwich. When the smoke from the salutes had died away, Horatio espied his brother. Tomorrow was Maurice's twentieth birthday, the twenty-fourth of May. Horatio spun his yarn to the lieutenant and got leave to go ashore. As the jollyboat bobbed over the water, the boy stood like a starfish, waving his arms.

'Dinna rock the boot, mon.'

'It's my brother!'

'I dinna care whither it be the King's Majesty.'

Maurice and he embraced each other with glee, then repaired to an inn and ate a fine dinner at Maurice's expense, chattering news the while. When the time came to part, the younger could not help but ask spiritedly:

'Do you not envy me?'

'Yes—and no,' said quiet Maurice honestly. 'I'd be no hand at the work you must do. Goodbye, brother. Bring me back a piece of the Pole for a walking-stick.'

And Maurice smiled crookedly, and walked away to catch the London coach.

Now it was the last week in May. Commander Lutwidge, to relieve his labouring sloop, shed six more guns and some gunner's stores; and despatched thirty-two supernumerary men and their victuals. The company was now eighty instead of ninety men. By noon on the thirtieth of May they at last joined their leader the *Racehorse* who had anchored at the Little Nore. Horatio was ready to lower the Captain's gig, and at one o'clock Commander Lutwidge waited upon Captain Phipps.

Still things went on arriving on board. A timekeeper brought to them by its maker, a certain Mr Arnold, was found to have stopped. It was one of two watch machines sent by the Board of Longitude: Captain Phipps had one made by a Mr Kendal upon the famous Mr Harrison's principles. Mr Arnold, observing mildly that his had stopped for want of being sufficiently wound up, set it to mean time at Greenwich, warned Commander Lutwidge that it might lose two and a half seconds a day, and delivered him an order from Captain Phipps for making observations on it.

On June the first there was a thunderstorm; on June the second when both ships weighed and came to sail for an hour, the wind went round to the north; on June the third, Dr Irving came aboard to finish the operations for distilling salt water into fresh: he merely captured and collected the steam from the ship's boiling kettles and coppers by the use of a simple tube. James Allen tasted some of the result and found it to his palate like barley water: though not unpleasant when made into grog or mixed with wine.

Finally and appropriately, the commodore loosed his tops'ls at five in the morning of June the fourth the King's birthday. At six-thirty both ships were sailing, and by midday the impatient midshipman saw himself to be further north off the east coast of England than he had ever been before. They were still frustrated, however, by northerly winds. And Commander Lutwidge brooded, suspecting that the *Carcase* was a prodigious poor sailer.

Her performance up the east coast while the winds continued contrary confirmed his fears. It cannot be a pleasant situation to find yourself in command of an indomitably slow ship: and Commander Lutwidge was often maddened when the commodore sent his boat on board to suggest remedies: or ran up a signal desiring them to make all the sail they could: and neither jibs nor staysails nor studding sails kept the *Carcase* up with her leader. James Allen made a matter-of-fact catalogue of the ship's misdeeds and shortcomings in his log. There was another member of the crew quick to deplore her laggardliness: thinking of the *Mary Ann* in the trade winds Horatio soon remarked:

'This ship ain't much of a sailer, is she, Robert?'

'That she ain't, so thought I, Horace.'

Horace had dreamed of seeing landmarks he would recognise as they ploughed up the Norfolk coast, but they stood far out, and he was disappointed. Early on the fifth morning, both ships anchored in Robin Hood's Bay to wait tide, then spent the day working into Whitby. By four o'clock the *Racehorse* was snugly inside: not so the slow old *Carcase*, obliged to anchor without the bay and await the next morning's flood. From Whitby they took on not only some fresh beef, but six live sheep and a load of hay for them sent from Captain Phipps's family estate at Mulgrave nearby.

By now there was a greenish light all night, an experience new and amazing to Horace, who found that he could write in the log in the middle watch without a lantern. Captain Phipps came on board one evening to examine the timekeeper, and found that it varied five minutes from the true time.

'Five minutes slow in ten days?' Captain Phipps said.

'Yes, half a minute a day,' replied Lutwidge, 'not two and a half seconds a day, as he warned me. How goes yours? Is yours one of this Mr Arnold's also?'

'No, mine is a Kendall. Have you followed this business of the timekeepers?'

Commander Lutwidge knew of Mr Harrison: the commodore imparted what the messenger from the Board had told him.

'This Mr Larcum Kendall (approved of by Mr Harrison) made an exact copy of Mr Harrison's watch (his fourth timekeeper). They are alike as are twins. Its performance I am told is nigh perfect (as is Harrison's.) But the Kendall I have on the *Racehorse*, his second, is not exactly the same.'

'Why have they not sent you the first, the perfect one?'

'Because it is about to go with Captain Cook, no less, who sails again for the Pacific, this summer. Meanwhile, we test this second one.'

'They might have given you the Harrison?'

'Poor Harrison. The Board hold it at Greenwich, until the Longitude prize is settled. You heard of that? Much heartache has it caused.'

'Does this Arnold clock follow the Harrison principles?'

'Judging by its first ten days, it appears not,' said Captain Phipps with a laugh.

The Captain went back at about half past nine in such a glorious sunset that he was moved to describe it in his log, the clouds to the northward making a beautiful appearance long afterwards. By that evening, June the fourteenth, they spied Shetland: where they dallied a day or so in calm fair weather, within sight of Hangcliff Hill. Seven boats of excited Scottish fishers came off to go trawling, and plied with drink on the *Racehorse* promised fish in return. In Horace's memory the good fish for breakfast mingled itself with the first (and last) punishment the commander ever decreed: one Richard Dingle, caught thieving, was to run the gauntlet at eight o'clock in the morning. There was precious little space (the ship being so built up fore and aft) but there the crew stood in a double line, and when the boatswain's mate had given him a dozen with the long thieve's cat, he stumbled round the circle, prodded from behind with a dirk, every man trying to get a cut at him with their 'nettles', three-tailed knotted ropeyarns. Dingle was well nettled: but no man would ever mention his offence again.

That afternoon the light clear weather gave place to a fog, the first fog of many: the two young mids upon the quarter-deck could see but a few yards across the oily sea into the wall of white whence the commodore had disappeared. At half past four she fired her gun and the *Carcase* answered: they repeated the signal often. By ten at night the fog was so thick and the guns' reports so muffled, that they took to their drums and their horns, each ship pushing into the unknown enveloped in the noise of the fair-ground, to the despair of those turned in. At eight, coming up to see what went on before breakfast, Horace heard the huge slow mysterious shout of a voice over the hailer, commanding them (as if from heaven or hell) to steer north-east. By mid-morning it was clearing a little, by noon they could again discern their consort.

A fresh southerly gale got up and blew all the next day, and the *Carcase* set all her sail in the hopes of keeping up: but in the course of her efforts carried away in succession both the main and the fore topmast studding sail booms. Commander Lutwidge ground his fist into his palm upon the poop, deploring both the timbers and the timekeeper, whose slowness steadily increased. (It was to be nearly three hours behind Greenwich time by journey's end.)

Next day, the people received the warm slops allowed by the government: flannel waistcoats, fearnought jackets and coats, milled woollen caps and stockings and mitts, and great boots proof against wet, big enough to contain several pairs of stockings. Horace looked at his clothes with some consternation. No doubt turning up and the judicious use of the shears would achieve something.

Upon the night of June the nineteenth a clear sky at twelve enabled the officers to take their first good observation by the light of the midnight sun. Horace noted down the readings and thought how strange it was, how beatific, to see the sun shining upon the blessed sea at midnight! What poetical philosophies would it draw forth from his papa! And next day when they saw the first whale sending up water spouts, Horace could hear his father's voice declaiming with wonder about leviathan!

Both ships brought to very early the next morning, the commodore

66

having sighted a sail and fired a gun to attract her. It appeared there was a more urgent reason than letters for speaking her: on board the *Racehorse* was a passenger, a gentleman of fortune, who urgently wished to go home. They found the vessel to be a whaling snow, flying Hamburg colours and homeward bound with seals. It was a pity she was not an English ship: but she undertook to put the gentleman and his servant ashore at Bergen and it was a measure of his discomfort and desperation that he agreed. The snow's boat took him on board about seven.

'Who was it?' someone asked in the mess.

'A Mr William Wyndham of Felbrigg, came for pleasure, meets nothing but foul weather and heavy seas and fog to boot, and suffers continual seasickness 'tis said.'

'Felbrigg!' exclaimed young Mr Nelson, feeling for Mr Wyndham: his own sickness making constant returns upon him in high seas.

'Ay. Where's that?'

'In Norfolk, my country. Why, I passed Felbrigg every time I took coach to school and back.'

'And do you know Mr Wyndham?'

'Not I. But I think I heard my father speak of the family.'

And Horace fell silent, suddenly in the chaise again with Papa and William on that first journey to North Walsham, jogging along the January lanes, fearful, cold, some great icy sorrow about his heart: Mamma. Mamma had just died.

Now the beer was out, and grog was served instead: and the *Carcase* carried away another studding sail yard in the next gale: and a cold spell developed, which the master noted as finger cold: and Commander Lutwidge ordered the *Articles of War* to be read for the first and only time: and both Captains had fires in their cabins: and a four-day cloud and fog caused the master to write that they saw neither sun nor moon since Monday noon. The salt junk seemed dreary and the people were issued with their pepper and mustard; the first snow and sleet fell and there was a smell of ice on the wind; they bent the ice tacks and sheets instead of the ordinary ones; and one of the seaman caught a small land bird, resting for a spell from the flocks chucking and whistling anxiously overhead. He brought it tenderly in his rough hands, near fainting, to show the master.

'Very curious. Red head, grey wings, blue back, white breast and tail, as big as a small linnet.' It was thought to be an arctic red-poll. The next day they saw other birds, large flocks of sea parrots, puffins and sea pigeons, and knew that the land must be near.

On June the twenty-ninth at ten in the evening the look-out called the land, spread from north-east to south-east snow glinting upon it: Spitzbergen. Horace and Robert looked at the chart. Beyond it lay another island, North East Land; north of that again a scatter of small ones known as the Seven Islands. The very tip of Spitzbergen was in eighty degrees north: the line of the continent of ice north of it was assumed to extend in a great arc from east to west; a line changeable with the seasons. Next morning they saw high barren black rocks, some bare and pointed, others covered with snow, their tips appearing above the clouds. When the sun shone it was diamond bright, the water was glassy smooth, the brilliance of the northern light exhilarating.

'Look, sea beasts!' Robert said.

The appealing, enquiring muzzles of a family of seals could be seen off the ship's bow, diving and gambolling ahead. The two boys turned and punched each other, animal spirits rising.

A Greenlander hailed and sent a gift of deer for each Captain: she was the *Rockingham* and thirsty for news. She reported the ice to the west, sixteen leagues away; several ships had been crushed by the ice closing suddenly upon them. She was convinced they would never reach the Pole!

The first few days of July were such warm and pleasant weather, the Captains let out their cabin fires and flung open their ports. They were sailing northerly upon the coast of Spitzbergen, and when they stood in close to the shore, saw the valleys between the high cliffs sometimes filled with solid ice. Many sails were now in sight, whalers coming back from their season's hunting, whose boats would sometimes visit them. Was there not a war afoot, asked one, the sight of warships being strange in these seas?

One Sunday afternoon, July the fourth, the *Racehorse* had anchored because of the calm in a small island bay about two miles from the land. Commander Lutwidge bade Horatio take him aboard her, while boats from both ships filled up their casks from the rushing streams. Horace had not before been aboard the *Racehorse:* how aggravating it was that a ship so like her consort should yet be (as her name implied) a swift sailer, while the poor old Carcase forever laboured to keep up. Upon the quarter-deck he spied a midshipman set to an easel engaged upon taking a view of the land: a cliff of ice, sharp and green, about the height of the ships' topsails, formed the back cloth to the bay.

'Am I permitted to look?' Horace asked from a discreet distance: he judged the young man to be several years his senior.

'By all means.'

'Excellently good. Are you employed for the purpose?'

'I'm a midshipman, like yourself. But Captain Phipps is glad to have all the records I can make. You are from the *Carcase*?'

'I am. I have brought Commander Lutwidge across.'

'What think you of that ship?'

"Very little!' Horace laughed.

'Her performance is the cause for both complaints and laughter here.'

'I can well imagine it. I fancy Commander Lutwidge may be more inclined to oaths.'

Horace learnt later that the midshipman was Phillip D'Auvergne from Jersey, a young man also much interested in the timekeepers, and in charge of the meteorological records. Folk said his father was a Duke.

Next day their friend the *Rockingham* ran under the stern of the *Racehorse* and reported the ice to be about ten leagues to the north-west of Hakluyt's Headland, an island off the Spitzbergen shore. So now they were within reach of it: both ships, enshrouded in fog, pursued their way northerly till a hail from Josh Edwards, the ice pilot, brought the watch up from below.

'Islands of ice to larboard, bearing nor' nor' westerly!' he called again from the masthead.

'What did he say, ice?'

'Look! Floating along, like an island.' Horace studied the ice in his glass, green, opaque and sombre through the mist.

'There are several, in a row.'

Like a rear guard left behind the main army, the pieces of ice floated in purposeful procession to the north-west: tall and forbidding, they seemed sometimes to sway back and forth in the water.

'Ahoy, *Carcase*! Steer now nor' nor' east!' the commodore hailed through the fog.

'Ahoy, *Racehorse*! Steering nor' nor' east!'

The thick fog would clear a little every now and then teasing out like wool. Horatio stood with his glass raised, determined he should miss nothing, while behind the creaking and groaning of the ship another sound formed itself into a roar. A great roaring like a huge surf beating on land.

'Hark to the sea upon the ice!'

'Is that what it be? I thought it was a wind.'

From the poop Commander Lutwidge hailed Captain Phipps.

'Ahoy, *Racehorse*! Do you hear the noise of surf?'

'Ay, *Carcase*. Desire you now shorten sail. All hands on deck to haul according to need. Watch our motions!'

'Ay, ay, sir, will do so.'

The *Racehorse* was taking down her studding sails, and appeared to be moving under her three topsails. The master of the *Carcase* ordered likewise.

'All hands! Up here and out! All hands on deck!'

The thunderous roar became louder, the teasing fog cleared away, and there was revealed only a quarter of a mile distant a huge lofty continent of snow-covered ice, compact yet uneven like craggy land, with the great surf beating thunderously against it. It lay from north-east to north-west, its arms extended as if to embrace them. They hauled their wind to the westward after the *Racehorse:* but she could not weather it, and quickly hailed:

'Ahoy, *Carcase!* Going about!'

'All hands, ready her, going about!' yelled the commander of the *Carcase* with a note in his voice that made the men fall upon their braces like demons. The ship had less weigh than the *Racehorse,* but was slower to answer the helm. An age went by after the master's shout at the helm, the ship taking her laggardly time; while the shore of the ice seemed dreadfully clear and the surf beat louder and louder. But they got her about, the men hauling on the mainsail for their lives. When her head was round, Allen looked back at the ice with narrowed eyes.

'About a cable and a half and that's all!'

'God's providence the wind was light!' said the officer.

'Ay, so. And the fog just then cleared. Here it come again now, thick.'

The *Racehorse* had put on all the sail she could carry. The *Carcase* did so too, tacking from the ice to the south-east. All that afternoon and evening they stood on and off to the ice, in case the weather should lift enough to see if any way through it to the north appeared. In the morning the fog cleared, and the ice lay in a great curve: distant and shining, the ice pilots would talk of the 'blink of the ice' as if it lifted its eyelid at them. By noon they were sailing north-easterly in fair weather (the *Carcase* a great way astern and to leeward) towards the vast expanse of pack ice north of Spitzbergen. That night, lying snugly in his berth under both his fearnought jackets, Horace was rudely brought to by a bumping and cracking, a bombardment of jostling thumps, a more than usual groaning of the *Carcase's* timbers, a hollow slithering of lumpy obstacles against her sides, which seemed all too near.

He sat up. The next thump against her shuddering timbers caused him to exclaim.

'Robert! What ails this ship?'

A further shock and crack got the midshipman from his berth.

70

'I'm going up to see,' Horace said, struggling into the fearnought jacket and the fearnought slop and the huge pair of boots, and going on deck into the green light. Some of the men on watch greeted him with laughter: his tousled head scarcely emerging from the too large coat.

'Hey, Mr Nelson, ye'll have to grow a little, there's nowt else for it!'

'What is it, ice? I thought my last hour had come! I've come up to view it,' Horace explained, his long nose questing the icy air.

'Ay, well, we're in the midst of it, the shock's had one man off his feet already. There's a fine piece a-sailing this way now.'

They were surrounded by flotillas of sailing ice turning as they sailed, making small whirlpools, cracking with loud reports as they met each other. The large piece noted by the seaman touched the *Carcase* lightly amidships and exploded with a small roar.

'It's going with us!'

'Ay, so'tis. 'Twould be worse if it were agin us!'

Horace lowered his glass, waved to the watch, and stumped below to his bunk. His boots were far too big. The men smiled at each other, watching him go.

'Don't miss much, that little fellow,' said one.

When Horatio came up at four in the morning they were sailing along the side of solid ice to find an opening. At seven, following the *Racehorse,* they hauled into the ice and sailed eastwards.

You could feel it the minute you were within the walls of ice, the cold, still threat of calm. The water was glassy green, smooth as a mirror. At last they were in the ice, they would pick their way through it to the Pole! He felt strangely exultant that they had entered it close at last. But even as he lifted his eyes, the sails began to flutter.

By eight the *Carcase* was idling and the *Racehorse* was far, far ahead, only her tops'ls visible above a shoulder of snow.

'This won't do,' pronounced Commander Lutwidge coming up from his breakfast. 'We shall have to tow the old lady, Mr Baird, I think.' What with a laggardly ship and a losing timekeeper, he was sorely tried.

'Ay, sir, so thought I. Shall I proceed?'

'The sooner the better.'

Horace watched the furling of the courses and the lowering of the cutter. He had long had his eye upon her, wanting to learn to handle her. He determined that he would exert himself at the first opportunity to command her. Men were being stationed at the sides with ice-hooks. All the morning the boats towed the ship towards the *Racehorse:* the sun shone upon miles of gleaming ice glistening green and blue like jewels; and the men in the boats tossed up several small pieces one of which Horace sucked.

'Owch! It's fresh, not salt! Why is it fresh, Mr Allen?'

'That always is, they say, bor. You'll have to ask the scientific gentlemen aboard the *Racehorse*, I reckon.'

At three a fresh north-westerly sprang up, they hoist in the boats, set the sails and by five o'clock had got up close to the *Racehorse* whose boat awaited them.

'If you please, sir. The commodore desires your two ice pilots to confer with his own immediately.'

'Very well. Mr Edwards, Mr Preston!' called Commander Lutwidge up the rigging. 'Make all speed, *Racehorse* boat waits you!'

Commander Lutwidge surveyed the expanse of grumbling cracking jockeying ice.

'Mr Wykham, Mr Allen! I do not like the sound and movement of this ice: leave the sails, keep her handy, what think you?'

'Ay, ay, sir. Nor do I.'

'The wind's a -blowing fresh, sir, there be a right swirl of ice aft!'

An ominous creaking and cracking was heard as ice met the timbers aft, clutched them and was overridden by more ice driven up from the west.

'It's freezing up, aft.'

'I reckon it's freezing up on every quarter!'

'Shall we try to move her? Shall we sail? Is there open water for'ard?' the commander called.

'Here come the pilots back, sir!'

The *Racehorse* boat was seen pulling towards them fast and hard, steering with difficulty between the swirling ice, the water surface in places cracking as they met it. The ladder was down amidships and the pilots ran up as soon as they touched.

'Haul her up, haul her up, she'll set fast else and crack against us!' ordered Mr Wykham. The *Carcase* people had their slings ready, the crew of the boat made them fast. The crew bounded up, and the boat was quickly hoist in after to save her.

'Captain Phipps orders we get out to the westward with all speed, there's no way through the pack ice to the east and it is not safe to linger,' said the pilots.

'We are very near set fast as it is!'

'Ay, we must use the ice anchors and poles and warps and bear her through.'

Some of the people were quickly stationed with their ice poles and ropes upon the ice. The commander and the master in control, the officers at the steering, they bore and warped the ship through a channel towards the sea, south of the one that had closed up behind them. The ship was hove through by main strength and was clear of the close-packed ice by seven, the *Racehorse* an hour later. Now there sprung up a breeze at north-east; both ships set their sails, made for the open sea amongst the drift ice, and stood to the northward through the night. But at eight in the morning it fell calm and they saw the ice very close upon their lee bow, a great swell setting them right upon it. They lowered their boats to tow off: and though a breeze rescued them, it was quickly followed by a fog. The commodore had almost decided to go into harbour in the nearby sound, when a useful wind made them take their way westerly once more.

By the afternoon of the next day they were amongst drift ice again, in the road of the whalers, approaching the main westerly pack, leviathan blowing his water spouts on every hand. The wind whistled so shrill from the south-west, it was like a thousand witches. Huge pieces of ice now met them, drifting south-east, some of two or three miles' extent, which the ice pilots called floes: being north countrymen they pronounced them 'flaws', and thus Commander Lutwidge and his clerk spelled the unknown word. Now having pushed their way to the limit in the west, they turned eastward again and at midday on July the tenth stood out of the ice and saw it stretching away to the east mile upon glittering mile. Captain Phipps began to conceive that it was one impenetrable body, having run along it from east to west more than ten degrees.

Passing through the clear water to the north of Spitzbergen and the islands, he now led the way for the second time into the ice eastwards; but, again, the pilots aloft found no way through and turned the ships once more into the open sea. For two days and a half they battled with swell, calm and current, until a westerly gale struck the *Racehorse* and got her under treble-reefed top sails into the harbour of Vogel Sound. Commander Lutwidge took in his own reefs before the wind struck, and by six in the evening the *Carcase* too was turning into the haven.

It was a good roadstead, lying between the two islands of Vogel Sang (the Dutch had called it Bird Song) and Cloven Cliff, whose northernmost point was a sharp cleft rock like a cloven hoof, hence the seamen called it Devil's Island. The sound stretched south-westerly towards Hakluyt's Headland: Fairhaven, the old English navigators had named it. Next morning the boats were to go ashore watering, and Horace saw his chance. Might he be allowed to command the cutter, learn to handle her in these safe waters? The cutter was four-oared and deep, being built-up or raised upon on its deck, but Horace soon got the feel of her sail and clung to her jealously once he had made her acquaintance. They led the water to the casks by means of hoses laid into the rushing streams of melting snow which ran down the rocks. Great drifts of ice floated past the mouth of the sound from the north-east.

There followed four days of bright clear weather. The sun shone warmer and warmer, on the hottest days a thermometer held in it would rise from the thirties to the eighties, and the tar on the timbers would melt. The sky was blue, the clear deep water reflected it. The streams were noisy with melting snow, the snow-covered rocks glistened, great blue shadows lodged beneath them. Taking the cutter to the watering, the mids took a sounding and found five fathoms twenty yards from the shore: they could see large stones upon the bottom but no sign of a fish. Ashore, the two midshipmen ran for the rocks, tempted by the pure folds of snow. Where it had melted, small hidden flowers were coming, white saxifrage, grey-green rosettes of delicate mouse-ear, bright green creeping willows, lichens and grasses.

A great flock of bright brambling flew over, swooping and chirping, to one of the rocky islands.

'Now,' said Horace, reaching the ledge he had aimed at, 'we can take a good view of the whole sound.'

There lay the two sloops, their sails loosed and drying in the breeze. There went the longboat from the *Racehorse,* taking a load of gentlemen including Commander Lutwidge towards the small rocky island where Captain Phipps had set up his tent with an astronomical quadrant and other instruments. Gulls and sea swallows wheeled and screamed in the sky, drifts of pied eider duck floated in the water. Several whalers were at anchor or making out of the harbour. On the deck of the *Racehorse* Horace could see the sailmakers busy amongst piles of canvas. A halloo came from the cutter far below them.

'Ahoy, there! Going aboard!'

One day Horace came on deck to find the second lieutenant, Mr Pennington, standing over two seals he had shot. The round, grey whiskered heads were like loveable dogs.

'Are they good to eat, sir?' Horace ran his hand over the prickling fur on the leather skin.

'I don't know: it's the skins I want. A sealskin waistcoat's a fine thing, eh, young Nelson?'

'I suppose so, sir.'

What an idea! What a great thing it would be to shoot some animal, and take its skin home!

The story went that Dr Irving, struggling up the highest point on the island of the instruments, had been followed all the way by a barking black dog. Horatio told the tale to the carpenter of the *Carcase.*

'Poor animal, that was off one of the fishing ships, got left behind, I'll be bound,' said Abraham Purcell working away at a model he made. 'He should have tempted it, coaxed it, it wanted company and food, that's what it wanted, poor beast.'

The watering took two days. At ten o'clock in the morning of Sunday July the eighteenth, when the commodore made the signal to weigh, the splendid weather had changed to fog.

Early in the morning of the nineteenth, they stood into the ice eastwards for the third time. Finding no passage through, and the wind changing to easterly, they stood to the westward again searching for openings. They were further north on July the twentieth than they had yet been, in the latitude of eighty degrees. Snow fell: huge flakes like stars and all different landed upon Horace's sleeve and were slow to melt. Icicles formed upon the rope ends, snow hung much about the rigging. The wind blew from the north: extra brandy was issued to everyone. Fog enveloped them on July the twenty-second from early morning till noon: but this time the *Carcase* did not lose her consort, as she had done so often before, their agreed system of gun signals proving perfectly satisfactory.

Twice more did the ships haul into the eastern ice and running ever south-easterly found that at last they had rounded Deerfield, the north-east point of Spitzbergen, sought for so long. It was the afternoon of July the twenty-fifth. A fine clear sea lay open to the north-east: the mountains around were lower, the colour of the land was reflected in the names on the chart: Red bay, Red hill, Red beach. The weather had turned fair. At supper in the cockpit Charles Dean reported that the commodore was of the opinion that they now seemed to have the most flattering prospect of getting to the northward.

'To the Pole? Does he mean to the Pole?' demanded the youngest midshipman, his voice breaking in his excitement.

'Who knows? Why not?' said John Creswell.

'None of the Greenlanders thought it possible,' said Toms.

'That's true. They all entertained the most gloomy ideas of our success,' added Mr Rushworth.

'That is because they were not attempting it themselves! I say we shall get to the Pole! Robert, what say you? Shall we not?' Horace exclaimed, addressing himself to his food.

'Why should we not?' echoed his friend.

Why should they not? They would reach the North Pole: they would be the first of His Majesty's subjects to do so: they would return triumphant, there would be levées at the court, the King, the Queen, the First Lord...He would be welcomed and fêted in Burnham, Papa would be proud of him...my son Horace, who has just returned from the North Pole, you must know...

Horace lifted his shining eyes to find his companions smiling upon him round the trestle.

CHAPTER SEVEN

'...I exerted myself to have the command of a four-oared cutter...'

That night, idling in a calm up the ice northerly from Deerfield, the ships brought to and Commander Lutwidge sent the master of the *Carcase* back to Moffen Island which they had just passed, to make some measurements. (James Allen understood it to be Muffin Island, memories of the muffins of his childhood entering his head.)

They landed at half past ten o'clock at low water and found it to be nothing but a shingle bank two miles round, with a pond in the middle froze over. But the birds! As they tramped up the shingle and reached high water-mark, a storm of wings enveloped them, flapping whirling wings, white and grey, brent and dusky, as the geese, ducks, eiders, snipe, sea swallows and all manner of sea fowl rose up frightened and angry from their nests. One of the officers took shot at them.

'Terrible fishy to eat,' said another. 'I've gotten my boots all over egg!'

The eggs so blended with the stones as to be often invisible. Brave terns screamed, diving upon the intruders' heads, geese hissed furiously, a raucous squawking arose. Near the pond they found the grave of a Dutchman buried in July 1771.

The tide had begun to flow and the men were measuring, up to the water-mark, when somebody looked behind to the sea's edge and yelled. Three large white bears were plodding up out of the foam. Allen had never before seen a white bear: brown bears, yes, in fairgrounds and circuses. He was mightily struck. The magnificent great white shoulders of the beasts, the black polished sniffing muzzles, the long gleaming fur! The officer who was quick to his musket was preparing to shoot. Allen was not at all convinced of the propriety of shooting at so large a creature, flanked by two more. He retreated up the shingle. The lieutenant's shot went ill, the bears took fright and plunged back towards the sea. Now fog was beginning to descend; they speedily finished their observations and were aboard again before two.

'What, Goldilocks, no bear?' Mr Wykham teased Mr Pennington, having heard the tale next morning.

'Never fear, I shall get one in the end.'

Horatio hovered, picking up the conversation. The second lieutenant seemed a demon for sport.

That afternoon, the weather being still calm and hazy, Commander Lutwidge ordered a boat off to the north-east to take soundings and try the current. Lieutenant Pennington quickly volunteered: Horace Nelson as quickly.

'Let him do a little navigating in the ice, Mr Pennington, 'twill improve his education. Don't force an argument with ice taller than the cutter, Mr Nelson,' he added smiling.

'I will not, sir,' said the eager midshipman following the men down.

In fifteen minutes or so, they were entering the jostling drift ice, where Horatio's wits were fully exercised to steer the boat clear of it while measurements and soundings were done. Then Mr Pennington, spying a lone prostrate black body upon an ice floe, ordered the cutter towards it and fired a shot. It was Horace's first sight of a seahorse. It reared up upon its flappers, its lugubrious black head lifted in alarm above the two long tusks which gave it so quaint an appearance of melancholy, before it slid smoothly into the sea.

For the next three days the two vessels were close to the main body of the ice, turning up towards North East Land; frequently tacking for ice, the wind all the time in some point of the east. Often they were plagued by fog. In foggy weather the ice would hang about the rigging, the ropes would rattle with it, but if the next day were fair the sun would melt it in a trice. Such were the calm bright days at the end of July, as they tacked along the continent of ice, making for Snowhill, visible upon an island off North East Land and hoping for a way through towards the Seven Islands. Upon the ice floes seahorses stretched baking in the sun, within the throw of a biscuit when the ships stood in to take their soundings. Two splendid beasts with tusks of an uncommon brightness and size caught the attention of the midshipmen of the *Racehorse,* who was as usual a good way ahead of her consort. Mr Midshipman Floyd and a party lowered a boat and made for them but the seahorses heard them coming and disappeared. Their disappointment was great: they had heard tales of Mr Pennington's attempt: the animals seemed to afford easy sport. There was scarcely a breath of wind, and it was a remarkably fine sun-shining night. It was midnight.

'Let's row back to that island we passed.'

'Ay, 'tis but a mile and a half or so, and the ship's dawdling.'

'I see the *Carcase*, floundering along half a league aft.'

'Very well, then, before we are stopped. Quickly, lads, row hearty.'

They rowed off into the warm sunshine over the smooth sea. They had gone near three miles (the island was much further back than it seemed) when they heard the *Racehorse* fire a gun: but all decided they were at too great a distance to discover whether there was a signal out for them to go on board. As they rowed up to the island they perceived their target upon a piece of ice. This time they approached more cautiously and fired.

The startled animal floundered into the sea, but came up at once near the boat with a number of others. The sea was a boiling cauldron of foam and blood and angry whiskered muzzles: with their round heads, their broad shoulders and their sharp tusks the incensed creatures attacked their attackers, heaving, blowing, bellowing, diving beneath the timbers, appearing below the oars. The two midshipmen shouted orders, sometimes contrary; the seamen half rose, and staggered; the boat bounced. One stout animal, enraged to heroic strength, grasped an oar beneath its tusks and wrested it from its owner. It was this scene that caught Mr Baird's eye in his glass, while he stood on the quarter-deck surveying the island in the midnight sun as the *Carcase* idled towards it. He lowered his telescope quickly and his glance fell upon Mr Nelson below the poop, having just recorded a sounding of one hundred and fifteen fathoms in soft ooze.

'Mr Nelson!'

'Sir!'

'D'you see the *Racehorse* boat, southerly off Low Island? She's in trouble, with seahorse I think. Take the cutter, waste no time. It almost looks as if she's lost an oar.'

Horatio looked, summoned his crew, lowered the boat and was away.

As they approached, he manoeuvred the cutter in a circle, then turned alongside the *Racehorse* boat and drove his own as fiercely as the men could row athwart the reeling animals. The arrival of the second boat dispersed them, and they dived snorting out of sight. Someone leaned out and recaptured the oar. Mr Floyd hailed Mr Nelson.

'Thank you indeed! You saw the fight?'

'The officer on duty looked out.'

'Ah, lucky for us!'

'Did you shoot one?'

'Ay, but he got away!'

'Is the boat sound?'

'Ay no harm, only the oar and a few splinters.'

'Do you purpose to land?'

'We do, there may be deer to shoot. Will you join us?'

Horace wished dearly that he could, but deemed it would exceed his orders. No doubt, the lieutenant still watched.

'Cannot, I'm afraid. Good luck!' he said with some regret.

'Thank you again. Goodbye!'

As he turned the cutter around once more and set the men for the ship, the absurdity and delight of the situation suddenly smote him: here was he in smooth arctic seas, in warm sunshine in the middle of the night, in bright daylight! In command of his cutter which he had used to some advantage. What would Maurice, what would Papa, what would they all say could they see him now? He laughed aloud. The men looked up in surprise and echoed the laughter, as the oars plashed peacefully over the shining surface of the sea.

The weather continued calm and clear, fine and warm. They drifted gently amongst the ice to the north-eastward, where they could see the main body joined to the Seven Islands and no appearance of open water between them. Towards midnight Captain Phipps sent Mr Crane the master of the *Racehorse* to an island ahead, to survey the prospect to the north-east. Commander Lutwidge decided to follow: looked around for Horace Nelson (who was turned in that night), found himself a substitute and set off towards the largest of the Seven Islands. To be sure, it was all very delightful, so calm, fair and warm. The boy Nelson had been quite exuberant about some jaunt he had made last night, to the help of a *Racehorse* boat. But it would not stay like this forever, or there would have been no difficulty in persons reaching the Pole centuries ago. Lutwidge was not a man of sensibility, but he divined what the boy had felt. Several times they had to haul the gig over the ice, but there was a passage up to the shore of the island, the *Racehorse* boat lay there. Commander Lutwidge set off over the crisp snow to climb one of the many small hills and before long fell in with Mr Crane.

'A good morning to you, sir.'

'And a very good morning it is Mr Crane, and no mistake.'

They climbed together to the top where they could survey the prospect. Here, they gazed in silence over the silver expanse to the east. It was entirely frozen over, not like the ice they had hitherto coasted, but a flat even surface as far as the eye could reach. A compact body of ice lay joined to all the islands and land in sight, and no appearance of water except the stream along the North East Land, the way the ships came in. Commander Lutwidge swung his glass once more round, from the distant ships to the far distant eastern horizon. Then he lowered it, and looked at his companion. Both men shook their heads.

'Ten leagues of ice, would you say?'

'At least that, sir.'

'So would I.'

They made their way back to the boats, through much drift wood and cask staves and plenty of deers' horns lying upon the ground.

'Look at these tracks, sir! These be bear, an' all.' Great deep rosettes showed where the bears had gone.

'I've seen not the smallest sign of grass?'

'There's a few patches, where the snow's melted and the earth has slipped.'

Commander Lutwidge reached the *Carcase* at six in the morning to find drift ice from the north-east had nearly beset both ships. The *Racehorse* was made fast to a large piece of it. He went over to report their survey to Captain Phipps.

The master of the *Carcase*, basking like the seahorses in the fine warm sunshine, was surprised to record a latitude of eighty degrees thirty-six north. The men were filling the ships' water casks from ponds upon the ice like wells, and all fresh water. There was the lightest of winds from the north-east, often a complete calm. The men, in the intervals from their work, were playing on the ice all day, snowballing, sliding, leap-frogging, laughing and shouting in the greatest exhilaration and contentment. Th younger midshipmen joined them. Philip D'Auvergne set up his easel, surveyed the idyllic scene, and drew it in pen and ink wishing he had colours: the fine rigging of the two ships against the azure sky, one of the boats upon the ice, the water barrels at the wells, the men playing leap-frog, all caught in the brilliant light of the calm sun. The smell of fresh venison issued from the galleys; Mr Floyd and his party had shot a deer on Low Island. At ten o'clock the *Carcase* warped to the same icefield as the commodore was fast to; and in the calm and sunshiny midnight hours Commander Lutwidge walked over the ice to visit Captain Phipps. He had heard his ice-pilots talking, he wanted to enquire what the commodore felt: the ice-pilots were alarmed at being beset much further to the east and north than they had ever been at this advanced season.

'Why 'tis August tomorrow. That's autumn to us. We're always away by July!'

''Tis August today,' said Preston looking at the time.

'I've been a whaler twenty years, we all have. We've never been in eighty degrees and more at this season, in all our whaling years!'

'But we are on a voyage of exploration!' exploded Captain Phipps. 'And you admit it can change very fast!'

'Ay, let's hope it does that, sir.'

At eight o'clock in the morning a large white bear came plodding over the ice towards the ships. A wail of frustration went up as a *Racehorse* shot got him.

They lay fast moored and becalmed under the blue sky in this large bay, beset by the ice as far as they could see. Horace like many another found it difficult to feel anything but well-being. But Captain Lutwidge remarked that by midnight the calm had given way to a north-westerly wind which blew directly in upon them from the open water. As he noted this for the log, he pondered.

By four o'clock in the morning of August the second there was a thick fog; though it was not so thick but that those aloft could see that the smooth ice where they had played so merrily two days before was now in many places forced higher than the main yard, by the pieces squeezing together. It soon became clear that it was hourly setting in stronger. When the fog blew out the ice-pilots at the masthead reported no open water except a little towards the west point of North East Land. The Seven Islands, the North East Land and the frozen sea formed almost a basin, leaving only about four points opening for the ice to drift out in case of a change of wind. Apart from handing the sails there was little for the men to do. Inactivity led to speculation: a slight sense of unease crept amongst them. In the afternoon the wind blew more and more freshly from the west or north-west, the fog came thick, the ice set strongly upon them in a large body. In the early hours of the third of August the *Racehorse* drifted from the *Carcase* to the south-east about a cable's length. It began to be evident from their repeated bearings that the ships were being driven far to the eastward with the wind and current. Captain Phipps noted that the western passage by which they had come in was now closed up. He sent a message to the *Carcase* to warp nearer; and consulted with Commander Lutwidge and the ice-pilots. They decided to employ both ships' companies in cutting a passage through the ice for the ships to haul to the westward. A hawser was secured to make fast the *Carcase* to the stern of the *Racehorse,* and the men were armed with saws and axes and attacked the ice before the leading ship. A great noise of sawing, splintering and hacking filled the morning hours; shouted orders arose, as they heaved at blocks eight or twelve feet thick; when they had breath, they sang. Laughter arose when anyone went heels in the air. There was now a light breeze from the south-east, and by noon the sun burst through, so remarkably warm that Commander Lutwidge noticed the tar beginning to run upon the side and anchor stocks of the *Carcase,* yet the water the opposite side was freezing as they worked. Horace looked about him in the sunshine and noted the landmark he had made when they began.

'Mr Baird, sir,' he said to the officer who passed.

'Mr Nelson?'

'We have worked four hours, sir, and moved only from that lump of ice aft there which looks like a capstan!'

'Ay, true. What think you, a hundred yards?'

'No more, sir. Meanwhile, does not our ice drift faster than that, north-eastwards in the current?'

'Much faster, so the bearings suggest.'

'Might we not drift to the Pole with the ice?' asked the midshipman, ever hopeful. The first lieutenant said comfortingly:

'Ah, but the wind will change, you will see. We shall get a gale from the east in the end, will blow us clear and loosen the ice.'

The lad looked disappointed rather than otherwise, there was no whit of alarm in his face. Mr Baird went his way, admiring his lack of fear yet wondering at his simplicity.

By eight o'clock James Allen noted they had got but a few fathoms by reason of the west ice coming so fast that it filled up as fast as they cut. Captain Phipps reckoned it to be about three hundred yards: meanwhile the current had driven them, with their ice, far to the north-east, and had forced the loose ice from the westward between the islands, where it became packed as firmly as the main body. Officers and people turned in exhausted with their fruitless labours; and only the morning watch were on deck to see the bear who came close to the ship at six o'clock, lifting his nose to inspect. On their going towards him he went away.

So came the fourth of August: the wind had gone round north-westerly again, the weather was pleasant. But every bearing they took showed them that the ice was driving them relentlessly eastwards. By four in the morning of the fifth the fog had returned, by noon it was so thick no land was in sight. Life aboard the *Carcase* had been interrupted at about eleven by the arrival alongside of a family of bears. A large dam more than six feet long was seen leading her two whelps, sprawling, toddling and slipping over the ice towards the ship.

'Oh ho, Mr Pennington, three bears in the offing!' called Mr Wykham from the quarter-deck.

'One shot amiss and we lose the lot.'

The mother rose on her hind legs to prospect, her polished black nose wriggling with enquiry. The shots echoed, the two cubs plunged and fell, the dam reared up growling at the ship, then fell dead between them.

'Pore creetur, pore faithful creetur,' muttered Abraham Purcell who loved the animal creation.

Thwarted it seemed of the Pole, Horace began to dream of a bear.

Upon the *Racehorse*, Captain Phipps conferred with Commander Lutwidge. The winds that had brought back the fog were still coming mainly from the north-westerly quarters: the sloops were still drifting badly to the eastward. He must keep ever in mind his primary duty and concern, which was to endeavour to preserve the people, and have plans ready to this end, if necessary abandoning the ships. But first they decided to send a party away to survey westward. Captain Phipps sent for a midshipman he trusted, Frederick Walden, an AB.

'Mr Walden.'

'Sir.'

'We desire you to take with you the two ice-pilots and another man, with a similar party from the *Carcase*, and walk north-westerly to the island which we have been calling West Island in our bearings, a hill of some height from which you should be able to see the state of the ice, and if there be any clear water by which the sloops may get out. We reckon it to be about twelve miles off, do not you?'

'Ay, sir. 'Twill take near twenty-four hours' rough going over the ice.'

'Take plenty of food. Be as expeditious as you can.'

By two o'clock the party of eight men, well booted and jacketed and slung with bags of food, went off into the mist. Horatio and Robert watched them go.

'Should you have wished to be one?' said Horace to his companion.

'Not I. They must walk all night. But you would!'

'Ay,' Horatio laughed, 'I would.'

After the two had turned in that night the noise of shots awoke them. Mr Nelson scrambled into his boots and hurried up to see what went on.

'A bear,' he reported on his return. 'Right alongside. They say they are sending it to the commodore. Robert! If we could but be alone on deck when a bear comes alongside!'

'Why, are you anything of a shot?'

Mr Nelson sniffed doubtfully: he had on occasions hit a target.

'I daresay I could do for a bear close at hand.'

'We've no muskets.'

His friend slept, while Horatio deliberated upon the acquiring of some.

Mr Walden and his men returned about half past nine the next morning, August the sixth. The ice, they said, although close all about the ships, was still open to the westward round Black Point, off North East Land, by which the sloops had come in. Moreover, upon the island they had had a very fresh wind from the eastward, whereas the ships had been in near calm all day. This cast everyone's spirits down a good deal: for it lessened their hopes that an easterly gale would extricate them. Captain Phipps now sent for all the officers of both ships and put to them the alternatives: he was something of an orator (being a member of parliament).

'So,' he finished, 'either we sit here, gentlemen, beset in the ice, drifting over to the east and north, waiting for a change in wind and weather to free us, and in constant danger of driving upon rocks or shoal ground, which if we strike we shall be crushed by the ice or overset.' He paused for their melancholy situation to be fully taken in. 'Or,' he went on, 'we abandon the vessels and betake ourselves to the boats.'

'My intention,' he concluded when the murmur of opinions had died down, 'is to prepare the boats for going away, and as expeditiously as possible. The situation may change, in which case we shall be spared the difficulty. Order all the boats and the two launches to be lowered after dinner, and we will set about fitting them for hauling over the ice.'

Everybody fell to his task, thankful for something to do. The launch, the cutter and the gig were lowered on to the ice. Purcell produced billets of wood from his stores, saw to the making of light stanchions to fix round the top of the gunwales and instructed the gangs in fixing them with wedges and mallet. The sailmaker unrolled his yards of tarpaulin on the ice, measured and cut it, for each small vessel to stretch round the stanchions. Then he spread out a spare studding sail, which he ordered the men to hold firm and cut up into strips.

'What's these for, Sails? Bandages?' said a young seaman perched upon the studding sail.

'Belts.'

'Who for?'

'You. To drag the boats with. See? Like harness.'

'Oh, ay. 'Twill keep us warm.'

The work on the boats went on until the evening meal, and was resumed again afterwards. By seven o'clock there was a thick fog which made their labours the more difficult, and snow and sleet for good measure. While the men still worked, cries came from the two vessels: the pressure of loose ice had forced the *Carcase's* bows aboard the *Racehorse,* carried away her bumpkin and done other harm. Both companies must set to work to warp the ships apart and resecure them: and at ten o'clock the crews broke off at last to rest. At midnight the officer taking the sounding noted the water from twenty-five to only fourteen fathoms: and could perceive the drift of the *Carcase* even by the lead.

'Just look at that line, Mr Allen.'

'Ay, she driffs badly, sir, she do.'

'The whole pack must be drifting at some pace and into shallow water!'

'Ay so't must,' said Allen stolidly. 'But if the wind goo round 'twill driff the same manner west.'

Captain Phipps had already given orders to sound wherever there were cracks in the ice, so that they should at least have notice before either the ships or the ice took the ground: by which they must instantly have been crushed or overset.

At six o'clock in the morning all hands were turned up, breakfasted, and fell again to their work on the boats: while some were set to the cutting up and sewing of eighty canvas bags.

'Stitch, stitch, stitch,' remarked one seaman struggling with the palm, an implement he had little practise with. 'What are they for, any road?'

'Bread bags, man. For us to carry.'

'Twenty-five pounds o' bread to a man.'

'That'll be a tidy weight.'

'Ay, over the ice an' all.'

'We shall need it, every crumb.'

'I hear the cooks be boiling beef to take.'

'The more the better says I.'

Meanwhile the *Racehorse* launch being ready to go, Captain Phipps had set off earlier in the morning, a long line of men harnessed to the towing rope and pulling with a will. They got her two miles to the westward before turning back to be in time for the men's dinner.

Now they met the launch of the *Carcase*, a line of men hauling her, Mr Baird encouraging them, some people pushing each side her stern, a midshipman aboard aft as if steering and a small band of music mustered by the officers. Midshipman Phillip D'Auvergne had drawn a picture of the scene.

The *Racehorse* party cheered them. Captain Phipps heard the news from Mr Baird that the ice seemed looser near the ships, and that Commander Lutwidge was thinking to hoist the sails. The commodore hurried back the faster, ordered all the sails to be set, and by one o'clock with a light easterly wind and with the *Carcase* in tow, they were sailing. They sailed and warped and bore the ships through the ice for five or six hours, yet got them less than a mile to the westward, taking aboard the men from the *Carcase* launch party at three o'clock. Towards evening the ice began to close again like high rocks about them and it was impossible to get any further. Captain Constantine Phipps and Commander Skeffington Lutwidge conferred.

"Let us keep all the sails upon them, so that we be ready to force through when we can tomorrow.'

'Ay, so I think too.'

'How are your men?'

'In good heart. Full of japes. Preparing to pile on all their clothes and some of the officers' cast-offs, since you say none is to carry but what he can wear! How are yours?'

'The same. Behaved very well in hauling the boat. They seem quite reconciled to leaving the ships if we must. They show great confidence in their officers.'

'It is the seventh today. The boats cannot be got to the water before the fourteenth, by my reckoning. If the ships' situation doesn't alter by that time, I think we are not justified in staying any longer by them. What think you?'

'If we stay too long, we shall find all the Dutch whalers departed, on whom we rely for a passage home.'

'Just so. I'm resolved to carry on both attempts together, moving the boats constantly, but without missing any opportunity of getting the ships through.'

'Yes. That seems the only course. But in view of today's wind, we may still hope for release.'

'So we may, it blows fresh from the east this evening. I shall take some sleep. Goodnight to you, Lutwidge.'

'Goodnight, Captain Phipps.'

Mr Midshipman Nelson, having taken down their bearings from the officer's readings (including West Island, soon to be called Walden's so rumour went) stood upon the quarter-deck surveying the ice through the thickening haze and gnawing his knuckles. When the company were being allotted their places in the various boats, he had quickly exerted himself to have command of his cutter, with twelve men. He found himself almost disappointed that they might not need to leave the ships after all, for he had fancied the navigating of her. But whether they hauled or whether they sailed, they would not remain here stuck in this ice with white bears a-posting over it on all occasions. (Several bears had been seen in the last day or two, lurking near at hand, attracted by the smell of cooking; but everybody had been too occupied to hunt them.) Their departure seemed imminent. They had been issued with their muskets. Spread upon a grating below the poop was a splendid white bear skin drying, which Horace had pictured before the fire at Burnham. It was very nearly midnight, when the watch would change. He went in search of Robert, who had just returned from fetching the officer a hot noggin from below. He led him towards the ship's side.

'Robert!' began Horatio in urgent tones.

'Ay? What?'

'Will you come with me on a bear hunt? We have our muskets!'

'When?'

'Now, tonight! When the watch changes, go below, get our guns, steal up again later.'

'They'll see us.'

Horace flung his arm towards the already shrouded ice.

'Fog coming. We can slip over. It may be the last chance. We shall soon be hauling the boats, or sailing if the ice should loosen.'

'Ay, I suppose so. Who is to have the skin?'

'Whoever shoots the bear,' said Horatio, confident that it must be he. 'Or we may both get a bear!' he added encouragingly.

Robert laughed.

'Very well, I'll come.'

'Good. There's that ladder down amidships on to the ice. We'll go down when they're all up here.'

Eight bells struck from forward, the relieving watch came up, the boys went below with the rest.

Less than an hour later Horatio led the way over the crisp snow which covered the ice. He walked stealthily, it crunched as they stepped. It was not easy going, for great blocks of broken, jagged ice had reared themselves up everywhere and frozen hard together, to be covered by the frequent showers of snow. Robert paused to look at the ships rapidly vanishing behind the fog.

'At least we can follow our footsteps back,' he said, 'if we lose sight of the ships.'

'There's a slight chasm here, beware,' said Horace leaping it.

'How long do we search?' Robert asked, after nearly an hour had revealed no bears.

'Till we find one,' said Horace with determination. 'We know there are plenty here,' he said airily. 'It cannot be long before we come upon one.'

'Let us try another direction,' Robert suggested, after a further long tramp over the ice. 'Let us turn by this great castle of ice and subscribe a circle back towards the ships.'

'Very well, so we shall,' said Horace turning. 'And what do I see!' he exclaimed with excitement when they had gone upon this tack some time. 'A lucky turn of yours! Do you observe?'

'Ay, I do. At last. Let's get nearer.'

'Quickly, quickly! He has a brisk turn of speed, we shall scarce catch up with him,' said Horace with exuberance. The bear paused a few minutes, half turned and snuffed the air. The two hunters skidded and slid over the ice towards him. The bear set off as purposefully as before.

'Let us take a shot from here, or we shall lose him!'

'Ay, very well, let's. I've not much hope of these ancient-seeming weapons.'

They loaded their muskets, stood, aimed and fired. Many shots chased each other over the ice. The fog was beginning to clear. But the rump of a rapidly moving white bear against a backcloth of misted snow is a poor target. The shots went wide, the bear was roused: he turned, surveyed the ice behind him, then trotted off in an unconcerned manner once more.

'Come on, after him! We shall have to stalk him,' ordered the intrepid Mr Nelson.

'I've used most of my fire,' said Mr Hughes breathlessly.

'I, too. We must get nearer this time.'

They pursued the bear until he scrambled across a narrow chasm, shook himself, and turned to stare at them. The fog had blown clear, it was nearly four o'clock in the morning, they could see the two ships at no great distance. Robert found that he had indeed used all his ammunition; Horace tipped the last of his powder into the pan and prepared to fire.

From the bows of the *Carcase,* where he was conferring with the master about the probability of the hawsers which attached them to the *Racehorse* breaking with the hard pressure of the freezing ice, Commander Lutwidge chanced to look out over the ice through the thinning mist.

'Who's that out there, on the ice? Is that those two midshipmen reported missing?'

For the absence of Mr Nelson and Mr Hughes had already been noticed and some anxiety felt as the fog thickened.

'It is, I reckon, sir,' said James Allen looking through his glass.

'What on earth are they doing?'

'Attacking a large bear, sir.'

The commander snatched the telescope.

'The devil they are! Fire a gun for their immediate recall.'

On the ice, Horatio drew a deep breath, took careful aim and fired. There was a feeble flash and splutter: and no more.

'Hang it, hang these confounded rusty pieces!' he screamed, half laughing. 'It's not gone off!'

A signal was fired from the *Carcase*. Robert looked anxiously round.

'We're seen. We're ordered back. Come on, it's no good, Horace. There'll be hell to pay if we don't go at once.'

But Horatio was examining his firing-piece intently.

'It's flashed in the pan. I've no more powder. Never mind, do but let me get a blow at this devil with the butt-end of my musket, and we shall have him.'

And he made as if to leap the chasm at once. His friend put an arm out to stop him, astonished at his simplicity.

'Horace!' he shouted. 'You are a shrimp, the smallest boy aboard, you cannot take on that great beast! You've taken leave of your senses! Besides, they order us back.'

Horatio stared, his mouth open. He stared at Robert. At the great bear who watched them with some interest. At the ship. And again at the bear. It had reared itself up. It was within a step, it was so near.

'Well, *I'm* going back and I think you're a simpleton. You do not know when you're beaten!' Robert yelled in tones of angry amazement, walking quickly away over the ice. Horace watched him go and turned again to look at his prize. There it stood. Surely, there was some way of conquering it? He felt he had never wanted anything so much as he wanted this bear. He could not endure to be beaten.

From the *Carcase* at the commander's order Mr Pennington fired a shot calculated to miss the boys and dismiss the bear. It echoed over the ice. Alarmed for the first time, the great beast plunged around and made off.

Only when he was following Robert to the ship's side did Horatio's disappointment give place to some apprehension.

The commander sent for him at once, and being pressed with many more important matters addressed him forthright and furious.

'Mr Nelson!'

'Sir.'

'Here are we all, engrossed night and day in the duty of extricating ourselves from a hazardous situation, and you, an officer in the making, to whom I have lately allowed the command of one of the boats should we take to them, can do no better than to go off over the ice on your selfish concerns, endangering your own life and that of your companion, in pursuit of a bear. What possible motive can you have for hunting a bear, sir, at such a time as this?'

Horatio flushed from his throat to his forehead. He was cut to the quick at the suggestion that he was unworthy of his position and had failed in his duty: that he should also be deemed selfish was the last turn of the screw. He thrust out his lower lip in a way he had when distressed, drew back his head and uttered his reply in such tones of self-righteous and outraged innocence that the commander was forced to lift a hand to hide his smile.

'Sir, I wished to kill the bear, that I might carry its skin to my *father*,' the boy said.

'Very well. Don't be so foolish again. You may go.'

'What were you doing, firing shots over the ice at four o'clock this morning?' enquired Captain Phipps of Commander Lutwidge when they took an early breakfast together to concert their plans. 'I was up collecting a party to explore to the westwards.'

'You will not guess. My two youngest mids stole away after a bear in the fog, which when it cleared, we saw them standing up close to the brute, though with a chasm between. They had fired their muskets to no purpose and were all set to kill it by hand, it seems. That young Nelson was the leader, Hughes went with him. We fired the signal to order them back. Hughes obeyed but Nelson lingered. Then I had Pennington crack a musket at the bear, who mercifully made off. And the boy returned scowling to the ship.'

Captain Phipps led the laughter, Dr Irving and the rest joined in.

'I like a boy with spirit,' said Constantine Phipps.

'Maybe, so do I, but how am I going to confess to Maurice Suckling that I have lost his slip of a nephew down an ice crack?'

'Or had him eaten by a bear, like the man in *The Winter's Tale*!'

Captain Lutwidge knew not *The Winter's Tale*, but nonetheless assented.

'Quite so. Therefore I was stern with him, and he pushed out his lips at me and looked wounded: offering the excuse that he wanted the skin for his *father*.'

'Ah! A worthy motive. Is he a good boy?'

'Excellent. Full of activity and diligence. Most capable already with the cutter and my gig.'

'Present him to me when occasion arises. I like to meet the bright sparks.'

The *Racehorse* party returned at about nine o'clock, one of the ice-pilots, Mr Floyd, the mid, and three seamen. The fog still hanging about when they started, the ice-pilots had directed their walk westerly with a compass. They had got to four or five miles ahead of the ship, then followed their prints back.

'And the state of the ice?' enquired Captain Phipps.

'Large fields of ice, very hilly and close, sir. Very troublesome walking, sir, especially with the boats, but it is possible to pick a way round.'

It was the morning of Sunday, August the eighth. Captain Phipps now gave orders that everything should be finally got ready upon both ships to go in the boats, and that the launches should be hauled further westward today. The launch hauling was exceedingly hard work: but they got them above three miles more westerly before they turned again for the ships.

Meanwhile those left upon the ships ran up from their dinner at sudden wild cries from the look-outs.

'The ice! The ice is opening! A wee bitty! D'ye see that small stream of water north-west?' the *Carcase* look-out hailed the man on the *Racehorse* top.

'Ay, 'twas not open an hour since.'

'Is it enough for us to get going?' called Commander Lutwidge surveying the ice from the poop.

'Ay, sir, we can bear them through, with the warps and the poles.'

Those left on board now fell to work eagerly to hoist in the small boats, then to warp the two ships through the opening channel. As the afternoon wore on and their progress increased, Commander Lutwidge ordered a swivel to be fired to let the launch parties know where to find them. The *Carcase* was still made fast to her leader. The cook put his head from the galley in surprise, and noted their stately progress.

'I've been a-boiling all the beef we hoist up o' Saturday, two hundred pieces, to go in the boats. And all the bags o' bread be packed ready!'

'Never you mind,' said the master 'that'll get eat. I never did know nuthen so unsartin as ice, not no-how,' he added.

Soon after six o'clock, both launch parties returned. Captain Phipps, noting the ships' progress through the ice, saw that the pack itself had drifted even more to the westward: but he decided that it was not such as to justify giving up the idea of moving the boats on ahead of them.

By eight o'clock however the Captain's caution seemed unnecessary. The easterly wind blew fresher. He hailed the *Carcase* with glee:

'We are making sail! I propose to cast you off. Make all sail and follow!'

'Ay ay, sir,' called the master. 'Mr Cunningham! All hands!'

Soon the *Carcase* also was sailing through the ice after the commodore. Ropes coiled down and all ship-shape, Mr Nelson peered out into the mist over the side. You could not see very far but you could *hear*: the constant jostling of the ice near at hand, the more distant thunderous roar as it split, cracked and shattered; and sometimes, in between, the slap and plash of flowing water. As if by magic, the heavy ocean of ice was everywhere loosening and pulling apart!

Someone called a sounding: twenty-five fathoms. They had left behind the shallows near the rocky shores of the land, they were drifting with the ice to the westward. The weather was dirty, the fog was thickening, but aboard the ships there were sounds of exultant joy and relief. At eleven o'clock that night all had extra brandy.

Through the fog and calm of the next day the two crews bore and warped the ships through the opening ice in the strong westerly current. When the fog cleared they saw they had overtaken their launches: and sent twenty-five men from each ship to bring them aboard. Both ships were moored to the ice: it was very cold: the cordage was frozen. Now it began to snow. Thicker and faster fell the huge starry, frozen flakes all night. Every rope about the ships was as thick again as its natural size: and the rest of the launch party picked their way aboard gingerly at two o'clock. Captain Phipps made all his fatigued people turn in for a few hours: but by nine o'clock they were sailing once more through heavy, jostling ice, their timbers shuddering as they struck. By ten the snow had stopped. The strange floating structures of ice caused shouts of astonishment: a magnificent archway large enough to sail through: the domes, pillars and windows of an ice-made church; a flat table with icicles around it like the fringes of a cloth.

By noon the ice was opening fast, the look-outs cried joyfully at the sight of the open sea. By one o'clock they were through most of the floating pack and standing to the north-west; by eight there was no land in sight, though they saw the great arc of the ice from north to west at midnight. Eight hours' sailing brought them abreast of Cloven Cliff. By ten at night they were safely in Smeerenberg Bay, under the stern of the commodore, with four Dutch whalers lying near them.

CHAPTER EIGHT

'...I found that a squadron was fitting out
for the East Indies...'

Smeerenberg or 'Greasy Mountain' was thus called because the Dutch
had been used to boil their whale oil here in coppers: and the remains
of some of these were found upon shore. The anchorage was deeper
and the hills higher and sharper than Vogel Sound, often with summits
as pointed as pines. To gales, snow and sleet they set to work to re-stow
their gear, and see to the ship. Then the weather became serene, though
Captain Phipps noted that in these parts some quarter of the sky was
nearly always loaded with hard white clouds. The longboat took bearings
and angles from Hakluyt's Headland and then went ashore watering;
Horatio took the cutter to sound round the ship and to the south-west.
The gentlemen from the *Racehorse* from their tent on the shelly shore
of Smeerenberg Point, took their observations and a survey of this side
of Fairhaven, to the pleasing smell of freshly baked bread coming from
the *Racehorse* cook's oven set up on shore. On the land opposite to the
instruments lay a valley between two high black mountains entirely
filled with a near perpendicular body of ice, of a very lively light green
colour: a cascade of crystal water tumbled out of it. Great pieces of ice
broke off and crashed into the water: there was one floating there now
of the same brilliant colour. This, Captain Phipps was informed by a
guest from one of the Dutch whalers, they called an 'iceberg'.

The *Carcase* people sat peacefully on deck in the hazy sunshine
drawing and knotting yarns, and wondering at the thought of their
being fast stuck in the ice but ten days ago. They rieved the proper
topsail sheets and put away the ice sheets: and by ten o'clock on the
morning of Friday August the nineteenth weighed and worked out of
the harbour.

Some consternation was caused amongst the people by the ships'
taking their way northward again: in the midshipman's mess Horatio
informed Robert that he supposed the hope of the Pole was not quite
given up. The main body of the ice lay in a great circle north of them
on Friday afternoon: and they stood to the west north-west along it

that night. But Captain Phipps, being persuaded he could do no more on his mission soon turned to the south. By Tuesday they were headed for home in light airs and clear weather, and there followed two weeks of calm sailing in which all had leisure to rejoice.

'I wonder if our expedition will be counted as anything of a success?' said Mr Nelson to Mr Hughes one calm night on the quarter-deck: regretting his vision of the levée at court should they have returned triumphant.

'In that we were not forced to leave the ships to be crushed to pieces, I suppose it was not a total failure,' said his friend judiciously.

'In that we did not reach the Pole 'twas not much of a success,' complained Horatio.

'Ay, true. No way was found.'

'And in that I did not shoot that bear 'twas a wretched failure' Horace decided.

Robert laughed.

'I suppose a great many astronomical observations, surveys and soundings have been achieved,' said he, 'judging by all the instruments.'

'At all events,' Horace added with some satisfaction, 'you and I have been in Arctic waters and seen the wonders of the ice. Which we may never do again.'

Captain Phipps noted with pleasure that Jupiter appeared in the sky upon the night of the twenty-fourth. (The great Galileo, he knew, had discovered how to find longitude by Jupiter and its moons, but it only worked on land.) Mr Allen noted the star too, and left a space in his log for its name, never to be filled in. Should the ships be separated Commander Lutwidge was to make his own way to the Nore, but now the good breezes and moderate weather made this seem unlikely.

On September the seventh the wind went round as it had often done before from the south-east to the south-west, causing the *Carcase* to wear ship about five in the evening. It was at eight o'clock that night that James Allen first noted the great sea from the southward. Horatio noted it too, for it made him feel sick: a head sea quickly brought on his sickness. At two o'clock in the morning of the ninth, Commander Lutwidge noted once more the heavy swell from the southward: and remarked to Mr Baird that either it had blown, or it must blow, very hard from that quarter.

'Ay, sir, the sea waxes larger and larger. Something's afoot.'

By eight in the evening the master noted the confusion of the sea, fighting with itself and running with foam. By midnight, however, the weather had moderated and the watch turned in hoping for some sleep.

So that all were unprepared for the violent squall which hit the ships suddenly at about one o'clock, and carried away the mizzen boom of the *Carcase*. The wind had gone round more westerly, and the great swell reached them from this quarter. By two o'clock it blew so strong that the men below could scarce hear the bo'sun's summons when it came. The timbers shuddered, the wind screamed, the water thundered, the deck tilted so madly they could hardly put on boots and jackets. Horatio scrambled up with the rest. The wind clapped a blow at his open mouth like an angry hand. A bitter lash of spray struck his cheek. His stomach rose as the ship fell down the steep side of a wave. Someone bellowed in his ear to hold fast, hold fast all the time, never let go. The sea had risen to a great height, the waves must rear huge above them, though he could feel rather than see their raging presence in the gloom. The lanthorns swung wildly. Men up on the tops of the main and fore were reefing or furling. Horatio followed the crew of the mizzen, happier to feel the ropes in his hands and beneath his feet than the plunging deck. They fought with the mizzen top sail to furl it. The mate's commands being blown away off to Norway the work could not proceed orderly, but each man must watch his neighbour awaiting the moment to roll it, while mastering its flapping fury and riding the rigging like a drunken man. The sloop heeled over, the maddened water reached up to the men on the masts. It was nearly an hour before the topsails were in.

The wind blew west by south ever the harder, and the waves chased the ship, an endless army pursuing on the starboard bow. Every now and then one reared terribly, and dashed a part of its crest upon the deck as they rose to it. At four o'clock the *Carcase* still buried her side deep in the water.

'Send down top-gallant yards! Strike top-gallant masts!' roared the commander through the hailer.

The topmen, soaked, frozen and buffeted, proceeded to obey the command. The gale caught the ropes and spars as they were lowered and rattled and swung them wildly.

'Hand main topsail!' ordered Lutwidge, when the top-hamper was down and stowed. The men on the main top fought and furled the topsail, and descended on to a deck deep with swirling water where they were instantly wetter than aloft. Those below had been soaked to the skin long before.

'The pump! Hands to the pump! Keep the pump going!'

One pump was now going continually. Gear and barrels and spars were beginning to work about. It was six o'clock and a mate struck it, but the bell swung so wild he could scarce do so.

'Secure the boats! Lash the booms!'

Repeated tumbles of foaming water made the work difficult. Horace and the cutter crew struggled to re-lash their boat, while the seas poured beneath and shouldered up the spare booms where it lay.

'Casks overboard!'

'Empty barrels all over! Clear the decks!'

All the lumber washing about loose was hustled to the lee side and over. The main deck now was continually full of water, never clearing itself as the ship rose.

At eight o'clock the gales were as strong or stronger, the sea as great.

'Scuttle the launch on the main deck!' bellowed the commander to the lieutenant at hand.

'Ay, ay, sir.'

The seamen hoist her down, cleared her out, and let the water in.

Wet to the bones, the people clung or crouched where they could, cold, exhausted and beginning to be hungry. Horace was most conscious of tiredness: the roar of the wind, the perpetual diving of the ship, his efforts up above, made him feel as if he moved in a dream. Yet he knew still that one second's carelessness might dash him into the boiling torrent of the sea. The bowls of cold burgoo were better than nothing, but little comfort to a sick stomach.

By ten o'clock the master noted that the sea was making a free passage over them. It wrenched loose the harness that held the steep-tubs full of pieces of beef. The cook roared, seeing them go.

At noon the commander had leisure to look for the *Racehorse* and spied her four or five miles to leeward of them and bearing south-south-east. By one o'clock the gale had lessened slightly. They saw the commodore set his main topsail. At three o'clock the *Carcase* set hers, by half past it had moderated enough to set those on fore and mizzen. Now they bore away for the commodore. By four o'clock:

'Out third reef topsails! Set the jib.'

Between five and six they were near enough the *Racehorse* to hoist the colours to the commodore. As she answered the ensign the men cheered. Release from the storm of howling wind made many of them jocular. Horace went below innocently thinking to get dry and soon observed there would not be a dry clout aboard. Wet he was and wet he would stay until the sun and the breeze dried him. Without any warning of its coming, he had weathered his first bad storm.

At seven o'clock, attending upon the first lieutenant, the midshipman remarked:

'That is the first considerable storm I have ever been in Mr Baird, sir.'

'Och ay, laddie, tha' will no' be the last,' remarked that officer who was scanning the waters for the *Racehorse*. She had left them behind again.

'Was that a tolerable bad storm, sir?'

'Ay, that was a daicent blaw,' said Mr Baird somewhat grudgingly. 'It's a splendid thing there's ever a deal to do Mr Nelson, for it leaves nae time for fear and fashin' yersel. There she is noo! D'ye see? South-east by south four miles awa' to my reckoning.'

'I do. Is she driving south-east?'

'Looks so. She'll be to Norway at this rate.'

At half past eight those on duty could still see her light, bearing south-east, but by nine the wind had shifted to the southward and they had lost sight of her. They stood to the south-west to join her, supposing her to stand that way when the wind shifted. At ten, seeing no light, they fired a gun. They got no return.

They were in fifty fathoms, with brown sand. The gale was still fresh, with frequent showers of rain. At four in the morning, James Allen noted the great sea again from south-westward. But there had been no sight of the commodore.

'Send a man to the mast head every half hour to look for her,' ordered Commander Lutwidge at nine that morning. It was Saturday, September the eleventh.

But see her they did not. As the look-outs descended from the mast with blank faces, so anxieties began to arise. Mr Baird had not liked the way she was driving when he last saw her. Commander Lutwidge, chancing once to view her during the storm, had thought she was labouring worse than they. This was a strange irony, if their fast-sailing leader should be less able to ride out the rough weather than the old *Carcase!* She must, he supposed, have been forced to bear away to try to rid her decks of water. She was bearing away toward the rocks of the Norway coast when last they had seen her light.

In the cockpit the young midshipmen talked it over.

'Do you suppose our noble leader is lost?' Horatio began in a low whisper, warming his ever damp hands at the flickering lantern.

Robert looked quickly over his shoulder.

'Hush, I am sure 'tis ill luck to say so. What thought you of the storm, Horace? It is the worst I ever was in.'

'It's not only the worst, 'tis the first *I* ever was in,' said that young man. 'I thought it a decent blow,' he added carelessly.

'Were you afraid, it being your first?'

'Not exactly. Why, there was no time. Mr Baird said it was a good thing there was always plenty to do.'

'Ay. The more storms you live through, the more you suppose you *will* live through, I daresay. I would not like to be caught below when a ship went down,' Robert reflected.

'Nor I. I would rather meet my end in the waves.'

'You would not breathe very long in waves like those.'

'You would not. 'Twould be all over before you got to Thy Kingdom Come,' Horace imagined.

'Is that what you would be at, saying the Lord's Prayer?' Robert asked.

'I might well. We can't tell what we would be at.'

'Gasping for breath,' said Robert miming it.

'Trying to swim,' mimed Horace, knocking the other in the face. 'I wonder how long you keep your senses?'

'Not long at all,' said his friend wisely.

'Which is a merciful providence,' said Horatio pulling a long face like his father in the pulpit.

And having got the measure of their watery grave and distanced their terrors with their banter, they broke into a loud laugh and turned to other matters.

The gales, the squalls and the rain continued. The wind was south-west and at eight the master noted the heavy sea from that quarter. By nine the wind had gone round west by north and blew stronger. By ten fierce gales were upon them: and all was to do again. The water poured over the ship, till by half past eleven she was almost waterlogged from the weight on her decks. In two hours, she looked past help. Horace, cold, tired and sick, had a guilty thought that it was no good thing to joke of a storm. What did you do for relief when thus washed over? How fearsome to be the commander in such a tempest, the lives of all eighty of them in your hand! At midnight he was to realise what you did, when they lowered the gaff (the fore-and-aft sail) of the mizzen, furled its slack upper portion, which was called balancing it and brought the *Carcase* to under this balanced mizzen alone, with her head to the south-west. Now she lay riding the wild, cold storm, several men at the helm struggling to keep her head towards the relentless procession of the waves.

There was always something (until the very last) that you could do, the boy thought. To be the commander or the master was to foresee, to know, to decide quickly in each peril *what to do*. He felt some triumph in seeing the ship reduced almost to her bare poles fighting her battle.

He caught Robert's eye as they waited at midnight for their extra spirits. Both saw what the other thought, neither spoke, a subdued smile passed between them. The brandy glowed in the throat, made an island of warmth in the sodden, aching misery of the howling night.

Neither the violent gale nor the huge sea abated by a jot through the next two watches but rather grew worse. Many on board thought of the *Racehorse:* if she scarce conquered the first storm, what would she do with this?

Not until the morning of Sunday did the north-westerly wind moderate, to allow them to sway up the yards once more. At midnight they wore ship to the westward, and the gales and the rain went on.

On the morning of Monday September the thirteenth, a look-out saw a sail to westward. The commander and the officers, the mates and the mids all ran up to look.

'Can't tell. It may be she.'

'Water's too high to see, sir.'

'She's a great distance off.'

'I think 'tis she!'

Lutwidge now ordered the private signal to be made and a gun fired.

But there was no response. She proved to be a Dutch ship from Archangel to Amsterdam: she had no news of their consort. A Prussian fishing boat likewise knew nothing: Mr Pennington going on board her returned none the wiser as to the *Racehorse* but the richer by some fresh mackerel and herring.

Those coming up at four the next morning were soon aware of the distant ominous whine from the west.

'Here we go again.'

'Let you not *whistle*, you lubber.'

However, a certain amount of confidence prevailed, following the ship's performance previously. The storm was neither so fierce nor so long as those before: Horace supposed to Robert that they would be by the time they got home proper north sea men. By the afternoon all reefs were out and they proceeded for the next twenty-four hours sounding all the way. Flamborough Head lay sixteen leagues to the south-west. The gales and squalls of rain went on.

First light on Thursday brought bright weather.

'Oh dare, oh dare, that do you good and no mistake,' remarked the master, stretching his arms in the sun as he came up at seven. 'Sails about, too.'

There were several fishing vessels in sight. Commander Lutwidge, choosing to disregard the articles of clothing that had already begun to flutter in the fore part of the ship, now decided to speak to one. She proved to be a smack from Yarmouth. At nine o'clock they sent a boat and took on board her master as pilot, leaving a man in his place. By noon, Horace noted with content from the deck log that Cromer was but twenty-eight miles off.

That evening the wind blew up once more into a gale. They lost the fishing vessel despite the poop lanthorn lit to guide her, and at eleven they fired a gun, and brought to under the mainsail.

The fourth storm hit them at four o'clock in the morning. The strong south-westerly gale roared, the wind lashed the sea up once more into those great, mastering waves. But it was short and sharp. By six they were setting the main topsail, at seven they saw the fishing boat and spoke her, by eight it was moderate and fair.

'Land ahoy!' yelled the look-out cheerfully.

Horatio was up with his glass with the first. Why, it was Norfolk land, it was his land, curving south-west to west, a silvery gold line in the sun. He stood there straining to make out the coast, imagining he saw the sand dunes of Burnham and Holkham, the inlet of Wells! By noon they sailed in light winds and fair weather with all their canvas towards Cromer lighthouse four or five leagues off. They worked into Yarmouth Roads in the morning of Saturday, September the eighteenth.

The first thing Commander Lutwidge did was to go ashore and make enquiry for the *Racehorse*. The next was to send an express to the Admiralty with the copy of the *Journal of the Proceedings of the Voyage*, which Mr James Robinson, his clerk, had made ready.

'No intelligence of the commodore here,' he said to Mr Baird, coming aboard again.

'If she be driven far south, sir, she will no' touch this coast as northerly as this.'

'Very true, so thought I. We may find her much nearer home.'

'Ay, sir, so we may, ye're richt.'

There was something infinitely pleasing, Horace decided, in getting oneself dry, ordered and comfortable again after being wet, miserable and storm-tossed. They stayed in the Roads five days, and he wrote chirpily to Papa to announce his Arctic freezing, near-drowning and present safety. The ship work done, the water loaded, they sailed again on the twenty-third. Against the prevailing south-westerly winds, in weather still often wild and stormy, they worked their way along the coast of old England to the south-west: Southwold (where James Allen wrote 'Sole'), Dunwich, Aldeburgh, Orford upper lighthouse, Orford Ness light, Balsey Church. It was at four o'clock on September the twenty-fifth that Commander Lutwidge lowered his glass from a long study of a vessel to windward, let out a bark of laughter, and shouted shortly from the poop:

'Mr Baird, Mr Allen! The *Racehorse*, I do declare!'

' The *Racehorse*, sir?'

'The *Racehorse* it is!'

'The *Racehorse* ahoy!'

'*Racehorse* to westward, lads!'

The news was around the *Carcase* in no time, most people saw her for themselves, the ship's side quickly filled with men all smiles and wonder. When they thought they had been seen, they hoist the ensign. The *Racehorse* solemnly answered.

'If that ain't like her, to be ahead arter all.'

Commander Lutwidge retired to the cabin smiling, and sent for the officers to share a bumper.

Early next morning they spied her at anchor off Harwich and worked up and spoke her, anchoring close: before long Mr Nelson took Commander Lutwidge to wait upon the commodore.

'Upon my soul, Lutwidge, I am happy to meet you!'

'I must say the same to you, Captain Phipps, sir! I lost sight of your light at nine o'clock on the evening of the tenth, and saw you not until yesterday! How did you fare?'

'She took it ill, poor lady. There were six or seven mighty storms—!'

'Six or seven! Where have you been, sir?'

'Maybe four or five! Joined all between with as ill weather as I ever experienced—'

'Four, I think, we weathered, the first two being by far the worst. The second we brought to under the balanced mizzen.'

'Ay, so, I think it was the worst storm I ever was in. And we by far too near the Norway coast, having borne away to rid the ship of water—sit down, take a drink! Dr Irving, Mr Lyon, Mr Harvey, Mr Adamson come and drink to Commander Lutwidge, he not being with Davy Jones as we feared!'

The commander of the *Carcase* smiled, and forbore to say that he had consigned Constantine Phipps to the same locker and with perhaps more reason. The details of the hazards they had suffered went back and forth between them.

At eight o'clock that night, the two ships had anchored in the Swin: where last year, Horatio reflected, he was making his first exploration of this channel and Thames mouth. It seemed a long, long time ago. Working up the Swin next day, the landmarks swam easily into his memory: Whitaker Beacon and Shoe Beacon (James Allen wrote them as he said them, 'Bacon') where they anchored for the night.

At eleven the next morning the *Triumph's* boat came aboard with their orders to repair to Deptford. At noon they anchored at the Nore and after dinner the commander sent for Horatio.

'Mr Nelson.'

'Sir.'

'Your uncle would like to see you. You may take the cutter. We will fire a gun when you must return.'

'Ay, sir. Thank you, sir.'

'Carry him my kind regards.'

'I will, sir, thank you, sir.'

'I am sorry you have no bear skin to present him.'

Mr Nelson allowed himself a deprecatory smile.

'But you may tell him from me that I am well pleased with your progress otherwise.'

'Ay, sir. I thank you, sir!' the boy said warming, and retired.

It was September the twenty-eighth 1773, the eve of his fifteenth birthday. Captain Suckling seeing his nephew looking tolerably rosy and fat remembered, and referred to it.

'Well, Horatio! I do declare you begin to look more near your age at last. How did you fare? They seem at least to have fed you well!'

'Oh thank you, sir, yes, they did that, sir. A hot breakfast and meat *every* day when we were in the cold parts and you should have seen the barrels of stores we loaded in! Though a good deal went by the board coming home, sir!'

'So! You had these late bad gales in the North Sea. Now you know, I daresay, how to ride out a storm?'

'Ay, sir, we had at least four. And in the very first lost our consort and never saw her again for two weeks. I think Commander Lutwidge feared she had foundered.'

'I daresay he did. And what of the Pole, Horatio? Sit down.'

'To tell the truth uncle, we were up and down and back and forth that ice for weeks. We made at least four entries to the east. The fourth time we got through to an open sea, and went further and further east and there were bears and seahorses, some of the officers shot them. And then it froze hard, and the wind and the current drove more and more ice in upon us from the west in great blocks and we were set fast near *two weeks,* sir! We thought we must leave the ships and drag the boats back to the water. I was to have command of our cutter, with twelve men.' He paused for breath. His uncle listened spellbound. The boy told the tale well. He had never been in the Arctic himself.

'And then?'

'Then it melted, like a miracle! The wind blew from the east, and we were out in two days or so. All the whalers were for home by then. We were in the harbour with them a week and then we sailed.'

'I hope you kept a good log.'

'Ay, sir,' Horace said, 'when I was able.'

'Have you written to your papa?'

'Ay, sir, from Yarmouth.'

'Good.' Captain Suckling surveyed his nephew with some satisfaction and pleasure. He was fit and growing fast, he was doing very well in fact. He should not be surprised if the boy brought real credit to him if he continued this way. 'Now Horace, as to your future.'

'Yes, sir?'

'There are two ships fitting out to go to the East Indies. To join the squadron already there. Sir Edward Hughes is to be commodore, I believe. How would you like to go on a frigate called the *Seahorse*? It would seem appropriate,' said his uncle, with a rare flash of wit.

The boy laughed.

'I should like it very well, sir. Is it a war, sir, in India?'

'We trust not. An eye is being kept upon the French, my boy, in the Indian Ocean, I know not quite why,' and his uncle winked and looked mysterious, unwilling or more probably unable to elucidate the situation further. Horace had always considered the French his implacable enemies and any chance to help in the confounding of their knavish tricks filled him with satisfaction.

'When do I leave, sir? And shall I be long away?'

'I think it may be two years or so. I expect you would like to see your family? The ships lie at Portsmouth and I understand will be leaving in November. Let me know when the *Carcase* is paid off and I will write you Captain's servant on this ship for the period of your leave. You should have time to take a week or so. Will that suit you?'

He could not help comparing this eager young man with the mutinous lad he had sent home more than a year ago. But last year's disaffection seemed in another life to Horatio, who seldom thought of it now.

'Very well indeed, sir, I thank you. Shall I go on leave straight from Deptford, Uncle?'

'Ay, I think so. Seek out your brother. You will have enough money? You may choose to go to Norfolk together? Or perhaps Mr Nelson would come to Kentish Town? I am sure my brother would welcome you all. See what is best.'

'Thank you indeed, sir.'

'You must be in Portsmouth the last week in October. Captain Farmer is in charge of the *Seahorse* frigate, and her master is Mr Surridge. I will write to Mr Bentham in the Navy Office and ask him to use his good offices in commending you to Mr Surridge, who is an excellent master.'

'Thank you, sir. And my clothes, Uncle?'

'The same kind of thing you took to the West Indies, and take plenty. Here, I will give you some money towards it. You know where to go? Maurice will help you.'

'Yes, Uncle, thank you. I will fit myself out.'

'And buy them large enough, my boy, you have begun to grow. Now Mr Boyles would like to see you, I'm sure; you may seek him out.'

Horatio was by no means averse to entertaining some of the young lieutenants of the *Triumph* with his tales. By the time the *Carcase* fired her gun, Charles Boyles, a reliable young man but not greatly adventurous, was almost envious of his lively countryman from Norfolk. He slapped him on the back saying goodbye.

'I dessay when you get back from India you'll find me still here,' he laughed. 'Come and see us!'

'I will!' Horace called from the ladder. 'Goodbye Charles!'

That evening they sailed up the river, anchoring in Long Reach for the night. A hoy came alongside next day and they loaded out all the guns and powder and gunner's stores, and continued their journey. They made Deptford that night: and for the next two weeks saw the *Carcase*, their home throughout such surprising adventures, reduced to an empty hulk; sails, top-masts, spars; anchors, cables, rigging; booms and boats; barrels of unused provisions; the carpenter's stores, the bo'sun's stores, all got up, surveyed, checked and returned. They washed her down on the thirteenth, returned the longboat to stores on the fourteenth, and on the fifteenth were paid off at half past noon by the commissioner.

That evening found Mr Horatio Nelson in the welcoming clasp of his brother Maurice.

CHAPTER NINE

'I was placed in the Seahorse*…with Captain Farmer…'*

Good Peter Black drove William back to school on a late October Sunday, cool and crisp, with the trees showing bright signals of red and bronze and yellow amongst their green. Summoned by Papa, William had got leave to go home on Saturday to see his brothers. All had burst into the yard, hearing the mare's hooves. Papa jocular and cheerful to have 'his wanderers' home; Maurice and Horatio themselves, the one thin and quiet, the other stalwart and talkative; Edmund and Suckling without a great deal to say for themselves as usual, William thought with scorn. Both the older girls were absent; Sukey in Bath, apprenticed for three years to reputable milliners named Watson, an arrangement made by Papa who had visited the city more than once since 1770; Ann, now thirteen, away at a better school for a few years. Only little Kitty, irresistible at six years and a half, imposed her female sway. Apart from that imposed by Mary Blackett from the kitchen.

By Wednesday, William reflected, his younger brother would be speeding to Portsmouth, to Portsmouth…To join his ship for yet another adventure to the ends of the earth. William sighed. He could not help but be cast down, sixteen and grown young man that he was: it was so slow, jogging back to Mr Jones and school, it was so prodigious *dull*. Yet he would not care for being frozen hard in ice floes, nor sailing along in a fog, nor climbing ropes, nor lashing sails. Horace made it sound so enlivening, so bold.

'Master Horace, he looked as well as ever I seed him,' remarked Peter. 'Right stout.'

'Plum duff and salt beef, Peter,' growled even stouter William, for his questioning had elicited the information and his brother's indifference had irritated him. 'Every day. Save when it was venison and dumplings.' And he laughed savagely. They had all thought Horatio looked well: filling out, firmer in the face, often rosy. 'He goes to the East Indies you know,' William said grandly though somewhat grudgingly.

'Ay, so he told me. More cheerful than last time, worn't he? I reckon he'll do well, our little lad.'

William pouted, torn between jealousy of the affection his brother invariably called forth and between a natural desire to profit from his prowess at second hand. At home he had several times interrupted the flow of excited narrative with a Latin tag which only Papa could understand and translate, so that Horace could appreciate the scholar. Which he was eager to do, William now admitted. Always so affable, so generous, seldom surly as he felt himself to be. Ready to laugh at his clowning, to pull a face in answer. Oh how he wished, he wished...he knew not what he wished.

'I go to Cambridge next year, Peter, you know,' William stated.

'Oh ay,' said good Peter, not even dimly aware of what a young man did in Cambridge. 'Then I reckon you'll do well too,' he added with natural kindness. He had seen the two boys grow up. 'What do a young gentleman do in Cambridge then?'

'I go to college there and study and be a scholar and then I become a parson like Papa.'

'You coul'nt be a better nor a kinder man nor your papa, Master Will'am, not nohow,' said Peter fervently, grasping on to something he did understand. Even the vicarious approval comforted poor William. He relinquished his envy: and a few minutes later guffawed so suddenly that Peter held the reins in tight.

'That bear! That tale of the bear! Did you hear that, Peter?' he snorted.

'I din't, how could I now? You tell me, Master Will'am. I like a good tale. Tha's greedy to keep 'un to yerself. What manner of a bear?'

So William launched into all the tales, of the ice and the fog and the seahorses and the bears. He told them as Horace had told them, sometimes even more wildly: knowing he should entertain his fellows thus when he reached school and should warm himself with their admiration for his most enviable absent brother.

Dusk had fallen when the London coach descended to the town of Portsmouth and turned into the George in the High Street. Horace was stiff, cold and a little anxious: finding his own ship brought back painful memories of lonely Chatham. But at the office of the Port Admiral he found out that the *Seahorse* was anchored at Spithead, and he must find a boat to carry him over from the sally port. He was rowed out against a fresh southerly gale, the town looking grey and shadowy, only a flare or two and some lanterns swinging as he left. The frigate seemed scarcely more welcoming in the cold choppy water; but once aboard, the creaking and swaying, the smell of the varnish, the thud of feet, recalled him to his seaman's life for good or ill. The officer on watch directed him to the midshipmen's berth, which on a frigate it appeared was in the steerage right aft the mainmast. Horace descended from the half-deck.

In the dimly lit cabin were several men and some mids, one of whom he quickly sensed to be about his own age, peering at a book with a candle. He smiled shyly at Horatio, his fine sensitive features and high forehead looking more scholar than sailor. Horace dumped his chest.

'Just arrived?' The mid's voice was as gentle as his looks.

'Ay, Horace Nelson mid,' said that young man, determined to seem the sailor to those who listened.

'Tom Hoar, the same.'

'Where shall I encounter the purser? I never was on a frigate. I've been on a sixty-four, a seventy-four, a merchant-man and a sloop—' said Horace for the benefit of the listeners.

'May I conduct you?' Hoar blew the candle out and led Horace up to the half-deck once more.

'You're a hardened seaman then,' he said, ' yet you don't look older than I—'

'I'm fifteen, but I joined when I was twelve.'

'I'm fifteen too. They wrote me on a ship's books at twelve, but I knew nothing to the purpose so I was put to school to learn navigation.'

'Is this your first ship then?'

'It is.'

The two boys lingered, eager to talk. Tom, a Yorkshire boy, was the very opposite of Horatio in that all his sea-learning had been at school. After his first Latin school in Durham, he had been put to a preparatory navigational one in his native Stockton, then to a nautical academy in London.

'But this year I have been at Christ's Hospital where I've learned more than all the others put together. A friend of my papa's, Captain Phipps, presented me there—'

'Captain Phipps! Captain—the Honourable—Constantine—John—Phipps?' announced Horace slowly, in shrill delight.

'Yes, he. Why, do you know him?'

'I am but just come back from the Arctic with him!'

'I heard of it! I heard he was to go, in the spring! In search of the Pole!'

'Just so. We never reached it however: the ice was too closed.' And Horace proceeded to impress his companion with a brisk account of their adventures before enquiring again for the purser.

'You say you're fifteen? You're much taller than I, but alas so everyone is.' Horatio pulled a long face.

'I believe many of us youngsters tell him eighteen: but I don't know what good it does,' said Tom Hoar.

So Horatio told the purser eighteen and gave the place of his birth: the purser, whose name was Alexander Ligerwood, said 'Norfolk' would do, the Captain came from Norfolk (Horace wondered if he was a friend of Uncle Maurice) and entered it all down under October the twenty-seventh 1773.

Tom Hoar soon made Horace acquainted with the 'two Georges', the other mids in the berth. There was George Hicks from Norwich, a pleasant enough stolid young man of nineteen, slow to talk but friendly.

'I was at the grammar school at Norwich,' Horace informed him. 'Only for half a term though.'

The other was George Farmer the Captain's son, seventeen, and rated a captain's servant. George Farmer was a solemn ginger-headed boy, knowing nothing yet but what he picked up from a naval papa, and the more inclined to remember his position as Captain's son. His lack of confidence made him often haughty, and not popular with the rest.

The other inhabitants of the berth were the master's mates, the captain's clerk and several more.

The next morning, Horatio having promptly protested his ability to navigate a longboat or a cutter to Mr James Drummond first lieutenant, he and Tom were engaged upon the familiar task of watering. Horace surveyed the town of Portsmouth from the stern of the longboat. Ports Down, whence the London coach had descended the night before, rose above it to the north. The buildings crowded down to the wall, which now at high water seemed to meet the sea. Some fine handsome buildings stood out, amongst many that were small and mean on the western side which fringed the harbour. The church tower was surmounted by a belfry, and that by a domed cupola with a small spire carrying a gilded vane. A-top the vane a glittering three-master took the air. They sailed past the saluting platform and the square tower and powder magazine at the bottom of the high street, towards the sally port where Horace had embarked last night and the narrowing entry to the harbour. A round tower lay on the Portsmouth side, a fort upon the other.

'All this beyond the Round Tower,' Tom said as they passed it, 'is called the Point, I have learned.' At the tip of the Point inlets ran in easterly towards the town, forming quays. North of it, Horatio could see the dockyard and the gun wharf. They moored near the victualling quay and the two seamen began to load barrels.

It was soon discovered that the *Salisbury's* boat was at hand engaged upon the same occupation. A round-faced rubicund midshipman, smiling confidently, walked over towards the two boys as they stood on the quay.

'*Seahorse?*' he asked.

'Ay.'

'I'm Charles Pole mid, of the *Salisbury.*'

Charles proved to be a Devonshire lad, who after his grammar school at Plymton had had the good fortune to be sent to the Naval Academy here in this very dockyard. He turned and pointed to it as he told them. He was a friend worth making, for he knew his way around Portsmouth: added to which he was sunny-natured and one took to him immediately.

'Follow me,' he murmured, 'and I will show you the best haunt for mids upon the Point. We've just time.'

The three lads slid away from the quayside like water down a drain-hole. Charles led them back into Capstan Square (through narrow streets which Horace, country boy that he was, would always remember as dirty) and into a hostelry behind a pair of blue posts. There was a crackling fire in the coffee room and a throng of noisy midshipmen consuming piles of buttered toast. While the three newcomers did likewise, they discovered that Charles after two years at the academy had been for a year with a Captain called William Locker, in the *Thames* of thirty-two guns. He spoke as warmly of Captain Locker as Horace spoke of Commander Lutwidge. The *Salisbury* was Charles's second ship, and it was quickly made evident by Horatio that his own experience had outdone Charles's. Wiping butter from their chins they hastened back to the boats, vowing to repeat the meeting as often as they could.

'Oh-ho! Way-oh! Mr Surridge! Mr North,' cried the officer of the watch from the quarter-deck, 'I think the longboat is in some trouble! Oh-ho! Over she goes! Mr Drummond, Mr North, the longboat is overset!'

A south-westerly gale had carried the watering expedition briskly towards Portsmouth on this early November afternoon: but a sudden squall going into the harbour had upset her. She lay over, some of her sails in the water, her men clambering upon her gunwale in an effort to right her. Oars, spars, empty half-hogsheads bounced upon the water around the struggling boat. Lieutenant Drummond bounded up on deck to look.

'She'll need some help, she won't right herself I doubt. Take the pinnace, Mr Drummond, sir! She may need a tow,' said Mr Surridge the master.

'Ay. She's shipped a good deal. Lower the pinnace!' cried the lieutenant, quickly picking his men. 'Look alive, people in the water, no day for a swim. What is it, Mr Nelson? Ay very well, get along down. You may thank your stars you were not in charge. It's Mr Hicks is it not? Is Thomas Troubridge with them? Ay, so I thought. I don't suppose any of you would have done any better.'

Horace did not suppose so either but always felt an irresistible urge to throw himself into the midst of things. The pinnace reached the longboat within two minutes, picked up the soaked and shivering men (not without some jests), assisted in righting her and lowering her sails, fixed a tow-rope and carried her up to a quay where they might rid her of her water. A bluff blunt-faced lad, his curly fair hair dripping with water and a determined set to his mouth, jumped and beat his arms upon the quayside.

'What happened?' asked Horatio. 'Are you Thomas Troubridge? Mr Drummond has his eye on you!'

But Thomas could only confess that they had met a squall, too sudden to forestall it: it was Horace's first encounter with Thomas Troubridge AB and the start of a warm friendship.

Mr Surridge the master had been watching the behaviour of the midshipman pointed out to him as Horatio Nelson. He had noted his eagerness to be off watering, had seen him volunteer to go with the pinnace crew, had approved his behaviour at hammock drill, gun inspection and other day-to-day tasks of the ship. He seemed a clever, cheerful, sensible, healthful lad, and of this the master was glad. For a day or two after Horace's arrival in the ship, Mr Surridge had received a letter commending Horatio Nelson to his especial interest: and no man cares to have his interest commanded on behalf of an unsatisfactory pupil, though most will exert themselves for a promising one. The letter had come from his agent Mr Kee, who explained that a Mr Bentham of the Navy Office had written to him for a recommendation in favour of Horatio Nelson, a nephew to Captain Suckling, the master being a necessary man for a young lad to be introduced to. Mr Bentham's letter, Mr Kee said, had been dated October the twenty-eighth: he had wasted no time in writing and hoped the letter would reach him safely before the ships sailed. One day, Mr Surridge approached the midshipman.

'Mr Horatio Nelson?'

'Ay Mr Surridge, sir.'

'I have received a letter from Mr Kee my agent, recommending you to my interest, Mr Nelson.'

'My uncle said that he would arrange such a letter, sir. He is Captain Suckling.'

'So I understand. I propose to put you in my watch, Mr Nelson. You seem well forward and eager to learn.'

'I am very eager to learn, sir. I thank you very much, sir.'

'We shall soon discover how to bring you on further, and what you need to study and practise.'

'Yes, sir. I am very much obliged to you, sir. I have quite a thirst for maritime knowledge, I do believe, sir,' said the young man in his light eager voice.

The master smiled.

'Ask me anything you wish to know at any time,' he said, and went about his business.

A company of marines arrived with a lieutenant, a sergeant and a corporal. HMS *Panther* arrived from Newfoundland, and the *Arethusa* from Boston. After dinner they ran out the guns and fired fifteen, because it was the anniversary of the Gun Powder plot; and the next morning Commissioner Gambier came aboard and paid the ship's company two months' advance. Now they were getting ready for sea. Beef was loaded, and five boxes of portable broth, 'whatever the deuce that may be,' remarked a master's mate; and one hundred and seventy-four gallons of port wine for the company was fetched in the barge. The *Lively* and the *Thetis* arrived from the westward, and the *Rainbow* sailed out of the harbour. Horace would stand when he was idle and sweep the whole anchorage with his glass saying the ships' names over. The little *Weasel* which had been dodging in and out of the harbour for the last week or two, got caught by a strong nor'-nor'-westerly and drove in the *Seahorse's* hawse: they had to veer away on the cable of the best bower. The next day the longboat fetched her last turn of water: for the following morning they unmoored at a signal from the *Salisbury* and hove short. On the morning of the nineteenth they weighed and sailed at the *Salisbury's* signal, and left riding at Spithead HMS *Barfleur*, Admiral Sir Thomas Pye; and with him the *Royal Oak*, the *Centaur*, the *Egmont*, the *Asia*, the *Worcester*, the *Panther*, the *Rainbow*, the *Diana*, the *Lively* and the *Weasel*.

Lying at Spithead for three weeks amongst all these, Horace had felt for the first time the sense of the navy as a powerful living force, like the heart which sends its life-lines through the body. Some ships came, others went, some seemed always to be at anchor. Small boats brought supplies, sloops brought men or messages. You watched, to know who went, who came; you guessed as to their movements, were proved right, or wrong; you asked about their captains, you heard about their history, you learned their secrets by hearsay; who was swift and who was slow; you remembered what you were told of their triumphs or their troubles. It was an endlessly absorbing game and the more you played it, Horace discovered, the more you felt a part of this vast, floating guardian of Britain.

At ten o'clock the stately departure of the two ships for the east was somewhat marred by the wind going north-easterly and the cutter having to be hoist out to tow. At half past ten, clear of the island, they set the studding sails; at half past eleven, Sir Edward Hughes hoisted his red broad pendant upon the *Salisbury*. The *Seahorse* hastened to salute it, whereupon the wads of the two foremost guns went through the lower fore studding sails and shot them away. They were hastily hauled down and Sails was set to repair them. With such mock heroics the journey to the east began.

❧

The *Seahorse* was a frigate of twenty guns, one of those speedy small ships who were the eyes and ears of the fleet, not a line of battle ship. She carried one hundred and fifty upwards of officers and men: that is to say, she felt to Midshipman Nelson bigger and more crowded than the bomb ketch *Carcase,* though nothing like so large and peopled as the *Raisonnable* or the *Triumph.* Beside them all, the little *Mary Ann* haunted his memory in having so small a handful of people that she seemed as homely as a party in a parlour. (They had spoken a merchant vessel from London for Jamaica in the channel, on the day they left Spithead: surely it must be, thought Horatio on watch, Captain Rathbone in his *Mary Ann*! But it was not.)

When they caught the trades, Horace to his infinite satisfaction found his position reversed from that in the *Carcase:* the *Seahorse* must frequently shorten sail for the commodore. The main topsail would be laid back to the mast to slow their progress and await the other ship. But speedy though she often was the *Seahorse* seemed often in trouble, a right crank old ship, George Hicks called her. The first gale, a day out from the Lizard, washed away most of the ledges and the necessary-stools in the head: to the discomfort of the people, for they were not repaired for a fortnight. Four times in three months did they find the fore top mast trestle trees sprung: and renewed them, the commodore this time awaiting them. So were her masts a trouble: first the mizzen was found sprung, and Horace watched the carpenter fitting a fish for it. A 'fish' to all intents and purposes was a splint. Later on they found the main mast sprung in five places, and as they neared their journey's end the foremast went too. They carried away the main top-gallant royal mast in a gale and the starboard crossjack yard arm in a squall: and the sails constantly split and flew to pieces.

One day, judging his friend Mr Surridge to be in an amiable mood, Horatio ventured to remark upon these disasters.

114

'Mr Surridge, sir?'

'Ay, lad?'

'I never did see such a ship for parting her canvas and springing her timbers, sir?' he remarked questioningly.

The master regarded his somewhat short but fairly rotund pupil with indulgence.

'And how many ships have you had the acquaintance of, may I ask?'

Mr Nelson once more surprised himself by counting out the ships he had known: the *Raisonnable,* the *Triumph, the Mary Ann,* the *Carcase...*

'Well, she's an old ship Mr Nelson, she's a quarter of a century I'm thinking.'

'Is she so?'

'Ay. She has a brave history. She was more than *ten* years old if I remember, when she went up the great river to Quebec. You'll not remember about Quebec? In the marvellous year of '59?' Mr Surridge asked, packing his clay pipe.

'Sir, I was but one year old. But I know about General Wolfe and the siege of Quebec,' Horace affirmed.

'Well, 'twas the fleet that enabled the general to take Quebec. And she was there,' the master said, slapping the ship's timbers beside him as if she were a horse. 'And she was in the East Indies at the taking of Manila in the same war if I am not mistaken. Perhaps she begins to feel her battle scars, lad.'

'Maybe she does, sir. Is twenty-five years *very* old for a ship, sir?'

'That depends on the ship and what she has suffered, you see.'

But whatever the ship suffered was turned in true naval tradition to good account by the ingenuity, the assiduity of the master and his mates and the bo'sun, Mr John North. They shored the booms with a broken spritsail topsail yard; they used half an anchor stock to make a second fish for the main-mast. Once when an excessive hard squall had carried away the starboard crossjack yard arm, they hoist the spritsail yard up for a crossjack yard, used the driver boom for a spritsail yard, the spare main topsail yard for a driver boom, and set the carpenter to make a new top-gallant out of the broken crossjack. They woolded the fishes to the damaged masts with half-worn clew lines or halyards, reeving new clew lines in their stead. They used for scupper plugs a sprung main top-gallant mast. Nothing went to waste until it could safely work no more. Nor was it only used: it was written in the log to have been used. The young midshipman noted these things with satisfaction: and grew very soon to like and admire Mr North.

❧

Before they had been a week at sea, Horatio and Tom Hoar saw the carpenter and his mate setting to to measure and make a wooden staircase for the accommodation ladder.

'What's wrong with the other one, Mr Carpenter?' Horace asked.

'That's iron, lad. That draw the compass, I'm told.'

Mr Surridge, passing by at that moment, seized the opportunity to instruct both young men with a lesson at the compass: with some questions and answers about the difference between true and magnetic north, and a prompt study of the compass needle, shown by him to be pulled off the magnetic meridian by the local attraction of the iron ladder.

'So, you see. We will have wooden steps. We have enough calculations to do without adding that one, have not we?'

'Ay, sir.'

Mr Surridge, indeed, was meticulous in his calculations and observations. Nearly always once a day and often twice, the mate keeping the log or the master himself would enter in the '*variation per azimuth*'. What a slippery word was 'azimuth'! Horace knew that the imagined circle from directly above his head which cut the horizon at right-angles was an azimuth circle, a quarter, a quadrant of a great circle of the sphere. An azimuth was the angular distance of any such circle from a limit such as a meridian. You could measure the true azimuth of any convenient heavenly body. But every heavenly body had also its magnetic azimuth, between the magnetic meridian and its great circle: you compared the true with the magnetic azimuth to find the variation of the compass and so to adjust the course set. Captain Farmer was particular that the midshipmen should all keep their own logs and work each for himself the day's work, the finding of the ship's position by account or dead reckoning. There was no skimping your calculations under Mr Surridge. Then there would be the checking of the current and the leeway made, by the hoisting out of the cutter, and the corrections in course and distance attendant upon it. Horace had known of these things in the Arctic: under Mr Surridge he took more responsibility.

Mr Surridge was always particular to state in the exact and literal phrase whence he had taken his bearing on his departure from land.

N.B. at 5 p.m. I take my departure from Funchall, he wrote, meaning not simply that he had left Madeira, as landlubbers use the phrase. From Funchal, from Tenerife, from Bonavista, he took his successive points of departure on his journey to the Cape of Good Hope.

But, used enough to taking an altitude or a double altitude upon the sun, what Horace had never seen practised with such assiduity before and was always to remember was the taking of lunar observations to find the ship's longitude at sea. Ships carried Greenwich time as best they could upon the watch and from this, by comparing the apparent time at the ship got from altitude observations, they could work out their longitude position. But it was a rare watch that did not vary, did not lose or gain with the tossing, the temperatures, the contingencies of a long voyage. (Horatio had heard about the behaviour of the time-pieces the Board of Longitude had sent upon the arctic voyage.) This master, Mr Surridge, seemed never to miss the chance to take an observation upon the sun and moon, or the moon and a star. With a self-conscious zeal that he was to regret, Horatio once asked Mr Surridge the method. The master's grey eyes glittered. By the time he had explained to Horatio step by detailed step this method, by ten equations, the midshipman's face had taken on the stunned and vacant look of one who has lost his bearings. His glazed eyes looked past Mr Surridge at the heaving ocean, while his brow set into an agonised frown. Mr Surridge's mouth moved at the corners.

'Do you follow, Mr Nelson?' he said.

Mr Midshipman Nelson blushed, but judged it advisable to be honest.

'Not the method, sir, only the conclusion, I beg your pardon. But, sir, would not a timekeeper that kept perfect Greenwich time be a very great benefit to a ship? I heard my uncle speak of such.'

Mr Surridge considered his pupil.

'Dr Maskelyne's opinion is that the timekeepers may serve to make the observations the better but will never supplant them. For those who dislike hard work it would lessen the labour, that's certain. But do you know what they cost, Mr Nelson? I have heard that Mr Kendall's first watch, copying Mr Harrison's, cost four hundred and fifty pounds. It would be a rich sea captain who would expend such a sum?'

'Yes indeed, sir.'

'Until somebody can make one as perfect but much cheaper I cannot see them coming into common use.'

Horatio was always to remember Mr Surridge as a very clever man, and years later was to give it as his opinion that his log book of the *Seahorse* was almost if not *the* best in the Navy Office. Nothing pleased the master more than that Aldebaran should be conveniently visible or that Aquila should offer itself for measurement, both stars being amongst the seven tabled in the *Nautical Almanac*. He himself trusted the lunar method more than any watch. He praised Mr Nevil Maskelyne's *British Mariners Guide* with its clear rules for finding the moon's position and distance: and his *Nautical Almanac*, which had tables of the moon's longitude and latitude computed for every twelve hours. Only last year Mr Maskelyne and Mr Whichell (who was master of the Naval Academy at Portsmouth where Charles Pole had been) had published three tables for clearing the lunar distance, which was the worst part of the whole process. Last year too there had been published a work continued on the same plan, giving tables from which the correction to clear the lunar distance could be taken: it had been done by a Dr Antony Shepherd, Plumian professor of astronomy in Cambridge, with additions by the astronomer royal himself. Mr Surridge admitted that he had found upon enquiry that it was large, expensive, and ill-adapted for use at sea. (It was not until years later that Horace connected the impractical Professor Shepherd with the gentleman he considered to be the persecutor of Mr Bryan Allott, at Burnham Market. But he it was.)

Neither could Horatio know that the reverend Dr Maskelyne's assiduity in furthering the age-old lunar method with the publication of all these tables (admirable as it was) was due in part to a mean desire to put down the rival method, now enshrined in the accurate and beautiful timekeepers of Mr John Harrison (four, no less, before 1760 and he said to be working on a fifth.) For Nevil Maskelyne hoped to win the longitude prize himself. He had moreover bullied and wronged the ageing Mr Harrison in a manner worthy neither of his cloth nor his status in astronomy. All Horace knew (and would remember) was that Mr Surridge was a confirmed lunar man: and that Captain Farmer left these complicated matters to him.

CHAPTER TEN

'...and watched in the foretop...'

The island of Madeira rose abruptly from the sea, and next day the town of Funchal appeared, its white walls shining amongst still-green trees, a castle behind it, and high above it a glistening mountain church. Neat vineyards patterned the hillsides. Horace remembered Barbados: should he ever grow used to the excitement of green land after weeks at sea?

They spent six days in Madeira, taking in stores and doing repairs. A marine by the name of Thomas Harrington caught thieving received his first punishment: he was to become famed for punishment as the voyage went on. A day's sail after Madeira, the rocky islets called the Great Salvages, then the Canaries, or Fortunate Isles as many seamen call them: and now they were drinking good Madeira wine instead of sour English beer. In the steady trades they sped on south-westerly and on Christmas day spoke the *King of Prussia* from Liverpool to Africa. The ships began to dawdle as the trades began to fail. It grew hotter: the quarter-deck and poop awnings were fixed: and fishing for shark became the occupation of the idle.

In the Atlantic, the second day of the New Year was ushered in with hard rain, thunder and lightening in the middle of the night. The wind veered and took the ship aback: there she was rolling to a stand, until the helmsman bore away and the mast crews trimmed the sails. It was to happen so often while they lingered in the doldrums that the cry of 'All aback for'ard!' became familiar in all their ears.

One morning the commodore came aboard the *Seahorse* to present them with a second lieutenant. Sir Edward Hughes was plump and good-natured in countenance, a man of about fifty, easier in manner than their own Captain. He spoke to most of the officers, and had a smile for the midshipmen.

'My son, George Farmer,' said the Captain, 'and Mr George Hicks, from Norwich; and Mr Thomas Hoar; and Mr Horace Nelson, nephew to Captain Suckling.'

'Well, Mr Nelson, you look to be the youngest, I hope you are therefore working the hardest. I know your uncle,' said the commodore with good cheer. Horatio thanked him, wondering if his friend Robert on the *Carcase* had aught to do with Sir Edward, but he did not dare to ask.

While the Captain read Mr Samuel Abson's commission to the ship's company Horace watched first Lieutenant Drummond, who eyed the newcomer speculatively, weighing him up.

With light airs, cloud and lightening to the eastward the ships crossed the line, where Neptune and his court appeared, ducking the Captain's son and Mr Hoar and Thomas Troubridge and many another untried seaman. Mr Surridge wrote with some complacency a note in his log:

> N.B. I think it worthy Remark^s that the Ships Comp^y has been Remarkable Healthy since we sail'd and this day when we cross'd the Equator there was but 3 men on the Sick List with slight ailments.

One night in February the watch below were awoken to an unusual roll and heave, a splintering noise and a rending of canvas. Horatio darted up on deck into the warm wind and came upon Thomas Troubridge, whom he had grown greatly to like and admire in the past weeks.

'Taken aback, and we've fallen on board the commodore,' gasped Thomas running breathlessly forward: they had carried away the spritsail topsail yard and split the sail badly.

That Sunday prayers were read to the ship's company for the very first time upon that voyage. By the middle of February, they were running out of wine; the longboat plied to the commodore and fetched two pipes more. But at least they were no longer idling: gales of wind, squalls or fresh breezes from varying quarters drove them towards the Cape: once, indeed, the frisky *Seahorse* lost all sight of the commodore for several hours.

Half-past three on Wednesday the second of March.

'Land ahoy,' came a yell from aloft. 'Land bearing east nor' east. Distant fourteen or fifteen leagues!'

There was an immediate scudding of officers and men to the starboard side. Nobody was sorry to see the land. They had suffered strong gales the day before, Horace had felt sick as usual, he viewed the distant grey blur with relief and some surprise. They were approaching from the south, he had expected that they would sight the land due easterly?

'Ay lad,' the master's mate explained, 'but we set the course southerly on the trades to reach the westerly gales. The roaring forties, ye'll learn to call them. Then we run down our easting before them, 'tis the quickest way, and turn northerly again to make Good Hope.' Three hours later the famous landfall was beginning to take shape.

'That's the Cape of Good Hope, north-easterly,' the mate told him. 'And the flat high land beyond it is Table Mountain. When there's cloud upon it we call it the tablecloth! We run in to Table Bay.'

Sails were shortened, anchors unstowed, the ship tacked. By eleven o'clock there was little wind at all and they hoisted out the longboat and the cutter to tow her, which they did for four hours before a fresh breeze came on and the Captain had the boats veered astern. A strong but variable gale blew as they worked themselves towards the Bay, the two boats in procession behind. When the wind went round easterly against them the ship was soon in stays.

Sudden cries of alarm were heard from the longboat and the cutter.

'Ahoy, there! The longboat! The longboat's drove under the counter!'

A squall had driven the boat under the overhanging stern of the now stationary ship, one of her masts was caught, she was in danger of overturning. While the hands on deck were all studying to move the halted ship, overset she did and took on much water, the two men clinging to her side.

'The longboat's gone over! She's upset!' yelled Thomas Troubridge from the cutter.

'Cut her adrift! Cut her rope, sir, she'll be pulled under the ship!' The order, seeming necessary, proved fatal.

The officer cut the tow rope, the longboat was floated sideways clear, her men vainly trying to right her. She drifted off westerly before the gusty wind.

'Go after her! You men in the cutter, keep sight of her! Rescue the people. Keep her afloat if you can and tow her back.'

The cutter crew pulled off into the heaving sea after the wounded longboat. Horatio watched her into the cloudy, darkening west until he could see her no longer. Thomas was in her.

The two ships anchored in sight of the great, smooth, tawny-green headland called the Lion's Rump. In the morning Tom Hoar and Horatio, fetching bread and beef from the shore in the pinnace, met the cutter returning alone.

121

'What happened?'

'We could not save the longboat, we could not float her nor tow her—'

'Where were the men?'

'Gone. No sign. It was dark when we reached her.'

'Drowned before you arrived—'

'I suppose so,' said Thomas Troubridge miserably.

Horace remembered the seaman drowned in the Kitthole.

They were three weeks at Table Bay on repairs and renovations and the damaged sails. One evening in March Thomas Troubridge put his cheerful yellow shock head in at the cockpit where Horace and Tom Hoar made up their logs.

'Here am I,' said Tommy, 'and here's my chest,' he added, heaving this in after him.

Horace stared. 'What? Are you messing here? What's happened?'

'I'm appointed mid! From tomorrow!'

Horatio sprang up and walloped his friend's shoulder.

'The devil you are! What a splendid thing. Now we shall all yarn together and see more of you!' exclaimed Tom Hoar.

'What confusion will arise,' Horace went on. 'Two Georges, two Toms! What a very great pity none of you bear distinguished names, such as Horatio,' he shrieked, ducking to avoid Troubridge's fist and dancing round the berth. 'I shall call you Thomas or Tommy. He,' indicating Hoar, 'is Tom!'

The berth happened to be empty and a letter to Horatio's papa soon done. He sealed it and directed it.

'You write to your father,' Hoar said.

'Ay, have you written to yours?'

'Yesterday. I wonder if they will ever reach home?'

'Stale news, when they do.'

'Horace—' Troubridge now began, having stowed his chest. 'Both of you—'

'Yes?'

'What do you think to Mr Drummond? How is he to work for?'

Tom said at once: 'I notice nothing, but Horatio—'

Horatio swung round on his chest, rested his elbows on his knees, and stared at Thomas thinking. He had become aware of a slight sense of unease in his approaches to the first lieutenant upon whom he must constantly dance attendance. He had mentioned it to Tom Hoar.

'It depends upon his mood,' he replied. 'Sometimes he seems surly as a bear, other times as friendly as a brother, will even fling his arm about me. Why do you ask?'

Thomas shrugged. He had overheard a small group of the seamen sniggering about the first officer. He had not altogether understood the import of their remarks.

'I should not fancy his flinging his arm about me. I dislike that kind of fawning. So I had best keep a polite distance.'

'Nor do I like it either. But one must not offend one's master,' Horace said.

'He never does it to me,' said Tom mildly.

'You are such a gentleman; that distances him perhaps. Is he a tyrant?' Thomas went on.

'Not more than many a lieutenant. I rather took against his pinching my cheek...' Horace confessed.

'You didn't tell me that!' Hoar exclaimed.

'If he pinch my cheek I shall raise my fist,' declared Troubridge.

'...After which I tried to keep more cold and distant. His friendliness seemed pleasant enough at first.'

'Ay. Well, thanks for the warning.'

'Do you suppose it is my wretched smallness, making me look such a child?' Horace complained.

'That is certainly possible,' agreed Tom Hoar.

The next week, to salutes from all round, the two ships ran out of Table Bay on an easterly wind, the *Seahorse* as usual soon out-sailing the *Salisbury*. Captain Farmer sent for Midshipman Nelson and apprised him of the fact that he was now to be rated AB for a while, the Captain's son becoming a midshipman in his place. Horace had no lack of confidence in his ability to carry out all the duties of the seaman and was not particularly averse to the change (even though the pay was less): but his face wore a somewhat laconic smile as he went to tell both Tom and Thomas. Their messing all together had been short-lived.

One of the things Horatio was always to remember with satisfaction about his days as an AB was his being made a topman. The topmen were the best sailors in a ship, he knew this from his earliest days. Working the sails above the lower yards, they must be the handiest, the surest, the strongest, the most agile, the most daring of all. (They must also be the quickest, each mast racing the others; some captains were rumoured to punish the last down). It was not a job given before you had been two or three years at sea. Mr Surridge had watched Horatio and knew him to be fearless, smart and competent. When Captain Farmer changed his rating, he spoke to the leader of the foretop men in Horatio's watch, that master's mate to whom the boy talked most.

The mate knew the young man's worth: Horace now worked in the foretop under him. It was not only the greater responsibility which pleased him, it was the sense of larger freedom he came to have, being often up aloft.

In moderate or fresh gales from west and south they took their way south-easterly. Often there was dark squally weather and a great sea following them. Horace would survey behind him this enormous swell, this vast procession of rolling grey waves breaking beyond into huge expanding nets of foam. Sometimes the sight of the following ocean filled him with a strange elation, sometimes with a melancholy loneliness that seemed unbearable.

By mid-April they met the trades, having set their course northerly at last. The wind blew steady and often strong, but the blue and glorious days of those trades which drove the *Mary Ann* to Barbados were absent, south-east trade weather being cloudy and rainy and often sunless.

On a Monday in late April, Horatio noted the cutter hoist out at mid-morning and heard the pipe as the Captain went down into her. It was common enough for the cutter to go to the *Salisbury*, less usual to see the Captain go in her. The cutter was back at one without him.

The Captain was aboard the *Salisbury* all day. At six in the evening the studding sails and the top-gallants were ordered down: and the mids were sent once more to fetch the Captain. Captain Farmer, his face flushed and gloomy, retired at once to his cabin and sent for Lieutenant Drummond. Lieutenant Drummond did not appear again, either in the wardroom, nor upon the quarter-deck: neither that night, nor the next morning.

'What's happened to Mr Drummond?' asked Tom Hoar cheerfully in the mids' berth the next day. The silence indicated that some knew. But none spoke. At that moment Tommy Troubridge came in.

'There's a pair of marines on guard outside Mr Drummond's cabin!' he said.

'Under arrest,' muttered someone shortly, rising and going off up on watch.

'Suspended from duty?' Tom whispered.

'Ay, so I believe,' said George Farmer, a question upon his pale face.

The next morning was fair, the people sat in the sun drawing and knotting yarns, some men started to paint the barge. But there was a dark sense of unease about the ship, strange contrast to the sunshine. The people whispered: the news was around. In the mids' berth sat Thomas Troubridge when Horace put his head in, one eyebrow raised.

'Have you heard?'

'Ay.'

'What do you make of it?'

'The same as you do.'

'I know not what to make of it,' said Horatio simply. 'I suppose we shall hear the fault?'

Thomas shrugged and half smiled.

'If the fault is not too disgraceful,' he said.

'What do you make of it, Tom?' Nelson said as Hoar came in. Tom looked at Troubridge and flushed slightly.

'I can make a guess,' said he.

'Is anyone else confined?'

'Two or three seamen, I have heard.'

'Ah. Well, you never did take to that party,' Horace remarked to Troubridge, darting away.

That evening the bo'sun summoned the officers and company, The Captain stood forth on the poop and announced to all (what the master had known and noted the previous day) that Mr Drummond, first lieutenant, was ordered under an arrest and was suspended from all duty by order of the commodore Sir Edward Hughes.

Now they lost the trade wind, and it became hot and sultry, as sultry as the mood upon the *Seahorse*. Fishing lines were issued, the smell of blood and fish invaded the ship; then the sour, clean taint of vinegar when the people washed between decks. They noted seaweed pass, birds in flocks appear: the master's mate drew them upon the log, a flock of fluttering V-shaped signs. The master observed the star, Aquila, and began a series of remarks about wind, weather and current which described their passage northerly across the Indian Ocean, being set constantly to the eastward by the current.

At six o'clock on the morning of May the fifteenth they saw the land, west-south-west about eight leagues off. Misty and still, blue gradually dawning to green, Horatio watched the coast of India take shape. One, two, three, four strange towers sailed into sight, towers with storeys which descended like the flounces of a lady's dress.

'The four Chillamburn Pagodas,' said the mate at his side.

The reefs were all out and the studding sails set. Headlands, buildings, forts, pockets of blue-green trees, green swards and silver sand sped nearer.

'The flagstaff of Porto Nuovo north by west,' called the look-out.

They unstowed the anchors at eight.

'The flagstaff at Fort St David's north-west by west!'

Fresh breezes and fair weather at midday.

'The flagstaff of Pondicherry north-west half north seven leagues,' noted the master at noon.

As they gazed upon that romantic landfall, most men forgot the officer cribbed and cabined in his berth and the seamen in their chains in the dark hot belly of the ship.

That evening they anchored at Sadras. The next they were running into Madras Road further north. As the sun went down at six o'clock, the commodore saluted Rear Admiral Sir Robert Harland upon His Majesty's Ship *Northumberland* riding in the harbour: while the barrack buildings of Fort St George south of the city glowed red, the flagstaff rosy on top; and a cupola above the town clock caught the rays of the dying sun.

In Madras Road, between repairs and ship work, they exercised great guns and small arms; and on oak-apple day in that far-off harbour hazy with damp and heat, the British ships remembered the return of King Charles and fired him twenty-one guns.

The next morning the signal went up for a court martial upon the *Salisbury*, the officers gathered, deliberated all day, broke up at seven in the evening, and dismissed Lieutenant James Francis Edward Drummond of the *Seahorse* from His Majesty's Service. The day after, another court martial was held upon the *Salisbury*, whose dire outcome was not known until three days later. 'Three men,' wrote the master's mate in the log, 'received 25 lashes each alongside us, being part of the 200 sentenced each of them by a Court Martial on board the *Salisbury* 31 May.'

Horatio had seen it all before; the ghastly procession of boats, with their victims tied and waiting, the solemn beating of the drum by the marine guard, the fearful effects of the bo'sun's cats. But Tom Hoar and Thomas Troubridge who had not were shaken in their different ways. The intermittent drumming was heard all the morning as the deathly boats plied round the anchored fleet.

'What becomes of them? Can they live?' Tom said in a low voice.

'It is to be hoped not. They are cut to pieces,' Horace informed him. 'I've seen the start of such floggings before.'

Thomas was more vociferous. He jumped up and ground his fist in his hand. 'Horace, Tom, why should that crimp-haired dandified scoundrel get off scot-free? It must have been he who sought them out, *they* would not begin the affair!' he whispered furiously.

'Did you note we were not even told what was the affair?' Horace said.

Troubridge looked at Hoar, raised an eyebrow, then spoke.

'You cannot be so innocent! There is but one crime that is not spoken of. All others are openly announced when the Captain reads the articles and orders the punishment. Drunkenness, insolence, neglect of duty, theft, striking an officer—'

'So you think—'

'You must know what I think!'

Horace in fact had the vaguest ideas about the matter; but he now remembered Maurice warning him in terms that were strange to him then. *You may meet some men who want to use you as men should only use women: watch out when they are kind and make much of you.* The sense of unease he had felt with Mr Drummond slid into place: yet Mr Drummond had not seemed a bad man so much as a moody one.

'That man,' Thomas went on, 'has the deaths of three to answer for and nothing to pay!'

Horatio considered this.

'Oh but he has. Will he not feel terrible remorse at their deaths, should they die? And the disgrace! He must go home, tell his parents—'

'Ay, what must his thoughts be like now? I can imagine nothing more painful,' added Tom.

'Two hundred lashes is a deal more painful,' said their practical friend sardonically.

'Where is he? What will he do, do you suppose?' Hoar questioned.

'I neither know nor care what he does,' Troubridge said. But Horace's mind dwelt upon the officer. Dismissed, disgraced, put ashore in an unknown country perhaps with little money, how lonely he must feel! If he were to meet him by chance upon the ship, should he not salute as became him and wish him farewell in kindness? But the test never arose. Drummond was already gone, smuggled off the ship after dark upon the same night as he was sentenced with no farewells from anyone, and put ashore with his belongings to find his own way.

Very early on July the fourteenth, at five o'clock when the sky was pale honey pink, they unmoored to a signal from the *Salisbury*, and weighed and came to sail in company with the whole squadron: the *Northumberland*, Rear Admiral Sir Robert Harland, the *Salisbury*, Commodore Sir Edward Hughes, the *Prudent*, the *Intrepid*, the *Warwick*, the *Dolphin*, lately arrived from Trincomalee, and the *Swallow* sloop. They sailed south and at ten o'clock anchored in a line two miles offshore opposite Chepank House, in nine fathoms. The palace of the Nabob of Arcot was a plain classical building of white and red stone, standing in gardens well planted with groups of cypress and palm and glossy shrubs and bushes. There was time to survey it through one's glass, to follow its shady walks and stone steps and flowery arbours.

A boat was lowered from the side of the *Northumberland* and went ashore bearing a letter from His Majesty. In due course His Highness the Nabob of Arcot fired twenty-one guns from the cannon concealed in his floriferous gardens. It was answered by the roar of twenty-one guns from each of the squadron waiting out at sea and followed by a second salute in the same manner. Then the whole squadron weighed and sailed back to their former berths.

Five days later the contents of the letter became apparent. At dawn the admiral gave the signal to unmoor, and the *Northumberland*, the *Prudent*, the *Intrepid*, the *Buckingham* and the *Warwick* did so. In the afternoon the *Northumberland*, the *Intrepid* and the *Warwick* sailed for home, Rear Admiral Sir Robert Harland was recalled. Salutes of farewell to the departing admiral and salutes to the new commodore followed. At sunrise next morning a little country ship called the *True Briton* added her loyal salute, which the commodore returned. The country or local trading ships, as Horace was to discover, all sailed under the British flag.

A Mr Thomas Henery had taken Drummond's place. The luckless Thomas Harrington was punished again and again for insolence, for petty theft, and even for selling his clothes, feeling the absence of any need for them in the tropical heat. Twice was fresh beef condemned and returned as carrion. Rats ate the spare sails; a seaman called William Orton died and was buried. The people repaired and painted up the *Dolphin's* yawl which they had received in poor state instead of their lost longboat; they made covers for the boats, renewed the awnings, and sewed new red ensigns and pendants. And while a wholesale condemnation of carpenter's, bo'sun's, gunner's and armourer's stores went on, much being returned to His Majesty's naval storekeeper at Madras or converted to junk, or even thrown into the sea, Horace would gaze at the alluring coastline and long to get ashore.

CHAPTER ELEVEN

'…I…visited almost every part of the East Indies…'

Surveying the turbid and muddy River Hooghly, the sand spit of Kedgeree Point to the south-west, and a few houses strung along the bay between, Horatio reflected that it was an odd place to be having his sixteenth birthday: and thought of his father and his family, with a small pang of sorrow.

They had left Madras in mid-September, the *Seahorse* leading; joined by the *Salisbury*, the *Dolphin*, and a local snow, perhaps enlisted to guide them, they made their way in often wild and squally weather across the Bay of Bengal. The most interesting hazard had been their getting into a strong tide setting to windward by which the ship would not keep to, although she went two knots ahead. At noon the next day they had anchored at Kedgeree.

The abiding memory of Kedgeree was to be the largest, most wholesale refitting and renewing of a ship that Horace had ever known. It was breathlessly hot and the seamen began mending up their seine net which had been torn trawling for fish.

The sultry estuary was enlivened only by the comings and goings of ships and the salutes that followed. An East Indiaman anchored, soon known to be the *Anson* and to have on board her the judges. Next arrived the *Ashburnham* Indiaman carrying the gentlemen of the Supreme Council: she too visited each of His Majesty's ships. On the Sunday after all this, the commodore shifted his broad pendant from the *Salisbury* to the *Swallow* sloop, and the little *Swallow* weighed anchor and stood towards Calcutta with Sir Edward Hughes aboard.

'Calcutta,' said Tom to Horace. 'I suppose we shan't get there.'

'I doubt we shall not,' his friend replied, watching the sloop disappear up the river. 'What do you suppose he has gone for?'

'Maybe for new masts and spars, I heard there are shipyards there. Someone told me it is a splendid city, glistens like marble. Spires and domes and pillared buildings and some steps down to the river.'

'You make me long to see it. But what about the infamous black hole which I was once taught of?'

'Any road,' said one of the master's mates behind them, 'I reckon we can now get on, now all that's over.'

The main and foremasts of the *Seahorse* had indeed been condemned: and all the ships' boats towed the old *Seahorse* alongside the *Salisbury* and hoist out the faulty masts by use of the *Salisbury's* main yard. Within the week the broad pendant flew again from the *Salisbury*, the commodore was returned and, not long after, there arrived new masts from Calcutta.

Now the beginning of a bad fever or flux struck the *Seahorse:* and within a month she had sent twenty-two men on shore to the hospital. Meanwhile, shipwrights were everywhere. Caulkers and carpenters were at work, bricklayers repaired the fireplaces; the galley was re-tinned; the fo'c's'le repaired; a decayed hand-pump renewed. The forge, mended on shore, was re-installed. The pinnace was repaired. Tarring began. All the sailmakers of both ships had gathered upon the *Salisbury* to make new main and mizzen sails. The gunner carted his wet powder on shore and set about sifting and drying it. The worm-eaten rudder and the platform of the magazine were renewed. One day the *Seahorse's* best bower anchor got stuck fast in the mud: and repeated attempts to weigh it caused exasperation to those concerned but no little amusement to the rest.

The new masts being got in, they set to getting the rigging and the topmasts back. The *Swallow* returned from Calcutta; and men began to appear pale but recovered from the hospital. They heeled the ship over and scrubbed starboard and larboard, the carpenters repairing some of her sheathing. Painters came from Calcutta; and bamboo to make studding sail yards arrived. They discovered sails and loglines eaten to shreds by the rats. Nonetheless on the twenty-fourth of December the ship was declared ready for sea.

'Christmas tomorrow, Tom,' exclaimed Horace, meeting his friend as he came down off the rigging. 'Would you think it possible?' And he wiped his brow.

Tom Hoar shook his head gloomily, the thought making him homesick. Christmas was taken little note of: though fresh beef arrived, there was no service read: and Horatio thought of snow and frost and keen Norfolk winds and the polished holly, and Papa and the others walking to church. And Mamma not there.

Towards the middle of January, a pilot came aboard to carry them down the Hooghly River to Inglelee Road. Here were swung on board eighty-nine chests to be stowed in the afterhold, a certain reticence as to their contents prevailing. The master's mate was seen drawing their mark (the shape of a heart, with the initials E.I.C. upon it) into the log: East India Company. Thomas Troubridge made enquiries.

'It's treasure,' he muttered to the others later on, assuming a fine air of mystery.

'What, gold?' asked Hoar.

''Tis said to be ten lacks of current rupees. You must know what is a rupee: but don't ask me what is a lack.'

'It's clear what is the lack,' put in Nelson at once; 'we three lack the rupees.'

'Clear enough,' Troubridge said, and with a loud and sudden guffaw at this schoolboy wit, the three went about their business. The next day they were on their way back to Madras.

From Madras harbour (where they watered and provisioned for a three months' trip yet knew not their destination) they sailed on the twenty-ninth of January 1775, stood to the south-east, and rounded the island of Ceylon. All the landmarks were cried: the rocks called the Little Basses, Mount Chimney, the Elephant Rock, the Great Basses, Dondra Head, Point de Galle. Horace sought them out upon the master's chart, and when they turned north-westerly:

'We shall see Bombay!' he informed his friends.

The weather was mostly pleasant, their only enemy the calms which caused the ship to turn her head all round the compass again and again off the south-west coast of Ceylon: once they had even to hoist out the boats to tow.

One morning at nine o'clock when they had left Colombo to the south-east they discovered a ship in company who drew near enough over the next two hours to speak them. She proved to be the *Dodley* bound from Batavia to Bombay, a ship of the country trade, handsome as were many of her kind, often larger, speedier and better built that the usual East Indiaman. Horatio found Mr Surridge at the rail.

'She's a handsome ship, sir?'

'Ay. She'll be built in Bombay, native shipwrights, Parsees, they say. They copy our ships and they often make 'em better. And the teak wood is all here abouts you see.'

'She's bigger than the country ships in the Hooghly?'

'For why, *they* must get up and down to Calcutta. They're built up there. Great shipyards in Calcutta, and Burmese carpenters. I'm told it's a bigger fleet trades from there, though smaller ships.'

Horace had learned a little about the country trade as they lay in the Hooghly and saw the ships going and coming. Anyone, European or Indian, could trade between India and the Indies, China and the gulf of Persia, though the Company had the general control.

'Are the ships all British, sir?'

'Just as often owned or part owned by the Parsees. They have English officers however, and native crews.'

'What do they carry, Mr Surridge, sir?'

'Cotton in great part, from Bombay I believe. Raw cotton. Sandalwood, that smells right sweet up the coast of Malabar. Pepper. Spices they pick up in the islands of the East Indies on the way to China. And you can guess what they bring back.'

'Tea!' the boy said. 'All the tea in China!' It was one of Papa's oft-used expressions: Horace could hear his very voice.

'Ay, and porcelain cups to drink it out of. And silk and satin. From Calcutta I believe the cargo is largely rice. How did you fare with the dried salt fish and rice of Kedgeree?'

'I have tasted dishes I like better, sir,' admitted seaman Nelson. Mr Surridge laughed, nodded, and strolled away.

The *Dodley* flew the British flag, as did all the country ships. Whenever occasion presented itself, they sought the convoy of a man-of-war and expected its protection against enemy or pirate. Thus did the *Dodley* now.

On the afternoon of the twelfth of February they sighted Cape Comorin on the southern tip of India. Calms still enfolded them: there was much tacking and wearing; and often for some part of the night they would come to on the stream anchor and await the breeze of morning. On the fifteenth they were running in to Anjengo, the most southerly English factory upon the Malabar coast. Horatio saw the town from aloft. At one extreme glistened the Fort with the British flag flying, at the other the Portuguese church, and along the shore a native tomb. Palm trees waved their delicious fronds over all, rooted in the silver sand. A great rolling surf beat the shore below Anjengo, braved only by the shallow native boats: and to the north beyond the tomb rose romantic red cliffs. After sunset in the quick dusk, there came on a partial eclipse of the moon: all wrote in their logs the discomforting fact that it was not visible in England. Calm enfolded them; the scents from the shore were mingled, sweet odour of spice, rank smell of drying fish used on the rice fields. At one in the morning they weighed and made sail in a light north-easterly breeze from the land. The *Dodley* was still in company.

On Sunday February the nineteenth, having been at anchor all night, they sailed early in the morning and were taking their course north-westerly, when at seven o'clock the look-out cried:

'Two sail on the starboard bow. Standing toward us. Two sail to starboard!'

The officer of the watch, the master who was come up before

breakfast, the Captain himself who took his airing on the poop, all clapped their telescopes to their eyes to see.

'They're Bombay cruisers, ain't they?' said Captain Farmer.

'They are ketches, any road,' said Mr Surridge.

'I cannot distinguish any colours,' muttered Mr Abson.

The country ship *Dodley* lying well astern plied her way innocently after the *Seahorse* in the hazy morning sunshine. At half past seven the two ketches hauled their wind to the southward and stood after the *Dodley*. At the same time they hoist their colours.

'What are they about?' said the master.

'Those are the colours of Hyder Ali!' shouted the Captain. 'Rouse all hands, tack the ship, stand after them and give chase!' roared Captain Farmer.

'Mr North, all hands!' cried the master.

The bo'sun's pipe shrilled, the watch tumbled up from below, the orders rang out. The *Seahorse* turned her head and stood after the two ships. Half an hour later, within reach of them:

'Fire a shot, fire several shots, to bring one of them to!' the Captain ordered. 'They must be native ships of the Mahrattas, no doubt. They must answer our summons.'

They were slow to do so: but eventually a boat was lowered from one of them which came on board the *Seahorse* at nine o'clock.

'We ships of Hyder Ali,' announced the messenger. 'Hyder Ali, he great prince. We out from Mangalore.'

'I care not where you are out from, nor for Hyder Ali,' muttered Captain Farmer. 'Why do not those ketches bring to, nor shorten sail, at my fire? I wish to speak them. Do not they understand the command of a British ship?' he said raising his voice, as if loudness ensured understanding.

The boatman could only shake his head in bewilderment and repeat 'Hyder Ali,' and shrug his shoulders.

'Several other vessels heaving in sight, sir!' called the officer. 'Perhaps they have consorts!'

'Ships on the port bow,' shouted down the look-out. 'Two, three...Three ships to port, standing towards us!'

'Mr Gunner, trundle out the guns, man them, and be ready to give these ships fire. I'll Hyder Ali them,' snorted the Captain. 'Mr Surridge, Mr Abson, give chase and get the ship where she may do her worst. I doubt the intentions of those ships. If a ship will not declare her intentions, she shall be peppered till she do! Carry on!'

And before anybody had time to question why, the *Seahorse* was preparing for action. The gun crews ran to their stations, the decks were cleared, the carriages rumbled out, the powder boys lined up at the magazines below. Every seaman at his rope ready to work the ship as the officer might order; Horace at the foremast with the topmen; the master warily at the wheel, the Captain surveying the ketches.

'Mr Abson, they read our intent, I think they put on sail!' shouted he.

'Ay, sir. We give chase.'

It appeared the ketches made as if to fly: but the *Seahorse* was fleeter. Horatio watched with some excitement the expanse of sea steadily narrowing, was aware of the gunner's orders below him, saw the cook stand out of the galley his hands to his ears: but was nonetheless shaken to his bones by the first roaring of the guns.

Round after round from the nine-pounders in turn cracked and roared over the water, the lesser voice of the smaller guns barking in between. Smoke billowed back over the deck, reek rose to the rigging. Horace choked with the rest, his eyes blinded and weeping with burning stench. The ketches sailed on, seemingly in no mind to bring to. On the *Seahorse* they were scarcely aware of the return of any fire so boisterous was the noise from their own guns. The high singing of splintered glass filled the space between the roar of two guns: panes shattered and fell. Drawing up close, the *Seahorse* sent a knotty explosion of grapeshot into the enemy's rigging. Horace was aware of a silence like death on his wounded ears when for a space no sound fell. A cracked and hoarsened voice called an order, a seaman struck six bells.

Then the uproar began once more, swallowed up the whole morning in a deafening chaos that seemed to achieve nothing. Just before noon, however, in a lull, the first officer shouted:

'Nearest ship bringing to, sir!'

A pause.

'Strikes her colours, sir!'

'The devil she do,' muttered Farmer. 'Give the order to cease fire! Bring the ship to. Mr North, a boat.'

Orders filled the ship, mast crews to their ropes; gun crews drooping, swabbed their faces; a mid, Troubridge, to the cutter with his crew, Lieutenant Henery following down.

The cutter returned with the news only that the two ships were as they had protested armed cruisers of Hyder Ali. In a flurry of wounded self-importance the *Seahorse* made sail: the *Dodley* had pursued her own way and was not to be seen.

Young Nelson ate his dinner on the still reeking mess deck and reflected that he had been in action. For years as a green boy, as Captain's servant and youngest mid, had he longed to hear the boom of guns in earnest. Now it had crept up on him unawares: and he knew not the reason and neither did his neighbour.

'Hey, Tom! Tommy!' Horace said at the first opportunity. 'What a to-do was that! Can you tell me why we chased them? Who, pray, *is* Hyder Ali?'

'Tommy knows, he's asked Mr Henery,' Hoar said.

'It's all to do with the French,' Troubridge began. 'Hyder Ali is a nabob who has an alliance with the French—'

'Confuse and confound the French,' Nelson put in. 'This is why we are here, this is what my Uncle Suckling told me! I recollect now, we were to watch the French...'

'Ay. Our commodore, Mr Henery said, is to spy out French plans and ambitions and communicate direct with the Secretary of State. Because three years ago the French had a plot to land twenty-thousand men at Pondicherry—'

'Where's Pondicherry?'

'It matters not: they gave it up. But do you know how we discovered this plot?' Tommy paused.

'How should he? Get on,' said Hoar.

'A Captain, a real swash-buckler called Lockhart Russell crashed through the surf into a harbour in Mauritius, after a hurricane, on the wind. And there were all the ships laid up, *transports*. And he asked and got intelligence!'

Horatio's eyes widened and shone.

'*That* is the stirring sort of commission that I long to undertake!' he cried.

'I too,' Thomas agreed. 'When we are captains may the Lord allow us such an action!'

Tom Hoar, less of a firebrand than either, smiled and said naught.

'To crash through the surf into a nest of enemies!' Horatio could not exult enough. 'And coolly walk up on shore!'

'And get off again it seems, unknown!'

'Ay! Fortunate Captain, the hero of such a chance!'

Horace came back to earth.

'So Captain Farmer was suspicious of the ketches because this prince is in league with the French?'

Troubridge nodded.

'Mr Henery said that all British captains can be relied upon to harbour suspicions of hostile behaviour on the part of Hyder Ali's fleet.'

'And our Captain thought they were going to board the *Dodley* full of tea from China?'

'Not a great prize,' agreed Hoar.

'What if they wanted her out of the way?' Troubridge suddenly cried. 'I have just now thought of it! The treasure!'

'A-ay,' Tom Hoar agreed. 'So! Eighty-nine chests of the company's rupees, no lack of rupees...'

Horace was immediately caught up.

'Captain Farmer must be more than commonly sensitive to its presence!' he shouted. 'Only suppose, they might have boarded us, having dealt with the *Dodley*, seeking our treasure. They might have heard tell of our treasure? Spies. In the Hooghly. We should have had a fight!'

'We did have a fight!' roared Troubridge.

'I mean a serious fight. They would have been joined by those three others, it would have been five to two!' Nelson cried busily arranging the encounter. 'We should have been surrounded—'

'What we have missed!' sighed Hoar, raising satirical eyes to heaven.

Troubridge and Nelson had the grace to laugh.

Meanwhile the master's mate entered in the log the stores used in the action: 57 Roundshot 9pounders; 15 Grapeshot 9pounders; 2 double headed hammeredsshot; 25 Roundshot 3pounders; 2 grapeshot 3pounders...And the carpenter gloomily mended the panes of glass.

The calms continued. What winds there were now met them from north or north-west, so that there was much tacking or wearing, they being on a northerly course. In the still nights they would put down the stream anchor: there was a magic warmth and mystery in being awake in this latitude in the middle watch: often enough the abundance of stars in the deep blue sky was veiled with cloud, then blazed forth in splendour to dazzle a young seaman on watch, then was misted again. Soundings brought up blue mud. Another of the master's mates, an old shellback who knew the coast, would tell Horace what to watch out for, regale him with tales of the Malabar settlements. One morning they saw the flagstaffs at Calicut against the overwhelming background of the huge Ghat Mountains towering stupendously behind. On the beach before the palms was a small sprinkle of huts, in the harbour rode a few ships. No fort, no church, no temple appeared.

'Calicut's not much then, is it?' he asked his friend later.

'Not now, lad. But ha'nt you ever heard of old Vasco da Gama? That's where the Portuguese first come, the first traders from Europe. They say that was a fine splendid city in those times, till much later. But d'you know what happened?'

'No, what?'

'That all went under the sea, Lord bless you. Four miles of it. I've seen waves breaking in Calicut Road where no waves ought to be, on the temples and palaces underneath you see. That's why Calicut Road's not so safe, unless you know it. Nothing much now but what you saw, and the smell of shark's fins a-drying before the coconuts.' And the mate sighed at the vanity of human endeavour. 'Did you ever see a fowl with black bones, eh? And there's a race of monkeys. And water-snakes. Did you ever see a water-snake? Reeling around in coils. I've seed them in Calicut harbour.'

Next day at noon they were running into Tellicherry Road, as grand as Calicut was humble. It stood on rising ground above the shore surrounded with a modest wall, a handsome mountain behind it. There were two forts, and the English flag flew proudly upon a handsome building. Fish was good here, said the mate, sardines and oysters in particular. Tellicherry Fort saluted with thirteen guns. The *Seahorse* returned as many. Horace longed to set foot on the sand of Tellicherry: the mate had told him of a glorious wild lily that ran over the bushes and shrubs as brilliant as flame. But the watering was done by the boats from the shore and they sailed away leaving Tellicherry in the pearling dawn. That afternoon five seamen received twelve lashes each for drunkenness: had someone laid hands on arrack from a shore boat? Nobody told.

Through calm and haze they idled northward. As they tacked past Mangalore the main seaport of Hyder Ali nabob of Mysore, they saw a fleet of ships at anchor: its river entrance was dangerous because of the rapid current in the narrow channel. It was defended by batteries and a fortress.

'There crouch our friends,' remarked the Captain to the officers, 'licking their wounds, I trust.'

St Mary's Island, Pigeon Island, the Karwar river, the Oyster Rock, were idled by: and at last the notable Cape Ramas hove in sight and the high northern point of Goa Bay.

They sounded their way up the coast, bringing up blue mud. On the fifteenth of March they saw Kanary Island, and at sunrise next morning the lighthouse on Old Woman's Island, seven or eight miles off. By noon they were standing in for Bombay.

Horace never forgot his first sight of the grand and noble harbour of Bombay, looking across its spacious waters to the mountains of the main continent of India. It occupied a southerly island of a group which formed the western boundary of the harbour. Now as they entered the Road the face of the city appeared: a handsome dockyard including the Admiralty building, the Marine House, the church with its neat temple-dome above the tower, the great paved pier running out from the Bunder house, a circle of lesser houses joining this to the castle, which was solid if not lofty and surmounted with the flagstaff. Beyond the castle, the Dungaree Fort, or Fort George. Palm trees waved around Fort George, but none waved as high as the British flag. The blue sky was broken by piled white clouds, a moderate breeze slapped the water into wavlets, several large ships lay at anchor and numberless small busy vessels made their way back and forth. From this harbour went cotton from Surat and many another part of India; and silk and muslin, pearls and diamonds, ivory, sandalwood, pepper, cassia and cinnamon from within the great continent. To it came pearls from Ormuz: and from Bussorah and Muscat in the Gulf of Persia raw silk and wool, dates and dried fruits, rose water, attar of roses. Coffee and gold, drugs and honey came from Arabia. China sent tea and porcelain, sugar and wrought silk, in exchange for cotton and bullion. From the islands of the Indies spices came, and perfumes and ambergris, arrack, and sugar. From Africa came drugs and ivory and slaves.

It was a scene such as Horatio loved, full of activity, bustle and enlivenment. No sooner had the ship made her appearance than the salutes began. The guns roared out from all over the harbour, the decks of the *Seahorse* shuddered with her replies. They had arrived, and they were welcome! The Fort added its final fatherly voice to the rest and saluted them with thirteen.

The main business of the next day was to send on shore the treasure of the East India Company: Captain Farmer watched it go with some relief. Later on, the government and Council of Bombay made their way to what somebody spelled as their 'yatch' and the gunner hastened to give them fifteen. Meanwhile the *Seahorse* was scrubbed and blacked and tarred and renovated; new stores came aboard and water, wood and provisions for six months.

'Six months' stores?' Horace muttered to Tom, who was counting in from the boat he and Tommy had brought alongside. 'Any idea where we go?'

'Heard nothing as yet,' Hoar answered. They were never told.

Two companies of the EIC's troops and a party of their train of artillery came aboard, to be conveyed to Surat: and early one March morning they left Bombay on the land breeze in as cheerful a flurry as they had entered it, to the farewell salutes from the Fort and from a country ship nearby. At eight o'clock, as they ran out to sea southerly, the look-out reported a fleet of ships at anchor to the southward. When later the *Seahorse* tacked ship and stood to the northward again, she passed clean through this fleet, sailing for Bombay on the sea breeze: merchantmen and grabs, cruisers and country ships, their canvas filled from the west, their wakes widening behind them. As the *Seahorse* neared them guns began to boom out, and the *Seahorse* answered. Up the rigging, Horace shook like a spider.

Surat was one hundred and twenty miles north of Bombay. The merchant ships preferred the convoy of an English cruiser, said the old mate, because of a horde of pirates called the Coolies who came out from the gulf of Cambay to the north in swift sailing ships, infesting the navigation and falling upon those who sailed alone. In two days and a half they were running in for Surat Road, the Tappee river lying north-north-east. That evening one of the Company's ketches lying in the road hoist a broad pendant. Captain Farmer, apprised of this, called to the gunner.

'Fire a swivel shot at that ketch, we'll see if she knows the nature of her transgression.'

The shot was fired, but the pendant remained flying. The Captain waited, muttering to himself upon the quarter-deck.

'Mr Henery, he shouted at last, 'take a boat, board that ketch and confiscate that pendant.'

Horace stood watching all this with some admiration. He had noted before the Captain's precise attention to flag etiquette, and approved of his uncompromising decision. The ketch should know her business. Lieutenant Henery returned with the pendant looking, himself, a trifle embarrassed. It seemed that while His Majesty's frigate the *Seahorse* lay in Surat Road, the shipping of the world had better mind its manners.

Early the next morning a boat was wanted to ply up to Surat for bullocks and wood and water for the ship. Troubridge was in charge. Horace quickly volunteered. As the sun rose ahead of them, they came suddenly upon the city round a bend in the river. It lay on the south bank and seemed strangely more of the orient than was Bombay, despite the factories of the English, Dutch, French and Portuguese each side of the old Mogul castle, flying their flags upon their buildings. For Surat (as they learned later) was governed jointly by the Mogul and the East India Company, their two flags flying upon the towers of the castle. In the outer wall of the city were towers bearing cannon, and holes for musketry. There were two walls and between them houses with gardens, growing every kind of vegetable and salad. The mate had told Horace of bazaars with costly merchandise and exotically mounted strangers from all parts of the globe: Turks and Persians upon Arab chargers, native nobles upon elephants and camels, merchants upon mules and horses, ladies in carriages, and hackeries drawn by oxen. He had talked of certain gardens of the Nabob where different flowers of like height were planted in patterns to resemble a rich Turkey carpet. He had told him of a hospital for animals where sick and injured beasts and birds and insects were tended, and beggars were hired, as food for vermin. He had talked of the weavers of fine stuffs sitting under the trees, the embroiderers, jewellers and painters, and those craftsmen who inlaid ivory and ebony and sandalwood into their pieces. But the boat crew had scant time to explore, and within an hour they were returned to the ship with a load of wood and another boat following with bullocks.

They left Surat Road one morning in April, with three country ships in company for Cape St John, who parted at dusk that afternoon. From then on their course, as Horatio noted from the deck log, was ever west or north-westerly. He studied the chart.

'I give it as my opinion,' he announced to his friends, 'that we are sailing for the shores of Araby!'

A strange richness lay in the very name.

CHAPTER TWELVE

'...from Bengal to Bussorah'

High above the Arabian sea, in bright hot sunshine which warmed his bones, and a fair light breeze from the north-west which lifted his pale hair, Horace surveyed the water from the foremast, saw nothing but a flurry of flying fish, and was happy. In his memory lay the journey of the *Mary Ann,* recalling other happiness. A certain rich and fresh excitement was now overlaid: for it was evident they were bound for the pearl fisheries, the pirate haunts of the Persian Gulf.

'There's always been pirates in these parts between Arabia and India. They comes across this sea. From Muscat. That's a regular nest of Arab pirates, is Muscat. Or was,' the old master's mate had told the boys.

'Shall we see Muscat?'

The mate winked and looked wise. 'I've heard plenty of tales of company's ships grabbed between the Coast of Malabar and Bombay by Muscat Arabs. Grab's right, too: you've noted the Bombay grabs? They're Arab ships, grabs.'

'Ay, they're square rigged, two masts, with a great stern behind and no bowsprit?' Troubridge said.

'That's it. Terrible cruel people, them Arab pirates. The things they do, to poor innocent sailors. I heard of them sewing up a Captain's mouth with a sail needle and twine. He was simple enough to lecture them, when they fell upon his ship! 'Twas only between Bombay and Surat, too. Arab horses, he had on board. Dumped him and the men ashore, burnt the ship and the wretched horses with it.'

'Damnable villains!' exclaimed Tom Hoar.

'Now you see why Captain Farmer was quick after the ketches. They did not show what they were. There was that most desperate pirate from the Gulf...Name of Muhanna or some such...' went on the mate.

'What did he do?' Hoar prompted.

'Got himself fixed on an island, Kharag they call it, drove off the Dutch, and was a regular hornet, till we joined with the King of Persia, and took two or three years to dislodge him. He escaped to Basra, but they captured and killed him by the order of the King of Baghdad.' To the mate all rulers were kings.

'There are Englishmen not above being pirates,' remarked Horatio.

'Ay, so there be. What are smugglers but pirates, in a manner of speaking?'

So the look-outs were ever on the watch for pirate sails. Early one morning four ships to the northward were sighted carrying triangular sails, with banks of oars as well. On deck there was some altercation as to their name.

'Calavats I call 'em' said the master's mate, who had written them thus in the log.

'Galliots I thought they were,' observed the officer of the watch. 'Or galleywats…'

'Gallivats,' said Mr Surridge with decision, when appealed to. 'They carry swivel guns. Are they still in sight? Ay. Coming along there.'

'Exercise the small arms,' said Captain Farmer with a smile to the gunner, looking at the vessels through his glass.

They did so. And at three o'clock the great guns.

The exercises were regularly repeated almost every other day as they crossed this ocean. One of the master's mates drew a flock of crosses in the log and noted 'several' large birds about the ship: 'several' being anything up to two hundred to a man from Norfolk. Mr Surridge had out his instruments one day, observed the sun and moon, and worked his intricate calculations of time and longitude. Next morning land was cried, a long uneven shore of very high land, hazy and somehow sinister, six leagues distant: the high land over Muscat. That afternoon the cutter fetched the pilot, an Arab from a ship lying at anchor, a silent brown-skinned man, his robes tucked up and his head turbanned. Calm fell, and they anchored.

At four in the morning they hoist out all the boats, to tow the ship over a remarkably clear sea showing a clean sandy bottom. The calms which interspersed the breezes, the haze, the sultry brooding weather, all in Horace's imagination added to the sense of threat he felt as he rowed with the rest along shore for Muscat harbour. Next morning they saw Muscat Point eight or nine miles off, singularly like the Start Point at home; and the mate drew a finger in the log and said so. As they ran in for the harbour a little country ship called the *Betsy Gally* saluted them promptly with eleven guns: she was to become their companion for many weeks.

Dark rocky pinnacles enclosed the harbour of Muscat, rose high behind the glistening honey-coloured city and disappeared into the haze inland. Upon a separate steep rock stood the castle, a turret at each end of it. It was the calm of high tide, it was hot and hazy. The rocky pinnacles, the turrets of the castle, the towers and mosques and houses of the city, even the masts and rigging of the *Betsy* riding there, were reflected in the astonishing clear water. The sea lapped the very edges of the buildings and covered the strand which would be revealed when the water fell. Flights of gleaming white sea birds flashed against the shadowed cliffs. Forts perched on menacing crags. Boats were anchored near the rocky shore. The place seemed full of menace to Horatio.

They stayed but a day and a half in Muscat, then made the signal to the *Betsy Gally* to weigh, for she was to come with them for Bussorah (or Bushire): and sailed at eleven that night.

At noon next day they signalled to a little group of trankeys, pearl fishing vessels, lying to the west, one of whom undertook to lend them a pilot. He arrived soon afterwards and in high spirits mimed the pearl fishing: diving, gasping, throwing up his hands in amazement, to make known to the strangers the marvels in the oysters they brought up. The summer's pearl fishing was begun: and many a sailor sweltering in the *Seahorse* would gladly have changed places with the cheerful men in the trankeys. For the weather was for the most part disagreeably heavy and sultry: and despite windsails to carry the air below, the crew was often fagged out with heat. Early in May they were rounding Cape Musandam, which guards the entrance to the Gulf of Persia on the west.

This strait bears the name of Hormuz: but no man upon the *Seahorse* remarked it in the log. Ormuz, whose pearls are extolled by poets, whose opulence, pleasures and prosperity had become a fable, whose people wore silks and precious stones, and feasted sumptuously to the sound of sweet music, grown rich with 'plentie of pearls': Ormuz had blossomed for two hundred years, then fell into the hands of the Portuguese, whence the English East India Company and the Persians together wrested it. It was quickly ruined, even its stones carried off. The navigator of the *Seahorse* knew not even its name, given to the straits: passed the small barren island with the ruined castle upon it, but made no mention. Ormuz the diminished lay on beyond the large isle of Quishme, which also had known a greater day.

The Gulf of Persia, Horace was to remember, is full of islands and their shallows. Here lurked the pirates, here bred the pearls: small groups of trankeys were often in sight. Sounding between the isles, the *Seahorse* observed the Great Tomb and the Little, noting the reef running out to the west; and Quais, a pearl island lying under the highland of

Kharag, whose port had been great long before Ormuz, but lay now (the pearl pilot pointed) in ruins on its northern shore.

Twice, assaulted by gales and squalls from the north-west, they ran in for shelter. Fogs and hazes often enshrouded them, heavy dews surprised them; calms forced them to anchor; hot winds off the land parched the seamen filling water barrels at the shore. The *Betsy Gally's* slowness hindered them. One day, suspecting a shoal, the cutter went ahead to sound in discoloured water. Horace saw Tommy smiling as he returned.

'Thirty-six fathoms, sir, and no less!' shouted Troubridge. And he held up on an oar a long streak of yellow-coloured jelly: 'Fish spawn!'

Thus in the month of May they beat their way up the Gulf, until they sighted the highland of Halileh, and Bussorah Point.

They ran in for Bussorah Road and said farewell to the cheerful coasting pilot from Muscat, putting him down into a trankey with his friends. The *Seahorse* now made a signal and fired a gun for a pilot to carry her over the bar. Not until the fifth request was a boat seen to be coming out, and an excitable Persian pilot climbed aboard full of gesticulations and excuses.

'We have been waiting out here the past three hours,' protested the Captain holding up three fingers and shaking them at him. 'What goes on in Bussorah that you have no one to answer a ship's signal?'

'Sah!' exclaimed the pilot, waving his arms above his head. 'Bussorah, she at war! Men, army, soldiers! In Bussorah, Sah, tirty-tousand Persians!' and he held up both his hands and shook his fingers long and vigorously: the while his bare brown feet trampled the deck.

'Thirty-thousand Persians!' exclaimed the Captain. 'What for? Where is this war?'

'We invest Basra, we make siege, we wake the sleepy Turk—say our Khan…'

'What has happened to the English agent and factory?' said the Captain, speaking loud and slow.

The pilot threw up his hands again. 'Gone! I know not. Ah, quit, I hear rumour. All gone!'

The Captain considered him with some disbelief.

'We shall soon see about that. Let us get on. The water is falling. We are too late, with all this delay, we shall not get over the bar tonight.'

The pilot, who had been aware of this for some time, nevertheless urged a trial to save his face.

'We try, we sail.'

They bore away for the inner road and, as they drew nearer, Captain Farmer's feelings were somewhat comforted by the sound of guns: the Company's armed vessels seeing their approach, saluted with thirteen each. They sounded, two and three-quarter fathoms only.

'We not make harbour tonight,' said the pilot shrugging sadly. By now it was dark.

'So I told you,' retorted the Captain. 'We'll lie to on the stream anchor, Mr Surridge, and wait tide.'

That night, the mate wrote a most portentous NB in the log:

> Upon our arrival here found that the English Chief and Factory of Bussorah had been obliged to quit it, in consequence of the Turks and Persians being at War and Bussorah being at this time invested with 30,000 Persians.

They got over the bar with the high tide in the early morning. Riding in the harbour were the Company's armed vessels and five merchantmen, one of whom saluted them now. When they were finally moored the fort of Bussorah lay due south, and in the town beside it Horace picked out the English flagstaff. It being high tide, some quite large vessels had drawn right up to the houses of the town, where people hurried about on the quays and landing stages: though the *Seahorse* was moored far out. Streets of flat-roofed stone houses, mosques and distant forts rose behind. Three-quarters of the town was surrounded by the sea, and that towards the land had a wall with cannon upon it. The going and coming, the flocking of people, seemed no more than one might expect of a busy port at high tide: nothing indicated the presence of thirty thousand Persians. Towards eleven o'clock a boat was observed approaching containing several Englishmen and the gunner made ready to salute.

Mr Moore, the agent in Bussorah and the rest of the gentlemen of the English factory (as the East India Company's settlements were called) were soon cabined with Captain Farmer and his senior officers.

'We rely on you for news, sir,' began the Captain at once. 'The Company in Bombay has had some account of troubles between Turks and Persians: and the main reason of our cruise is to see how the English factories fare. Imagine my astonishment to be told by the pilot yesterday that Bussorah was invested with thirty thousand Persians and that you were obliged to quit the factory!'

'It is Basra he was speaking of. No doubt the name was misheard. Basra is besieged,' said Mr Moore smiling. 'There have, to be sure, been large numbers of Persians assembling in this town (though hardly that quantity) and there was an occasion when some were in our place overnight. As to our quitting the factory, we have come and we have returned so often over the last twelve years that I wonder not the fellow is confused. He may have heard our agent has left Basra, which is not yet so.'

'Why do the Persians besiege Basra?'

'Kerim Khan Zand who has ruled most of Persia for about twenty years, has picked a quarrel with the Pasha of Baghdad about the treatment of his merchants and pilgrims in Baghdad and Basra. He is said to have sent letters to Constantinople many times, and has grown angry. He often grows angry, we have had many occasions of his anger ourselves. He has sent a large force to Basra led by his brother Sadiq Khan and says he will open the eyes of the sleepy Turk!'

'So our pilot reported. What has happened to the factory there? You say the agent has not left?'

'The Company's agents have migrated between here and Basra for years. They will come here if they need to.'

'They may need to be conveyed here? How long has the siege held?'

'Four months or so. If I were to recount, Captain, the history of the settlements at Bandar Abbas and Basra and Bussorah, you would never believe the vicissitudes! The Gulf is a region of perpetual disturbance and war.'

'We should be very obliged to hear, Mr Moore. It might enlighten me upon how I may carry out my general orders. Bandar Abbas did you say? I never heard of a factory there.'

'No, it is before my time also. It was finished off by the French, in the war in 1759. We abandoned it in 1763 and took everything to Basra, where we established a residency and the Turks recognised us as a consulate. This made the Persians jealous (Bandar Abbas is Persian) and their sheikh quickly made an agreement with us for exclusive trade in the Gulf, unbounded, with total liberty, no customs, a monopoly in woollen goods; and no other Europeans to settle in Bussorah for trade while we were there. It was all confirmed by a grant from Kerim Khan himself. They even built our factory here you know, where the colours fly, there's a fine garden and a burial ground and twenty one guns! It all went on quite peacefully I believe, with our having a factory in both places for about five years until 1769—when we managed to fall out with Kerim Khan and it seemed prudent to withdraw to Basra.'

'What was the quarrel on that occasion?'

'There were various difficulties arose. We had joined with him in the attempt to dislodge a notorious pirate from Kharag island. Some of the differences may have grown out of that. At all events he was bitterly offended at our going from Bussorah and the loss of trade to Persia. Three years later there was a severe plague.'

'A plague! Where?'

'Basra, Baghdad, all those parts. We could only return here while it lasted. We left the houses and the factory in the care of the governor up there, and loaded the stock and the treasure in the *Tyger* and the *Drake* from Bombay. Kerim fell upon the *Tyger* and took her, and kept two of the Company's servants in prison for a spell!'

Captain Farmer was outraged at this.

'What were the Bombay Marine, what were *we* doing?' he demanded.

'No one was at hand to help. Moreover, Kerim was eventually susceptible to reason. When the plague was clear we went back to Basra and re-opened the factory. This was eighteen months ago. On the whole, it has seemed more politic for one of us to stay here as if at least in earnest of restoring the trade at this factory.'

Captain Farmer arose to pour the gentlemen another glass of wine.

'My orders are to assist the Company,' he said 'in any place where I happen to be where there is a settlement, should the Company's servants request it. Do you need help, Mr Moore? I am prepared to convoy any British vessels to Basra and protect them while there despite the siege.'

Mr Moore considered. 'We must wait and see, Captain,' he said at last, 'what falls out. You may be sure I will visit you again if we need your services.'

'Do, sir, pray do. We shall be here at least a month, with the work on the ship.'

And the Company's servants departed.

There was much to do on the ship. The discomfort of all was increased when the wind turned to gales, for then the weather would become thick, occasioned as the mate often wrote 'by the dust flying off the desarts.' A disaster was discovered in the afterhold: a puncheon of arrack had leaked out forty-seven gallons 'where the rats or other vermin had eat the cask'. On Saturday morning Mr Moore came out again suggesting he arrange a visit from the Sheikh to inspire respect and consolidate friendship on both sides. Captain Farmer was glad to agree and added that it would do no harm to exercise the great guns and small arms 'very regular'.

With trumpeting and some clamour the Sheikh of Bussorah came out to visit the ship. All were lined up to greet him, the guns fired, and Horatio watched a man of some agility come aboard. He wore billowing pantaloons beneath his cream robe, a golden girdle, a high, bright green turban and scarlet shoes. He and Captain Farmer expatiated upon the wisdom of friendliness and the advantages of trade: but since their deliberations were through an interpreter, and since a good deal seemed said on both sides more than was translated, neither was greatly enlightened in detail; though they parted, when the Sheikh had seen the better parts of the ship, in amity and in the general hope that the English factory in Bussorah might flourish once more.

The seamen fished in the harbour, adding fresh fish to their dinner. The pearl fishers came and went singing their pearling songs, swaying together as their little boats returned at evening to the beat of their drums, their purple or red robes tucked into their girdles, their white turbans catching the light till the last.

Parties of men were allowed ashore. Hoar and Troubridge took Horace, climbed the steep streets, peered into the courtyards of mosques, wandered round the market stalls of colourful merchandise, leather girdles and shoes, dates and fish, fruit and wine. It was evening, and the shimmering heat flaked away to dusk. Every man upon the quayside hearing the call to prayer, washed himself and went down upon his forehead in devotion. The three English boys were struck to silence with the rest.

By mid-July, no desperate news being received from Basra that might have persuaded Captain Farmer to stay, they were ready to sail. A pilot came on board to carry the ship to the outer Road where they anchored, firing a gun and making the signal for all masters of merchant ships wanting convoy. By three o'clock all were collected and they weighed and made sail with the *Eagle* snow (an armed cruiser belonging to the Company); their faithful friend the *Betsy Gally,* and her companion country ship the *Fatty Elsy:* a schooner also called the *Betsy;* and two ketches, the *Euphrates* and the *Tigris.*

Now Horace was to observe the difficulties and necessities of a numerous convoy over a long distance. Next morning they must shorten sail for the first of many times for the rest. When it was necessary to tack, they must all tack, attracting each other's attention with guns and signals. For the first three days, all the convoy were in company: but next day they tacked at a signal from the *Eagle,* and found they had parted company with the *Betsy Gally,* and must bear down to the *Fatty Elsy* far to leeward, and order the other ships under their stern. The *Betsy Gally* had caught up by noon.

'Well may that tub be the *Fatty Elsy!'* exclaimed Thomas Troubridge when the three chanced to meet at the side. 'Why cannot they all keep up?'

'Why do they not carry more canvas?' Tom Hoar suggested mildly.

Horace remembered the *Carcase.*

'Little do you know,' announced he, 'what it is like if a ship's a bad sailer! I have lumbered all the way up the east coast of England in the *Carcase,* that slow ship, being harried to put on more sail by Captain Phipps, your patron, Tom: till *our* commander tore his hair!'

With frequent gun signals, with shortening of sail, and the gathering of wayward members under her stern, the *Seahorse* rounded Cape Musandam and ushered her company into the Gulf of Oman. At noon on the twenty-seventh of July all were in company: but at half past three the *Seahorse* tacked and lost sight of them. At six the next morning only one was to be seen.

'Which is that ship, Mr Henery?' roared Captain Farmer from the poop, arisen early and enraged to find but one of his chickens in sight.

'Mr Troubridge?'

'*Euphrates* I think, sir.'

'The *Euphrates,* sir!'

'Then speak her and bid her keep close!'

Whether by command or no the ketch did so in solitary state as they approached Muscat and anchored in its pellucid water.

Now began a contest on the *Seahorse* to sight the missing ships.

'*Eagle* snow coming in now,' called Mr Abson at five.

'*Fatty Elsy* rounding the rock sir!' said Tom Hoar at six.

But it was six the next day before the *Betsy* schooner hove in sight: and not till the day after that they saw the *Tigris* outside the harbour, and fired a gun and called her in from the sea.

'Now where in the world is that *Betsy Gally?*' said Lieutenant Henery scanning the harbour later that afternoon.

It was John North who sighted her.

'*Betsy Gally* in sight, Mr Henery! In some trouble, near the Rock where the fishing boats are!'

'Ay. Driving on to it! The boats, Mr North,' said the officer.

Horace tumbled down into the cutter after Tommy and rowed for the Rock. The two boats secured cables to their friend the country ship and towed her away from danger and into harbour. The *Seahorse* greeted her arrival with a cheer.

The next afternoon the *Seahorse* stood out of the harbour and made the signal for all masters of merchantmen at the port, to acquaint them of her sailing. They sailed for Bombay on Sunday morning, the sixth of August, and with them this time came the *Indian Queen* a country ship, the *Eagle* snow, the *Betsy* schooner, the *Fatty Elsy,* and, to every man's satisfaction, the *Betsy Gally.* The *Euphrates* had bidden them farewell with thirteen guns the day before, being left in the harbour. Nobody noted what happened to the *Tigris.*

All went tolerably well with the small convoy for the first three days: though the *Betsy* schooner proved slow and the *Fatty Elsy* slower, they having to bear down and gather her in no less than four times.

'I wonder how long the old man will put up with this,' muttered Troubridge to Hoar. 'Not long, says I.'

Thomas was right.

On the ninth, a huge swell was apparent from the south, on the tenth the weather turned cloudy and threatening. Fire guns as they might, they could scarce keep all the ships under their stern for long together. At one o'clock Captain Farmer, an irascible man, lost patience. He summoned his officers, took their opinion, and decided to leave the convoy to their own devices. The mate protested breathlessly in the log:

> …at 1, upon finding the *Fatty Hoy* sailed so heavy and the wind hanging in the Southern Quarter, it was unanimously agreed by the officers that it was necessary for us to make the best of our way to Bombay and not wait for any Convoy otherwise it might endanger losing our passage to Bombay upon which we parted company with the Convoy.

At noon the next day the *Eagle* and the *Betsy Gally* were still in sight, and kept with them two days. Going on watch early on the thirteenth, Horace espied but one ship. 'The *Betsy Gally* still in company!' he cried with some glee.

She stayed with them, altering her course due east as they did when in the latitude for Bombay. The *Eagle* came in sight once more and the next day all three ships stood in for Bombay harbour and the cheerful salutes of the vessels riding there.

CHAPTER THIRTEEN

'...in time I was placed on the quarter-deck...'

Curtains of rain approached and fell hard upon Bombay, sizzling into the sea around the ships: the last of the monsoon. Within ten days the *Seahorse* was away again, standing down the harbour one morning to salutes from the Fort and the grab. Next day two deserters, found lurking below decks, must be put into a Company's cutter for Bombay. The following afternoon, they must lie to for a boat which came from Bombay with letters.

'What next, whatever next!' sighed Horatio, feeling his usual impatience to be off.

At last they were away for Madras, the journey enlivened by nothing more than the beating of poor Harrington yet again and the getting up of the old bread on deck, to put aside what was over-infested with fat white maggots, too much even for the iron will of Captain Farmer to impose upon his men: for after they reached Madras two thousand five hundred and sixty pounds of it was condemned. Horace and his fellows loaded the vile stuff into the boats and returned it into the store, along with quantities of sails and ordnance likewise condemned.

About a week after their arrival midshipman Thomas Troubridge, checking on board some rice and sugar which seaman Nelson and his crew had brought out in their boat, whispered in his friend's ear.

'Trouble in the wardroom again.'

'Oh? What?'

'I think the first lieutenant is under arrest!'

'Lieutenant Henery!'

'I was told his duties were suspended. Besides, an officer from the *Coventry* has arrived and is on the quarter-deck even now—' Thomas glanced upward. 'An acting-Lieutenant Gossart. I've not seen Mr Henery since this morning—'

'What's he done, what is it this time?'

'No idea. They say it's because the gunner's lodged a complaint against him.'

'You and Tom find Mr Henery agreeable, do you not? I liked him perfectly well.'

'Perfectly.'

'Perhaps he has offended the old man?' Horace mouthed silently, raising an eyebrow.

Thomas nodded. Try as they would, none of the three could warm to Captain Farmer and were often aware of the same sentiments in others. Horatio realised that he had always, albeit secretly, laboured under a slight sense of injury since he had lost his midshipman's rank to the Captain's son: the more particularly when he noticed its duties performed less well by that young man than by himself. The arrest of Mr Henery did nothing to ease his feelings towards the Captain.

❦

An unexpected command to sea came at noon one late September day and reached the men after their dinner.

'Huzzah, heaven be praised!' exclaimed Horace to his neighbour at the mess table, finishing his grog with a flourish and banging his tankard down.

'Oh you, you always must be doing! We're well here, up the junk renewing the rigging. Easy peaceful work, is knotting ropes.'

But Horace watched with eager interest the arrival aboard of some hundred East India Company troops and their baggage. A pilot came too, who took charge of the ship.

'All I know is we're going north,' Tom Hoar replied to his enquiry when they met. 'Not far, a few days, taking these men.'

At seven forty-five that evening they were sailing. At sunrise Horace recognised the two hills north of Madras they always used as landmarks; Pullicate hill, Armigan hill. That afternoon there was a summons to punishment: Harrington, it appeared, had possessed himself of two shirts belonging to the soldiers and had been simple enough to wear one. Clean and fresh, it drew the immediate attention of Mr Midshipman George Farmer.

They came to anchor that evening for the night: and in the early hours a seaman called John Giffy died. When the watch was changed at four they tried the current and found none. At six all were summoned, the funeral read, and John Giffy, disguised in cloths and flags, entrusted to the sea as the sun rose redly over the eastern horizon. The splash of the body clearly heard seemed to Horace an occasion of dire melancholy. To be thrown overboard! So far from home, one's family unknowing! Pray heaven he was never thrown overboard! He yawned nervously as they trooped off for breakfast and realised that it was his

152

birthday. He was seventeen, a man. He had entered into his eighteenth year, the age that he and Thomas Troubridge had pretended to at first. Had Captain Farmer suspected? Was this why George, two years his senior, had moved into his place? It was his miserable height, why could he not grow taller! Always, always it had provoked him to be so short.

That afternoon the cutter was hoist out, Lieutenant Abson took her, and Horace quickly made himself one of the crew. They were to go towards the shore looking out for a vessel with a message that was expected. The *Seahorse* shortened sail, hoist a Union Jack at the foretop-gallant flagstaff and fired signals for the shore boat while the officer and his crew approached a roadstead: two white pagodas made a splendid landmark and beyond them lay Pandarly village with hilly country behind it. But between the ships lying at anchor and the shore itself they saw a curling barrier of violent surf rolling landwards, beyond which they had been bidden not to go. As they rode here waiting it grew dark. The *Seahorse* herself anchored in Pandarly Road at about seven-thirty: they could see her lights and made towards her. Then they spied the bobbing light of a catamaran coming from the land: they hailed her, informing her they were from the ship, but her people pursued their way unheeding. So the two craft reached the ship together. The cutter was hoist in, the catamaran delivered her letter. Horace had enjoyed the trip and counted his birthday well spent.

The next morning in a pink and pearly dawn freshly cool, all boats were hoist out, the pinnace, the launch, the cutter. The troops stood in a line handing along their baggage and the boat crews stowed it. By six o'clock they were away with orders to wait 'to the back of the surf' where mascula boats would meet them to land the baggage.

Misty morning sunshine gilded the almost colourless water, the line of surf was a creaming, seething turmoil, the beating of the rollers upon the distant sand a continuous dull roar. As Horace sat watching the surf dazed into a kind of dream by the noise, a whole row of shallow pointed shore boats manned by shouting Indians shot over the boiling surf line and paddled vigorously towards the boats. The men's lithe brown bodies, like polished mahogany, were laced all over with foamy water. Horace was entranced at the sight.

'Mr Troubridge, sir!' he exclaimed to Thomas watching them come. 'What would I not give to be in one of those boats, through that foam, and rolling towards the palm trees! Would not you?'

'That I would too,' agreed Thomas heartily. 'But they say they need practised handling.'

'Ay. Glorious! Glorious it must be. Could not a man lie on a plank and be borne inward thus on the foam?'

The baggage was loaded, the Indians set forth towards the surf, waited for a rolling crest, then rising upon it with active paddles and loud cries were carried triumphantly shorewards. Horatio watched, longing to be one of them.

They were back at the ship by eight o'clock to carry the troops: and before noon the *Seahorse* weighed and sailed for Madras.

That afternoon Harrington sidled on deck clad in a pair of breeches of a certain colour and a conspicuous smartness: he half-smiled, poor fellow, when the accusation was made and the punishment ordered: the breeches were lost forever to the soldier.

They were five days in Madras. On the last morning when they were ready for sea Mr Surridge ordered Horace and Midshipman Farmer to carry him across to the *Nottingham* Indiaman, shortly bound for Europe.

'Ship's books, lad,' he said seeing Horace's eyes upon the large canvas bag he bore. He put it carefully under the bench and took the tiller. 'Going home to their Lordships at the Admiralty.'

'I see, sir. Is it the Muster Rolls, Mr Surridge, sir?'

'Ay and the Accounts; and some of the Logs. For the last year. Heat and damp don't do books much good.'

Watching the two young men pull, the master studied Horatio's pink eager face with pleasure. Interested in everything, he was. Every detail. Intent upon informing himself in every direction. Character was beginning to show in that face: the long nose, the complacent lips so determined when closed, the alert commanding eyes deeply set and wide apart. The cheeks were still rounded with puppy fat, when the boy laughed he was but a boy. And being short made him look the more boyish. But when he looked thoughtful you could see the man. George Farmer said nought, looking haughty and affronted as if he thought seaman Nelson had best keep quiet. He was less at home in the boat. Young Nelson was due for the quarter-deck, he was ripe for a little command again, his seaman's duties had strengthened and matured him, given him confidence. Overdue, Mr Surridge thought. He must wait his chance and draw the Captain's attention.

'How would you like to see Trincomalee, lads?' Both young men looked up, pleased.

'I have seen the flagstaff, sir, several times!' Horace said. 'Are we to see the harbour?'

'Finest harbour in the world,' was all that the master would now say, smiling.

Tom Hoar meanwhile had taken the cutter, carrying the sick surgeon to the hospital on shore. He was the second surgeon they had had: the first, a Mr John Bullen, had been discharged a year ago with ill-health. For the moment the *Seahorse* had no one.

On October the twenty-first they saw from the *Seahorse* the high land near Trincomalee in the island of Ceylon, and by that evening had anchored within sight of Flagstaff Point. Horatio, noting it in his journal, reflected that it was their family day, the day of Uncle Suckling's triumph. He wondered if Papa still kept it, he wondered how they all were at Burnham? He longed that he should have some triumph to report, to make his father proud. Here was he but still a seaman, though he flattered himself an increasingly able one. Surely soon, now he was seventeen, he must make the quarter-deck again, he must be noticed? He was well, strong, in high spirits, happy: he must do all in his power to further himself. He knew what he wanted and should gain it. He had entirely outlived his feelings against the navy of two years since.

They were working in for Trincomalee at eight o'clock next morning when the land wind died and the boats were all hoist out to tow. From aloft where the foretop men worked the prospect ahead was enticing. Flagstaff Point rose steeply out of the sea, its bare cliffs bright with sun. To the north of it glistened the inlet known as Back Bay where a number of large vessels lay at anchor: to the south, the smaller inlet called Dutch Bay. The town of Trincomalee, white roofs dotted amongst heavy foliage, lay behind the headland: and beyond it westwards Horatio caught the misty gleam of distant water, a vast expanse, the great harbour itself. All around rose hills clad in bosomy green foliage: which was to separate into the dark velvet of polished trees, the glossy satin of bushes, the lace and feathers of many palms. Far inland, he could just descry the high blue mountains of the southern interior. A brisk sea breeze at last got up and by noon they were running under sail southerly for the Round Island, the point of entry to the harbour. It stretched before them, a calm lake, heavenly beautiful, with hilly headlands rising steeply, softened with thick foliage where now and then cascades of blossom fell. Secret inlets lurked between the headlands, a man longed for a boat, a day of freedom to attain those sandy shores. Another fort, another flagstaff, on the western point of the isthmus guarded the entrance to the harbour: Ostenburg Point. To larboard, a little island nestled in the arms of a great neighbour. Here they anchored and moored in twenty-three fathoms of crystal clear water upon a sandy bottom, off the north-east tip of Great Sober Island. The *Coventry* was riding near at hand and hailed them as they swung the ship around. As dusk fell, sweet and spicy unknown scents were borne on the land breeze to the ship.

Next morning a wooding party was called. (Trincomalee, it was said, provided the best wood and water in the Indies.) It was a pleasant day, not too hot, for it had rained in the night. The boat dropped them down to a sandy beach on the bay opposite the little island, with their hatchets and their hammocks, their tent stuff and their food. As he leapt into the warm water to help pull the boat up Horatio felt himself abounding with energy, almost dazed with joy.

'This is the life!' he exclaimed with glee as they beached the boat.

'Ay so it is!' agreed Lieutenant Abson leaping into the deep white sand, followed by solemn George Hicks and cheerful Thomas Troubridge, exulting with his friend.

'Dry land,' said he, plodding after the others to choose the tent site. 'How I love dry land, Horace!'

'I love it all, the sand, the sea, the sky! All these trees!'

'Begin unloading!' Thomas called.

Above the tide-line (the tides it appeared were small) they pitched their tents in a cosy place backed by bushes. The ship was now out of sight, for a high wooded ridge ran from east to west across the north of the island. Just below it rushed a good clear stream, they had landed not far from it. Behind their camp the land rose to tree-covered hills in the middle of the island. Across a quarter mile channel sat the Little Island, a neat bush-clad rock.

The tents up, the baggage stowed, and the cook and his mate already collecting their firewood, Horatio led his band to the furthest point of the bay. The glossy-leaved shrubs and bushes that covered the slopes and overhung the beach provided a tempting abundance of dead dry undergrowth. The men worked with a will, the staves and branches cracking and clattering under their hatchets, the piles of wood along the foreshore growing, the wind from the sea cooling their bodies, their only threat the flies and mosquitoes arising from the scrub as they worked.

The shells, the shells in the sand! Horatio marvelled, walking back from the wood pile and stopping to pick up a few. How his father would love these shells, green and pearly snails, pointed conical shells like winkles, bright brown, spotted, green, or red like a strawberry! There was one with pointed ends; one like a corkscrew, another with pale ridged flounces like a little pagoda, many with points at one end and frills at t'other! He tipped a few quickly into his pocket. Ah! One with spines all round, like a starfish. He must needs tear himself away to hack wood.

The next day a smaller shore party with another tent was disgorged near the stream, Mr Midshipman Farmer in charge, followed by all the empty water-casks and a number of ironbound buckets. The launch with Tom Hoar in command came and went, collecting their wood and the others' water. The smell of the midday meals drifted along the shore. At nights, Horace and Thomas wandered along the water line, picking up shells in the warm moonlight. At dusk and dawn strange birds whistled and shrieked from the undergrowth, small animals chattered, fish plopped in the clear water.

There was one day they had occasion to remember. Sitting over their meat, a marine of Thomas's party suddenly cried out, 'Where's Ward? Where's my mate, Ward? Not like him to miss his dinner—'

'When did you last see him?' Mr Troubridge asked.

'When he knocked off, sir. Said he was going for a wash to cool himself down—'

'Where?' Thomas said, rising to his feet. The water was quickly deep in parts. They had been warned of it.

'Opposite Little island. Said he knew a place—'

'Come on, three men,' said Mr Troubridge and stumped off along the shore. Horatio quickly followed with the man's friends.

They found him out of sight of the camp, floating face down, the sea gently nudging his body on to the strand which he could so easily have gained had he been alive. They turned him over. The man's trunk was bare. Thomas felt his heart.

'He's as dead as yesterday,' he said, his face pale. 'Couldn't he swim?'

'I never knew,' said his friend kneeling down. 'God help us! Poor old John.' He swayed back and forth, his face screwed up. Horace looked about, appalled, trying to counter their shock with explanation.

'Perhaps he fell off that rock near the pool.'

'No knowing. You'll wash in parties in future, and people who cannot *swim*...' Thomas's voice failed. Many seamen could not swim. 'Bring him,' he said.

John Ward was carried between the three of them. They laid him in a tent till Tom came with the launch and sent him back to the ship with the wood and the water barrels. Tom Hoar's fine drawn face looked bleached as they told him what had happened.

They were on shore a week. Horatio's wood pile was always the largest (he had told his men that it was to be so and his enthusiasm had kept them at it). Apart from the melancholy of Ward's sudden drowning they were happy and contented all day, none against his neighbour. Things were otherwise it seemed at the watering place, where yells and roars one day sent Mr Abson along to inspect: he found Mr Midshipman Farmer in furious altercation with a marine called John Mears, who disagreed with his superior officer about the steadiness of the latter's labours in comparison with his own, his own being deemed insufficient.

'I'll have that man thrashed,' young Farmer muttered to the lieutenant, 'for insolence and quarrelling!'

'Are you having trouble with your men?'

'I find Mowll asleep, and this fellow idling, in the middle of the morning!'

'Where were you?'

'With the rest, at the water side!' Farmer raised his voice. 'Sir,' he added as an afterthought. Abson walked back wondering.

When they went aboard again Horace looked back with some nostalgia to their Crusoe camp – the shore, the trees, the rocks which had been their landmarks, the clear stream where they had drunk – suffering a pang to leave it: like all camps, it had become 'home'. That evening the Captain sent for him.

'I hear good accounts of you on all sides, Seaman Nelson,' said Captain Farmer without more ado. 'Tomorrow when the muster is called you will notice yourself named as Midshipman again and will henceforth take your place on the quarter-deck.'

Although it was what he had hoped for so long, Horace was stunned, his ready tongue searching for words.

'Thank you, sir, thank you indeed, I am…much gratified, sir,' he managed to say.

'Very good. I have no doubt of your capabilities, Mr Nelson, and wish you well.'

'Thank you, sir,' the young man repeated as he saluted and withdrew.

Mr Troubridge and Mr Hoar, lurking without the cabin, knew from their friend's face what had occurred and haled him off at once to the cockpit to celebrate noisily and joyfully what both averred should have happened long since.

The muster next morning which confirmed Horatio's promotion revealed also that four seamen had deserted from the wooding party taking their hammocks with them, and nobody had noticed. The purser detained Mr Troubridge, Mr Hicks and Mr Nelson.

'When do you last remember seeing them?' Mr Ligerwood asked: 'William Pigot, Absolom Bodley, Charles Sidney, John Clark?'

'Bodley was with me, he came back to dinner,' Horace remembered. Each man it appeared was remembered by someone at the meal.

'And you struck the tents in the afternoon? They wouldn't leave it till then to take their hammocks: they must have made off after dinner?'

'Ay, while we rested round the fire. That'll be it,' said Hicks. 'They'll be hiding up till we sail.'

Horatio thought of them for weeks, wondering how they made out. He could understand their longing to stay there upon the island. Water they would have. But food? (The fresh beef of Trincomalee had been a pleasure to them all: the ship was even now invaded with the sad bellowing of two live bullocks.) If they fell in with native seamen, they might be carried across to Trincomalee where a living could be made. But how would they make themselves understood? And if they fell in with British seamen, would it not quickly be supposed they were deserters? He imagined them peering out from the wooded hill ridge watching the *Seahorse* preparing to depart, as she bent the main and studding sails that afternoon and unmoored, hoisting in the boats at dusk.

The *Coventry* signalled at five in the morning and the two ships sailed at six, the boats towing, the airs so light they could sail but little. In the Great Bay south of Trincomalee Harbour they fell in with the *Terrible*, a Company's ketch, who said she had dispatches for the commodore and the Squadron, so they agreed to keep company with her. On an afternoon in November they were running in for the familiar palm-crowded shore of Anjengo and her bright red cliffs. The *Terrible* was already there.

Two days later the *Coventry* made the signal and sailed onwards for Bombay: but upon the *Seahorse* the tar pot was smelt from near the galley for'ard: the people were set to picking oakum, great piles of worn ropes beside them. They patiently teased the strands of hemp into a mass of loose fibres with their sharp hard nails or some small favoured spike of a weapon. The carpenter and his mates collected the stuff, wedged and forced it between planks and in holes and covered all with tar, caulking the pinnace and the main deck. The topmen were often up aloft loosing the sails to dry after frequent storms of rain. The midshipmen were busy about water casks, pounds of fresh beef and bags of peas, for re-stowing.

One evening the *Salisbury* arrived, anchored far out, and was saluted at sunrise by the Fort guns. Lieutenant Gossart saw her cutter coming across.

'Go and speak the *Salisbury*'s cutter, Mr Nelson,' said he, 'and see what she wants.'

'Ay, ay, sir' Horace replied, eager for news of any kind.

A stalwart midshipman, tall and fair, was sailing the cutter. He looked up at Horatio when he had drawn alongside, gazed and then smiled. He seemed familiar in face. An older man sat in the bows. The boat appeared to be full of old rope.

'Mr Horace Nelson!' the mid called.

'Ay...? Mr Charles Pole!'

'Not set eyes upon you for months!'

'No indeed, years. How are you?'

'Well. We have brought you five hundred weight of junk—'

'The people *will* be pleased!' Horace said tartly.

'And our carpenter wishes to borrow a topsail yard!'

'An unequal exchange! Good morning, Mr Carpenter, sir,' Horace greeted him as he came aboard. 'You'll find our carpenters painting the pinnace over there, to starboard.'

Horatio summoned some seamen to haul up the rope.

'The *Salisbury* has sent you a present, my men, for which I trust you are grateful!'

'What, more junk!' The seamen groaned, laughing.

'How do you get on, Mr Nelson?' Charles Pole asked.

'I have just made the quarter-deck again after a year and a half as AB!' called Horace cheerfully.

'And you are glad of the change?'

'Upon the whole. Though I love the work up aloft!'

'Ay. I hardly knew you, you are grown. How is Tom Hoar?'

'Very well, always thinking, in his clever way. He would like to see you!'

'Do you come to Bombay?'

'We rather suppose so.'

'Then let us meet! Let us meet at Bombay!'

'So we will! If we appear! Goodbye!'

The two carpenters had arrived with the top'sl-yard, the cutter pushed off.

'I have encountered a friend of ours,' Horace said to Tom as they sat over their good beef at dinner time in the cockpit. 'Guess who. From the *Salisbury*.'

'Not Charles Pole?'

'The same. Came across with the cutter. While you were in the holds this morning. We have an assignation to meet him in Bombay.'

'Excellent,' Tom said. 'Is Thomas to be of the party?'

'Certainly, if I know anything,' Horace replied, elbowing Troubridge.

The older of the master's mates looked up from his plate and pronounced:

'I would expect any assignation in Bombay for lads of your metal to be with some party of the fairer sex. That's what I would expect,' he said solemnly, nudging the other mate beside him who responded with a belch. Mr Hicks winked at the three boys, hoping they would take the bait: Mr Farmer wiped his mouth and favoured them with a faint and supercilious smile, watching Mr Troubridge's colour rise.

'O there's time for that,' Tom Hoar said casually.

160

'God bless you, Mr Pole has that all arranged,' said Mr Nelson as cool as you please. 'Mr Pole promises to have the cream of Bombay society, the fairest of their sex, at our disposal.'

Thomas looked at him in surprise: but Horatio enjoying the effect he made, wriggled his long nose, picked delicately at his meat, and with great gravity added: 'I was not able to ascertain, while we hauled up their load of old junk, whether these were to be the dusky beauties with the dark eyes we see ever about us: or the daughters of the Company. Either, for my part would be agreeable,' he finished airily.

'Some of each,' supplied Tom, assuming Horace's tone.

'Ay, take your pick,' said the confounded mate much amused. 'Who is this Mr Pole? I should be happy to make his acquaintance.'

'A dog, a great dog,' Horatio confided. 'We knew him in Portsmouth.'

This casting of honest, stalwart Charles Pole in the character of a dog led Tom Hoar to explode into a loud guffaw, whereat the company joined him, causing Mr Nelson to choke upon his wine.

The next morning they heard that the *Salisbury* had departed for Bombay in the night. Horace smiled to himself, remembering his nonsensical talk of Charles. How all men joked about such things; he had lived with the seamen many months, smirking dutifully over lewd jests, an outsider, waiting for this urgent absorbing force which exercised them all so much to exert its power over him. Even as he joked yesterday, he yearned: the fairest of their sex, the soft, the sweet. What were they like, what was it like to kiss them, should he not be terrified, how was he ever to discover, stuck upon a ship with all these men? How he wished his foolish words true, about Charles! The men were coming down from aloft, he shook himself out of his melancholy, and smiled as each came.

'Smartly done, men, you are first down. I can but commend you to more clawing of rotten rope.'

The mizzen men laughed, trooping back to their oakum.

Further for'ard, Mr Midshipman Farmer was having words again with Nicholas Mowll, coming off the mainmast last and stumbling drunkenly as he came. Mowll was answering back, raising his voice, a thing a man was rash to do.

Horace worried much, upon re-attaining the quarter-deck, about the seamen whom it would now fall to him sometimes to command. At first he had watched men with whom he had worked and joked, running past him with their faces solemn and their eyes avoiding his. This would not do, these were his friends, his workmates, the same as ever they were! He himself had felt constrained, to be thus set over them. Soon he was greeting them cheerfully as they passed naming those he knew well and making them take notice. They responded at once, all smiles and winks.

He supposed that he might some day have to roar at a man in anger, turn him over to the sergeant of the marines, recommend him for a beating, as Farmer appeared now to be doing. He dreaded this event.

'When I came back from the West Indies you know,' he said to Tom that evening 'I never wished to be an officer at all.'

'You told me. You longed to stay in the merchantman, and your papa would not let you. You were crazed with the Captain.'

'Ay, I loved Captain Rathbone and all the men too,' Horace said simply. 'I hated the navy, I can tell you.'

'Then you've changed your tune, lad. How do you think to being an officer now?' asked the master's mate.

'All very well, save for getting men beaten,' Horace confessed. They had all that afternoon witnessed Mowll beaten. 'And getting men pressed,' he added.

'You'll not make no kind of an officer if you don't make your men obey you,' growled George Farmer, flushing.

'I daresay thrashing's a harsh necessity,' said the mate, admiring his tarred cane basket with a lid, bought from Anjengo. 'For some men. What about Thomas Harrington, eh?'

'Captain Rathbone thought it brutal and useless,' Horace remembered. 'It's strange that when all I wanted was to stay with the seamen I was not allowed to. And when I had got perfectly used to the notion of being a mid and proceeding to an officer, I was sent for'ard again.'

'That's just the contrariness of life,' said the mate, 'which the longer you live the more you'll notice.'

Tom Hoar dealt the cards with an expert hand. 'It's all a matter of chance and luck,' said he sententiously.

'The seamen on the *Mary Ann* used to say aft the most honour, for'ard the better man,' Horace reflected.

'*That's* often true enough,' said Thomas Troubridge bluntly.

One breezy morning on his way back from taking a message to the gunner, Horatio chanced to encounter Lieutenant Henery, a great deal of whose time was necessarily spent in a gloomy pacing of the decks. Horace smiled and saluted his superior with unaffected pleasure.

'Good morning, sir!'

Mr Henery peered at him from a closed and clouded countenance. Who was this, who addressed him from the world he was banished from as if all were well? Most other officers, particularly junior ones, averted their eyes and mumbled their greetings when they met him. Against Horatio's smile, his face eased into something like his former pleasantness.

'Why, good morning, young Mr—Nelson, is it not?'

'The same, sir. I hope you are well, sir?'

'Never mind about me. You seem in high spirits enough?'

'Yes, sir. I have just been upon a message to the gunner to fire a rebuke at a grab ketch wearing king's colours,' the young man began for something to say—and then gasped, remembering that Thomas had reported somewhat between the gunner and Lieutenant Henery.

'The gunner can go to hell for aught I care,' Henery rejoined, amused at Horatio's blunder. 'I understand you are raised again to midshipman?'

'Yes, sir, from the end of last month.'

'Not before time, and sorry I am not to be up there commanding you.'

'I am sincerely sorry myself, sir, and may that matter be quickly remedied,' said Horace, whose wits always responded to his spirits. Lieutenant Henery smiled and nodded his thanks, diverted from his own concerns for a little. There was an extraordinary directness and warmth about that youth, his greeting had been as spontaneous as a child's might be, so that at first he had supposed him ignorant of his own miseries. But this was proved not so.

The evening they left Anjengo they had unmoored at five and were ready to depart with the wind, when someone spotted a ship in the offing: Thomas Troubridge was immediately despatched with the cutter for intelligence. When he had not returned by eight they burnt false fires and fired a gun to tell him to come. They were, however, still waiting on the wind. The cutter returned at nine, the midshipman ran up, rosy in the face and somewhat abashed, and reported her to be the *Alexander* from Bengal to the Red Sea.

'Oh, ay. Any intelligence?'

'Only that Sir John Clarke is going to have the *Dolphin* surveyed, sir.'

'And a merry time you've had, sir, to bring me some useless information. Still, I'm glad you enjoyed it,' Mr Surridge added kindly, as Thomas darted below to hide his laughter.

All up the Malabar coast they sounded, sometimes every hour. So emphatic was the master about this that his mate echoed his words in the log and wrote:

'Keep that lead constantly going'

more than once. Mr Surridge had shown great satisfaction at Horatio's promotion (rightly assuming that his own recommendations had been largely responsible for it). Now he did everything in his power to put him in the way of experience.

'We must get you able to tack the ship, sir,' he told him. 'Mr Troubridge and Mr Hoar have taken her about, and it must be near second nature to you after all these years. Watch carefully each time, practise the commands with the lieutenant, and when you feel ready he'll let you take her.'

Full of spirits and confidence, Horace saw his chance one afternoon when the ship was tacking occasionally and informed the master and Mr Gossart that he would like to take her around. When the men tumbled up next at the sound of John North's pipe, he was ready. The Captain had come up, the master was below near the helm, the men were running to their stations, loosening the braces off the pins and coiling them on the deck. Mr Gossart handed him the speaking trumpet and said quietly:

'Carry on from here.'

'Silence fore and aft, every man to his station!' said the midshipman, surprised at the sudden volume of his own voice. When every man was ready and still and waiting:

'All ready!' he cried, more loudly. He paused as he had always seen the officers do, gave a quick look all round again, then ordered the helm down. As soon as the master reported it down, Horatio repeated:

'Helm's alee!'

Now the fore and head sheets were let go and overhauled, while Horace kept his eye upon the mainsail, waiting for the flutter, the flattening that showed the wind was out of it.

'Raise tacks and sheets!' he cried. His voice was light, but determinedly clear, he wished he could roar. All but the foretack were let go. The men were gathering-in the lee maintack. Now was the moment. Better too soon than too late or her head would pass too far round.

'Mainsail haul!' The men hauled.

There was a pause, the yards dawdled a little swinging round, his heart beat uncomfortably. He judged he had been a little early. But she went around. John North let go the foretack, the men yelled as they hauled upon their braces. When all the braces were belayed, the yards trimmed, the tacks boarded, the bowlines hauled out, Horatio, looking serious, turned to the lieutenant.

'Order the watch below,' said he with a smile. Horace had forgotten this.

'Go below, the watch!'

While the watch still on deck were coiling down and clearing up, Mr Surridge joined them.

'I was a bit too soon, sir,' the boy said, looking from one to the other.

'Perhaps a trice,' said Lieutenant Gossart.

'It didn't matter. It's a nice point, to judge the moment. It was fair enough for the first time,' the master said. 'We must see he does it often, Mr Gossart.'

Horace practised whenever opportunity arose. Once he had taken her about at night, he felt he was really learning the feel of her.

They had passed by Cochin and Calicut, but ran into Tellicherry for a night and a day. And this time they went right into the great bay of Goa, slowly passing the low white buildings of the monastery on the southern point of the harbour mouth, as the boats towed them. They anchored south-east of the Al Guarda fortress at dusk. Horace was roused by the salute of the fortress at sunrise and ran up to see the prospect. It was a clear, calm morning. The huge bay rippled smoothly in the early sunlight. Land-ward to the east, it was bounded by a chain of little hills fringed with palm and mango. Below these opened the river entrance that led up to the city. A huge Portuguese man-of-war rode regally at anchor.

Thomas and Horatio took the launch across the bay with a party of men for water. Coming back, they stood into the river mouth, the morning breeze off the sea taking them easily amongst all the craft. A bend in the river disclosed the city high above on several hills, full of noble buildings, palaces, mansions, churches and convents surmounted with crosses: yet strangely quiet, strangely empty. Parts of the holy Christian city of Goa were deserted and weed-grown, the houses and grand buildings ruinous. The Portuguese trade was in decline: the Jesuit mission two hundred years and more in the past.

They left Goa after four days with three English merchant ships and two snows in convoy.

Six o'clock of a squally grey morning found them working into Bombay harbour, Old Woman's Island behind them, the *Salisbury* and the *Coventry* riding at anchor ahead.

'I see no bevies of fair ladies lining the quayside,' whispered Tom Hoar to his friend when Horace came up.

'Oh they are still abed,' said that young man jauntily, ' having their beauty sleep.'

Chapter Fourteen

'Ill health induced Sir Edward Hughes…
to send me to England…'

The sun between the eastern mountains pierced the haze and lit upon the glittering white buildings of Bombay: the bold Admiralty, the balustraded top of Government House, the church tower with its pretty neat cupola, the great Bunder House whose stone pier ran out into the water, the flag upon the Castle at the north-western extreme. Horace, running his glass along the whole water front, felt a great longing to explore the town. Blown by the offshore breeze, the palms above the buildings tossed. The town was walled, and below the wall there was a sea-water ditch. Though they had lain in this harbour twice before, his duties had never taken him further than the pier or the shore of Old Woman's Island which ran out to the south. Charles Pole had suggested a meeting. He was now a petty officer, could accompany his two friends and meet Charles's as an equal. His health and strength were never better, his spirits bursting.

'Let's get ashore Thomas, let's get ashore!' he said to Troubridge, lowering the spyglass.

'Ay, there'll be plenty of boat duty, unloading. We seem to have become a regular tramp, a baggage ship.'

Horace's chance came that afternoon when he and Tom Hoar took the cutter to unload the bales of sepoys' clothing taken on board at Anjengo.

'You report to the barracks, Horace. You will like to see the Green,' Tom said quietly.

Horatio thanked him, thinking what a gentleman he ever was, leapt ashore, saw the boat fastened and walked up the burning hot slope of the pier, past the bales and casks, towards the Bunder House. He soon found himself for the first time upon Bombay Green, the wide expanse of grass lying behind the quayside buildings. The church had a rounded apse with large coloured windows, a neat wall and railing round it, a large mango tree outside it. He thought suddenly of the church at Burnham with its yew trees whence he had stolen a twig on a winter night. The trim and regular fronts of new red brick houses with pillared colonnades reminded Horace in a certain way of Uncle William Suckling's house in Kentish Town. Polished trees and shrubs sheltered the smaller houses round the green, which was now a scene of such bustle and variety that the boy stood still awhile to take it in. A line of the Company's soldiers in dark coats and white breeches marched and drilled in the distance; silk-coated Indians met and greeted one another, English ladies strolled arm-in-arm beneath pale parasols, a white man was carried in a litter with a canopy by four loin-clothed bearers, another sat in a kind of sedan chair, but upon wheels and drawn by oxen. Thinking of red kine in his father's glebe, Horatio picked his way past some lean elderly cream-coloured oxen grazing mildly upon the Green and made for the barracks. How like to England it all was: yet how strangely unlike! For the first time he was old enough to be sensible of the meeting of such different ways of life, the romance of the Indies was ballasted by the familiar and comforting appeal of what the British had built and established here. He was a boy of his time, he never doubted but that the British imperial ways were superior: he nonetheless relished his opportunities to see other ways. As a child he had drunk in the West Indies at a gulp, without thought. Now he found himself remarking and considering the differences.

An English servant came to the quayside with him to count in the thirty-six bales, turbaned sepoys in curious short, white pants (such as Horace had never noted before) loaded them upon pale oxen.

Two days before Christmas the gunner and his mates got out the guns (for re-painting) and all his stores, into the pinnace and the cutter. Mr Hoar took the pinnace, Mr Nelson the cutter, and when the stuff was unloaded saw to the hauling up of the two craft, which were to be repaired on shore. The work was finished an hour before Mr Troubridge was expected to pick them up. The two mids found their way to the main street of shops known as the bazaar: here were counters and stalls loaded with goods from all over the world, kept by the people called Parsees. At tables beneath awnings worked jewellers; in dark shops silver-smiths beneath lamps fashioned the soft metal into flowers and leaves. Pearls and jade, bangles and necklaces made Horace long for money to spend upon his sisters. The patterned shawls, the sandals, the flowing dresses! Scents overcame them, attar of roses and jasmine. Arrack, the wine of the Indies, in tall flagons and vessels of stone.

'Horace, come quickly, we are late!' Tom said at last.

'Thomas will wait!' Horatio scuttled after his longer-legged friend.

Now they must use lighters, the boats being up for repair. Upon Christmas Eve the mids unloaded condemned bo'sun's stores on the shore: and the cook killed two bullocks, the last of seven taken on board at Fort Victory down the coast.

Christmas Day promised at first to be as colourless as it always was. The people cleaned the ship fore and aft and then were idle. The cook made a brave attempt to roast the beef to be festive.

'You would think we might get leave to go ashore,' said young Nelson, finishing his grog. 'Shall we essay it?'

'No cutter. No pinnace. How are we to *get* ashore?'

Thomas rubbed his shock head, frowning.

'The Captain and the officers will no doubt use the launch,' added Tom Hoar.

'There are the shore boats if we can command one,' Horatio continued, his determination increasing.

In the end, cries up above produced the information that some boats from the *Salisbury* were on their way. It seemed a ships' visiting was afoot: all who would like a trip to the *Salisbury* should come. A party of the *Salisbury's* people came aboard grinning shyly, soon to be borne off to the lower deck amidst cheers and back-slapping.

'Come on, come on, now or never,' shouted Horace returning to the berth, reporting all this and seizing his belt and hat.

'Who do we know on the *Salisbury*?' demanded Troubridge.

'Tom and I know Pole and you soon will. Come on, look alive.'

He rounded up his friends, waved cheerily at the two Georges left upon duty, slapped the surgeon's assistant on the back, shook hands with the master's mate wishing him yet again a merry Christmas, and left the steerage in laughter behind him.

'You haven't got leave,' Troubridge protested at the side.

'We have. General leave was given, I heard it, for visiting the commodore's ship. First come, first served. Leave to go, sir?' he said hastily to Lieutenant Abson who seemed to be counting them down.

'Mr Nelson, Mr Hoar, Mr Troubridge. Carry your drink with care, I warn you. Let me not have you rolling aboard tonight, you midshipmen,' he added in an undertone to Hoar who wore his dress jacket and was much too hot. 'It's a pity your friends don't dress up to you,' said the officer.

'This Pole,' Thomas announced in the boat, 'will have gone ashore I'll wager.'

But Charles Pole was waiting for them upon the *Salisbury's* deck, some of his friends with him.

'I swore you'd come, I knew you would if you could!' he said, greeting Hoar and Nelson with glee.

'Here's Thomas the second, Thomas Troubridge, the third of our trio,' Horace said. 'I assure you he ain't so shy as he affects.'

169

The troop of mids disappeared down below to enjoy the grog, the games and the songs of the *Salisbury's* cockpit. Near two hours later, with a sense of enormous effervescent elation, with a notion he might float over to the *Seahorse* did he so wish, Mr Nelson grasped the hand of Mr Pole from the top of the *Salisbury's* ladder.

'We meet again sometime near the New Year at the barracks, you to send a message of the day and hour and supposing we can all get leave,' he said very carefully, repeating Pole's invitation: and saw the fiery face of Charles nodding as if from a great way above him. Sea water dashed into their red faces brought them all to before the boat touched.

After Christmas the clearing of the ship for dock went on apace. The carpenter's stores and the powder barrels went ashore in lighters. They cleared the forehold, got the water and the ballast out, the foretopmast and foreyard overboard. Poor Thomas Harrington tried to desert from one of the shore parties and was duly beaten. Mr Midshipman Farmer took all the empty water casks to Old Woman's Island to be repaired; and came back with the cheerful message from a mid on the *Salisbury's* boat met upon the shore that the party at the barracks was to be on New Year's Eve: all midshipmen who could get leave were heartily invited. Horatio went to his chest in some excitement, but struggled into his dress clothes with dismay.

'Look at this, look at me!' he announced, strutting into the berth and raising his arms from his sides. The frilled cuff of his shirt scarce showed below the jacket sleeve, the sleeve itself exposed inches of bare forearm, the front edges of the coat could not, it seemed, ever meet.

'Hold on. Brace up!' Troubridge stooped before him, tugging at the garment each side.

'Drop your yards, man!' commanded Hoar, holding Horatio's arms to his sides as Thomas buttoned the young man in, helpless with laughter.

'Loose a reef, be quick, or I shall burst, I shall stifle!' yelled Horatio.

'Wear it open then, you lubber. Cannot you do better than that for a shirt?'

'None others left, decent.'

Hoar (who had plenty of money and clothes) lent him a shirt when the day came, too large but better than his own. Mr Surridge, watching the jovial party of mids going down to the launch, caught his pupil's eye and smiled.

'Grown out of my coat, Mr Surridge, sir!'

'So I observe, Mr Nelson. It would not be right at your age *not* to grow, however,' he said comfortingly.

The small parties of midshipmen from the *Salisbury*, the *Coventry* and the *Seahorse* met on the pier, and converged upon the barracks, where Mr Pole's acquaintances amongst the junior officers of the Company's troops ushered them into their mess and plied them with arrack, sweetmeats and tobacco. The sailors talked of their travels, of Calcutta and Kedgeree, Madras and Trinco, Muscat and Bussorah in the Gulf: the soldiers talked of marches into the hills, bargains in the bazaar and soft-eyed damsels: the Scots talked of home and snow and first-footing over the threshold on New Year's Day. Somebody suggested cards, the table was cleared of glasses, the baize cloth laid. They embarked upon the simplest of games, a mere matter of wagers upon the order in which the cards would turn up. Horatio had but four crowns in his pocket and caution at first held him back. But as the game proceeded, as he watched his friends enter at the behest of the persuasive officer holding the pool, and saw the glee of those who swept in their lucky share, and the intense, silent absorption round the table he found himself caught up into it. He should lose his crowns, but what did it matter? He was not a great money-spender upon his own behalf but had always dreamed of making money for his family. At the next wager he backed the card he fancied, laid his coin down and within five minutes to his amused surprise was possessed of two. When after six or seven games he had still not lost but always added modestly to his pile he began to feel a certain confidence in his luck. Soon Pole and Hoar, sitting each side of him, observed his unfailing fortune.

'Horace!' muttered Tom. 'Look at you! Beware, it will turn, it must turn!'

'Must it indeed?' Horatio thought, and grinned with satisfaction when it repeatedly failed to do so. Other players further off now noticed his luck, men began to wait upon the card he named. As the excitement grew and the games went faster, so the lucky few (who had steadily amassed what small wealth was to be found in the pockets of poor mids) began to risk higher stakes. The young subalterns it appeared had more to gamble with. Horace, furtively counting his gains after an hour's play, found he had fifty pounds! With an air of dashing assurance he waved his frilled wrist in the air, said that the six of clubs would appear before the knave of hearts and wagered his fifty upon it. Hoar tugged at his sleeve and told him he was a fool, Pole laughed at his assurance, Troubridge looked glum having lost the little he had. A red-faced subaltern took him up, silence fell, the dealer turned the cards, the six of clubs duly arrived to a roar of delight and rage.

Enjoying the sensation he made, Horace collected his gains with a modest smile, and a twitch of his long nose.

'Come on, come on, do we end there, lads? Will you see the navy take all your wealth and keep silent? Come on now, who'll lay the next wager? Let's see this young man's luck broke!'

171

'Ay, give the poor red-coats a chance,' jeered one of the mids bitterly. 'They have a slow enough time of it to be sure.'

'What, Mr Pettigrew, I can't think you're finished?'

Mr Pettigrew who had lost his fifty eyed Horace with some animosity and named his card.

'And one hundred upon it,' he said.

'I take you,' said Mr Nelson with as much insouciance as he could put into his tone; and named his.

'Double it!' snapped Mr Pettigrew.

Mr Nelson nodded sagely, entirely sure he would win.

'Ay, very well an' all. Two hundred it is.'

A gasp was heard from the navy. Tom Hoar looked over Horatio's fair head at Charles Pole, his eyebrows raised high above his aristocratic roman nose. The cards were turned, the navy triumphed, the army was routed. Pole looked quickly at Hoar and nodded. They rose.

'We thank our hosts,' shouted Mr Midshipman Hoar when the uproar had quieted a little 'but we are sorry to announce that the carriage is at the door. In other words,' he said drawing forth his pocket watch with some ostentation, 'the launch will be waiting.'

A last drink was partaken of, new year greetings exchanged and the evening's main winner seemingly unconcerned and closely flanked by his three stalwart friends was marched over the Green to the pier, a sum jingling in his pockets equal to three hundred pounds.

'Not a word now,' said Tom Hoar as they bobbed over the water. 'Thomas, not a word from you neither, to a soul. Horace, keep your tongue fast on the *Seahorse* or you'll not save a penny! Harrington will have the lot!'

They laughed immoderately, nearing the ship. Horace turned into his hammock, the money beneath him, in a kind of fantasy of confidence about his good fortune. He bore, it seemed, the charm of fate, the smile of chance, no one could break his luck and he had *known* they would not. How had he known such an extraordinary thing? He was asleep before considering the question and did not even hear eight bells.

Just before midnight he awoke with a shock, in a state of cold horror. What had woken him, was it simple habit? The bells had not yet sounded, the bo'sun's pipe was not shrilly summoning him on deck. What thought had struck him so cold? What was this uncomfortable lump beneath him? He put his hand down and felt the money, tied up in his spare black neckerchief. The whole of the evening before came to his mind in a flash, and the shocking thought with it: *Supposing he had been the loser and not the winner where would he have found the money to pay?* Write to Papa and confess that he had gambled and lost? Beg from Uncle

Suckling? They were both too far away. From whom, then? Go to the Captain, whom he somewhat disliked? The idea was appalling, it was sufficient to ruin his career, his eyes were wide open staring into the dark. The red-faced young officer he thought, had had to borrow from his friends. He would never do such a thing again, he swore to himself he would not. He remembered that it was the first day of the year of 1776, an opportune day to make such a resolve. He swung out of the hammock, locked the money in his chest in the steerage under all his clothes, dressed and washed, and was ready to go up for the middle watch in a most sober and repentant frame of mind.

The stripping of the *Seahorse* went on. Horatio took the launch ashore loaded with the main rigging, and with it Mr North the bo'sun and a party of men to help him at the rigging loft. Early in January the master attendant came on board and they warped the bare *Seahorse* into the dock.

The next day Mr Nelson was sent down from the ship with a party of men to the cooper's yard upon Old Woman's Island. The coopers worked below the wall amongst their piles of wood and withies, with their particular and intricate tools, bending in new wood to the casks, or hammering in fresh bottoms, or binding and caulking the sides. They were a quiet group of craftsmen, many of them English, wearing old sailcloth or straw hats, stopping sometimes to mop their brows or dash insects from their faces and arms.

'Damned musquitoes!' said one, greeting the tars with a smile and pointing to the casks that were ready. 'Never leave you alone.'

Beyond the yard was the watering place where a fresh stream ran with a water-mill beside it. There were stretches of marshy, muddy land below the town wall upon Old Woman's Island, reminding Horace of the marshes at home, as they stood awaiting the casks and filling them.

The *Seahorse* was in dock twelve days. The people worked at the rigging loft and on the ship new-rigging the masts. Horace brooded upon his money wondering how he could safely keep it until he got home. And when should he get home? None knew, it was better not to think of it.

As work proceeded on the ship, John North the bo'sun fell ill of a fever, the kind of sickness that had struck many. Some weeks the sick bay was full of groaning, panting sailors. It was said the *Salisbury* had sent twenty-six men to hospital before Christmas. The illness was a kind of ague, a tertian fever, and seemed to spread. Horatio remembered his shivering ague fits as a child and with the memory there arose slowly the sweet loving sense, almost a bodily presence or a scent (now seldom recalled) of his mother who had cared for him. He sighed at the nearness of the memory which nudged him and yawned a huge aching yawn, feeling so tired this morning that he yearned to be in a small white bed at home with that gentle presence to comfort him. Why should he be so tired? He stretched his arms and his back muscles. They ached. His legs ached, feeling like lead. He shook himself, and went to the side to count in the beef. The baskets full of joints of fresh red meat smelling strong roused distaste rather than appetite in him. When it was all aboard he found he had forgotten the quantity.

The new gunwales were fitted, the coppers came back from repair on shore, both anchors were catted and their cables bent, the foremast woolded, the rudder hung. On January the eighteenth they came out of dock, slipping the mooring chain and dropping anchor again in the harbour. Horatio thought he would feel better to be away from the land: there was more air, a fresher cooler atmosphere altogether on the water. The bowsprit, found to be much decayed, was hoist out by means of the foreyard and a midshipman ordered to take it ashore one afternoon in the launch to be fished. Mr Nelson having volunteered to go could not be found (he was in the quarter gallery, his dinner having made him feel sick that day as had happened several times lately) and Mr Troubridge put himself forward instead.

'I am taking the launch Mr Troubridge,' shouted down Horatio, looking pale and furious as he arrived amidships. 'It was arranged this morning.'

'You were not here and the men were ready, Mr Nelson,' replied Thomas coolly.

'I am here now, sir.'

'And so am I, sir. We are away and you may stay behind.' Thomas now looked red and truculent.

'I am better able to command that vessel than you, sir,' screamed Horace down to the water.

'That I deny. I have my orders.'

'I had *my* orders I tell you!'

Tom Hoar, watching with astonishment this sudden furious contention between the two friends, suddenly saw the officer coming and went to Horace's side.

'Ware!' he muttered. 'Gossart in the offing. You have no chance of persuading Thomas, what has got into you? What matters it who takes the launch?'

'It matters very much to me, sir,' cried the enraged midshipman rounding on him huffily so that the smile upon Hoar's face faltered. 'How dare he rob me of my duty!'

'Horace what ails you, you look ill?'

'Tell that Mr Nelson from me,' came a cry from below, rather nasal in kind, 'he's a damned proud, conceited prig and I'll fight him tonight in the—' Thomas Troubridge's words coming clearly over the water as they took the boat out suddenly stopped. He too had seen Lieutenant Gossart. Horatio turned about following Thomas's gaze, saluted, and stumped off glumly to the companion way.

'What goes on?' said the officer.

'All's well, sir,' said Hoar airily.

'It sounded so,' said Gossart.

That night the strong cheese for supper made Horace feel sick again: he ate none, but sipped a little grog and felt better. He had no doubt he would soon get over what had upset him. He felt bitter animosity against Thomas, whose behaviour must have worsened his sickness, he believed.

Next day his head ached, throbbing noisily as he encouraged the men at their rigging. The carpenters and caulkers were about again, the ship smelt of tar. It was the tar, he thought, made him feel so sick! You could not escape it. He could only nibble at his meals. The surgeon's assistant who messed with them watched him covertly. Next day the order was given to smoke the ship for rats. The braziers were lit, burning some especial substance got by the Captain from the dockyard, recommended with great acclamations and gesticulations by the stall keepers who sold it. The acrid smoke curled and billowed into every hollow in the belly of the ship, the men directing it stood with wet cloths over mouth and nose; the stench nauseated Horatio, he fled up to the side and hung his head over, his empty stomach heaving painfully. Everything was against him: why must they smoke the ship today? Behind him the *Seahorse* was full of the squealing of rats, the scampering thud of their feet, the yelling of seamen as they ran to destroy them, the thumping of the wooden billets upon the victims slaughtered on the decks. Some leapt live into the water. Sharks came slicing towards the bodies, making a turmoil in the bloodstained sea. The master's mate, who liked exactitude, later stood counting a pile of bodies and adding in each man's tally as he reported it.

'Four 'undred and sixty-seven I made it. Think of that now,' he said later with satisfaction at dinner. 'That's a fair lot of rats to be rid of.'

'Why *count* them?' groaned Midshipman Nelson.

'Why not?' said the mate. 'I shall put it in the log. You look sick, lad,' he added kindly.

'I was. I am recovered, no thanks to you and your doings.'

'Are you eating nothing?' asked the surgeon's assistant.

'No, I thank you. I cannot. I have a headache.'

After dinner, a party of men was wanted to go ashore and pick over the bread. The thought of the maggots in their nooks and holes was more than Horatio could bear. This time he begged *not* to take the launch. Hoar volunteered. If only he could forget the vision of the rats and the crawling bread he would be better, Horace told himself. He went to the side and breathed deep.

He could not be rid of the headache, his eyes ached with it, his skin felt stretched. Turned in, he could not sleep for it, and the aching of his limbs grew worse and worse.

CHAPTER FIFTEEN

'...in the Dolphin*...with Captain James Pigot,*
whose kindness at that time saved my life.'

In the morning, the sickness and the headache were as bad and he was
aware of an awful cold. He was afraid there was nothing for it, he had
succumbed to the sickness. He stumbled up before breakfast to the
fo'c's'le, to the sick bay ahead the galley. The surgeon's assistant was
already there, amongst his patients.

'I thought as much,' he said grudgingly as he saw Horatio.
'Headache?'

'Yes.'

'Backache? Legs ache?'

'Yes.'

'Sick?'

'Ay.'

'Cold?'

This time the midshipman nodded gloomily, clutching his chest with
his arms.

'Get into that cot and lie quiet. As quiet as you can,' the man added
in a sinister afterthought. 'I'll bring you the medicine.'

There was no surgeon just now on the ship, he was exceedingly
busy, and gave frauds short shrift. But he could see this boy was ill.

Horace crept to the cot, swung into it, pulled up the blanket and
felt the relief of giving in. The headache worsened, the chill gripped
him, the sickness went on. He thought of the agues of his childhood.
This seemed much worse, but he forgot what they were really like, they
were so long ago. If only his head would stop pounding like a gun, he
might sleep! Somebody greeted him, commiserating. He thought that
it might be Mr North, better and up on his feet and walking, but his
eyes would not open and he could only groan. He was scarcely aware
of four men stumbling in later in the morning panting after
punishment, swearing and yelping as their raw stripes were treated. He
had his medicine, the bitter bark, diluted but bitter as gall, and was
clenching his lips to keep it down. He was deathly cold.

In the agues of his childhood he could remember shivering, he suddenly recalled Mamma holding his chattering jaws in her kind hands. But this was a terrible still cold, a paralysing cold, and he felt dazed and feverish at the same time. Someone brought him hot, weak grog and held him from behind while he drank,. He drank it gratefully, and at first it comforted his empty stomach, but it soon turned to tenderness, pain and a dreadful nausea. He spued it up upon the deck, distressed at the trouble he gave. They tried the medicine and the hot grog with regularity: at first he seldom kept them down for long. After an age of cold he entered such terrible burning heat that the blanket was flung upon the deck, he started up panting, the cot creaked with his tossings, he heard his voice changed to a croak begging for water. The tepid water seemed cool compared with his heat: someone bathed his face and his forehead with cool cloths but his hot skin burnt the cloths dry, his skin that seemed pulled tight over his face bones. After the age of heat, suddenly his sweat burst out upon him. Sweat ran into his eyes, from his nose into his mouth, he lay slippery in a drenching of sweat The relief was so blessed, he sighed with it and slept. But awoke into another age of cold.

The days and nights ran into each other with no pattern (he could not remember how many days): the cold, the heat and the sweat came and went, linked by sickness or by sleep, by the appetite for the drinks brought him or the nausea so often following it. Once at the beginning he heard his name called in a loud whisper and opened an eye to see Tom Hoar standing at the entrance trying to smile at him, saying something. He lifted his hand from the blanket to show he had seen him. Sometimes the throbbing pain in his head beat time with the noises of the ship. Hammer, hammer, hammer, hammer. He groaned at the hammering and heard once again his name called.

'How are you lad?'

He thought that it was the master this time.

'…noise hurts my head,' he croaked.

'It's the carpenters building a sail room between decks', explained Mr Surridge, as if this might help matters. 'They'll soon have done.'

Horace tried to smile at him. His throat at this stage being cracked and burning he could say no more.

After what seemed an age of this chaos of suffering (it was in fact but five days or so) there came a day when he felt better. He felt so much better he had beef broth and a little soaked bread, as well as grog. He reclined in the cot knowing that ease after pain which causes the sufferer to smile with relief. Thomas Troubridge saw the smile, peering in from the doorway that day. (He had been before, but seen his friend in a state of dreadful fever. And it was a difficult matter evading the assistant surgeon and his nurses, who made it their business to chase out visitors and never allowed them across the threshold: the sickness, they assumed, being spread by contact.)

'Horace!' said Thomas. 'You are better!' He had suffered cruel remorse at his furious quarrel with his sick friend.

Horatio opened his eyes and his smile widened. There stood his good friend Thomas, there was some reason why he was touched to the heart to see him, he almost shed a tear.

'Ay. You'll see me aloft before long I promise you. I feel much better today. But tired,' he sighed.

'Good. Here comes the guard, I must go!'

Horace only remembered the quarrel when he was gone and laughed weakly at the thought of it, brushing away the tear. But Horatio's hope of recovery and the return of his strength were soon denied. At noon next day he was gripped once more by the terrible coldness, and lay in dismay knowing what would follow. The shouting of men working up junk, the top-gallant masts being swayed up, the hauling of stuff aboard, the clanking anchors, the slapping cables, all slid back into another world. Here there was pain and sickness and the torment of heat. The next day his hopes rose, for he was once more better. Hoar came and stood at the cabin door and waved at him.

'What are you all doing?' said Horace feebly.

'We've got a harbour boat now for our use. The launch is going on shore to be repaired, Thomas has taken it. A lighter brought some wood. The people are blacking the tops, and so on. How are you? Thomas said you were better, and then—'

'Ill again yesterday.'

'Perhaps that will be the end.'

'I hope so.'

But the fever struck him again next day, in the way of a tertian fever once it has settled itself, coming on at noon.

'You'll feel better tomorrow, lad,' said the man who tended him, which was true: but you waited in apprehension, the boy now knew, for the fever to come again. When two days had passed however and it had not come nor had he been sick, he dared to hope. Thomas came.

'Are you better?'

'A little. I have had two days better.'

'Praise the Lord.'

'Amen. What are you all doing?'

'Well, the lighter has brought gunner's and carpenter's stores. Tom has taken the harbour boat watering. They're white-washing the gunroom and the magazine.'

'Perhaps I shall soon be allowed up. Thomas, what can be the date? How long have I been ill?'

'It's the fifth of February by my log. When were you ill, now?'

Horace's head ached as he thought. Then a landmark appeared.

'The day after the rats?'

'Ay, so you were. You must have been ill near two weeks.'

'It feels longer than that.'

Thomas grinned, waved and quickly disappeared: the assistant surgeon came in.

'You are a little better, Mr Nelson.'

'Yes, sir, so I am.'

'You shall try your feet in a day or two, if this continues.'

The boy sighed with contentment and lay back to rest. The next day he fed like a horse: wine, meat, good shore bread, beef tea, nothing went against him. All his extra fat was gone, he was slight as he had been as a child, he reflected that his best jacket, even, might fit him. In the afternoon they let him up on deck and he saw the spritsail rigged and got across. The petty officers gathered to congratulate him, the seamen he had known saluted his appearance with smiles. He begged next morning to take the harbour boat watering.

'No, no, nonsense,' said Lieutenant Abson. 'You are not yet fit. But you may go with Mr Troubridge if he will have you. He is not to work the boat, mind,' the officer told Thomas, who took his friend aboard eagerly. Neither said a word of the last time they stood at the side together, but both had it in mind and smiled sheepishly. They landed at the watering place on Old Woman's Island, Thomas bidding his friend stay aboard and not exert himself. But Horatio would come, walked shakily up to the stream and the mill and looked in upon the coopers, exulting in his recovery. He felt very tired at night, he was not on watch yet, but he was getting better. That afternoon they saw the *Dolphin* anchor in the harbour.

The next evening at sunset the *Seahorse* hoist the commodore's broad pendant instead of the *Salisbury*, and for three weeks was to fire the evening and morning gun and make the weekly signal for accounts. The commodore himself however was seldom aboard, preferring to live ashore. The painters began painting the ship, and Horace still found the smell nauseous. He was eating sparely but regularly, and he had not been sick again. As the week went on, and his legs got stronger and his tiredness less, he rejoiced. He looked at his neglected journal, counted the days in his mind and realised he had been up for a week and a day.

When the fearful cold and sickness overcame him again on the morrow, he would not believe it, he thought it must pass, it was only the smell of the paint. But by noon he had stumbled to the fo'c's'le, Tom Hoar holding his arm, to give himself up to the fever once again. His disappointment was grievous, he was entirely silent with despondency, the other's cheering words went unheard; he lay sick, weak, tears rolling down his cheeks, his head hidden in the blanket. Mr Surridge came next day when the fever had abated, and shook his head sternly.

'Up too soon, lad. They'd no business letting you carry on like that.'

'But I felt better, sir.'

'May be, but look what's followed.'

'I'll be all right tomorrow, sir,' the young man said, wondering.

And tomorrow brought the fever again. The next day brought Hoar, with some tale of the little *Betsy Gally* coming into Bombay and returning into the stores the exact amount of hawser they had lent her in Bussorah, which the stores had passed on to the *Seahorse* yesterday. The invalid smiled sadly, wondering if tomorrow would bring the fever or relief from it. The pinnace (Tom told him next) was back, repaired and just launched. Horace swore to himself he should soon sail her: and the fever overcame him next day.

On the morrow, lying weak and sick after an attempt to take some porridge for breakfast, Horace heard eight bells strike. The bell being on the fo'c's'le before the galley sounded loud and clear in the sick bay, where many a sick man cursed its noisy regularity. Immediately following it was a gun signal and when a quarter of an hour later he heard the bo'sun's pipe begin its wailing, he slid out of his cot and staggered round the galley and beyond the forehatch. The crew were lined up, somebody of importance was coming aboard. It was the commodore, Sir Edward Hughes. He was followed by four captains of whom Horace recognised but one, Captain Marlow of the *Coventry* whom he had once seen in Trincomalee. One of the others later proved to be a Captain Pigot of the *Swallow* sloop which had recently anchored: not the dreaded Hugh Pigot who was succeeded by Horatio's uncle upon the *Triumph*, but another called James. Now what would all those officers be about? It looked like a court martial: he remembered Lieutenant Henery. Horace crept back to bed. Tom woke him out of a doze at half past three in the afternoon.

'There's been a court martial.'

'I know, I saw them come.'

'You did? Trust you. Henery is honourably acquitted.'

'I am very glad to hear it, I always thought he would be.'

'But I say Horace, the joke is there's a rumour going around that Henery has laid a charge against the old man himself!'

'Captain Farmer?'

'Ay. Wherefore, do you imagine? Thomas and I can't think.'

Horace thought and his head began to ache.

'If I were Lieutenant Henery,' he said judiciously, 'I should bring a charge against him for keeping me waiting so long before trial. He's been in misery and suspense since...Can you remember?'

Tom thought it was when they had last been in Madras.

'Back in September. Before Trincomalee, before my promotion.'

'Ay, I think so.'

'Disgraceful, is it not?'

'I suppose it is. Are you better?'

'Today I am,' said the patient wearily.

'You must be worn out, you look very thin. Can you eat?'

'Not much. I had some broth. I can drink more easily.'

Tom brought him some of the sweet arrack he had bought in the bazaar, diluted with water. It went down well and soothed his stomach.

The rumour about the Captain proved true. On an afternoon following a day of fever came Thomas Troubridge to see him. Horatio was to remember the day well.

'Horace!' Thomas hissed.

The boy opened his eyes.

'There's been another court martial!'

'What happened?'

'They've all gone. The court acquitted the Captain, it was announced.'

'But what was the charge?'

'We are never told. How are you?'

'Tired...oh, Thomas, if only I could throw it off!'

'You will, you will. Why, you've been up once...I hear voices, I must go. Keep your heart up, man.'

The voices proved to be the assistant surgeon leading another kindly-faced man, not old but of seeming authority. Sir Edward Hughes, visiting the ship for the two courts martial, had enquired of the Captain concerning his invalids. Captain Farmer had to admit that he did not like the look of his bo'sun, Mr North: and mentioned also Midshipman Nelson, Captain Suckling's nephew, whom he had heard was very bad. Sir Edward Hughes had today brought the surgeon of the *Salisbury*. This was he.

'Mr Nelson, here is Dr Perry of the *Salisbury* to see you. How are you now?'

Horace turned hopeless, pleading eyes towards the doctor as he took his wrist.

'Oh, sir, if only you could help me, if only you can tell me how to throw this thing off!' he said urgently.

'You are not in fever today, and your pulse is steady. How long has this attack lasted?'

'He's been bad for a week again. We had him up, we had him ashore, before that—'

'How long did the first attack last?'

'More like ten or twelve days was it not, Mr Nelson?'

'I should say he is improved today. Maybe this bout will be shorter. Drink whatever they bring you, for you lose so much in the sickness and sweating. Take heart, if you go through tomorrow with no fever then the bout is over. Do you take your medicine like a man?' he smiled.

'When I can keep it down, sir.'

'Ay, 'tis bitter stuff. Were you given to the ague as a child?' Dr William Perry sat by him on a cask they rolled up, unhurried and patient. Horatio told him his memories.

'I shall come again to see you make good progress. Now I must see the others.'

He had already seen John North; in his opinion the man was far from fully recovered and should go home. Next day the *Dolphin* was named as the home-going ship, Captain Pigot of the *Swallow* appointed to her, and Mr North fixed for her bo'sun. Meanwhile Horace, encouraged by Dr Perry, was better again, entering the berth like a ghost of himself, a shock to his companions. All made much of him, he was not yet to be allowed on watch, but must idly pace the decks. Thus occupied, Horatio encountered Lieutenant Henery, restored to his duties, his honour vindicated, but his temper soured.

'Well, Mr Nelson: I've seen you look better. What a fool's trick, eh, to succumb to disease, I think it unworthy of you.'

'I shall soon be well, sir. May I tender you my congratulations?'

'That I am vindicated you may. That he goes unpunished you may not,' he added in a sinister whisper. 'I have a plan to go ashore,' he went on in a kindlier tone. 'Will you accompany me? It would do you good. I hereby give you leave, and will expect you at the side in half an hour.'

Horace was pleased and accepted gladly. They wandered in the bazaar, drank wine in the shade of a tree below the wall, and ate food the poor invalid found too rich. Nonetheless, the trip encouraged him, and by the end of the week he had begun to pick up some strength. Dr Perry arrived to see his invalids, met his young patient on the quarter-deck and shook him by the hand.

'Well, my boy. You look better.'

'I think I am, sir, I thank you.'

'I wondered at finding you not with the sick.'

'I have been up a week, sir.'

'Are you working?'

'I am to stand a watch tomorrow if I am able, sir.'

'Good. I'll see you tomorrow.'

Horatio rose early, ate a modest breakfast and stood the morning watch. There was not much afoot. The masters came aboard again to survey Mr North's stores. Mr William Touch arrived as purser from the *Dolphin* instead of Mr Ligerwood who was also for home. The people were working up junk, Horace strode from mast to mast urging them on, Dr Perry saw him at work and was satisfied. At twelve o'clock he slid his chest up to the table for dinner, slumped down upon it and sighed.

'Horace?' Tom, following him in, watched anxiously. Horace said nothing but looked up with hollow, shadowed eyes, knowing all too well the meaning of the sickness in his stomach, and the terrible cold which felled him like a blow.

Sudden in its attack, the fever was slower in its progress. When the sweat at last broke from him next noon, he fell into a deep and helpless sleep. In this state Dr Perry found him.

'What a pity, what a pity. That's no healthful sleep but a kind of trance.'

'Ay so I thought, sir.'

'He may come out of it. I'll come tomorrow. Watch him carefully, see he drinks if he wakes.'

When he did awake he had no memory of his sleep or of the fever or even that he had stood his watch. He felt puzzled and as heavy as lead, and could not raise himself to drink without a man's arm to help him. It was only later when he tried to rise to relieve himself that it came upon him with a shock *that he could not move his legs*. His hips were like logs. They would not do as he told them.

He lay back. Tears rolled down his cheeks.

'What is it?'

'My legs. I cannot move my legs!'

'Hold hard, I'll help you.'

The man pulled his legs from the cot and stood him up, his arm around him.

'Now hold on to me. Can you walk?' Left standing, he would have fallen flat upon the deck had not the other caught him.

Dr Perry, discovering from Mr Surridge that the *Seahorse* was about to make a short trip north towards Surat, decided that his patient must not go.

'Now then Horace, this is a disappointment. You must go to the hospital, for I can't have you cruising without the power of your legs.'

'What has happened to me, sir?' the poor boy said.

'You've lost the use of your legs, I hear. Let me see you try to move.'

Horatio strained until the sweat started from him to move his limbs. They lay immovable.

'But shall I get better, sir? Or shall I never be able to move again?' he burst out.

'Oh I hope so, indeed. Patience, Horatio. You have had a bad attack but all's not lost. We'll get you ashore tomorrow. It's a good hospital and run by the Company. You will be well cared for. I'll see you there.'

In the morning Tom Hoar found two strong seamen, friends of Horatio's, to carry him in a blanket to the side. Lieutenant Henery watched from the quarter-deck with a glum frown. The tallest of the men hung the sick boy over his shoulder like a side of beef though more gently, and carried him down the ladder into the repaired cutter launched that day, where Thomas Troubridge waited. They laid him on his blanket, carefully wedged upon deck. He looked at the sky through tears and shut his eyes fast. Two other sick seamen were helped into the cutter after him.

Mr Surridge had observed all this from the side of the ship and stood clicking his teeth, feeling much downcast. The sickness on the *Seahorse* was such that he had had to ask for two petty officers and thirty men for tomorrow from the *Salisbury*, to get the ship ready for sea. Others than these three had already gone to the hospital. The *Dolphin* it was said had sent a number last week. Neither Captain Farmer nor Mr Surridge had kept a record of the *Seahorse* sick in their logs, both feeling it to be a kind of disgrace for a ship and preferring to make light of it while they could.

There were three large hospitals in Bombay run by the East India Company. Horace was taken to the one for Europeans which stood within the gates. There was a second on the esplanade for the sepoys, and a third for convalescents upon an adjacent island. The place was cleaner, airier and altogether more comfortable that the cramped sick-quarters of a twenty-gun frigate, and there were English and other white doctors and many Indian nurses and orderlies. Without the noisy background of ship life, time slipped all into a stream; he knew not how long he had been there nor what were the days. When he felt better, he missed his two friends stealing their quick visits to bring him the news. Dr Perry came over to see the squadron's sick several times and found that the boy's distress had thrown him into the depths of despair. The good man recounted several cases where the patient had recovered and was walking about now upon his business, well and jolly.

Horatio set his jaw, nodded his head, and gripped the doctor's hand as he left. Next day a recrudescence of the fever knocked him down.

He was in the hospital more than two weeks while the *Seahorse* came and went upon her six-day cruise. On the thirteenth of March the *Salisbury* signalled all the ships to send boats for the usual conference upon the squadron's movements. On the fourteenth she signalled to the *Seahorse* for a boat and Lieutenant Henery went over, taken by Mr Midshipman Hoar. Dr Perry had seen his sick men that day and decided that ten of them including Horatio had no hope but to be sent home, the sooner the better. The *Dolphin* would sail a week hence. The invalids were discharged that same day (the new purser wrote Horatio's discharge in the *Seahorse* muster book) and were to go straight to the *Dolphin*.

On the fifteenth Mr Gossart the acting lieutenant was discharged back into his own ship the *Coventry*, since Lieutenant Henery's position was established: and the *Coventry* left on a cruise next day. On the twentieth the *Seahorse*'s books were taken by Mr Troubridge in the launch over to the *Dolphin* to go home to the Admiralty: and any possessions of the sick men which could be collected. Tom Hoar saw to Horace's chest and hat, and other oddments belonging to his friend in the berth.

'If you see him bear him my good wishes and my love, Thomas,' he said to Troubridge.

'Ay I will that, poor old Horace.'

'I dearly wish I could say farewell.'

But when Thomas reached the *Dolphin* it was said the invalids were not expected till the next day. A watering party however was ordered upon the afternoon of the twenty-first and the two midshipmen both contrived to go, and hung about upon the shore of Old Woman's Island until they saw the *Dolphin's* boat coming off with the invalids. They followed her. A few of the sick went up the ladder alone, but most were half-carried aboard. They saw Horatio go, as thin as a skeleton in the arms of a seaman, his pale face and long nose sharp with sickness visible over the man's shoulder.

'Goodbye, Horace! Brace up man, get you well!'

'We expect you back soon! God bless you!' cried Hoar and Troubridge. They knew that he heard them for he lifted his head and smiled towards the cutter.

The *Dolphin* had lain at the chain moorings in Bombay harbour until the sixteenth. Now she was moored in mid-harbour, having run further out. The next day she completed all her provisions and received on board her own sick men, four of them, from the hospital. That evening she weighed and made sail, but at seven the flood made and it fell calm, so she must needs anchor again. At three o'clock in the morning of the twenty-third of March she weighed once more and set her studding sails and sailed from Bombay. By eight o'clock Kanary Island was five leagues to the north-east, and for the sick men the long journey home had begun. Midshipman Nelson was scarcely aware of it, for by noon that day he was gripped with the fever again.

CHAPTER SIXTEEN

'The spirit of Nelson revived...'

The *Dolphin* was a twenty-gun frigate as was the *Seahorse*, and her arrangements were much the same. The sick bay was for'ard of the galley on the fo'c's'le: the smell of the sick men (despite frequent swabbings of the deck with vinegar) was nauseous: the stench of the heads, beneath the bowsprit (where were the seamen's latrines) found its way up by the foremast: the effluvia of greasy cooking frequently entered from the galley. The fever having left him, Horatio longed for fresh air, for the sight of the sea and the surf along the shore, for they had told him they were standing not far out down the Malabar coast. With an enormous effort, with his hand beneath his shrunken buttocks, he tried to lift his leaden legs over the side of the cot. One of the surgeon's assistants heard his struggles and came over.

'D'ye wish to try your legs, laddie?' said he.

'Yes if you please. Will you help me?'

'Ay, ye're fit for a wee change of scene. Ye'll be feeble, mind,' he warned him.

He stood him up upon the deck.

'Grip fast to me now. Can ye move, can ye e'en shuffle?'

The legs were almost powerless.

'Might I not crawl? I cannot bear to be so helpless. Lay me down, let me try, please let me try.'

But the most he could do was to proceed upon his elbow, using his other hand fin-wise like a seal.

'Och, noo, tha's no way for a mon to get aboot. I'll fetch my mate.'

While he was gone Horatio persisted, moving slowly and steadily upon his hip. If he could but walk! What use was a man who could not walk? Dr Perry had said he would walk again. The two men linked arms and carried him to the side of the ship.

It was still early in the morning. The *Dolphin* was idling off Mount Dilla where she had lain-to the night before. Horace turned his sad eyes to the pearled coolness of the misty shore, felt the morning breeze on his face, looked at his helpers and smiled.

'I thank you. That will do me good.'

'Ay, that it will. Hold fast, now. There's our boat, look 'ee, going ashore. You watch her go and come.'

'I will.'

The boat had gone to order firewood. He watched her till she vanished in the mist: and later on, joined by several other convalescents, counted in fourteen small shore boats bringing loads of wood, as if it were his duty again. Two days later they stood in for Cochin Roads and anchored overnight there, to take on more wood. This time Horatio had managed to walk a few steps between the two men. When they came to help him back he was almost cheerful, staggering between them: telling them about Anjengo. Off Anjengo Captain Farmer of the *Seahorse* had chased and fought a ship of Hyder Ali's. The men were pleased to hear him prattle and encouraged him. They sailed away from Cochin and the next morning fell in with a Company's cruiser the *Revenge,* for whose boat carrying mail and news they brought to. Horace watched all this with the keenest interest longing for the return of strength: but alas, within an hour of their making sail he felt the dreaded chill upon him again and knew his respite was over. After a day of it, he could expect a day's relief. Mr John North the bo'sun from the *Seahorse,* having rejoiced to see his young friend upon the fo'c's'le the previous week, came to mourn his relapse.

'Then you're not so well again Mr Nelson, I'm sorry to hear?'

'Beaten again Mr North, sir. How are you? Are you recovered?'

The bo'sun did not look it: he was thin and yellow, not the man he had been.

'Let us but get quit of this hot, unhealthy climate and get home,' he said with longing, 'and I'll pull up.'

'I pray so, sir. Where are we?'

'Why lad, we're in Anjengo Road, I came to tell you. Do you know who has just saluted us, did you hear our guns answer?'

'Ay, I wondered. Who is it?'

'The little *Betsy Gally!* Do you mind the *Betsy Gally?*'

'The *Betsy Gally!* Indeed I do, with us all the way to…all the way to…'

'Bussorah, in the Gulf. And back to Muscat, and she hung on to Bombay!'

'That she did. I remember! We left them all behind but she!'

'Ay, bless her heart. Just think of that.'

Horace did think long of it; and was accompanied in his next paroxysm by strange hot dreams of the Gulf, of sand storms which cleared to reveal figures dressed in pantaloons of cream silk and red shoes, who brandished long knives, and one of whom to his horror had the face of Thomas Troubridge. Tom Hoar was there, coolly playing cards at a green table in the sultry desert: until Mr Surridge appeared with John North who whipped them all back to the ship, amidst flashes of summer lightening.

As Horatio emerged from a week of fever, the hot sultry weather and the lightening which had appeared in his dreams and half-conscious dozing, continued. Rain followed, a huge south-westerly swell made his tender stomach rise as several days of squalls, gales, split sails and confused seas struck them. Nevertheless as the days passed and his first week without fever led into a second, Horatio took heart and practised his walks upon deck in the intervals of calm. One day he made the forehatch, the next time the mainhatch, telling himself he would soon clear the mainmast and descend to the steerage and the midshipmen's' berth.

Captain Pigot enquired for the progress and watched the efforts of all his invalids, but took an especial interest in this boy who had come aboard so ill that he had expected to bury him along the coast. He was acquainted with Captain Suckling, he began to have a great desire to return the lad well to his uncle. He had heard from poor John North that he was well thought of by the master of the *Seahorse,* that he was active, willing, dutiful and fearless up aloft. He sent a message by the surgeon that when Mr Midshipman Nelson found himself able to walk to the cabin, he looked forward to drinking a bumper with him to celebrate the occasion.

This challenge reached the poor boy on a morning when a wracking headache, aching limbs, nausea and chill announced the return of the fever: even as the surgeon delivered it, he could have bitten out his tongue. Young Nelson was down again. How long could so frail a body resist such repeated attacks? The boy's despair and disappointment were grievous to see.

'No hope…I have no hope, sir, it beats me down.'

'Not so, you have great courage. You have been two weeks better. You will do it next time. Never give up hope.'

Never give up hope, never give up hope, never give up hope beat the pulse in his head. How much longer could it go on, how much longer could he hold out? Was it not much easier this time to let go, to slip his moorings, to give up hope, to die? But if he did so he would never reach home, he would never see his family again. The faces of his family crowded in upon him, not seen for so long, blurred, smiling or malformed hideously by his fever. His father said *My brave Horatio,* as he had said upon his first going into the navy. He could not disappoint his father. And the Captain, the Captain cared about him, had invited him to the cabin. Captain Pigot knew all about him and his efforts to walk. He would not give up, he must present himself to the Captain. Next time.

By the beginning of May he was better again, sitting up, eating his porridge, supping hot grog. After a great swell the day before, the sea was fallen, the weather seemed cooler.

'Where are we?'

'Nearing Africa, I believe. Distance took from Madagascar in the log.'

'Mr North never came to see me,' Horace remembered. 'He is used to come on the good days.'

'Ah, weel. Puir Mr North, he's no' fit...'

'Is he ill again?'

'Ay, laddie, he's a puir thing, tak to his bed again.'

'How long?'

'A day or two sin'. In his ain berth.'

'I'll visit him.'

'Ye'll do so. No' ower far today. Tak it aisy. We'll try your legs noo.'

To his surprise his legs had not forgotten all he had taught them. The first day he got to the mainmast. The second day he got to the half-deck, descended to the steerage and found the midshipmen's berth.

The bo'sun's cabin was next door.

'How is Mr North?'

'Very ill, they say. Is he a friend of yours?'

'From the *Seahorse,* yes. I came to visit him.'

'Peep in, then. He may like to see you.'

John North lay in his cot. Horace was shocked. His yellow skin was stretched tight over the bones of his face, his lips were back from his teeth. This was not the man he knew, this seemed a stranger.

'Mr North, sir!' he whispered several times.

At last the bo'sun opened a sunken eye.

'Who's that? Come in, can't see.'

'It's I, Horace Nelson, sir.'

'Ah yes.'

'How are you, Mr North?'

'Mortal ill, lad.'

'Then you may feel better tomorrow.'

John North shook his head, his eyes closed.

'Nay, I'll not get home,' he sighed. 'I'm done.'

Never give up hope, Horace thought. It was too late to say it to the bo'sun. He laid his hand, thin with illness, over the gnarled yellow claw with risen blue veins that lay upon the blanket. The man tried to smile.

Forced to tack southerly they found the weather grow cooler; there was a great sea from the south-west and a cold wind in that quarter, as they turned once more north for Africa. Despite the rolling of the ship, Horace set out aft the next day. Helped by seamen who watched his progress with concern, he made his way beyond the mainmast to the half-deck, beyond the capstan and the afterhatch, to the foot of the mizzenmast. A marine sentry polished a buckled shoe outside the Captain's cabin: he looked up in surprise, and seeing a midshipman he had never set eyes on before, stood to attention.

'The Captain sent for me.'

'When was that, sir?'

Horatio pondered.

'Last week,' he said simply.

'*Last week!*' said the man, hiding a smile. 'Very well, sir. Your name?'

'Mr Horatio Nelson, mid. Invalid,' he added.

The marine knocked at the door.

'A Mr Midshipman Nelson, sir, sez you sent for him last week.' There was a moment's startled pause.

'So I did. And I'm heartily pleased he has come. Come in, Mr Nelson,' said Captain Pigot, rising to welcome him and shaking his hand. 'You have had a dangerous trip aft, but reached port safely.'

'Yes, sir, I thank you. I did not choose to be any longer in answering your summons.'

The ship rolled, the boy staggered, the Captain caught him.

'Sit down, sit down, Horatio. I'm acquainted with your uncle. A glass of wine, to speed your recovery?'

'Thank you, sir.'

They talked. Of Horatio's illness and of Dr Perry's promises, of his early adventures, of Uncle Suckling, of his friends on the *Seahorse,* of his ambitions and his bitter despair in being sent home. It was the first of many talks.

'I have been to see our bo'sun, Mr John North, sir.'

'Ah, that is a sad story, I am afraid. But you have youth on your side,' the Captain said, showing him out. 'See this young man safely for'ard,' he said to the guard.

The next day was fair, with smooth water. As the evening wore on it grew dark and cloudy, with thunder, lightening and rain. Early in the morning of the ninth of May died John North, and in fair weather again Captain Pigot read the service and they buried him. Over the side draped in cloths. Horace watched bleakly. Thus might he go next time, if he grew worse. He had always liked and admired John North:

besides, he was a friend, he knew about the *Betsy Gally* and the set-to off Anjengo, they had talked about their *Seahorse* days. When he heard next afternoon the sale of the bo'sun's effects going on at the mast he turned and walked the other way.

Six days later as they approached Cape Agulhas and noted the remarkable tableland beyond it, the fever descended once more upon Horatio.

❦

The *Dolphin* took a week approaching the Cape of Good Hope in very hazy weather: and anchored in the afternoon of the twenty-first of May. Horace heard the guns from several ships boom, felt the *Dolphin* shake as she returned the salutes and knew they must have reached the Cape. Next day there was good soft shore bread for breakfast and he was well enough to enjoy it. He longed only for fresh butter, butter from an English dairy! The taste of butter was almost forgotten, it was a far-off legendary delight. 'Midshipman's butter', the soft spread from an avocado, tasted in the West Indies, was nothing to it.

'The wine's good too, laddie. Try it.'

Horatio sipped the drink they had brought him.

'And there'll be fresh mutton for dinner! All came aboard yesterday.'

'How long shall we be here?'

'Anything up to a month, I should guess. How d'ye feel?'

'Better again. May I get up?'

'If ye're well enough. I'll give 'ee a hand.'

On deck he looked over the water and recognised nothing, until one of the midshipmen told him where they were. Three years ago they had anchored in Table Bay, approaching it (to his surprise) from the south. He remembered his first sight of the tableland. Now the tableland lay to the north-west, and they were on the eastern side of the isthmus of the Cape, in the bay called False. On the shore he could see a tent where the coopers were mending the casks. As he picked up strength again Horace found that he was walking much more easily about the ship, forgetting sometimes to hold on at all. Captain Pigot stood watching him from the quarter-deck one day. The boy had been to the steerage to unlock his chest and find his telescope and emerged with it under his arm on to the half-deck.

'Now then Mr Nelson,' he called, 'just skip up here to join me if you please.'

Horace smiled rather palely, doing his best to be brisk.

'I'm glad to see you about again. You've been laid low once more I hear.'

194

'Yes, sir. Every time I think I am better, down I go again.'

'But your walking is much better. You are twice the man you were when they carried you aboard. You must keep your heart up, have hope.'

'Oh, sir, how *can* I keep hope when every time I am beaten down once more!' the boy burst out.

'This is the nature of the thing. But you will, you must win in the end. You are very much better than when we sailed. Do not you think so?'

Horatio thought back to the day he was carried aboard hoist over a seaman's shoulder. He thought he remembered Tom Hoar and Thomas Troubridge somewhere, he could hear their voices but could not see them. They were calling farewells and encouragement to him. The whole scene was enveloped in a mist of confusion and weakness and despair, isolated, no memory of fore and aft around it. He had to admit that the Captain was right.

'Then do not give up the struggle. You have every chance of recovery as we get into better climes. The periods when you are well are getting longer, are they not?'

Horatio cautiously admitted this might be true. He was comforted by the Captain's kindness and his friendly encouragement to talk. He told him of Tom Hoar and Thomas Troubridge and Charles Pole.

'Oh, sir, I *shall* be far astern,' he sighed. 'They will all outstrip me!'

The Captain laughed.

'You do not know what wind of fate awaits you,' he said.

One day, which was the tenth of his respite, another of the invalids died, John Gordon by name, who was sent to be buried on shore. Horace felt a pang of dread hearing the service spoken and as if it would try his courage the fever gripped him sooner this time. The twenty-one guns for His Majesty's birthday boomed with the throbbing of his head.

Captain Pigot missed his young friend, whose regular perambulations about the ship he would watch from the quarter-deck: he enquired of the surgeon and was concerned to note that the fever had struck again and sooner. He reflected upon the death of Gordon, and the tendency to despair he had noted in young Nelson. If the lad gave up, he was lost. He sent along a bottle of wine from the cabin and with it a kindly brief note: *Courage, Horatio! Do but hold on and you must conquer soon.* Horace read the message and let his tears flow since no one was by to see them. He held on to its sentiments and to the affection which had sent it, and in holding these held on once more to his life. On the first opportunity that arose Horace went to thank the Captain for his kindness.

'What did I tell you?—you are better again, young man. Hold on, never say die. Your constitution must be a stubborn one to have endured so far. Take a seat, pray, and join me in a glass of this excellent Madeira wine. What urged you, Horace, to join His Majesty's navy: choice or necessity?'

Horatio pondered, sipping the wine.

'Both in a sense, sir,' he said. 'My father is a parson as you know, and not rich: there are eight of us and my mother is dead long since. My uncles, her brothers, undertook to help us. When I saw that my Uncle Suckling was commissioned to a ship (it was the *Raisonnable,* sir) I begged to join him. I was at school, but I have always preferred active pursuits. It was at the time of the trouble in the Falkland Islands, sir.'

'I remember. That was the end of '70, we thought there would be war in 1771. So you joined in 1771?'

'Yes, sir. But there was no war after all.'

'So you have nearly served your seven years, my lad.'

'Oh, sir, if only I had not had to come home.'

'Never mind that, a sick man is no good, your best and only hope was to come home,' Captain James Pigot said briskly and turned the conversation. 'Now did you know of the *Dolphin's* part in the troublesome history of those same Falkland Isles?'

'No, sir, has she one?' Horatio said, interested at once.

'Ay. You will have been very young when the war with France was settled in 1763?'

'Only five, sir,' Horace smiled, 'but my mother used to tell us about the war. My uncle was in a victorious action off Cap François in the West Indies.'

'I heard of it. It appears that after the peace the French made a settlement at Port St Louis in the Falklands. A year later this old ship arrived, not so old then, commanded by Captain Jack Byron; you may have heard of him, he was a bold sailor. He made a claim upon the Falklands for His Majesty, and planted a settlement on another of the islands. I hear that the droll thing was, the English at Port Egmont and the French at Port St Louis did not know of each other's existence for some long time.'

'And this ship, this ship was the vessel?' Horatio was feeling some wonder at the way things were linked together in life: this ship bringing him home had had her part in the events which first sent him forth to join the navy.

'Ay this very *Dolphin!* She was, in truth, on her way round the globe.'

'*Was* she, sir?'

'Yes. And after that, two years later, she made another circumnavigation, when she lighted on the island of Tahiti: which is in the Pacific ocean you may know.'

Horace did not: but he was excited at the notion of the *Dolphin's* exploits and in discussing them forgot his woes, which had been the Captain's intention.

'Was that under Captain Byron too, sir?'

'I think not: and I cannot tell you who. But she's a much travelled vessel and getting elderly. Roomy though, and comfortable.'

Horatio assented, so far as the Captain's quarters were concerned. He had a fleeting thought that the Captain might not have found it so comfortable for'ard.

'How old is she, sir?'

'I think she was put down in 1751 at Woolwich. She was one of the first of the copper bottoms you know.'

'So she is twenty-five years old!'

'Ay, a quarter of a century. Getting towards her retirement.'

'Is that so, sir?'

'Probably, I should say.'

'The *Seahorse* seemed a very old ship, sir.'

'Yes, she served in that war too.'

'Mr Surridge told me she was with General Wolfe, before Quebec.'

'Was she now? You're interested in ships' history as I am.' The Captain stored the information about the *Seahorse* in his mind.

They sailed from the Cape on the twentieth of June. Horatio was in some spirits, counting the ships' salutes. He had been well a week, he seemed to feel better. As they rounded the Cape, he asked himself whether he had not a Good Hope that his sickness lay behind him there.

As they approached the island of St Helena at the beginning of July Captain Pigot began to keep a note of the men who were sick in his log. The death of Gordon had left him with thirteen invalids ill of the fever. (Mr John North had never been counted in the total number, for he had been ranked as 'bo'sun' from the start, not 'invalid' even though sick.) Alas, alas, his young friend Nelson was down again, one of the ten men sick that he entered on the fourth of July. He was much disappointed on the boy's behalf: he had been well more than two weeks. By the time they had anchored in St Helena Road next day and saluted the fort, the Captain had ruefully to observe that all thirteen were sick again.

They were in St Helena Road for two days. On the second, Horace was well enough to come out on deck and see Sugar Loaf hill to the south-west, while the pigeons and sea birds flighted and tumbled around the cliffs. They sailed in the evening; and two days later, a hundred leagues away in clear pleasant weather, the Captain had the satisfaction of noting only nine men sick. As they neared Ascension Island, only seven. On the twenty-first of July it was fair at noon with a following sea; on the twenty-second, four hundred and ten leagues from Ascension, eight men in the sick list and Horace Nelson holding his luck like an egg shell, two weeks well.

On the twenty-third ten men in the sick list, and Horatio one of them. The Captain sent wine and messages, knowing that the higher had been his hopes, the steeper would be his descent to despair. While the week of fever passed the *Dolphin* crossed the equator, and the master began to take their distance from Fayal in the Azores.

On the morning of the thirtieth of July at seven o'clock, when Horace, feeling better, was about to rise, he heard the cry of 'Man overboard'. A sudden skirling of the pipes of the bo'sun's mates filled the ship and a shouting of orders fore and aft and an immediate thudding of feet.

'Man overboard!'

'All hands, all hands! Watch below, all up, all out and up here!'

'Man overboard, man overboard, all hands man the ship!'

'Afterguard back the mizzen tops'l! Maintop-men, foretop-men, back the tops'ls!'

'Man the boats! Out the cutter, out the yawl to starboard!'

Horace entirely forgot that he had yesterday been ill, slid from his bed and went to observe the action. The officer of the watch spoke through his hailer from the quarter-deck, the acting bo'sun had ordered the boats down, the midshipmen and seamen were flinging themselves down after them, the Captain was out on the poop, his glass to his eye, finding and keeping sight of the struggling man in the water. As the men aloft backed the sails, the *Dolphin* lost weigh, slowed down, turned her head out of the wind and idled. The lieutenant joined the Captain on the poop.

'From amidships direct to starboard,' said the Captain.

'Row direct to starboard of the ship,' called the officer to the boats.

'Further to starboard,' said the Captain.

'Further to starboard!'

'Nearing him now!' the Captain said a minute later.

'Back your oars! Rope handy! Ship your oars!' yelled the officer.

The cutter reached the floundering seaman making his best endeavours to swim in a choppy sea, threw him the rope, pulled him in and turned about for the ship. Both boats were hauled up and stowed, the seaman taken below for rest and grog and dry slops; the sails hauled and the ship got under way again in much less than half an hour. All were cheerful at the outcome, many laughed and whistled, jostling each other as they went below, talking of the advisability of being able to swim. Captain Pigot smiled from the quarter-deck where the officer made a note of the occurrence in the deck log.

'What's his name? Here, you, Mr Mid. What's that seaman's name?'

'I don't know, sir.'

'Find out then, and enter it in the log.'

'Very well, sir,' said the hungry midshipman and forgot all about it. The seaman remained nameless.

Horatio marvelled, forgetting his illness. So ought a ship to be handled, a man to be picked up and rescued! So, one day, would he handle a ship if a man went overboard. He went through the motions and the orders in his mind, rehearsing what must be done. He almost hoped that he would have the chance. He stood there in his nightshirt miming the scene, muttering the words, oblivious of everything.

'Here, Mr Nelson, what are you about? You come back in here now, and get rigged. You were ill yesterday, mind. We'll have you overboard next; come on now, your legs are still a-stagger.'

The sick bay orderly took him reproachfully by the arm.

'Did you see? Did you see how smartly we did it? That was as brisk a piece of business as ever I've witnessed!' the boy said exultantly.

'You sound better.'

'Ay, I am better today. I feel much better, to be sure. I think I feel better than I have done yet,' said Horatio slowly, with surprise.

'Never you mind, you're on the sick list, how do we know but you'll be fevered again by noon, you stay close now.'

That morning they spoke a ship at eleven. Feeling no symptoms of illness, Horatio slipped on deck to watch. They sent a boat on board her which did not return until after dinner. She was a brig from Bristol bound to Barbados. She had not much news save that Britain was still engrossed in suppressing the rebels in America. Watching her go, Horace thought of Captain Rathbone and wondered where he was now. He still felt well, in a day or two they would take his name off the sick list. But he no longer dared to hope that it was for the last time.

Now it was August. The *Dolphin* had found the northerly trades and was sailing for the Azores. Eight men were still sick. Two hundred leagues from Fayal they spied a sail and sent a boat aboard her. She proved to be the *Fisher* from Angola to Liverpool and continued her journey in company with them. Another man fell ill again, making nine. The ship was one hundred and thirty leagues from Corvo, the small island to the north of Flores in the Azores. Three days later, eleven men were sick. Horatio watched and waited. As he waited a terrible depression of spirits assaulted and conquered him, its weapons a ghostly multitude of nameless dreads. Only two invalids were left on their feet today, in this fine breeze and clear weather. He supposed that next week he would lie in there again cold as ice, then burning hot until the sweat broke out of him. And what though, even if he dared not hope it, he *was* recovered, the fever *was* conquered? If he exerted himself he felt tired and heavy as iron. He went in dread, and dread of he knew not what. Never had he feared things! Did he dread the disease? He had met it and survived it often enough. Did he dread his future? He did not know. His soul seemed a battleground, he knew not what he dreaded yet all was dreadful. He would gaze for minutes on end into the green translucent sea in horror, as if soundings beneath the waves his evil and his good struggled together. What would become of him?

Thus Captain Pigot saw him one day gazing into the sea, and haled him along as usual to his cabin and regaled him with wine, and friendly chat. Horatio hid his dread behind pale smiles, tried to forget it, to feel that it was not there. He could not speak of it to the Captain, it must be hidden, he could not confide it.

'You have been well two weeks, Horatio?'

'Almost, sir.'

'Take heart. Have hope!'

'I try to, sir.' He would not tell the Captain that he fought an enemy as bad as the fever itself. Captain Pigot guessed his struggles, those of a soul climbing back to health as out of a pit. Weakness, tiredness and depression of spirits had him in chains. If he only kept well, time would cure him. He did not invade his soul, anxious though he felt, but asked him sometimes to dine in the cabin and often to join him for talk.

Horace restlessly walked the ship, the trouble with his legs was almost forgot. He would seek out places where he felt at home, where he could sit or lie and be alone with his thoughts. A place which had seemed welcoming one day might seem inimical the next. Driven by his dread, he would move from place to place. As he looked at dusk over the darkening sea he almost wished he had been the man overboard, that it had closed over him and freed him forever from his struggles.

What were they doing now, upon the old *Seahorse*? What was Mr Surridge about? Taking his lunar observations, on some cruise to the north or to the east? How he missed Mr Surridge, his interest, his admiration, his constant teaching and encouragement. What he had lost, in having to leave that ship! The master had already suggested to them, to him and to Thomas Troubridge, that they should now be working to be master's mates, that both needed only more practice and confidence, they were ready for the responsibility. Tom Hoar, though he had had more years of navigation school than either of them, was less ready to put himself forward. What a gentle, clever fellow he was, how Horatio loved him. And Thomas, too! How they had fought and argued, but what a good friend was Thomas, what a splendid midshipman, quick and determined, no dallying about Thomas, a boy after his own heart. Thomas would now have all Mr Surridge's attention: now that he Horace had gone, had failed, the master would bring on Thomas Troubridge. His heart seemed to weep with jealousy. And Pole, good Charles Pole: older than they, he must surely be a lieutenant soon. How he envied them all! Were they still visiting the Company barracks, gaming with the soldiers? Wandering the colourful, scented bazaar? He had liked Mr Henery, too, who had showed him kindness, and Mr Abson and Mr Gossart and his friend the master's mate who yarned to him of pirates in the Gulf. All his friends out there seemed better off than he, all would outstrip him. They would be master's mates, lieutenants, he would hear of them getting their first ships, while he still languished in and out of the fever. Even were the illness beaten now, how was he to get on? How was he to rise in his profession? Returning weak and sick to Uncle Maurice, what would his uncle do for him, what could he do more? There was no one else to help him. Papa had no interest at the Admiralty, and no money; his brothers and sisters were all coming up, to be settled in life. He had always dreamed of himself once he was a lieutenant being quickly promoted, hurrying home to Burnham with the news of his first ship. He had wanted, he had longed to be an admiral, to be in command of ships, to fight battles for his country. What of all this now, how could he reach it? His despairing mind in his weakened body was staggered at the difficulties he had to surmount. He shivered in his despair, even though it was a calm fair night. Supper was over long since, the sea glittered in the light of the evening sun in a clear sky. He had found himself a place where he could lie alone, and watch the water. The hammocks were piped down, the men on the second dogwatch came and went about their tasks. Oh who, who was there to help him?

He sat quite still, his eyes closed, feeling the warmth of the sun upon them, the radiance of it blood-red behind his lids. His tired mind subsided, gave itself up to a stillness near sleep. There swam into it then a notion that his King and his country were his patron, his helpers: he glowed with a sudden clear longing to serve his country, a patriotism he had never felt before burned in his heart as the sun warmed his face. His mind exulted in the idea. All seemed suddenly simple, all difficulties fell away: he would serve his country, she would receive him. He would be a hero, he would confide in Providence, he would brave every danger. A radiant orb hung in his mind's eye throbbing with warmth, pulsating with light. He must follow it to glory.

He did not know how long he sat with his eyes closed. When he opened them the great red sun was going down into the sea. He found himself smiling. Eight bells struck. There was a slight chill in the air. He hurried to his hammock, turned in quickly and fell into a deeper sleep than he had enjoyed for weeks.

They were three hundred and nine leagues from the Lizard. Horatio, brisker and chirpier every day, doing a little duty, making friends with the officers of the watch, stole frequent looks at the deck log. Now that they were truly approaching home, nearing old England, he could hardly believe it. A few weeks more and he should see his family, Papa and Maurice, William and Sukey, Ann, Edmund, Suckling, little Kittykat. (A pang went through him lest any of them were dead.) The weather had grown more English, too: it was evident the kind of summer they were having at home, wet, squally and cold. Now in mid-August they were meeting strong gales, constant hard rain, the sky as thick as winter. They were running under close-reefed topsails. Now and then it would moderate and become merely grey and cloudy. Their course was set for the Isles of Scilly.

On the twenty-seventh of August the officers wrote the Scilly lighthouse six leagues off: and the Captain with a grimace noted his invalids sick again, a round dozen of them. All but young Mr Nelson. At the recovery of this young man's health and spirits, Captain Pigot rejoiced. They were up on the poop at four o'clock on the twenty-seventh of August looking out for St Agnes lighthouse to the north-north-west.

'You have taken a turn for the better, my boy,' said the Captain, lowering his glass.

'Yes, sir, I thank you,' said Horace with perfect cheerfulness.

'Your health seems restored. You alone are on your feet today, out of the thirteen.'

'Yes, sir, I dare hardly believe it. But I do not think I shall be ill again.'

'I don't neither, I'm glad to say. Three or four more days, Horace, and we'll see Spithead.'

At four o'clock on the twenty-eighth, the Dodman; at six, Eddystone two miles off, and Start Point to the east-south-east. At half past nine that night the ship tacked, Eddystone Light being west-half-south three miles. A great swell at one in the morning and they took in two reefs. At three the wind came cheerily to the south-west, so at six out reefs and set the studding sails! Several ships around them all standing up the Channel.

On the evening of the twenty-ninth the look-out called the Isle of Wight east by north. At midnight they anchored in St Helen's Road, at daylight weighed and sailed and anchored across at Spithead. Horace arose to the exhilarating view of ships all around them. HMS *Barfleur, Resolution, Royal Oak, Egmont; Centaur, Exeter* and *Richmond* frigates; the *Vulture, Hunter,* and *Ranger* sloops; and several transports.

Southsea Castle glistened to the north-east, the gold ship on Portsmouth church caught the sun. Very soon after breakfast, the Captain went ashore in his gig. When he returned at noon he called the midshipman to him and spoke without ado.

'Your uncle, my boy, is here, and he is comptroller of the navy! Since April last. You are to visit him tomorrow. What is more, while we have plied our way northerly up the Atlantic Ocean, the rebellious American settlers have *declared their independence.* There will be a war, Horatio, of considerable proportions. I think it just possible,' he added, having learned the young man's misgivings about his future, 'that Captain Suckling will find a place for you.' He laughed, enjoying Horatio's surprise.

The next day, Horace visited his uncle in Portsmouth. It was three years all but a month since they had met at the Nore, on the return of the ships from the Arctic. Both were shy with the passage of time: the comptroller the more so, since Captain Pigot had made it plain that his nephew was restored from the dead. Horace saw his relation a little more portly, fleshier in the face than he remembered; Captain Suckling welcomed a young man, not a boy. Slight, alert, his thin characterful face dominated by the Nelson nose, his mouth determined, his eyes sparkling pale blue, his whole air purposeful, Horatio stepped forward.

'Uncle! My dear Uncle!' He could not be formal, he could not.

Captain Suckling's reserve melted at once.

'My dear boy! My dear Horace!' They grasped hands, the Captain held him warmly by the shoulders. 'I hear they gave you up for gone, down the Malabar coast!'

'Ay, I believe so. It went on and on until the middle of August, I thought I would never throw it off.'

'And you have. You look thin but well.'

'I am very well. I worried about my future, but Uncle, your position brings *me* hope as well as satisfaction on your account.'

'Thank you, Horace. Have no fear, a place will be found for you. I have written to the Admiralty today, and also to your Uncle William. Do you write to your papa and your brother Maurice and tell them that you are here. I hope the *Dolphin* may make Woolwich with time for you to have a few days to see them all. Would not that be an excellent plan?'

'Oh yes, sir, I should greatly treasure it, I thank you!'

'Very well, then. Now, you shall tell me about your East Indies adventures while we dine.'

They were at Spithead a week. The eighteenth of September found that old ship the *Dolphin* lashed alongside the Sheer Hulk at Woolwich, having tacked up the channel meeting variable winds. It was her last voyage, though none of her crew then knew it.

All the invalids were better except one man whom the Captain sent to the hospital next day.

As to Horatio, Captain Pigot summoned him quickly.

'Go and seek out brother Maurice,' the Captain said, 'and then go on to your uncle in Kentish Town. If you go at once you will have a few days before a summons comes, and the chance to see some of your family. Farewell, Horatio, I rejoice to see you recovered.' Horatio, being speechless, could only show his gratitude by embracing his kind friend.

Thus did the boy find himself in the London coach on the very day of their reaching Woolwich. His heart was full, he would never forget the Captain's kindness, which he believed had saved his life. Thinking of the warmth with which they had parted, he rehearsed all the Captain's goodness in his mind and was thankful for it. Then he fell to thinking with an almost breathless excitement of the joy Maurice would feel, to see him standing there outside the door, returned safe and sound! (He spared a moment in this daydream to hope that Maurice were not moved house.) Papa too would have had his letter by now. Supposing Papa were hastening to London and William with him…Where was William, still at school? He had had very few letters in all the time of his absence. Sukey, he thought, would be still at Bath sewing her elegant hats. She might be summoned, if Papa thought the occasion worthy. He would be eighteen in a week or so, a landmark in his life to be celebrated (though he thought that Uncle Maurice would have him aboard some vessel before that). At Kentish Town, Uncle William would roar with delight to see him, his cousins would wish to embrace him; James Price would be there, his eyes opening wide, his white teeth gleaming in his black face as he opened the door. *Why, Mas'er Horace…?* he would say, hardly recognising him.

As he thought of them all his heart seemed to expand, and to be filled with something of the same radiance as had entered it that night on the ship which he would never forget.

What was it then, why did the two things feel of the same essence? The light that had rescued him from his despair and the glow which illumined his family as he thought of them? What was this force which had made whole his tattered courage, which now filled his heart to overflowing?

Jogging along in the chaise towards the roofs and spires of London upon a fading autumn evening, the young man considered this matter soberly and decided that it was love. And it seemed to him as new, as vast, as amazing as it does to any young person on the threshold of life who recognises for the first time its glorious and all-pervasive power.

Bibliography and Sources

Primary Sources

Burnham Thorpe	All Saints Church Parish Account Book 1707-1793
	All Saints Church Register of Baptisms, Burials, Marriages
Burnham Sutton-Cum-Ulph	Church Registers No 2 and 3
Carcass, HMS	*Captain's Log,* S Lutwidge, Apr-Sept 1773, ADM 51/167/5659
Carcass, HMS	*Master's Log,* J Allen, ADM 52/1639/5659 XK 4368
Christ's College Cambridge	Archives; College v Allott in Chancery Allott v Wilkinson in Exchequer
Dolphin, HMS	*Captain's Log,* J Pigot, Feb-Aug 1776, ADM 51/259
Lloyds of London	New Lloyd's List, No 244, Fri, 26th July 1771;
	Lloyd's Lists No 3790, 10th, 17th July 1772;
	No 3792, 21st July 1772
Monmouth Collection	Autograph Letters of Nelson
Nelson, E	Rector, Burnham Thorpe, *A Family Historicall Register*, 1781 [Ptd *Norf and Norw Notes and Queries*, 1897]
Nelson, Lord	*Memoir of his Services*; Pt I [Ptd in Clarke & M A's *Life*, I]
Racehorse, HMS	*A Voyage Toward the North Pole undertaken by HM Command,1773*, C J Phipps [Publ 1774]
Racehorse, HMS	*A Midshipman's Log* [Publ 1879] T Floyd Includes officer lists
Raisonnable, HMS	A journal kept on board His Majestie's ship the *Raisonnable*...November 29th 1770 – May 25th 1771: ADM 52 1937 X/L01528

Raisonnable, HMS	*Admiralty Muster Books,*...1771: ADM 36/7669
Seahorse, HMS	*Captain's Log,* G Farmer, August 1773 – April 1776: ADM 51 883 X/K 4015
Seahorse, HMS	*Lieutenant's Log,* August 25 1773 – August 31 1774: ADM/L/S/222
Seahorse, HMS	*Master's Log,* T Surridge, 1773-1776: ADM 52 1991 X/K 4015
Suckling, Mrs Maurice	*Will, 22 December 1767,* PROB 11/936, proved 1st Feb 1768
Triumph, HMS	*Master's Logs,* 1771-1773: ADM 52/2052 X201528, 4257; ADM 52/2052 X/K 5056; ADM 52/2052 X/L 01528
Triumph, HMS	*Admiralty Muster Books,* 1771, 1772: ADM 36/7688; ADM 36/7689

Secondary Sources

Anonymous	*Journal of a Voyage to discover the North East Passage...* F Newbery, London 1774
Barker, D Wilson	*A Manual of Elementary Seamanship,* Griffin, 1929
Beecheno, F R	Papers on Henleys & Sucklings, *Eastern Daily Press,* 18th July 1923, Norf & Norw: Arch Soc XIX, 197
Bennett, G	*Nelson the Commander,* Scribners, 1972
Bewick, T	*Autobiography*
Blagdon, F W	*History of India,* London 1805
Boswell, J	*London Journal 1762-3,* ed Pottle, London 1950
Boydell, J	*A History of the Thames,* London 1793
Bradfer-Lawrence, H L	'The Merchants of Lynn', in A Supplement to *Blomefield's Norfolk,* Ingleby, London [1926]-1929
Brooke, J	*King George III,* Constable, 1972
Burchett, J	*Naval Transactions of the English...*London 1720
Clarke, J and M'Arthur, J	*The Life and Services of Horatio, Viscount Nelson, from his lordship's manuscripts,* 2nd ed, London 1840; 1st ed, 1809 Appendix 2
Clowes, W L	*The Royal Navy, A History,* 1897-1903
Coxe, W	*Memoirs of Horatio Lord Walpole,* 1802

Cross, F J   *The Birthplace of Nelson,* 1904
Crouse, J   *The History and Antiquities of Norfolk*; Norwich,
                        1781
Daniell, T & W   *A Picturesque Voyage to India, by Way of China,* 1810
Davy, J   *An Account of the Interior of Ceylon,* London 1821
Encyclopaedia Brittanica 1797, *Navigation:* Longitude at Sea
Eyre-Matcham, M   *The Nelsons of Burnham Thorpe,* London 1911
Faden, W   Map Publisher, Charing Cross, 1790s

Foley, T   *The Nelson Centenary...*East of England
(Florence   Newspaper Co, Norwich, 1905
Horatia Suckling)   *Some Notes on Barsham...*Pollard, Exeter 1906

Forbes, J   *Oriental Memoirs,* 1813
Forder, C R   *A History of the Paston Grammar School,* North
                        Walsham 1934
Foster, J   Alumni Oxonienses, Oxford 1888
Froude, J A   *The English in the West Indies,* 1887
Gamlin, Mrs   *Nelson's Friendships,* London 1899
Gardner, J A   *Above and Under Hatches,* ed C Lloyd, London
                        1955
Gérin, W   *Horatia Nelson,* Oxford 1970
Grindlay, R M   *Scenery, Costumes & Architecture of India,* 1826-
                        1830
Hakewill, J   *A Picturesque Tour of the Island of Jamaica* from
                        drawings made in the years 1820-1821
Hales, J   Letter to the author, 14 June 1974
Harrison, J   *Life of Nelson,* 1806
Harrod, W   *The Two Churches at Warham, Norfolk*
Hibberd, H   *A History of Burnham Thorpe,* 1937
Hilborough   All Saints Church *Guide*
James, B Rear-Admiral   *Journal* ed J K Laughton Navy Records Society,
                        London 1896
Ketton-Cremer, R W   *Norfolk Portraits,* Faber 1944
                        Country Neighbourhood, Faber 1951
                        Felbrigg, Boydell, 1962
Knight E C   *Autobiography,* ed Kaye, 1861
Long, E   *History of Jamaica,* the Years 1774-1775

Lubbock, B	*Round the Horn before the Mast*, Murray, 1902
Lynn Magazine, The	*Papers...during the Contest...*ptd 1768
Mackie, ed	*Norfolk & Norwich Notes & Queries I*
Marcus, G J	*Heart of Oak*, Oxford 1975
Masefield J	*Sea Life in Nelson's Time*, Sphere Books 1972
Moorhouse, E	*Nelson in England*, London 1913
Nares, G	Articles in *Country Life* 18th, 25th July 1957
Naval Chronicle, The	1799-1818, London
Nelson, Lord	*Letters from*, compiled G Rawson, 1949
Nelson, T	*A Genealogical History of the Nelson Family*, King's Lynn, 1908
Nicolas, N H	*Despatches and Letters of Admiral Lord Nelson*, 1844
Norie, J W & Co,	Map publishers: *A survey of the River Thames...and of the River Medway...*1826
Norfolk Chronicle,	The Years 1758-1771, Norwich
Northcote Parkinson, C	'The East India Trade', *The Trade Winds* ed, CNP London 1948
Norwich Mercury	The Years 1758-1771, Norwich
Oman, C	*Nelson*, London 1947
Ordnance Survey	Sheet TF84, 1966
Pares, R	*A West India Fortune*, London 1950
Pastonian	No 52, HN, measles; cattle plague
Peile, J	*History of Christ's College; Biographical Register of Christ's College*, Cambridge 1913
Pelican	*History of Art*, Vol 21, 1953
Pevsner, N	*North West and South Norfolk*, Penguin 1962
Price, F W ed,	*A Textbook of the Practice of Medicine*, Oxford 1947
Purchas, A W	'Wells Harbour', *Some history of Wells-next-the-Sea and district*, Ipswich 1965
Russell, J	*Nelson and the Hamiltons*, London 1969
Saunders, H W	*History of Norwich Grammar School*, Norwich 1932
Singer, C & Underwood E A	*A Short History of Medicine*, Oxford 1962
Sobel, D	*Longitude*, Walker Inc 1995
Southey, R	*The Life of Nelson*, ed Callender, 1922
Southey, T	*Chronological History of the West Indies* 1827 (year 1771)

Temple, R	*Views in the Persian Gulf,* 1813
Tracy, N	'The Falkland Island crisis of 1770: Use of Naval Force' *English Historical Review,* Vol 90, Jan 1975; 'The Parry of a Threat to India, 1768-1774' *Mariners Mirror,* 59, 1973
Venn, J	*Alumni Cantabrigienses,* Cambridge 1922-7
Walpole, H	*Letters,* ed Toynbee, Oxford 1903-1905 *Letters,* Yale edition, 1937-83
Walthew, K	From Rock and Tempest; the Life of Captain George William Manby, London 1971
Watson, J S	The Reign of George III, Oxford 1960
Wilson, A T	The Persian Gulf...an Historical Sketch, Oxford 1928
Woodforde, J	The Diary of a Country Parson, Oxford 1949
Young, A	The Farmers' Tour through the East of England, London, 1771 A General View of the Agriculture of the County of Norfolk, 1804

BOOK ONE

THE NELSON BOY

An Imaginative Reconstruction of A

Great Man's Childhood

£16.95 ISBN 0-9536317-0-2
Available from Church Farm House, Bottisham,
Cambridge, CB5 9BA

Pauline Hunter Blair

Horatio Nelson is one of Britain's great heroes and his later life is well documented. Pauline Hunter Blair offers us a rare chance to explore his childhood – through painstaking research and imaginative but plausible reconstruction. The scene is set in Burnham Thorpe, north Norfolk still (in its rural parts) very much the same. The rector, Edmund Nelson, is to be papa to eight youngsters, and his wife Catherine Nelson (of a family a smidge higher in the social scale) is the busiest of mothers. From this quiverful of children there begins to fly one, outstanding in spirit, wits, and character, who would fly far

Six well-authenticated anecdotes put milestones across Horace's childhood and boyhood: losing himself at Hilborough (where his paternal granny lived); riding to school through deep snow with William; finding the 'rare' bird's nest; picking a sprig of yew from the churchyard tree at dead of night; catching the measles at school at North Walsham; where he also, chiefly for his friends, stripped the master's pear-tree and never owned up. (Was this one reason why he was so keen to leave school aged just over twelve and a half and go into the navy?) The author dates these incidents more exactly by common sense and deduction and then sets them into plausible contexts.

The *Norwich Mercury* and The *Norfolk Gazette* of the time have provided an actual background tapestry of events, but the family's participation in them has to be largely imagined. (Nowhere does the author describe Horace's involvement in an event if that were circumstantially impossible.) We know the people, the neighbours, Horace was fond of when a child from the letters he wrote, the messages he sent, the enquiries he made as an adult, and thus the author lets them people his childhood.

Horatio Nelson's feeling for his father appears in many letters between them of adult life, yet not 'a scrap of a pen' survives from his mother: Pauline Hunter Blair suggests a huge bond between them, such as sets a person up for life. His relationships with his brothers and sisters, his tender love for Maurice, his and William's child-time devotion due to their near ages, not likeness; his recognition of the staunch faithful dullness of Susannah (Sukey) contrasted with the potential social brilliance of little Catherine (Kitty): these have been drawn in looking backwards from how he speaks of them, and to them, in later life.